ONCE A SPY

ONCE A SPY

Keith Thomson

DOUBLEDAY

New York London Toronto

Sydney Auckland

DOUBLEDAY

DOUBLEDAY and the DD colophon are registered trademarks of Random House, Inc.

Book design by Michael Collica

Library of Congress Cataloging-in-Publication Data

Thomson, Keith
Once a spy / by Keith Thomson. — 1st ed.
p. cm.
I. Title.
PS3620.H745O63 2010
813'.6—dc22
2009018120

ISBN 978-0-385-53078-1

PRINTED IN THE UNITED STATES OF AMERICA

1 3 5 7 9 10 8 6 4 2

First Edition

To M.S.T.

The price of freedom is eternal vigilance.

—Jefferson

Part One

Reasonable Paranoia

1

Brooklyn was booming. Elsewhere. Drummond Clark's block was still packed with boxy, soot-grayed houses, some settled at odd angles and all so close together they looked like one long soot-grayed building. At holiday time, the patchy displays of festive lights accentuated the cracks as much as anything.

On this bitter Christmas Eve, Drummond stood hunched in his small kitchen, alternately green and red in the reflection of a neighbor's tree, struggling to open a can of soup for dinner. He wondered how all the years had come to this. No friends, no family. He couldn't remember the last time one of the neighbors had invited him in.

Granted, a longtime widower wasn't much of a fit in an increasingly young and family-oriented neighborhood. Also the world was increasingly elitist and materialistic, and his station lacked luster: He'd worked in sales at a middling appliance manufacturer for thirty years. And, he acknowledged, *he* lacked luster—in sixty-four years, one gets the message. But none of that quite accounted for tonight.

He knew that there was another explanation. A glaring one.

"What is it again?" he asked himself.

He couldn't put a finger on it. He hoped the effort of getting his creaky can opener to do its job would jog his memory.

It didn't. But at least he got the can open. A cylinder of chicken and stars slid out and plopped into the pot.

Hunger and anticipation kept him by the stove. When the soup came to a boil, he lifted the pot from the burner and hurried to the worn butcher-block table. His bowl, napkin, and soup spoon waited in a neat row.

He bypassed the table and emptied the soup onto the waist-high plastic fern by the side door.

An electronic sputter burst over the pair of miniature speakers in the attic three doors up the block. The tenants in the house were four clean-cut young men who claimed to be Brooklyn Polytechnic grad students. The one who went by Pitman didn't know what to make of the noise. Sitting at the other end of the Ping-Pong table the "grad students" used as a desk, Dewart appeared equally puzzled. Like "Pitman," "Dewart" was a pseudonym, probably chosen at random. Pitman liked to think it had been inspired by Dewart's resemblance to Jimmy Stewart.

Glancing at his monitor, Dewart said, "Whatever the hell it is, it's coming from number six. Which is six again?"

"Checking," said Pitman. He pass-coded his way into a roster of electronic surveillance devices. "Probably one of the fiber-freaking-ops."

The fiber-optical microphones each operated using light waves transmitted by a cable thinner than a human hair, and they wonderfully defied metal and nonlinear junction detectors. But they were famously temperamental, with polymer lithium batteries that needed changing every nine days—best-case. On this job that meant sneaking into Drummond's house when he was out, which had been seldom since his disability leave began.

Ordinarily Pitman would have sent the devices in and out of the house's ventilation system fitted to crawlers, robots the size of a common cockroach. Or he would have used mikes that drew power from the house itself, wired into the back of a light switch wall plate, for instance. A pinhole video camera concealed behind a mirror would have been nice too. The problem with such "simple" devices here was their relative ease of detection.

"Yep, fiber-op," he relayed to Dewart, "in the planter in the kitchen."

"Any idea what's up with it?"

"A short, maybe?"

"How could that happen?"

"Maybe he thought he was watering the plant."

"All his plants are plastic."

"Good point." Trying to ignore his rising anxiety, Pitman mouse-clicked to the feed from 20-N and 20-S, nickel-sized pinhole video cameras he'd painted the local streetlamp-gray and wired onto streetlamps at either end of the block.

His display showed a block devoid of motion except flickering Christmas lights and a wind-tossed bar coaster—he could read the Schlitz logo. He could also see Drummond's side door dangling open. Drummond kept the door triple locked as a rule, except when taking out the trash. The alley was empty aside from garbage cans.

Pitman felt as if he'd been kicked in the stomach. "We need the JV," he said. His mind was a feverish montage of the potential consequences of losing Drummond, including several scenarios in which one of the "junior varsity" players climbed to the attic and, on orders from above, drew a gun—end of scene.

Yes, surveillance units lost targets all the time, even much bigger and more sophisticated surveillance units—Pitman had heard of an eighty-person team in floating box formation that lost its target when the wheel artist's car was cut off by a flock of kindergartners and a stubborn crossing guard.

But Drummond Clark wasn't just any target, of course.

2

At six the next morning, a disagreeably frosty Christmas, Charlie Clark was the lone passenger on the Q11 bus rattling past a desolate stretch of Queens Boulevard discount stores, fast food restaurants, and office buildings in decline or awaiting demolition. He saw that the driver, a pleasant, fresh-faced man around his own age—thirty—was looking him over in the rearview mirror. Even when Charlie wore old sneakers and jeans torn at the knees, like now, strangers mistook him for a yuppie.

The driver called back, "Going out to the island to be with family?"

Charlie weighed telling the truth. The thing was, over the engine rumble and the thumping of tires in and out of potholes, he'd heard a certain wistfulness in the driver's voice. Also, when boarding, he'd noticed the driver's thick wedding band and a snapshot of two little girls taped to the fare box. Charlie figured that, preposterously early this morning, the guy had had to pry himself away from the warm bosom of his family to come spend his Christmas breathing icy diesel fumes, dodging tipsy holiday drivers, and enduring the recorded voice's plodding recitation of the rules of disembarkation at every stop, even when no one disembarked. So probably he wouldn't be cheered to learn it amounted to chauffeuring an inveterate gambler to the track.

"I'm going to see Great Aunt Edith," Charlie said.

Great Aunt Edith was a filly.

The bus driver glowed as if his fare box had been replaced by an open fire. Charlie was warmed as well. To keep the poor bastard's buzz going, he got off a stop before Aqueduct Racetrack, at a neighborhood of

quaint but tired little brick and shingle houses that might well be popu-
lated exclusively by great aunts.

It meant walking a couple of extra blocks. He shivered, but not
because of the cold.

It was the debt.

The Big A opened in 1894. Many horseplayers called it the Big H, for heaven, especially on sunny days when the breeze lofted an aromatic blend of hay, freshly mowed grass, and horses into the sweeping, twin-tiered grandstand.

Charlie had spent a good part of the past ten years in the grandstand but developed no such sentiments. He thought of the ancient colossus as the weight of one more stubbly guy in a stained shirt away from col-lapse—when he thought about it at all. His focus was almost always on the races or the goings-on before and after: happy snorts, dragging hooves, extra steps. While stubbly guys all around him were crumpling tickets from the race that had just ended and muttering about their luck, he drank up clues.

A few months ago, he had noticed a colt take an extra step on the way to the stalls, avoiding a puddle. He read it as aversion to water and filed it away until six weeks afterward, when it was raining in Louisville, the Downs were mud, and the same colt was favored—the exact scenario Charlie had gotten out of bed hoping for every day in the preceding six weeks. Betting the consensus second pick netted him a sporty new Volvo, which was almost as exhilarating as the twentieth of a second during which the horse crossed the wire.

In a race last weekend at Gulfstream, with five horses already finished, Great Aunt Edith was lumbering behind by too many lengths to count. As usual. Charlie had already lost a hundred on the bay who finished fourth. Everyone else at the Big A viewing the simulcast, holding suddenly worthless tickets too, went into crumple-and-mutter mode. Charlie watched the entire race, as always.

With an eighth to go, he was rewarded by the sight of Great Aunt Edith's abrupt and unprecedented transformation into a locomotive. He smelled a rare ruse known as "hiding form," in which a horse racks up a record as a plodder but secretly is a bullet in workouts watched only by his owner and trainer. They intentionally hold him back in races with the objective of a betting bonanza the day they finally let him loose.

There was no better time to come out of hiding than the day after Christmas, when the betting pool was fattened by a grandstand packed with first timers and other fish who always pick the favorite. If Edith's people had such designs, her jockey would air it out in today's workout, and he could do so without the usual security precautions because Aqueduct was closed on Christmas.

Practically swollen with anticipation, Charlie hit the buzzer outside Aqueduct's administrative offices. His friend Mickey Ramirez appeared at the door. Mickey worked security here because, like most everyone else who worked at the track, he liked the horses too much. Otherwise he would have still been a successful private investigator in Manhattan. He was forty-two, of average height, and, because the refreshment stand eased the pain of bad bets, nearing three hundred pounds. His single attractive feature—thick and satiny black hair, worn long—emphasized the defects of the rest. His default setting—gloomy—worsened at the sight of Charlie now.

"You can't come in," he said through the glass.

"Happy Christmas back at you," Charlie said, unruffled.

"So you know it's Christmas?"

"No, I say that every day, just in case."

"You do know it's the one day of the year tracks are closed, right?"

"I didn't want you to have to spend it alone, old friend. Also, by the by, I want to see the workouts."

"It'd be my ass if I let you in, man. You know that."

"I know, I know, but here's the thing: I've had a run of rotten luck lately—"

"Don't get me started on hard-luck stories."

"—and I'm into Grudzev for twenty-three G's."

Mickey softened. "Shit."

Charlie breathed some warmth back into his hands. "Assuming Phil at the pawnshop has the holiday spirit, I'm short by north of fifteen. If I don't have it by tomorrow night, Grudzev's going to fill a cup with sand."

"And make you drink it?"

"Why would I care if he's just filling a cup with sand?"

"That could kill you, couldn't it?"

"Either way, it's a decent threat, don't you think?"

"Fuck, borrowing from a dude like that—what were you thinking?"

Charlie felt foolish. "That the horse was going to win," he said. He could have cited several times that Mickey had been in a similar predicament. Once he not only bailed Mickey out, he paid his rent. Which, come to think of it, he'd never gotten back.

"I hear you, man," Mickey said. He opened the door a crack but didn't move to let Charlie in. "You'll cut me in, yeah?"

This meant Mickey would allow Charlie inside if, in return, he related anything he saw that might affect the outcome of a race. Charlie bristled at the notion. For him, the thrill of winning was being right when everyone else was wrong. Where in the world but the track can a person get that? The thrill was diluted when other handicappers copied his homework; for the same reason, he was loath to bet based on another horseplayer's tip, even if it were to come by way of the horse's mouth.

"Cutting in" had a cost too. Odds at the track aren't set by the house, like at casinos, but rather by the money bet per horse—the more bet, the lower the odds. By cutting someone in, Charlie was lowering the odds on his pick, which was tantamount to giving away his own money, which was tantamount to nuts.

He thought of it simply as the price of admission today. Mickey could blab to everyone in his wide ring of tip traders, and still Great Aunt Edith would pay ten to one, more than enough for Charlie to pay off Grudzev and—what the hell—give him a Christmas bonus.

———

There were train compartments bigger than Mickey's office. Charlie huddled with him by a monitor that showed a skewed, gray-green security camera feed of Great Aunt Edith's supposedly private workout. The filly was running even slower than usual, like she resented having to work on the holiday. Charlie came to the nauseating conclusion that Gulfstream had been a fluke.

Mickey turned to him and asked, "What do you care about Edith for anyhow? I wouldn't bet her if she was the only horse in the race."

A jolt of excitement deprived Charlie of the ability to reply. The filly had accelerated to the point that a bullet would have had difficulty keeping pace.

4

"My name is John Lewis," the man said with certainty. He'd been just as certain a minute ago that he was Bill Peterson.

"Do you know where you live?" Helen asked.

The man shrugged.

"Do you know where you are now?"

"Geneva?"

"The town in upstate New York?"

"Don't know it."

Despite two sweaters, social worker Helen Mayfield sat huddled against her tiny desk at Brooklyn's Prospect Park Senior Outreach Center; at least the piles of folders full of lost causes provided a buffer against the draft. And the draft was no bother compared to the square dance class. The wall between her office and the rec room was so thin, it felt like the dance caller was hollering directly into her ear.

Not unrelated was the migraine, like a railroad spike through the base of her skull and into her left eye. Then there was the pharmacy three blocks away, where she might obtain a remedy. Closed December 25, sure. But also today, December 26.

For St. Stephen's Day!

She could help the man sitting at her desk, though. So everything else was relegated to minor annoyance.

He looked to be in his early sixties. Five-ten or eleven, weight about right, plain features. He had a moderate amount of white hair and an average amount of wrinkles and spots. His muscles were firm, but not so much that anyone would notice, except on close inspection. He'd spent the night here after volunteers in a Meals on Wheels van spotted him wandering Brooklyn yesterday afternoon in just the flannel pajamas and bedroom slippers he still wore. He had no wallet, no watch or jewelry, no identifying marks. And then there was his accent, or, really, the lack of one. He could be anyone from anywhere.

Still, Helen wasn't without clues. Each year the center cared for more seniors with neurodegenerative conditions than a neurologist typically saw in a career. Although he was relatively young, she suspected her John Doe had Alzheimer's. Its trademark was damage to the memory-retrieval process, manifested by a veil over the past and present. Symptoms also included humming and rocking without self-awareness. Mr. Doe: all of the above.

And the wandering was a classic. Alzheimer's caused minimal motor impairment. Ten years from onset, patients could tie a tie, bake a cake, even create a Web site. Driving a car was nothing for them. Except now and again, they departed for the corner store, only to be found halfway across the country. Such spells of disorientation often were prompted by unfamiliar surroundings. Out-of-towners visiting relatives frequently wound up as Does.

"Do you, by chance, have family in the New York City area?" she asked.

The humming ceased. The man sat ramrod straight. "Yes, ma'am. My son, Charles. Three-oh-five East Tenth Street in Manhattan, unless he's had difficulty making the rent again."

A few keystrokes at the social services database, and her computer screen filled with the driver's license data and a photograph of Charles Jefferson Clark of 305 East 10 Street. He was a year and a day older than she, five eleven and 170, with strong features and playful blue eyes that shone through scruff and tangles of sandy hair. In that shabby Yonkers Raceway T-shirt, she thought, he could be a rock star who dressed in defiant opposition to his means.

5

Feeling flush already, Charlie took a taxi to Aqueduct, stopping first at a Lightning ¢a$h. Into the gulley at window B, he dropped his driver's license and the key ingredient of his Great Aunt Edith wager: three Social Security checks made out to his mother, Isadora VanDeuersen Clark, each in the amount of $1,712.00. In a wispy cursive he imagined old-lady-like, he'd endorsed them, "Isadora V. Clark."

The first check had appeared in his mailbox in October, after what would have been her sixty-fifth birthday. If she hadn't died twenty-six years earlier. His horseplayer cronies were unanimous in the opinion that it was literally a gift horse. Still, he leaned toward notifying the Social Security Administration of the error. Until today.

Lightning ¢a$h looked and smelled like it was never mopped and never would be. The appeal was it accepted any check issued by the United States government without calling for verification; and the tellers paid so little attention to detail, they were likely to cash a check issued by the Confederate States of America. Usually.

It occurred to Charlie now that, given the run of luck he'd been on, today was the day the tellers would be replaced by undercover agents looking to bust deadbeats who cash their dead moms' Social Security checks.

Sure enough, the teller—a trim, middle-aged man with a self-assured air—licked his thumb and forefinger to enhance their adhesiveness, raised one of the checks to his lenses, and began to *examine* it.

Charlie tried to blink the horror out of his eyes. "My mom endorsed them to me."

The man muttered something in reply that sounded like "Yes, sir" but just as easily could have been a dubious "Yeah, sure." And continued his examination.

Hot acid jetted into Charlie's intestines.

An eternity passed.

Finally the teller opened his cash drawer and withdrew $5,058.96, the value of the checks minus Lightning ¢a$h's 1.5 percent fee. Charlie's acid ebbed and cool relief flowed in its place. The relief was mitigated by that blend of probability and superstition unique to horseplayers: You don't want to be lucky before the starting gate opens. It's that much less luck you'll have when you need it.

The sky above the Big A grandstand was an ominous, scowling gray. It would have taken a meteor shower to divert Charlie's attention from the oval. From the moment the stall doors banged open, Edith was a bullet. She finished five lengths ahead of the favorite. But two lengths behind a nothing chestnut named Hay Diddle, who won going away.

"There's a reason you never hear of anyone getting rich at the track," Charlie said to no one in particular as he crumpled his ticket. He left feeling heavier by a hundred pounds, the bulk of it melancholy and foreboding. On the stairs he used the handrail, the first time he could remember doing so, to counter the dizziness.

As the Q11 bounced him through potholes and back to Manhattan, the squeaky suspension sounded as if it were reiterating his exact thought: *Now what?*

He fantasized about staying aboard all the way to the Port Authority Bus Terminal and from there skipping town on the first Greyhound to Montana or South Dakota or someplace like that. He'd clear the damned horses from his head once and for all, then find steady employment, maybe go back to school at night and finish his college degree. Then he'd meet "her" and they'd buy the two-story brick colonial with a tidy lawn that had room for a swing set and sandbox. And he'd find a thrill less risky than the horses. Like skydiving.

Running now would only make things worse though. Grudzev's men would bring the sand to one of Charlie's friends.

Also, Charlie had tried fresh starts. Several times after a big score, he'd hopped a taxi straight to LaGuardia. But the *Daily Racing Form* was everywhere—once even at a beachside newsstand consisting of a milk crate nailed to a coconut palm. He developed a theory that money won at the track, like water to the ocean, found its way back to the track. Or, put another way: A gambler doesn't make the same mistake twice. It's usually nine or ten times.

His cell phone's ring ended his rumination. The readout flashed a number he didn't know, but the area code was 718.

Almost surely it was the Christmas Call.

As if today couldn't get any better.

The holiday had been yesterday, but his father traditionally didn't remember Charlie's birthday until days afterward. If at all. Charlie used to go see him on the big holidays, at places that could get them fed and out in under an hour, with televised ball games to minimize conversation. The last couple of years, it had dwindled to just the calls.

The old man had some means; he could bail Charlie out of the Grudzev thing without much hassle on his end.

Writing Santa would be a better bet, Charlie thought.

Reflected in the window across the aisle was a face so cross that, for a moment, he didn't recognize himself.

He let the phone keep ringing.

Walking to his apartment, where rent had been due a week ago, Charlie saw a Cadillac Eldorado idling in the handicapped spot. Sitting at the wheel was Karpenko. Forged in a part of Russia where men killed one another over as little as a dirty look, Karpenko was hardened well beyond his age of thirty-five. Word was he once shot a man just to make sure his gun was working. One look at him, at all his muscles and his sharp black goatee, and anybody would think, *Satan on steroids.* He had on a high-collared black leather overcoat, which actually made him *less* menacing; Charlie had seen Karpenko in warmer weather, when he'd worn just a tank top, displaying crudely rendered dragons and skeletons and other gulag tattoos.

Karpenko served as muscle for the man beside him, Leo Grudzev, a jack-of-all-criminal-trades whose favorites were small arms and narcotics trafficking and shylocking—his preferred term for high-interest moneylending. Not that Grudzev needed muscle. The forty-year-old's keg of a torso was joined to a proportionately sized head by a neck that would have been indiscernible if not for the thick gold chain and gold cross the size of a railroad spike. He had a sour face that jutted forward like a ski slope. Charlie thought of Grudzev as evidence anthropologists were wrong—Cro-Magnon man hadn't died out. Were Charlie to voice that, Grudzev probably would shoot him. If Karpenko didn't shoot first.

Charlie steeled himself as he approached. Behind the steel were bones and tissue that fear had turned to putty. Grudzev's window rolled down. Charlie was belted by musky cologne and garlic.

"Belated Merry Christmas," Charlie said.

"Same for you," said Grudzev through a thick Russian accent, "*if . . .*"

Karpenko reached into his coat, probably for a weapon. The glint in his eye alone caused Charlie's heart to jump.

Until Charlie hit upon a possible solution. "I have a plan to pay you by tomorrow with an extra five K on top," he said to Grudzev. "And if I don't, I'll go down to Brighton Beach and eat every grain of sand there."

Grudzev exchanged a shrug with Karpenko, then looked back at Charlie. "This plan better no got to do with a fucking horse."

6

The Prospect Park Senior Outreach Center was done in so many cheery pastels that the overall effect was depressing, the way a clown can be. The liniment in the air didn't help. Prior to pleading with Grudzev for a one-day extension, Charlie had listened to Helen's voice mail message, called her back, and gotten the rundown. If it hadn't included "durable power of attorney"—which would allow him to administer his father's finances—he almost certainly wouldn't be here now.

He almost didn't recognize the man hunched on the couch across the lobby. Usually Drummond sat straighter than most flagpoles, a function of rectitude as much as posture. His hair threw Charlie too. Charlie had correctly anticipated that, in the time since he'd seen him last, it would have turned fully white. The shocker was that it was unruly; Drummond used to keep it close-cropped, and practically regimented, by a standing weekly appointment at the barbershop.

The pajamas also surprised Charlie—not so much because of the incongruity of pajamas in a public place but because he simply couldn't remember having seen his father in nightclothes before. When Charlie used to get up for school, no matter how early, Drummond was gone. Often, the faint scent of talc was the only evidence he'd come home from the office the night before. More often, he was out of town, singing the praises of his beloved washers and dryers.

"Hey," Charlie said.

Drummond looked up, and Charlie saw the biggest change in him. His eyes had always been clear, sober, and sharp. Now they were the eyes of a man gazing into deep space and without a flicker of recognition.

"Dad, it's me," Charlie said.

"Oh," Drummond said pleasantly but without familiarity. "Hello."

Charlie felt as if an icy finger ran up his spine. "Charles," he tried.

Drummond looked him over, his eyes settling on the Meadowlands Racetrack logo on the sweatshirt peeking out of Charlie's jacket. Charlie wondered if, subconsciously, he'd put on the sweatshirt to provoke the old man. Although Drummond dabbled in the horses, the track had been their undoing, specifically when Charlie wound up at the Big A instead of staying at Brown for his sophomore year. There was a track axiom Charlie thought perfectly summed up Drummond's censure: "The gambling known as business looks with austere disfavor upon the business known as gambling."

Charlie decided now that the sweatshirt was merely a function of probability—a third of his wardrobe was racetrack giveaways.

"Charles!" Drummond exclaimed, as if aware of his presence for the first time. "What are you doing here?"

"Helen called—"

"The social worker?"

"She thought I ought to come pick you—"

"I see. Completely unnecessary."

"She said that you—"

"No, no, I'm fine. Completely fine."

"That's not what—"

"It's nothing you need to concern yourself with. Also, you should be in school."

Charlie was given pause. "You don't mean Brown, do you?"

"Clara Barton," Drummond said as if the question were inane.

"I graduated from Clara Barton twelve years ago."

Drummond rubbed his eyes. The vacancy remained.

"Oh," he said.

7

Helen Mayfield could turn heads, Charlie thought. But she was about something else. Her sunny blond hair was styled to be no maintenance. She wore a smart suit, obviously plucked off a rack, though, and not tailored in any of several ways that would have played up her figure. Her face was pale yet only cursorily made up. She was fully focused on helping others, he decided, and while not a practitioner himself, he admired it. Unfortunately, he thought, she was out of his league. And out of the league above that one too.

While Drummond dozed in a chair out in the hallway, Charlie and Helen sat at her desk, trying to talk above the Seniorobics class next door.

"Alzheimer's sufferers your father's age are a rarity," she said in a tone that was at once professional and compassionate. "Those his age already exhibiting his range of symptoms are statistically nonexistent. It's simply unfair."

She appeared to study Charlie to determine whether he needed a fortifying hand or a hug. He felt no worse than if Drummond were a stranger—some pangs but nothing that would trouble him tomorrow. Maybe it was denial. Maybe something was wrong with him. Maybe it was just the way things were. He lowered his eyes only because it seemed appropriate.

"So I guess a couple of aspirin isn't going to do the trick here," he said.

She smiled. "There are a number of Alzheimer's medications. Sadly, the best only slow cognitive decline, when they work at all. The neurologist will fill you in."

"What's a good-case scenario—if there even is one?"

"You might get lucky with donepezil or galantamine. Also you can expect some episodes of lucidity at random—sometimes five or ten minutes long, occasionally several hours. Still, the overall scheme of things is like child development in reverse. He's going to need full-time supervision now. I imagine you're too busy with your life to be his caregiver?"

"Something like that."

"What about other family?"

"They won't be much help. None of them are still alive."

She laughed, seemingly despite herself. "In that case, assisted living is probably the best option. It's not easy to find a suitable facility, in terms of the quality and quantity of staff, among other criteria. I'd be glad to help you."

"I'd appreciate that," he said, thinking of the time he'd get to spend with her. Left to his own devices, his criteria would be that the nursing home smell wasn't too bad and that his father could foot the bill. After Grudzev got his cut.

"Do you drink beer?" she asked.

He considered his response. Did she smell the Big A on him? Were his eyes bloodshot? Had she otherwise pegged him as a resident of Fringeville, meriting a call to the Durable Power of Attorney Department with a recommendation that they ink up the big rubber Hell No stamp?

"Sometimes," he said.

"Same. When we go over facilities, maybe we could have a beer?"

Charlie couldn't calculate the odds of this turn. He reined in his jack-o'-lantern grin lest it cause her to reconsider. "Maybe we could each have a beer?" he said.

From the sidewalk across the street, Dewart aimed a surveyor's level at the Prospect Park Senior Outreach Center. Most of his face was masked by the raised collar of his Dept. of Housing parka, along with his sunglasses, hat, and earmuffs. If someone still recognized him as one of the grad students rooming nearby, he had a story ready: He was moonlighting as a building surveyor to help with tuition.

The surveyor's level concealed a laser microphone. Directed at a second floor window, it measured vibrations in the pane and electronically converted them to the son's conversation with the social worker. The good news: Drummond had been located.

Hoping to ascertain that Drummond's disappearance had been benign, Dewart listened to the conversation through headphones concealed by his earmuffs—or rather, he tried to. Despite filtration software designed to eliminate ambient noise, he couldn't differentiate their words from the disco music blaring from the room next to her office.

8

Probably the biggest misconception about Brooklyn was that it lacked trees. Smack in the middle of the city was a two-hundred-acre forest—and that was only a fraction of the flora in Prospect Park, the masterpiece of the landscape designers Olmsted and Vaux, better known for one of their quicker jobs, Manhattan's Central Park. The treetops came into view above and between the buildings as Charlie walked Drummond out of the senior center.

"An interesting piece of information is that there are one hundred and fifty species of trees in Prospect Park," Drummond said. Once, he was a spigot of "interesting pieces of information," which, Charlie always thought, should have been billed only as "pieces of information."

Drummond was a shell of his old self, and out of whack in general, but the hour-long nap outside Helen's office seemed to have energized him. His eyes were clearer and there was vitality to his step—taken in shoes a half size too large, procured by Helen, along with a woolen overcoat.

"Say, let's let the taxicabs go on past and walk home through the park," he said. "It's such a nice afternoon."

It was dreary and forty degrees tops.

"Great idea," said Charlie. He would have agreed to do just about anything in order to capitalize on Drummond's relative and possibly fleeting coherence. He needed him to sign the boilerplate durable power of attorney document hot off Helen's laser printer.

Drummond spun abruptly and stared at a Department of Housing worker a half block behind them. The man was gazing into a pizzeria.

"Do you ever have the feeling people are following you?" Drummond whispered to Charlie.

Charlie had learned from Helen that paranoia was to Alzheimer's what sniffles were to a cold. "When I'm getting on the bus," he said.

Seeming to have forgotten all about the man, Drummond turned and resumed his course to the park. "Ah, a sycamore maple!" he said, pointing at the branches spilling over the gate. ·

In summertime, when attendance peaked and with the musicians, jugglers, and balloon sellers in full force, entering Prospect Park at the Flatbush and Empire gate was like walking into a parade. Now, as Charlie bought a pair of hot dogs and he and Drummond settled onto a bench to eat them, the crowd was limited to the lonesome vendor, a homeless man perched on a wall blowing into fingerless gloves, and a trio of construction workers quietly sipping cans of beer wrapped in paper bags.

A young father and a beaming little boy passed, hand in hand, probably on their way to the playground or the zoo or the carousel. Charlie was reminded how badly he'd wanted to go to those places as a kid. Drummond took him only to the historic house, where the butter-churning demonstration was as fun as it got.

Charlie tasted the same bitter regret now, which made broaching the topic of institutionalizing his father no harder than asking him to pass the ketchup.

"Dad, I think you'd do well to live somewhere with people to look out for you."

Drummond happily tore open his third ketchup packet. "Why is that?"

"You remember the business with the Meals on Wheels van, right?"

Drummond was focused on squeezing the ketchup onto his hot dog. Charlie felt like he was talking over a lousy long distance connection.

"Meals on Wheels, Dad?"

"Right, right. I suppose that in another culture, I'd be shoved out to sea on an ice floe about now, correct?"

Charlie hadn't anticipated nearly as much awareness. He hurried to unpocket the document. "Signing this gives me your power of attorney."

"That's reasonable, I suppose. What do you have in mind for me?"

"Helen recommended a few assisted-living residences."

"Eh. Those places are just waiting rooms for the cemetery."

"I'm not so sure about that." Charlie opened the manila envelope Helen had given him. "I personally would be delighted to move into any of these." He passed four brochures to Drummond, who grudgingly accepted.

They could have been mistaken for glossy advertisements for resorts, and the names would have done little to correct the misimpression— the Greens at Four Oaks, Mountain View Lodge, the Orchard, Holiday Ranch. Each brochure brimmed with striking, full-color photographs of ascendant suns igniting dewy fairways, hiking trails through forests at the blazing peak of New England autumn, and lakes that outshone most gems. Only Holiday Ranch hinted on the cover that it was a senior citizens facility, billing itself as "An Active Retirement Residence!"

"According to Helen, Holiday Ranch is incredible across the board," Charlie said. "But the really incredible part is they've just had an opening, which hardly ever—"

"What I want is to go to Switzerland," Drummond cut in. He pushed the brochures away as if they were junk mail.

"*Switzerland?*" Helen had said that Drummond initially thought he was in Geneva. As far as Charlie knew, Drummond had never been to Europe. Also Charlie couldn't recall him ever mentioning Switzerland, save a purportedly interesting piece of information about cheese. "What is it with you and Switzerland?"

"I don't know anything about it."

"For one thing, you just said you wanted to go there."

"Oh, that, yes. The facility I had in mind is in Geneva."

"That sounds great, but I have a feeling your financial picture doesn't include Geneva. Other than the one upstate."

"I can afford to go wherever I want," Drummond said with uncharacteristic defiance.

Helen had warned of delusions. "My guess is we're going to need to wring every cent we can out of Medicare to swing any of these places," Charlie said, "and that's before the shuffleboard fees. And assuming that

Perriman Appliances has a decent pension plan. *And* that you get top dollar for your house."

Drummond dismissed the notion with a flick of his hand. "I have nearly eight million dollars in my retirement account."

"Oh, really? I didn't see a picture of you in the *Daily News* holding up one of those giant checks from the lotto."

"Give me the power of attorney document."

Charlie happily handed it over, along with a pen, and flipped to the signature page. Drummond bypassed the signature line and began sketching, in the white space beneath it, what looked like a washing machine—which might cause the official responsible for approving durable power of attorney documents to question whether the signatory had been of sound mind.

"I think they're looking for a signature on that, actually," Charlie said, laboring to maintain his façade of cheerfulness.

"I need to show you something first," Drummond said.

He set the document on the bench and stuffed the remainder of his hot dog into his mouth, freeing up the foil wrapper. He smoothed the wrapper over a thigh, flipped it to the white, papery side, and began to draw again.

Another washing machine. This time, where the clothing would go, he added zigzags, squares, and circles.

"It's one of your machines," Charlie said. "I get it, I get it."

"You do?"

"Sure, you made eight million bucks selling washing machines."

"How on earth did you know?"

"You told me, like, a minute ago."

"Oh."

Drummond looked down at his picture without recognition. Charlie could practically see the fog rolling back into his mind.

"It's getting awfully warm," Drummond said with a shiver.

"Sign the thing, I'll get you a nice cold soda."

Drummond took up the document and wrought the firm signature Charlie remembered, the letters in perfect alignment, like a ship's masts.

As soon as they left, the homeless man descended from his wall. He dipped a grimy sleeve into the garbage pail by the bench where Drummond Clark and his son had been sitting.

The construction workers swapped smirks. Probably they thought he was searching for redeemables. Were they to have looked closer, they would have seen him bypass several shiny Coke cans in favor of two balled-up hot dog wrappers. A closer look still would have revealed him to be remarkably fit. Even at that proximity, though, his own mother probably wouldn't have recognized Pitman.

A glance at the inside of Drummond's wrapper was all he needed. In sketching the Device, even in this crude fashion, Drummond had effectively drawn his own death warrant, and possibly his son's.

Pitman pushed a frayed lapel to his lips. Into a microphone concealed by a dirt-caked button, he said, "I'm afraid our roof is leaking."

9

Charlie and Drummond crossed busy Bedford Avenue to Prospect Place, where Drummond lived. In the dwindling sunlight, the stucco homes looked like they were built of muck. This, Charlie thought, was the Brooklyn that Manhattanites had in mind when they wrote off the whole borough as depressing. Drummond's melodyless humming was a fitting sound track.

"We still have a few minutes before the bank closes," Charlie said, thinking of Grudzev. "I wouldn't mind getting them to cut a check for the Holiday Ranch deposit."

Drummond halted abruptly in the middle of the crosswalk.

"As a backup, just in case Geneva doesn't pan out," Charlie quickly added.

Drummond stared down Prospect Place. Any second the light on Bedford would turn, releasing a stampede of cars and trucks.

He was fixated, Charlie realized, on the gas company man lumbering out of a house halfway down the block. The distance and shadows made it impossible to tell whether it was Drummond's house or a neighbor's.

"What's the gas man doing here?" Drummond said.

"Something to do with gas?"

"They're never here this late."

Drummond leaped onto the sidewalk and ran toward the gas man.

More paranoia, Charlie thought. He ran too, for fear that Drummond would keep going and wind up in Cleveland.

The gas man shot a look up the block at Drummond, and at once turned and strode in the opposite direction.

"Wait!" Drummond shouted.

The gas man didn't look back. Either he hadn't heard, or, Charlie supposed, he'd had his fill of addled seniors haranguing him about soaring utility rates. He disappeared around the far corner onto Nostrand Avenue.

Charlie reached Nostrand just after Drummond. Of the two, oddly, only Charlie was panting. "I guess you forgot sixty-four-year-olds can't run like that," he said.

Drummond didn't reply, instead taking to prowling the block like a bloodhound. This part of Nostrand was solely residential. There was no vehicular traffic now and just a half-dozen pedestrians, none of whom wore the gas company's distinctive baggy white coverall. Drummond peered into shadowy doorways, the gaps between parked cars, even behind clusters of trash cans.

"He probably just went inside one of the buildings," Charlie said, hoping that would be the end of it.

"It's easy to find a parking space around here," Drummond said.

Charlie took it as a non sequitur. "So?"

"It's strange that he had no truck."

It was a decent insight, Charlie thought, particularly given Drummond's condition. The gas men drove everywhere, and if they couldn't find a spot within a short waddle of their appointment, they double-parked. If somebody gets blocked in for a couple minutes, their pragmatism dictated, them's the breaks. Yet there had been no gas company truck parked on Prospect Place, and there was no truck parked here or driving off.

"Still, there's a ton of good reasons he wouldn't have his truck," Charlie said. "Like, at his last stop, it got blocked by the phone company truck."

"What got blocked by the phone company truck?"

"The gas man's truck."

"Oh," Drummond said. "I hope we'll have as nice a day tomorrow." He turned and strolled back toward his block.

When Drummond had first come charging onto Nostrand, the gas man—really, Dewart—was on the sidewalk, just fifty feet away, one of the six pedestrians. On rounding the corner, he'd whipped off his cover-all and slung it into a trash can. Underneath he had on a black running suit that fit snugly over his slender frame. The tight knit cap, which he yanked from a pocket, compressed his thick hair, transforming the shape of his head dramatically, and even more so when seen from behind—Drummond and Charlie's vantage point. His intent was to appear to them, and to anyone else, as no lumbering gas man but, rather, as a trim yuppie en route to a jogging path in Prospect Park.

In fact he had visited Drummond's house on matters pertaining to gas. Before leaving, he lowered the thermostat to fifty-six. He figured Drummond would raise it when he returned home, at which point, on the opposite side of the readout panel, the thermometer coil and the mercury switch would rotate, sending current through the mercury and energizing the relay to the furnace two stories below. The burner would light a small amount of fuel, generating hot gas to warm the air in the house. The burner would also light the wick that was held in place, as of a short while earlier, by a nylon sleeve the size of a cigarette. The wick would set fire to a great deal of additional gas. Upon inspection, the resulting explosion would pass for a leak resulting from ordinary wear and tear. As the saying goes: Anybody can kill someone; it takes a professional to make someone die an ordinary death.

10

The house smelled to Charlie of his childhood: industrial-strength cleanser. As ever, the place had all the warmth of a chain hotel—no framed photographs, no bowling trophies, none of the knickknacks usually found in a home. The closest the old man ever came to decorating was shelving books in alphabetical order by author.

The only thing new was unopened correspondence, stacks of it, all around. After Drummond went to bed, Charlie nosed through it. He found numerous memos from Perriman Appliances, where Drummond had been placed on long-term disability leave. Charlie also found three unpaid utility bills. Adding them to his sudden awareness that the house was freezing, he figured he'd solved the mystery of the gas man: The guy had been here to cut the old man off.

Charlie climbed upstairs. Tiptoeing past Drummond's bedroom and to the end of the narrow corridor, he checked the thermostat.

Fifty-six.

So much for the gas man theory. On this cold night, Drummond must have *lowered* the heat. Charlie cranked the thermostat to seventy-five.

On the way back to the stairs, he paused at the doorway to his old room. The only remaining mementos of youth were the scale miniatures his father used to bring back from sales trips to D.C. Dust made it appear snow had fallen on the Lincoln and Jefferson memorials. Charlie again felt the chagrin of the birthday when he tore off the gift wrap, hoping for a PlayStation joystick, and found a Washington Monument.

His recollection was cut short by a gunshotlike crack that rippled into the night, leaving the mirrors and windows upstairs abuzz. He froze, until hearing the creak of floorboards in Drummond's bedroom.

Drummond had gotten out of bed in response to the cold, Charlie pieced together, then heaved open his bulky, spring-loaded window, which sounded like a gunshot.

Charlie stepped into Drummond's bedroom. In robe, pajamas, and slippers, Drummond stood at the wide-open window, gazing at the dark patch of a backyard a story below. Charlie joined him. There was nothing to see but the swing set Charlie's mother had given him, now just three rusty legs and a rusty crossbar.

Charlie said, "It'd probably be best to shut—"

The blast, which must have been heard for miles, made it feel as if the house jumped its foundation. Cupboards banged open. Doors jumped off their hinges. Drawers flew. Glass shattered.

A mass of bluish-red flame surged up the stairs, through the door, directly at Charlie. He was burning hot before it was upon him. He thought he would be incinerated.

Drummond dove, wrapping his arms around him and propelling them both out the window.

11

The explosion left walls charred on the houses on either side of Drummond's. Scraps of stucco and wood and metal littered the block. Burning hunks of timber fell from Drummond's eaves and glowed in the alleys. Waves of fire made a loud, crackling meal of the rest of the house. With coats thrown over nightclothes, dozens of neighbors poured onto the sidewalks and watched, through smoke and haze and heat, as the men of Engine Company 204 slashed the flames with shafts of water.

Among the spectators were Charlie and Drummond, uninjured but for bruises from run-ins with the swing set crossbar—fortuitous, because it slowed their descent—and the frozen ground.

Charlie was the only person in the crowd not wholly fixated on the firefighters. "Maybe something was up with the gas man after all," he said over the din.

"Oh," said Drummond.

The firemen reduced the blaze to a few stubborn sparks, and, eventually, just steam. The house was left a blackened skeleton.

While neighbors offered Drummond their sympathies and returned home, and soot-streaked firefighters coiled their hoses, Charlie shared his concerns of foul play with Engine Company 204's chief, a wiry man with a whisk broom of a mustache like those of his professional antecedents.

"We found the heat exchange tubing halfway up the block," the chief said. "Ten times outta ten, that means a fuel leak caused a boiler blow. We see it all the time with these older electric ignition units, especially with seniors who forget to check the fuel valve."

"Wouldn't the *gas man* have checked the fuel valve?" Charlie asked.

"We looked into that. The gas company hasn't got a record of any service here so far this month. Their nearest call today was way down on Bergen, at ten A.M."

Frustration heated Charlie. "Doesn't that make it *more* suspicious that the gas man was here this afternoon?"

The fireman smoothed one end of his mustache to a point. "All due respect, sir, gas men haven't got the exclusive on white uniforms."

Charlie turned to Drummond for corroboration. Drummond was hunched on a stoop, engulfed by an oversized, lime green down coat lent by neighbors who probably were in no rush for its return. He was watching the ribbons of steam blend into a purple sky. In his right mind he'd be distraught. His eyes showed only childlike wonder.

"If the guy were a house painter or Mister Softee or anybody else in a white uniform, it's still strange," Charlie said to the chief. "The way he glanced up the block, then rushed off—now that I think of it, it was like he was on the lookout for my father. Then he just *disappeared* onto Nostrand, which is a bunch of locked brownstones without alleys between them. There was no time for him to get inside a building. And we looked everywhere else; if there were even a manhole for him to have gone down, we'd have found it. So you have to think he had some kind of escape route."

The chief glanced at his truck. His men were all aboard now, impatient to go. Returning his focus to Charlie, he pursed his lips. "Sir, there are set fires that go past us, sure. It takes a real professional though, and I mean a heckuva pro. Why would a guy of that caliber be in this neck of Brooklyn picking on a senior citizen?"

Charlie weighed the odds that "HumDrummond" would be the target of a professional assassin.

"I guess you're right," Charlie said.

The fire trucks barreled off into the darkness, and Prospect Place reverted to its usual eleven P.M. form—the occasional taxi, the odd homeward-bound drunk, talk shows flickering behind window shades. Charlie and Drummond should have been in a taxi headed to Charlie's apartment for the night. But the gas man was stuck in Charlie's thoughts like a sliver of glass.

Settling alongside Drummond on the stoop, he asked, "Dad, have you been playing the horses lately?"

"Do you mean gambling on horse races?"

"Yeah."

"I've never done that."

"Are you sure?"

"I think so."

"There used to be *Racing Forms* around the house all the time."

"There used to be *whats* around the house?"

"*Racing Forms.* As in the *Daily Racing Form*—'America's Turf Authority Since 1894.' You used to pick it up at the magazine store or the newsstand in the subway, like, every day. You couldn't have been reading it just for your edification."

"I suppose not."

"I was thinking, what if you called in a bad bet, then forgot, for whatever reason, to pay up? The characters in that racket don't take it so well when they don't get their money—or so I've heard."

"Pardon the intrusion?" came a man's voice.

Charlie looked up to find a lanky twentysomething in a conservative, dark-blue suit and gray overcoat. He had fine features; precisely combed, wavy hair; and the earnest demeanor of a student body president. Charlie had noticed him before, among the spectators.

"My name's Kermit Smith," the young man continued in a smooth blend of country and urban refinement. "I'm an attorney—"

"He was thrown out of the bar," shouted a second man, walking the curb like a tightrope and failing, probably a function of the brown paper bag he clutched and the bottle of booze it surely contained. He was about the same age as Smith but shorter and stouter. He too wore a blue business suit and gray overcoat. His shirt collar was open and the knot of his tie was halfway down his chest.

"That's my friend, for lack of a better word, MacKenzie," Smith apologized to Charlie. "The bar he referenced is the Blarney Stone on Flatbush. Probably by now you've developed a theory as to which of us in fact was the problem."

Clever guy, this Kermit Smith, thought Charlie. But ambulance chaser all the way. In this part of Brooklyn, at this hour, the Samaritans were only bad.

Seeming to have read Charlie's edginess, Smith said, "Cutting to the chase, I overheard some of your chat with the fire chief. I'm with Connelly, Dumbarton and Rhodes, notable for winning twenty-four of twenty-four negligence suits against boiler manufacturers by convincing juries that the victims would have needed to be rocket mechanics to adequately maintain the dozen or so indeterminate valves on the older electric ignition units. If you're at all interested . . ."

The fire had made selling the house hugely problematic. Who knew how long it would take and how much work would be required to collect the insurance—assuming Drummond had remembered to make the payments? "I guess it couldn't hurt to know about, on my father's behalf," Charlie said, faking a yawn so as not to appear overeager. This was an arena in which a clever ambulance chaser could yield a big score.

MacKenzie griped, "Come on, we're gonna miss last call at Flanagan's."

Turning his back on his friend, Smith said to Charlie, "Why don't we step into my office for a moment?" He took a few steps down the sidewalk.

"Just give him your card already," MacKenzie said, prompting Smith to stray farther.

"Dad, please don't go anywhere for half a second?" Charlie said.

Drummond nodded. Charlie's concern was eased only a little.

Catching up to Smith, he noticed a sparkling new black BMW Z4 roadster four parking spots down. "I've always wanted to win a boiler manufacturer negligence suit and buy one of those," Charlie said.

Smith advanced to take the car in. "Well, this could still be your lucky night." He halted in a pool of shadows between streetlamps and reached into his coat, presumably for a business card or BlackBerry.

Smith's larynx was crunched by a fist, thrown by Drummond on a dead run.

So strange was this turn of events that Charlie closed his eyes, expecting that when he opened them, the hallucination would be over and Smith would be standing there, by himself, BlackBerry at the ready.

When Charlie opened his eyes, he found Smith teetering, his attempt to breathe resulting in a feeble croak. Charlie saw Smith had drawn from his coat not a BlackBerry but a pistol with a barrel capped by a silencer.

Drummond's right fist blurred into an uppercut, snapping Smith's wrist and costing him his hold on the grip. The gun hit the sidewalk with a metallic bass note and bounced away.

Drummond drilled a left into Smith's abdomen. The tall man reeled.

Eyes aglow with more than the reflection of the streetlamps, Drummond kept after him, heaving a roundhouse into his jaw and driving him backward. Smith stumbled over a cluster of full trash bags and appeared to lose consciousness in the tumult of cans and bottles.

Charlie looked on, cold air filling his gaping mouth. As far as he knew, Drummond had a hard time hitting a Ping-Pong ball.

Drummond meanwhile darted after the pistol. With it just inches from his grasp, he stopped abruptly and reversed course, leaping onto a stone stoop. From up the block came a muted cough. A bullet rang the metal banister inches above his head.

Halfway up the deserted sidewalk, Smith's stocky friend MacKenzie wobbled, no longer like a drunk, but rather, a concussion victim. A chute of blood from his nose glowed as he staggered past a streetlamp. Drummond must have started on him, Charlie figured, but hadn't had time to finish in his rush to stop Smith. In MacKenzie's hand was the paper bag Charlie had imagined concealed a liquor bottle. Protruding from it now was a silenced gun just like Smith's.

Charlie stood in place on the sidewalk and watched him advance. Fear jammed everything, not least of which was Charlie's mechanism for deciding what to do. The next thing he knew, he was falling.

He hit the sidewalk between the stoop and a trio of steel trash cans. Drummond, he realized, had reached through the banister spindles and pulled him down.

Another bullet hissed from MacKenzie's silenced barrel, stinging the sidewalk inches from Charlie's knees.

The most rudimentary survival mechanism enabled him to bunch himself so that the trash cans at least blocked him from MacKenzie's sight. From there he eyed the rest of the block. There were no pedestrians or motorists to provide help. Still, he thought, the neighbors would be deluging the 911 switchboard, as he would have himself if his cell phone, along with his coat, hadn't been a casualty of the blast. Then he considered, with a wave of nausea, that the neighbors had been given no reason to glance out their windows. There had been no roar of guns, no noise at all as cities go. And if someone happened to raise a blind, what would he see now? The shadows concealed MacKenzie's gun if the open lapels of his overcoat didn't. It would appear a clean-cut yuppie was ambling home.

Every part of Charlie trembled at the dull patter of MacKenzie's soles, the volume increasing as he neared.

Within thirty yards, or close enough that he was unlikely to miss, MacKenzie fired again. The bullet bored into a steel trash can on a direct course for Charlie's head. It exited on his side of the can and hit the stoop, ricocheting harmlessly away. Because Charlie was in flight, his elbow in his father's firm grip.

12

Nostrand was a still life, save the yellow cab idling in a parking spot halfway down the block. Drummond ripped open the rear driver's side door and dove in with Charlie in hand like a suitcase. A plump Middle Eastern man of perhaps forty-five sat behind the wheel, munching a kabob to "Jingle Bells" on the radio. "Where to?" he asked, as if their means of arrival were nothing out of the ordinary, which, Charlie thought, probably was the case in late-night Brooklyn.

Charlie turned to Drummond with the expectation that he would announce a destination. Indeed, Drummond pointed straight ahead and opened his mouth. But nothing came out. It seemed the words had stumbled along the way or gotten lost. And the glow in his eyes was fading, as if his power cord had been yanked.

"How about the police?" Charlie said.

Drummond appeared to think about it. Or he just sat there and said nothing. Charlie wasn't sure which.

Charlie's eyes flew to the movement in the rearview mirror. He whirled around to find MacKenzie in a crouch at the corner of Prospect and Nostrand, a hundred feet behind them, using the top of a *Daily News* vending machine to steady his gun.

A chunk of the rear window burst apart. Bits of glass sprayed inward, stinging Charlie's neck, ears, and scalp. A slug imbedded itself behind the driver's head in the inch-thick sheet of Plexiglas dividing the cab.

Drummond ducked beneath the window line. If PlayStation games represented reality with any accuracy, Charlie knew the car's chassis offered little protection against a full-metal-jacketed round traveling at near the speed of sound, and the seat essentially provided no additional defense. Nevertheless he dropped all the way to the floor and lay there, petrified.

"Just go anywhere," he managed to call to the driver.

Ibrahim Wallid was the driver's name, according to the ID rubber banded to his sun visor. He tried to reply, but no sound would come. He gripped the wheel and stomped on the accelerator, bringing the engine to a throaty roar.

But the taxi was still in park.

Drummond's headrest burst into particles of foam. Again a bullet bashed into the Plexiglas behind Wallid.

Trembling, the driver flailed at the gearshift arm. He clipped it with his wrist, snapping it into drive. With the accelerator already flush against the floor, the cab lurched forward like a dragster, laying half-block-long stripes of rubber. Another bullet sparked the top of a parking meter behind them.

Wallid ratcheted the wheel, turning the taxi at almost a right angle onto a clear Carroll Street block. Centrifugal force hurled Drummond into Charlie's spine. While explosive, the pain was a minor consideration because they were safely away.

Climbing back onto his seat, Charlie asked—shock had thrown off his governor so that it came out as a scream—"Who the hell were they?"

Drummond brushed bits of glass and foam from his hair. "Who?"

"The guys who tried to murder us a minute ago!"

"Oh, right, right, right." Some of the light returned to Drummond's eyes. "Tell me something? What's today's date?"

"The twenty-sixth."

"Of?"

"December."

"The last time I recall checking the calendar, the leaves had just begun to fall."

"So about two, three months." Charlie hoped this was leading somewhere.

Drummond waved at the shattered rear window. "This probably has to do with work." As if drained by the thinking, he sagged into a reclining position.

Charlie needed more. "I never thought of the appliance business as quite so deadly."

Drummond nodded vaguely.

"How about the way you knew how to handle yourself back there?" Charlie asked. "I'm guessing you didn't pick that up at the repair and maintenance refreshers?"

With a shrug, Drummond leaned against his window, content to use it as a pillow despite the cold and the rattling of the glass. His eyelids appeared to grow heavy.

"At least tell me how you knew that the first guy had a gun?" Charlie said.

Drummond sat up an inch or two. "Yes, the key was . . ." He stopped. He'd fumbled the thought. He recovered it: "The fellow lured you down the block with the thing they knew would most entice you, a monitor scheme."

"You mean a *monetary* scheme?"

"As I recall, the *Monitor* was a ship."

"I know. What does it have to do with anything?"

"The *Monitor* battled the *Merrimac*."

"Civil War, I know, I know. Was there a particular scheme the *Monitor* used?"

"The Merrimack is a hundred-ten-mile-long river that begins at the confluence of the Pemigewasset and Winnipesaukee rivers."

"You're losing me." Charlie suspected Drummond himself was lost.

"Franklin, New Hampshire," Drummond said, as if that settled it.

13

The precinct house was quiet. "It's so cold out there tonight, the pickpockets are keeping their hands in their own pockets," explained the duty officer as he led Charlie and Drummond down an empty, characterless corridor of mostly dark offices. The place had the same coarse, sour smell as all the municipal buildings Charlie had been to. He wondered whether the odor of all the humanity massed into these places was too strong for any cleaning compound, or whether all the places simply used the same inadequate cleaning compound. Either way, all things considered, he felt as if he and Drummond had reached an oasis.

They came to the squad room, a big, open space painted a drab beige with few of the wanted posters or softball trophies Charlie had expected and none of the chaos. Three detectives doing paperwork was it for action.

The duty officer directed Charlie and Drummond to Detective Howard Beckman, a man well into his fifties who looked to have been a bruiser back in his day. His thatchy gray hair was now parted ruler straight. Like his sport coat, his oxford shirt was crisp. His silk tie, knotted with precision, was of the quality usually seen on a cop only if he were commissioner. Charlie took Beckman for a warrior forced to the sidelines by age restrictions, striving to soften his edges with couture— though *couture* probably wouldn't be his term for it.

"So Murph says you fellas've got a good one for me," Beckman said with a smile as he gestured Charlie and Drummond into the chairs before him. Charlie liked the old cop right out of the gate.

Battling his own incredulity, Charlie delivered what felt like a thorough rendition of events. Drummond sat quietly, occasionally nodding in corroboration, mostly gazing at his slippers.

Afterward, Beckman cupped his solid jaw in a hand, evoking a general pondering a battlefield map. "Quite a day," he said. His tone was pure sympathy. Unfortunately his eyes divulged skepticism. He disappeared behind a giant computer terminal. "Let's start with the fire," he said, picking up the pace. "I see Chief Morris of Company two oh four ordered plywood over your windows and doorways to keep out looters, which is standard. He requested stepped-up police patrol—same reason, also standard. But there's no request for a look-see by a fire marshal, nothing like that. If he'd thought anything was fishy . . ."

"At that time the gas man and the boiler blowing up seemed like coincidence," Charlie said. "The two guys trying to shoot us made for a pattern."

The detective slurped hot coffee from a tall Styrofoam cup. "I've also got the report from the patrol car that the duty officer sent by." He dipped behind the terminal again and read aloud, " 'Resident officer saw and heard nothing out of ordinary. Officer observed no signs of gunplay, no casings, nothing out of ordinary.' "

Charlie had the same creeping, itchy sensation he did when a horse he'd bet began to let the lead slip away. "These guys, though, they clearly weren't amateurs."

"Then they would've tidied up, yeah. Understand this wasn't a full forensics team Murph sent over."

"What about the bullets in the Plexiglas divider in the cab?"

Beckman brightened. "That could be something, yeah." A burst of right and left index finger pecks at his keyboard and he relayed, with disappointment, "No new incident reports from Transit on the system."

"How long does it take for them to show up?"

"Not this long. It's the cab companies' first priority, if only so they can put in for insurance."

"Wallid said he was going straight to his garage, but I wouldn't be surprised if he stopped to get a drink first. My luck, the cab was stolen while he was in the bar."

"A lot of times, especially late night, the guy's an illegal with a borrowed hack license. Shelling out for the body work himself beats dealing with Immigration, you know?"

"Great," Charlie said. So the cab getting stolen would actually be better luck.

"We can still get to him," Beckman said. "I show three licensed cabbies named Ibrahim Wallid in the metro directory, plus a Wallid Ibrahim. We'll call 'em tomorrow, find out if one of their vehicles is out of service." He returned his attention to his coffee.

Charlie's anxiety escalated into a feeling like that of a cold coming on. "So I guess, from a procedural standpoint, this doesn't rate any more immediate action than a purse snatching?"

Beckman smoothed his tie. "The thing you gotta understand is, even on a slow night like this, we're gonna have half a dozen complaints where somebody's actually been shot. What the department would need to sink its teeth into yours is the *why*. *Why* would a sixty-four-year-old appliance salesman, even one who's surprisingly good with his fists, have professional hit men after him?"

All Charlie could come up with was, "That's the question of the night."

With an outstretched palm, Beckman put it to Drummond.

Drummond raised his shoulders.

Beckman massaged the bags under his eyes. "The best thing'd be if you fellas come back tomorrow when the flip-chart lady's here so she can sketch composites of your guys. They match anything in the system, we're off to the races."

"What do we do in the meantime?" Charlie asked.

"I'll put the write-up into play on the double. Maybe we'll get lucky and the name Kermit Smith, even if it's fake—or Smith in some combination with MacKenzie—will click somewhere in the system. Or, you never know, maybe a call will come in from an old lady on Prospect Place who was up late watching the Shopping Channel, saw two young male Caucasians in business suits pile into a car, thought it was suspicious that one of them had a bloody nose *or a gun,* and wrote down the tag number." Beckman plucked an ornately monogrammed leather card holder from his top drawer and dealt a pair of business cards across the desk. "Till then, if anything comes up, or if there's anything else I can do—"

The bulky dot-matrix printer on the stand behind him sputtered type onto tractor-fed paper, giving him pause and halting the activities of the other detectives.

"I'll get it in a sec," he told them. He was also telling Charlie and Drummond that their interview was over.

Charlie saw no remaining choice but to plead. "What if MacKenzie used the taxi's tag number to track us here? Or what if Smith followed us in his own car—like that new BMW, which, come to think of it, no one in his right mind would have left on the street overnight?"

Beside the printer stand was a window with a view of the street in front of the precinct house. With a tilt of the head that way, Beckman said, "Be my guest."

Approaching the glass, Charlie was irked by the reflection: The detective was rolling his eyes. All Charlie saw outside that he hadn't before was a *Daily News* truck delivering tomorrow's copies to the sidewalk vending machines. Nothing else even moved. Beckman's reaction no longer seemed unwarranted.

What the hell were you expecting? Charlie asked himself. MacKenzie lying in wait with a sniper's rifle? Smith revving the black BMW in preparation to mow you down?

As he stepped away from the glass, the message on the tractor-fed paper grabbed his attention.

12/26/09 @ 23:58:04

*.TXT SENT VIA NATIONAL LAW ENFORCEMENT
TELECOMMUNICATIONS SYSTEM*

TO: NEW YORK PD 107 STATIONS
FROM: DC FEDERAL BUREAU OF INVESTIGATION 100037870

CHARLES CLARK, 30, AND DRUMMOND CLARK, 64, SOUGHT FOR
QUESTIONING BY FBI RE: TONIGHT'S (12/26/09, AT APPROX 2330)
ARMED ROBBERY/HOMICIDE OF TAXI DRIVER WALLID,
IBRAHIM ELSAYED, 43, IN THE MACY'S PKG LOT ON FLATBUSH
AVENUE IN BKLYN, NY. MULTIPLE EYEWITNESSES SAW CLARKS
FLEEING SCENE.

14

Charlie grabbed the printer stand to steady himself, then looked over the message again, to find the words that in his harried state he must have misread.

He saw he'd misread nothing.

Poor Wallid, he suspected, had merely stumbled into the same dark pit he had. He wanted to study the message further, in hope at least of deriving some idea of what to do now, but he didn't want to risk drawing the detectives' attention. He was certain of just one thing: Staying here in the precinct house meant submitting to arrest, which would only make life easier for Smith and MacKenzie. If they—or whoever sent them—could either fake an FBI bulletin or get the FBI to send a real one, they'd be able to waltz into a holding cell here. They'd have Charlie and Drummond in their custody within fifteen minutes.

"Nobody out there?" Beckman called over.

Shaking his head, Charlie summoned an earnest-sounding, "Detective, thank you so much for your time. We won't take up any more of it."

"Okay," Beckman said with cheer that seemed genuine. He started up from his desk chair, headed for the printer.

At the same moment, the thick toe of one of Charlie's Converse All Stars caught the carpet at a bad angle. He stumbled and flailed wildly at Beckman's desk. Intentionally. The target of his flailing was the large Styrofoam coffee cup on the desk.

He struck it squarely, splashing at least ten ounces worth of potentially permanent stains onto the detective's dress shirt and silk tie.

"Of all the fucking ties," the cop said, pounding the desktop.

"I'm so, so sorry," Charlie lied.

With a prolonged grunt, Beckman launched himself out of the squad room, capturing the attention of the two other detectives. Just as Charlie had hoped.

Exigency overrode his nerves, allowing him to double back to the printer and tear along the perforation at the base of the page.

To his ear, the tear was loud enough to rouse area seismographs. The detectives, cackling as Beckman plunged into the men's room across the hall, didn't look over.

Charlie was hardly put at ease. Others in the precinct house would read the same bulletin. Alternatively the names Charles and Drummond Clark, which the duty officer had logged into the system, would "click." The phones here would begin ringing any second.

"We're leaving," Charlie whispered, pulling Drummond up from his chair.

Perhaps too hastily. The action drew odd looks from both of the detectives.

"I was thinking the least I could do is buy Detective Beckman a new cup of coffee," Charlie told them. "Can you tell me where . . . ?"

"Take a left outta here," said the detective nearer to him, "then right at the copier. End of the hall, hang another right, you can't miss it."

"Thanks, officer," Charlie said. "See you in a minute."

Entering the corridor, he turned right, toward the elevator.

"What about the coffee?" Drummond asked.

"That was an attempt at diversion," Charlie said. "We're leaving, actually, because we've been framed for murder, and if we're detained, we're as good as dead."

"I see," Drummond said, as if he got this sort of thing all the time. Or because he had no clue what was happening. He seemed in no hurry.

"You do get that we're fugitives?" Charlie asked.

"Yes, yes, framed for murder—I understand."

Charlie ran for the elevator and pounded the down button.

Drummond turned into the adjacent stairwell.

Just as well, Charlie thought, backpedaling and shoving through the stairwell door. His hurried steps resonated as if the raw concrete space were a canyon. Drummond doubled back to catch the door before it could boom into the frame, then he resumed his leisurely descent.

Maybe his pace was deliberate, Charlie thought. If nothing else, it was less conspicuous.

Nearing the door to the lobby, Charlie slowed too, just in time to avoid being spotted through the glass porthole. The duty officer was hurrying across the lobby.

Fighting the inclination to duck beneath the glass, Charlie continued walking toward the next flight of stairs, which led to the basement. He beckoned Drummond, who followed as if he had been headed to the basement all along.

Charlie glanced out again as he passed the door. Trailing the duty officer were two stern and determined-looking men in plain gray suits. FBI agents. Had to be. Charlie's heart erupted into a beat strong enough to give him away.

It all but stopped with the realization that he recognized the second FBI man: the father of the happy little boy in the park this afternoon. Unless his appearance now was a coincidence—and the odds were the same that a mule would win the Kentucky Derby—it spoke of an operation more elaborate than Charlie ever would have conceived.

The duty officer and two FBI types could be heard passing the stairwell and boarding the elevator. The duty officer, more deferential now, was launching into his pickpockets-on-a-cold-night joke when the doors clanged shut.

15

Charlie and Drummond exited the precinct house lobby onto a dimly lit sidewalk in the middle of a block of pitch-black stores and office buildings. There was no traffic. Alley cats were padding out from wherever they spent the day. The *Daily News* deliveryman was the only person in sight.

Whichever direction Charlie turned, he had the sensation that someone was sneaking up from behind. A cold gust sliced through his sweatshirt.

Taking Drummond by a sleeve, he headed downtown, if only to have the wind at their backs. He stayed close to the buildings so that someone in the squad room would have to open the window and stick out his head in order to see them.

On the slight chance Drummond's knack for evasion would yield an idea of what to do next, Charlie admitted, "Getting us out of there was as far as my plan got."

"There's an IRT station just two blocks away," Drummond said.

The Interborough Rapid Transit Company had discontinued service here, Charlie was sure of it. His only question was whether it had been before or after his birth. "It's closed."

"Oh, right, right."

There were two working subway stations in the area, each about a ten-minute walk. But by the time Charlie and Drummond made it to either—if they made it at all—they could expect a reception committee of transit cops.

"How about that?" Drummond pointed to the *Daily News* truck.

The twenty-foot-long rear loader sat at the curb two buildings down from the precinct house. Silver letters stenciled onto its driver's door spelled out HIPPO, which was apt. Its big rear door was wide open.

"You mean, stow away in it?" Charlie asked, hoping that Drummond had meant something else. Newspapers were stacked so high and tight inside the truck, it would be hard to hide, or even fit.

"No, take it."

Charlie mulled it over. Any second the "FBI agents" would finish conferring with Beckman and the other detectives, and the lot of them would stampede this way.

At the corner, the deliveryman loaded a stack of newspapers into the machine. He was the size of a grizzly. But Smith had been no peewee.

"You have another knockout punch in you?" Charlie asked Drummond.

"A knockout punch?"

"Remember how, like an hour ago, you flattened Kermit Smith?"

"By hitting him, you say?"

"I have another idea." Charlie kept to himself that it was a long shot. "Just stay put for a second."

Charlie was afraid. He recalled the horseplayer maxim: Scared money never wins. And as he did sometimes while sitting in the grandstand, he felt himself warm to the opportunity to defy the odds. He broke into a jog.

Nearing the corner, he called out, "Sir?"

The big deliveryman spun around.

"Sergeant Beckman," Charlie said. He flashed his wallet to show the business card the detective had given him, now in a transparent plastic pocket. He held it so as to give the embossed police department shield prominence. The shield glinted silver in the spill of streetlight. With a wave at his sweatshirt and jeans, he added, "Undercover."

The deliveryman stood unnaturally straight. "What's up, Sergeant?"

"I need your keys. Bomb Squad's got a special delivery with an ETA of sixty ticks. Your rig's too close to the entrance."

"No problem," the deliveryman said with a measure of relief. "Mind if I just get a better look at your ID?"

"Um—"

The revving of a mammoth engine drew their attention up the block. Drummond sat at the wheel of the *Daily News* truck.

The deliveryman showed only a little surprise.

Of course, Charlie rebuked himself. Because the keys were in the truck. Because why would anyone steal a truck like that?

"Looks like Sergeant Reilly's on it already," he said, hurrying back up the block.

Drummond opened the driver's door for him and moved to the passenger seat. "Best you drive, Charles," he said. "I don't have my license with me."

16

Stretching his feet as far as he could to operate the clutch and accelerator, Charlie had to strain to keep hold of both the gearshift and the wheel. The truck's girth made the four-lane stretch of Flatbush Avenue feel like a narrow path. Expecting half the police cars in Brooklyn on his tail, he looked to the rearview mirror to discover that the truck had no rearview mirror. There were two side mirrors; and in his, the closest thing to a blue and white cruiser was a teal Dodge sedan two blocks back.

Still, the cops would have no trouble finding them. The Hippo was as conspicuous as any ride outside Coney Island. Charlie decided to ditch it at the first place they could hail a taxi. Brooklyn College was just a few blocks away.

"So, Dad, now that we have a relatively quiet moment," he said, "would you care to enlighten me as to exactly what kind of crazy motherfucking shit you've gotten me into?"

From Drummond came no reply.

Warily, Charlie took his eyes off the road. Drummond was reclining in the passenger seat, watching a darkened factory bound past. He probably would have been asleep if not for the icy air whistling onto him through the cracked glove compartment.

"Sorry if I'm keeping you up," Charlie said.

Drummond shook his head, as if trying to align his thoughts. "I wish I knew."

"What about the eight million dollars? Does that have anything to do with this?"

"What eight million dollars?"

"You said you had eight million dollars in a bank account."

"Oh," Drummond said. No recollection.

He snapped upright, his eyes drawn to something in his side mirror.

Charlie saw a dark industrial block not much different from the last one or the one before that. Behind them was a Lincoln dating to Detroit's infatuation with the look of cruise ships, followed by a battered pickup. Next came a dump truck, then a late model Nissan. The teal Dodge that had been two blocks back was now even with the Nissan.

"Am I missing something?" Charlie said.

"This may have something to do with—" Drummond cut himself off.

"Work?"

Drummond fixated on his mirror but said nothing.

"What might we be talking about?" Charlie asked. "A customer really hot under the collar because his dryer takes too long to dry a load?"

"It's nothing like that."

"Okay, what is it like?"

"It's complicated."

"How about I get twenty questions?"

"I can't talk about it."

"Why the hell not?"

"For one thing, knowing would put you in jeopardy."

"As opposed to, say, *now*?"

Drummond nodded, ceding the point. He began to speak, only to stop.

"Come on," Charlie said. "The suspense is going to kill me first."

Again Drummond hesitated. "The truth is, Perriman Appliances is just a cover," he finally said in a whisper. "I really work for the government, in clandestine operations."

That would explain a lot of tonight. But knowing Drummond as he did—the man who complained the History Channel aired too much violence—Charlie couldn't swallow it. "So, what, you're a spy?"

"Company!"

"Like, the CIA?"

"Behind us!"

Charlie glanced at his side mirror. The players had changed only in that the teal Dodge had drawn half a block closer. "Which one?" he asked, doubtful it was any.

"The teal car," Drummond said, as if it should have been obvious.

"If you say so."

"Teal cars are very often rentals."

"I guess no one would *buy* a teal car . . ."

"They may fire."

"With all these other people around?"

Charlie's side mirror burst into particles of glass. The aluminum housing swung toward him, smashing a spiderweb into his window. He would have jumped if he weren't pinned in place by astonishment.

"Eyes forward!" Drummond shouted.

Charlie rotated his head to see a painter's van darting from a curbside parking space and into their path.

Reflexively he heaved the steering wheel counterclockwise, directing the Hippo into the left lane. There were buildings easier to maneuver than the Hippo. He sideswiped the van as the truck thumped into the left lane.

He barely registered the impact. His world had compacted into a tunnel that contained only the Hippo, the street, and the teal Dodge. Everything else was in soft focus, all sounds were muted. It took a beat to register that Drummond was speaking. ". . . we're fortunate to have a vehicle that's five tons of steel. Otherwise they could T-bone us."

Charlie had heard *T-bone* applied only to beef, but he didn't doubt its place in car chase terminology. Like Drummond's take on teal cars, it didn't seem like the stuff of delusion. So when Drummond added, "Stay as far to the left as you can," Charlie pitched the Hippo that way and only afterward asked why.

Drummond's response was forestalled by a hollow thud. A thin beam of light shone from a new poker-chip-sized hole between them in the steel wall dividing the cab from the cargo hold. A bullet must have first pierced the truck's rear door, then burrowed through the newspapers. The hole in the windshield told the rest of the story.

Every last cell in Charlie tensed in anticipation of the next bullet. "I guess they don't make five tons of steel like they used to," he said.

Drummond seemed unusually relaxed. "Did Grandpa Tony ever tell you about his apartment on State Street?"

Charlie feared a non sequitur to top the Merrimack River. "No."

"As you'll recall, he lived in Chicago during the Capone mob's heyday. Sometimes he'd hear machine-gun fire, and he'd peek out his window to see mobsters speeding by in a Cadillac that had been shot to Swiss cheese, followed by a police wagon that wasn't in much better shape. Always though, the vehicles were speeding, and the drivers were alive. The point is, it's extremely difficult to fire from one moving vehicle at another with any degree of accuracy. In all likelihood, they're just trying to fluster you. One of us getting hit by a bullet would be a matter of incredibly rotten luck."

"Then we're in trouble," Charlie said.

17

"**Get over** as far into the right lane as you can," Drummond said.

"The left lane, you mean?" Charlie wasn't sure he'd heard correctly; air was howling like a jet through the bullet hole. Also, he thought, albeit based on video game car chases, the idea was to obstruct the shooter's aim at the driver, not facilitate it.

"No, no, the right," Drummond said. "I don't want to let them get a line on our back right wheel well."

As if on cue, the Dodge drifted to that side. The man in the passenger seat nosed a gun out of his window, braced the stout barrel on his side mirror, and tipped it toward the Hippo's back right tire.

Charlie clocked the steering wheel. "Is he going for our gas tank?"

"Apparently."

"I thought, outside of B-movies, bullets don't ignite gasoline."

"In general that's true, but if he can put a hole in the tank, the diesel will gush out and soon we'll run dry. And in the meantime, if he can blow the tire, all it will take is one spark and—"

"Big blob of fire?"

"Essentially, yes," Drummond said.

Impressed by Drummond's knowledge, as well as flabbergasted by it, Charlie nosed right, just as the man in the Dodge pressed the trigger. Drummond's side mirror filled with the shot's white glare.

The bullet struck the Hippo's rear cargo door, decimating its upper hinge. Already ajar, the door swung outward. The lower hinge kept it dangling from the truck. It hammered the road, creating a comet tail of sparks, until swinging sideways and clipping the trunk of a streetlamp. Charlie felt the high-pitched clank in his teeth.

Severed from the truck, the cargo door flew at the Dodge like a hatchet.

The Dodge swerved to avoid it. The door gouged the pavement a few feet ahead of the Dodge, cartwheeled past its windshield, and slammed into a cluster of garbage pails, scattering them like tenpins.

Charlie would have cursed the luck, but the monstrous banging and rumbling in the cargo hold seized his attention.

"The newspapers," Drummond said.

"Or *Hippo* actually refers to a hippo," Charlie said.

It was quickly evident that Drummond was right: The stacks of newspapers were toppling, due either to the collision with the streetlamp or suction through the rear doorway. Bundles of papers could be heard bouncing around, like corn in a popper. The side mirror showed the cargo hold disgorging hundreds of individual copies.

The Dodge slalomed to avoid the bulk of this tabloid-sized confetti. Sheet after sheet slapped its windshield, flattened, and stayed put. The driver had to lower his window and stick out his head to maintain his course.

A still-intact newspaper clouted him in the face, bloodying his nose. A page clung over his eyes, blinding him. He kept one hand on the wheel and swept the other wildly in an effort to peel away the paper.

The passenger shouted and pointed. The driver cleared his eyes in time to see the dumpster. Too late to dodge it.

Charlie looked on like a baseball fan whose cleanup hitter has just sent one deep.

The driver of the Dodge jogged his wheel counterclockwise, so rather than head-on, he struck the dumpster with his right front quarter panel. The car bounced back into the street, its hood tented, the right headlight gone. The quarter panel flopped off.

Still, the car resumed its pursuit.

"They don't make dumpsters like they used to either," Charlie grumbled.

The newspapers had been a lucky break, he thought. Per horseplayer calculus, that severely diminished the chances of another lucky break, and it was hard to imagine escaping the Dodge, let alone lasting the night, without another half-dozen lucky breaks. As the horseplayers say, "Luck never gives; she only lends."

"Go right at Fillmore," Drummond said. "I have an idea."

Charlie took the sharp right from Flatbush onto Fillmore Avenue, requiring that he not turn the wheel so much as wrestle centrifugal force for control of the truck. The axles and tires moaned, and it felt like the Hippo might split in two, with the cargo hold continuing down Flatbush on its own afterward. The whole of the vehicle careened onto Fillmore without harm, save to Charlie's digestion.

Fillmore was a narrow, single lane through shuttered warehouses, or, as Charlie saw it, one big shooting alley. Without the cargo door, all they had to protect them from bullets was the cab's very penetrable rear wall.

What the hell was Drummond thinking?

Charlie opened his mouth to ask when the side mirror again filled with a muzzle flash. A bullet pounded through the cargo hold wall and ricocheted around like a hornet.

The Dodge sped to within a half block behind them. The gunman leaned out of the passenger window for a better shot.

"How's that idea going?" Charlie asked.

"Stop at the red." Drummond pointed at the traffic light dangling ahead.

"The rule is except when someone is shooting you!"

"Simple tactic. Listen, and we'll lose them." Drummond sounded intrepid and full of conviction. Like Patton—or at least unlike anything Charlie had ever heard from his father or thought within his range.

And it steadied Charlie. He threw the gearshift into neutral and pressed the brake. The truck slid, tires grating against the street and sending a whiff of rubber into the cab. They came to a halt on the crosswalk at the intersection with busy Utica Avenue.

"Now get ready to turn right when I say so," Drummond said.

Charlie clocked the steering wheel and tightened his sweaty grip on the gearshift knob.

A block to the left, on Utica Avenue, a green light loosed a herd of traffic led by an eighteen-wheel tractor trailer.

The Dodge, meanwhile, glided to a stop five or six car lengths behind the Hippo, close enough that Charlie could see the face of the man in the passenger seat—so mild mannered in appearance that hope flickered in Charlie that this was all some sort of misunderstanding about to be resolved.

With a grin, the man stuck his pistol out of his window and fired. Now that the vehicles were in idle, the report was earsplitting.

The round blew another hole in the cab's rear wall, buzzed past Charlie's right ear, and, on its way out of the cab, created a small cavity in the ceiling. Heart bouncing around inside his rib cage, he shoved the gearshift into first.

"Not until I say so," Drummond barked.

"But—"

"Just hold on."

The Dodge's driver rolled down his window. He was a fair-complexioned young man with hard eyes and thin bloodless lips set too tight to smile. He balanced his pistol atop the lowered glass. His shot pinged the doorframe by Drummond's head, creating a starburst. Drummond eyed it with an almost mocking indifference.

"Okay, we've held on long enough," Charlie couldn't help shouting.

"Just a few more seconds." Drummond pointed to the dense traffic rumbling along Utica from the left, led by the eighteen-wheeler.

The Dodge rolled closer, and another booming shot punched into the rear wall of the cab, creating a hole just inches left of Drummond's chest. The air filled with grainy orange haze that smelled of salt, the remains of a bag of corn chips on top of the dash.

The eighteen-wheeler rumbled to within a half block of the intersection. Any more time and the traffic would be in front of the Hippo, effectively turning Fillmore into a dead end.

"How about now?" Charlie meant the question to be rhetorical.

"Almost," said Drummond, fixating on the eighteen-wheeler.

Bullets rained against the Hippo. The smoke and the ear-wrecking reports and echoes made it feel like being inside a thunderhead.

"Go!" Drummond shouted through it all.

Charlie released the clutch and crushed the gas. With tires screaming, the Hippo bombed onto Utica. Its back end barely missed the eighteen-wheeler's front fender.

The truck driver reflexively slammed on his brakes, sending his gargantuan vehicle into an abrupt, sliding deceleration. All sound was lost beneath the howl of his eighteen tires.

To avoid rear-ending him, the young woman driving the Honda Accord darted to the right, into a lane that was parking spaces by day.

The trailer jackknifed right, filling that lane too. The Accord came to a shrieking stop a foot short of a collision.

The teal Dodge, flying onto Utica, needed to pass the Accord. To the left was the jackknifed trailer. To the right, the sidewalk. The Dodge leaped onto the sidewalk, a viable byway, if not for the streetlamp the driver had no way of seeing. With a deafening thunk, it stopped the Dodge dead.

In the remains of Drummond's side mirror, Charlie saw the streetlamp protruding from the teal hood like a stake. Much of the car was accordioned. Inside, the gunmen angrily swatted aside swollen air bags.

Exultant, Charlie said, "I hope that streetlamp is okay."

Gunning the Hippo away, he watched until the gunmen were specks. Left behind with them was his last shred of doubt about Drummond's claim. In place of it came awe and a thousand questions he was dying to ask.

"So now what?" he said for starters.

"This may have something to do with work," Drummond said.

Against a new tide of panic, Charlie said, "I know, I know—you work for the government. Clandestine operations." He rushed his words to make use of Drummond's last bits of light. "I need to know where exactly?"

Drummond sat up again. He eyed the bullet hole in the ceiling.

"I hope it doesn't rain," he said.

Part Two

Secrets of Appliance Sales

1

Fielding met Alice under strange circumstances.

He was in Havana, at a cocktail party. "Another woman asked to meet you, Nick," the hostess told him. "I'm going to have to start handing out numbers."

His physical appearance had something to do with it. He would have been just another bright-eyed, fortysomething surfer from San Diego, though, if not for his string of finds, which ranged from a cache of centuries-old gold coins to the wreck of a legendary pirate ship. And the thirty-room villa it bought him, which came with its own island off Martinique, didn't hurt.

At the same time, his success had made life tedious. The motives of others were increasingly obvious to him, and almost always economic. And he'd seen enough of the world to know it was the same everywhere. Drinking restored some of the edge—or so he rationalized it.

No amount of alcohol could make this gold-digger fest endurable, he thought. With the right woman, however, the night might be salvaged.

The woman he had in mind was Mariana Dominguez, aged ninety-four. She could be found on the veranda of the Hotel Nacional, rolling tobacco leaves from her own field into cigars that he believed were the finest on the island and possibly the world. "They're going to earn you sainthood," he liked to tell Señora Dominguez.

On the way out of the party, he traded the bartender a roll of ten-peso notes for a bottle of dark rum. He worked the foil from the cap as he strolled along the deserted Malecón. He admired the once-majestic Spanish town houses, now boarded up to keep out squatters. It was an especially dark night. If not for the slapping of waves against the seawall, Havana Bay could have been mistaken for a vacant lot.

Because of the waves, at first, he couldn't hear what the man ahead was saying, just the cruelty in his tone. Drawing closer, Fielding made out, "What's a matter, *puta,* you too good for us?" spoken with a heavy Cuban accent.

Fielding accelerated, soon discerning from the shadows a trio of street toughs surrounding a cowering young woman. The tough closest to her face repeated, "You too good for us?" A stout man with apelike facial hair, he reminded Fielding of Blackbeard.

The woman was a jogger and, taking into account the way her muscles swelled her running tights, a devoted one. Also she was lovely. *And* a redhead—Fielding's favorite. Minus the terror, he thought, her eyes would be spectacular.

The thugs reared on his approach, probably wondering whether he was drunk or crazy.

"*Buenas noches, amigos,*" he said. "I'm hoping you can direct me to the Hotel Nacional."

Blackbeard aimed a thick finger at the radiant, twin-spired colossus a half mile down shore. "See that?" he said. It was the only structure in sight bigger than a house. The other men sniggered.

"Thank you ever so kindly," Fielding said, starting toward it.

He halted when he came even with the woman. She didn't look up. Probably didn't dare. "Are you staying at the Nacional too, by chance?" he asked, knowing she had to be. It was analogous to running into a man on the moon: The lunar lander had to be his.

She cocked an eye toward Blackbeard, seeking permission to speak. He gave it with a shrug.

"Y-yes, as a matter of fact, I am," she said. Her accent was British. Fielding had presumed as much from what he would affectionately come to call her bathtub-white complexion.

"It's really dark between here and there, and possibly unsafe," he said. "Perhaps we ought to walk back together?"

The Cubans eyed one another, apparently trying to decide whether this was amusing or galling. Stepping his big chest into Fielding's face, Blackbeard said, "She's with us."

"How about I buy all of you a drink?" Fielding asked. He flashed his rum bottle.

Blackbeard grabbed a handful of Fielding's linen lapel, imprinting it with something oily. "How about you go to your hotel now?"

Fielding recoiled. "You had fish for dinner, didn't you?"

"That's it, *cabrón*." Blackbeard balled his free hand into a fist.

"Now, now, sir, please," Fielding said. "We can settle this without resorting to violence."

The second thug clucked his opinion that Fielding was chicken. The third called Fielding, "*Maricón*." Fielding knew enough Spanish to understand it as an appraisal of his sexual bent.

He told the group, "Recently I took a seminar called Emotional Balances, which, if you haven't heard, is like anger management, except it's conceived by accredited behavioral scientists. What we learned is that people feel better when they talk about their feelings. It eases the burden of facing our fears and offers us an emotional release. So what do you say we listen to one another, give it the best of our understanding, and see where it leads?"

The woman studied him, her mouth wide open in mystification.

She had beautiful lips, he thought.

"You a fucking crazy little *pedazo de mierda*, aren't you?" Blackbeard said to him.

Fielding turned the other cheek. "It's not easy, talking about your feelings, I know. But let's try, okay? Just try? One of my favorite sayings is, 'Every accomplishment starts with the decision to try.' "

He would have attributed the saying to "that great friend of Cuba, John F. Kennedy." But Blackbeard's fist was flying at his face.

He sidestepped it with ease.

"I tried," he sighed.

He set his bottle of rum on the wall in time to meet the advance of Blackbeard's confederates. He hit the first with a karate slash, causing the man to grab his wrist and cry out like an injured beast.

Fielding ducked the haymaker thrown by the second thug, then three-sixtied, gaining force, leverage, and surprise. To the man's exposed elbow, he delivered a karate strike with perhaps a little too much squash backhand. Still, it sounded like it broke bone.

Hearing Blackbeard rushing him from behind, Fielding whirled around and seized him by the waist, bursting the wind out of the big man. In the same motion he heaved him over the seawall. No splash rose from the bay ten feet below, just a heavy smack against a slab of sea rock.

Fielding spun around again, gearing up for the others' retaliation.

They were running away.

"The good news," he told the woman, "is now there's more rum for us."

She smiled, restoring some healthy pink to her face.

2

"**So who** sent you?" Fielding asked Alice.

He was fond of saying that the time they'd spent together—four weeks now—was like the mid–romantic movie montages that invariably feature the couple romping through the surf, except, despite a shared affinity for both jogging and the beach, he and Alice had yet to get around to that.

"*Sent me?*" She shifted uncomfortably on the silk-upholstered Louis XV settee in his den. Behind her, the exterior wall had been opened; the starlit beach appeared to be a mural. He paced before her, beneath the great white shark jawbone he'd kept above the mantel despite the decorator's pleas.

"Sent you, yes," he said. "Who sent you?" For the first time in a month there was no mirth in his tone. This, as opposed to some combination of the bare arms and legs protruding from her cocktail dress, the breeze off the sea, and the bamboo ceiling fans, probably explained her shiver.

Delicately, she said, "I'm not sure I know what you mean, darling."

"Let's save the trouble and pretend I've now asked, 'Who sent you?' ad nauseam, and endured all your variations of 'Sent me where?' and 'Why, nobody sent me anywhere, darling,' with you looking at me all the while like I've spent too much time in the wine cellar, shall we?"

"Okay, but I still won't know what you mean."

"All right, stick with that tack. I'll counter with a threat. But first, so you won't think it's an idle threat, let's broach for the first time the topic of what I do for a living. Alice, what do I do for a living?"

"You hunt for buried pirate treasure."

"Sometimes I do, yes. But have you ever thought about buried pirate treasure?"

"How should I think about it, Nicky?" She was playing along as though he were a seven-year-old.

He resolved to keep his emotions out of it. "Say you're a pirate. What sense would it make for you to take your treasure, which likely came at the sacrifice of lives and limbs, and dump it into an unguarded hole in the ground on a remote island you might never be able to find again?"

"What about the treasure of San Isidro?" she asked. His well-publicized search for the legendary pirate hoard was into a seventh month.

"Actually, the treasure of San Isidro is the maritime equivalent of an urban legend."

"How about your gold escudos, then?" He'd supposedly found the cache after weeks of searching along the Argentine coast. News photographs showed him neck deep in a hole on a beach, holding one of the coins aloft, its gleam matching the one in his eyes. A neophyte collector, Sheikh Abdullah bin Zayed al Saqr, bought the lot for six million dollars.

"I suspect you already know this, Alice—or whatever your name really is—but in case the brief you were given glossed over it, the truth is that the authenticity of the coins was questionable at best. Al Saqr knew that and didn't care. Because the coin deal was really a cover for . . . what, you tell me."

She looked away to hide her anguish. "Of course I've heard the rumors."

He stopped pacing, waited for her to look, then locked eyes with her. "Ever hear the one about Nick Fielding, illegal arms dealer?"

"Look, if that's the case—" She was embarking, he suspected, on an explanation of how she'd made her peace with it.

"It's the case," he said. "Moreover, as a dealer in illegal arms, one has to be ruthless, probably to a psychotic extent, though I'm probably an exception—then again, what psychopath thinks he's a psychopath? In any event, I had a man keelhauled recently. Know what that is?"

"I don't think I want to." Her eyes pooled with tears.

"Sorry, you've got to. 'Keelhauled' means dragged under a ship's hull so you drown, if you're lucky. Otherwise you're shredded by barnacles and whatnot. It would've been easier for me to put a bullet through the guy's head, of course; the keelhauling was something of a public relations move."

Weakly, she asked, "Are you going to keelhaul me?"

"Are you going to tell me who sent you?"

"Nicky, please, I—" Her voice broke into a sob.

"Then what good would keelhauling you do? You wouldn't be able to tell me who sent you."

"I wouldn't be able to tell you regardless. I haven't the first clue even why you think someone *sent* me."

"How about the night on the Malecón, when the Blackbeard look-alike said, 'What's a matter, *puta*, you too good for us?' First, the script was laughable. And how about the way he delivered the line a second time, just in case I missed it the first time because of the loud waves? Also, my dear honey trap, your hair was, and remains, red—my weakness for which is widely known. Now, before you accuse me of being vain, know I've done some homework. You claimed to be the only child of parents now deceased. You said you had an idyllic upbringing in Chiswick in West London, and you fled a tedious assistant solicitor's life in Bristol to study marine biology in the Bahamas. And your story held water, as it were. Whoever sent you did a bang-up job on your legend, if that's the right term. Probably you're one of those spooks with the single-mindedness of a mountaintop monk; you can set your real life aside for months at a time. Still, you're human, which means you can't entirely extinguish your feelings for your real life. I'm willing to wager that that will be so in the case of Jane."

Alice looked at him as though "Jane" were some strange-sounding word from the language of the indigenous Carib tribe.

She ought to have been curious which Jane he meant, though, for surely she knew several, let alone her de facto goddaughter.

"Poor play," he said. "You're masking your apprehension that I mean the little girl in South Yorkshire with pigtails the color of sunshine, who, on Christmas morning, opened an airmail package sent from this neck of the planet and delighted in its contents, a radio-controlled mermaid." He was certain this detail would get a rise out of her.

She didn't blink.

Could he be wrong about her?

"Well, then, that brings us to the evening's threat," he said. "Note the FedEx pouch over there on my desk. It arrived earlier from the UK, sent by a fellow limey of yours known as 'the Knife'—trite, sure, but if anyone deserves the moniker, it's him."

He strolled to his desk, automatically checking his computer screen for new e-mails. Nothing. Then he took up the sealed pouch. "This contains the pinky finger from Jane's left hand, removed late yesterday afternoon at the Rotherham rail yard, where she was found in what was believed to be a state of shock." Fielding disliked having had to dispatch the Knife to South Yorkshire yesterday to chloroform and butcher an innocent child, but he believed it was for the greater good. "As you may know, Jane had been warned repeatedly against playing with the feral dogs there. The dogs are currently viewed as the culprits. Now, unless you tell me who sent you, the 'dogs' will revisit Jane and tomorrow's pouch will contain—" Fielding stopped himself.

Alice had broken, though without the sobbing one would have expected based upon her maudlin performance to this point. "Fine," she said with the nerve of a different person altogether. "I'll tell you the truth. You're right. I was sent here by MI6."

"Okay, okay, good," Fielding said, preoccupied. What had caused him to stop himself mid-threat was the winged envelope icon that popped onto the computer screen, sent by one of his fellow members of Korean Singles Online. "I just need to take five, Allie. Hector and Alberto will take you up to your room. I've just received some, er, news of the hunt."

As soon as the two hulking servants led her out, he clicked open his message from Suki835. "Howdy, Cowboy232," the text began, then launched into the movies and music she favored.

He scrolled to the important part, her photograph. She had a plump, round face; pleasant eyes; and an effortless smile. She couldn't really weigh just 110, unless five four was the fib.

He moused to her silver left earring and magnified it several hundred times over, until he could read the text on the overlaid digital dot. Decrypted, it was indeed "news of the hunt," but not the hunt for the treasure of San Isidro as he had implied:

hounds lost rabbit and rabbit, jr., at utica and fillmore in bklyn at 00:35. rabbits driving ny daily news delivery truck north on utica. will unleash addl hounds asap.

Not good news, Fielding thought, but nothing to lose sleep over. How far could a feebleminded old man and a ne'er-do-well gambler get?

3

Charlie wrung another mile out of the beleaguered Hippo. When it felt like the truck was about to collapse into a pile of spent parts, he pulled into a down-market strip mall. The businesses—a supermarket, a carpet wholesaler, and five or six smaller stores—were all dark, save a few red exit signs and a display counter someone probably had forgotten to switch off.

He nosed the truck behind Sal's Cheesesteak Hut, a trailer painted to look like a giant hoagie. It sat on cinder blocks at the rear of the crumbling lot. Between the broken windows, graffiti, and garbage strewn all around, it appeared Sal had served his last steak years ago.

"I think it's closed," Drummond said.

"I like it anyway," Charlie said, "because it's big enough to hide this monster from the street, and it's just a block from here to the subway." He pointed to the elevated track, where a subway train was snaking toward the station. After midnight, the trains ran fifteen to twenty minutes apart. "We should hustle."

"Why the subway?"

Charlie jumped out of the truck. "I'm thinking, until we can figure out our next move, we'd do well to hide in Manhattan, where there are ten million people, as opposed to here, where it's pretty much just you and me."

Drummond remained in his seat. "Why don't we drive?"

There were too many bullet holes in the truck to count—the light streaming through them and into the cab resembled pickup sticks in mid-toss. Much of what had been the windows lay in fragments on streets between Fillmore and here. The rear tires were ribbons. Hurrying around the hood, Charlie left it at, "The truck's hot."

"I meant why don't we get a car," Drummond said.

"There's about a zero chance of even seeing a taxi around here now." His patience evaporating, Charlie yanked open Drummond's door.

"Our own car, I mean."

Charlie took Drummond by the elbow to help him from the truck. Or pull him if need be. "You really think it would be a good idea to go back to Prospect Place right now and get your Oldsmobile?"

"No, hot-wire a car here."

Charlie wavered between wonder and skepticism.

Of his own volition, Drummond slid to the pavement. "There have been weeks I changed cars more often than underwear," he said.

His delivery was sluggish, his eyes were overcast, and his shoulders were stooped. But if Alzheimer's sufferers retained the finer points of driving a car, Charlie thought, why shouldn't he remember how to steal one?

Light towers, one at each corner of the parking lot, transformed the area into an illuminated stage to passing motorists, of whom there were two or three per minute. Charlie weighed this against a mental image of transit cops and token booth clerks in all five boroughs currently scrutinizing his photograph. "Okay, why not?" he said.

Scattered around the lot were eleven cars and a van. Drummond pressed his face against the driver's window of the first car he came to, a late-model Chrysler sedan. With a dismissive nod, he left it behind. Same with the Kia coupe three spots down.

"Something the matter with them?" Charlie asked.

"I would need the ignition keys."

This disclosure coincided with the subway train's departure from the station. Charlie's stomach sank the same way it did when a horse he'd bet heavily fell hopelessly behind right out of the gate.

The subway fled his thoughts at the sight of the police cruiser rounding the corner. He heaved himself behind the driver's side of the Cherokee that Drummond had moved on to inspect. Drummond made no move to conceal himself; he remained standing by the driver's door and watched the cruiser. Which was what an innocent man would do, Charlie realized—too late. He was in the process of tackling Drummond.

They became a tangle of limbs on the icy asphalt. At least they were hidden from the cruiser as it zipped past.

"Sorry, I got a little carried away," Charlie said. "You okay?"

"I'm fine, thank you," Drummond said. "This one's no good either." He tapped the Cherokee with the newspaper he'd brought with him from the truck, presumably to read during the ride to Manhattan.

"You remember saying you could hot-wire a car, right?"

"Yes, yes, of course. But if the ignition barrel is encased in the dash, as it is on the newer models, it's much more difficult."

Before Charlie could ask what an ignition barrel was, Drummond was on his way to what had to be a suitable candidate, a boxy gray Buick from the days before anyone knew what "mpg" stood for.

Trying and failing to open the doors, Drummond dropped out of sight behind the hood. "An interesting piece of information is that locks with retinal scanners make exponentially fewer errors than iris scanners," came his voice. "There's no technology that allows the forgery of a human retina, you see. Also, if you kill a man, you can't use his retina, because it begins to decay immediately."

Charlie felt like crying. "So you're saying the lock on this car has a retinal scanner?"

"No, it's just an interesting piece of information, that's all." Drummond reappeared, having dislodged a softball-sized chunk of cement from the crumbling tire-curb. He flattened his *Daily News* over the back window on the Buick's driver's side, and hammered it with the cement chunk. The newsprint protected him from the spray of glass and blunted the sound—allowing Charlie to hear the yelp of brakes a few blocks away.

Had one of the cops thought twice about the unusual shadow movements he'd seen in the mall parking lot?

Sure enough, Charlie heard the garbled chatter of a police radio. Growing louder. It curdled his blood more than the siren would have.

"We have to go," he said. "Now!"

"I'm with you," Drummond said.

Charlie sprang toward the dark delivery alley between the supermarket and the carpet store. A trickle of streetlight at the far end promised a way out.

Hearing only his own footfalls, Charlie spun around. Drummond still stood by the Buick. Reaching into the gap he'd created, he opened the driver's door.

Charlie rushed back, intent on dragging him to the alley. Drummond dove past him, into the Buick, landing prone on the front seat. He flipped onto his back, snapped off the base of the ignition barrel, plucked two reds from the tangle of wires, touched their ends together, and brought the husky engine to life.

Scrambling into the passenger seat, he said, "Charles, we have to go, remember?"

Charlie shook off his astonishment—he could do nothing about his fright—and hurried into the driver's seat.

He shot the Buick down the alley, and, at the far end, turned out onto the street just as the police cruiser bounded into the strip mall parking lot. Again, he only heard the cruiser.

Driving away, he said to Drummond, "I'm impressed that you didn't have to change your underwear *every time* you changed cars."

4

"For now, the flooding appears to be under control—"

Charlie switched off the car radio. A water main break in Canarsie was the night's biggest news. No cabdriver murder story, no mention of the flight of the Clarks, nothing about traffic delays due to police blockades.

Nor was there sign of such blockades. The practically vacant Williamsburg Bridge stood just a block down Driggs Avenue. On the other side blazed Manhattan in all of its immensity and raucousness—a sanctuary, in Charlie's mind. Still his eyes bounced from mirror to mirror. The rest of him was as tense as rigor mortis in anticipation of police cars or, worse, a teal car.

Slouched in the passenger seat, Drummond registered little response to the radio or much else. His eyelids appeared weighted down.

Suddenly he cried out, "Bridge!" as if warning of an incoming missile. He plunged off the seat and bunched himself up on the rubber mat in the footwell.

It was too late for Charlie to turn back. To brake meant a certain rear-ending. The best he could do was slow the Buick. "What about it?"

Drummond looked over as if through thick fog. "They'll see us."

"Who?"

"I don't . . ." Drummond's voice fell off.

Charlie studied the steep on-ramp. A Volkswagen Beetle skipped across the threshold. At the ramp's peak, a stripe of light swept over a wrecker as it thumped onto the bridge's main span. Charlie's eyes jumped to the source of the light, the steel box mounted on the gantry above the span. The box contained a camera intended to photograph vehicles that sped or jumped red lights. Traffic cams had been blooming on gantries all over town recently. The photos were processed later— often months later—by the Department of Transportation. In cases of clear infractions, where both the license plate and the driver's face were captured, summonses were issued by mail.

"Please don't tell me that they—whoever they are—can tap into *traffic cams*," Charlie said.

"Maybe you should wear this." Drummond offered up the soiled New York Yankees cap that had been wedged into a pocket on the passenger door.

Charlie pulled on the cap. The bill draped his face in shadows. The cap itself compressed his pile of hair. A devout Mets fan, he'd always maintained he wouldn't be caught dead in anything with a Yankees logo. He never imagined he actually would have to make the choice.

The drive across the bridge and into lower Manhattan was uneventful— as far, Charlie reflected, as he knew. From Houston Street, he turned the Buick onto quiet Ludlow, intent on the quaint Italianate brownstone halfway down the block.

It was a few minutes to one. Lenore, who tended bar at the Four Leaf Clover, a horseplayer watering hole in Hell's Kitchen, ought to be home now, hopefully alone. He'd been to her apartment three nights ago. The visit lasted only as long as the nightcap that occasioned it. He left without much sense of whether he wanted to call her or whether she had any interest in hearing from him. They hadn't spoken since. So his showing up now and asking to stay the night would strike her as peculiar, to say the least. That he'd brought along his father would be off the charts. On the flip side, who would think to look for him there?

There was little activity on her block. The bodega on the near corner had no business. A middle-aged Asian man sat outside in the tent that protected the fruit and cut flowers from the elements. The portrait of boredom, he dipped a soup spoon into a small bowl. There was some movement on the other side of the blinds of the chess club on the second story. Farther down the sidewalk, a shopping cart lady had parked her cart and slept on a stoop by a heating grate. Otherwise the residential block was dormant.

Still, as Charlie drove onto it, his pulse doubled. Probably due to exhaustion, he thought. Also his blood sugar was on Empty.

No, it was the soup.

Like they say at the track, believe nothing that you hear and half of what you see. He shouldn't have been able to see the boredom on the man's face at all. There ought to have been vapor in the way, rising from the bowl. Hell, a night this cold, there ought to be a shaft of steam. Maybe Smith or MacKenzie or whoever learned about Lenore from one of the horseplayers at the Four Leaf Clover: Most of them would sell their mothers for the price of a two-buck ticket.

Or maybe the poor bodega guy's soup simply had gotten cold.

Drummond slept in the footwell. He might have a sense of whether the bodega man was something other than he appeared. But rousing Drummond risked drawing the man's attention, and more than likely Drummond would not have a sense. So Charlie simply drove past, watching the bodega in the rearview mirror.

The man shifted his position. He *was* watching the Buick.

But did that necessarily mean he was up to no good? What else did he have to do? He was bored—so bored, he probably had nodded off, allowing his soup to cool.

There was an empty parking space by Lenore's building. Charlie tapped the brake pedal.

The red taillights set aglow a circle, the size of a quarter, at the end of something the bodega man held to his right eye.

He was watching through some sort of night scope!

Shock nearly turned Charlie to stone. He fought an impulse to heave his foot at the gas pedal; he maintained the car's moderate pace. As he drove the remainder of the block, to his surprise, no bullets smashed into the Buick.

At the end of the block, he turned onto Delancey. The bodega man shifted his scope to the shopping cart lady.

While driving west on Delancey, Charlie felt regular sensation return to his body, but any sense of relief was negated by fear of what lay ahead, as well as uncertainty over which way "ahead" was. The fact that Smith,

MacKenzie & Whoever knew about Lenore's apartment turned Manhattan into an awfully tiny island.

And they were everywhere Charlie looked. Like the squeegee man on the corner. Didn't the city get rid of squeegee men last century? Or the electric company repair crew on the other side of Delancey, a common enough sight anytime. But how about the broad-shouldered guy sitting idly by the pneumatic drill while his coworkers were neck-deep in the manhole? Wouldn't he catch hell for gunning that monster in the middle of the night? Was it one disguise element too many?

Charlie turned uptown at the Bowery, only because he had no reason to, so theoretically there was no reason for anyone to suspect he would.

Hoping the ten minutes of rest made a difference, he roused Drummond. "Dad, I need some help," he said.

"My pleasure," Drummond said. In no way on the ball.

"Have you remembered, by any chance, who you work for?"

"Perriman Appliances—you know that."

Perriman was a perpetually debt-ridden Argentine manufacturer of third-rate washing machines, dryers, and refrigerators. Its early-'70s venture into automotives, a sedan named the *Chubut* for the southern Argentine province that was home to the factory, was greeted with wild enthusiasm and national pride. But reports of poor quality control— some Chubuts left the line missing parts—resulted in the nickname *Chupar* (Spanish for "to suck"), total sales of just 366 cars, and debt that nearly suffocated the company.

Perriman had had to move its midtown Manhattan office, where Drummond supposedly worked, to Morningside Heights, inconvenient to clients and prospective clients. But space there was ten to fifteen dollars per square foot cheaper than midtown. Charlie had always thought that Drummond had the brains for better; his issue was people skills.

"Tell me again what it is you do there?" Charlie said.

"You know: I demonstrate the appliances in the showroom, then go on-site with building owners and property managers to ensure that their specifications and measurements are met."

"Right, but that's just your cover, right?"

"*Cover?*"

Charlie exhaled in an effort to dispel his exasperation. It didn't work.

"How about this? When you're on all your sales trips, do you ever do any work on the side for, like, the CIA?"

"Not that I'm aware."

Which didn't rule it out.

"The NSA?"

"Not that I'm aware."

"I could get a list and call every place in Washington with a clandestine operations division, but if what we've seen so far is any indication about the resources of who or whatever's after us, odds are it'd probably be a case of the mouse calling the cat. So it would be really swell if you could remember anything."

Drummond sat up. "I think there is something about Washington."

In his excitement Charlie found himself mirroring his father's posture. "Yeah?"

Drummond massaged his temples, trying, it seemed, to stimulate the works within. "Something."

"You did go there on an awful lot of sales trips."

"A good percentage of North Atlantic Division's building owners and property managers are there. I go on-site to ensure that their specifications and measurements—"

"Oh, right, of course," Charlie said. But he was willing to bet that building owners and property managers had nothing to do with Drummond's trips.

"And nothing compares with the cherry blossoms."

There would be no cherry blossoms for months. The four-hour drive was worth it anyway, Charlie thought. D.C. was to spy agencies what Milwaukee was to breweries. And, if nothing else, as each pair of approaching headlights seemed to be saying, it was a good idea to get away.

5

The Fairview Inn was the type of motel once predominant on American roadsides, two stories of bricks, shaped like a brick itself, each upper-level room with an iron-railed balcony and each room on the ground floor opening onto a parking space. There were only four cars in the parking lot now, including a beat-up Toyota Cressida in the Reserved: Management spot behind the office. The Motel 6 on the other side of the New Jersey Turnpike had just two cars. And the Best Western Charlie and Drummond passed before that had had only a solitary RV. Evidently the holiday crowd had gone home, and business travel had yet to recommence. It was possibly the worst night of the year to be a fugitive, Charlie thought.

He brought the Buick to a stop beside the beat-up Toyota, out of sight of the Fairview Inn office. Over the rumble of the highway, he begged a sleepy Drummond, "Hang here for just a minute?"

Against his better judgment, he left the engine running so Drummond might stay warm, then he climbed into the stinging seventeen-degree night.

He rounded the corner to the side of the building that faced away from the highway. At the head of the row of ground floor rooms was a tiny office. The lights were on, but no one appeared to be inside.

Charlie rapped on the sliding window. Up popped a squat, middle-aged man, his doughy face flattened from sleeping against his desktop. His small eyes snapped to alertness, he smoothed the stripes of hair into place across his balding pate, straightened a clip-on tie bearing the Fairview's mountain peak logo, and slid the glass open an inch.

"Good evening, sir," he said. With a glance at his antique pocket watch, he added, "Technically, I should say, 'Good morning.' "

According to the letters packed into the placard, this was NIGHT MAN-AGER A. BRODY. Although other managers shared this desk, Charlie had no doubt that the meticulously trimmed miniature Christmas tree on the sill was A. Brody's work. Charlie usually felt a kinship to the A. Brodys of the world, miles below the station in life befitting their intellect. Now Charlie was far more interested in getting out of the cold.

"Hi, I'd like a room, please," he said. To diminish the chance of his being identified, he stayed at the outermost limits of the office's fluorescent haze.

Brody plucked a registration card from atop a neat stack, set it on his desk blotter, aligned it, and then tweaked it until it was exactly parallel to the edge of the desk.

"May I have your name, please, sir?" he asked finally.

"Ramirez," Charlie said, and, as soon as he did, cursed himself. His friend Mickey's last name, the first that had come to mind, was common enough around here. But even in the dark, with the bill of a Yankees cap pulled down to his eyes, Charlie was no Ramirez.

Indeed, Brody raised an brow. "And how many adults in your party, Mr. Ramirez?"

Charlie considered that the FBI bulletin might have reached the furthest outposts of civilization by now. "Just me."

Brody's brow stayed put, quieting Charlie's anxiety. "That will be fifty-nine dollars and eighty cents, please, sir."

Charlie paid with three twenties and received two dimes and a key card.

"Have a wonderful stay," Brody said with, Charlie thought, inordinate cheer.

Room 105 smelled of bathroom cleanser in combination with the flowery spray used to mask worse smells. The walls trembled each time a truck passed. Although worn, the beds were clad in crisp, clean sheets that promised sleep. And Charlie was starved for sleep.

"But how can we go to bed?" he asked as he paced the frayed carpet,

careful to stay away from the window. Drummond lay on the less con-
cave of the two beds. "Any second they could burst through the door
with guns drawn. Then what?"

Drummond sagged against his headboard. "That would be trouble?"

Charlie recognized that danger had preceded both of Drummond's
episodes of lucidity. Hopefully the threat alone would do the trick now.
"How about this? Say a sharpshooter takes a crack at us from out there?"
He waved at the window. The spotty vinyl shade filtered passing headlights so that they appeared on the inner wall of the room as giant, spi-
dery shadows.

Drummond was captivated by the shadows.

"Dad, if you could just remember a name. Even a phone number
could make a difference in whether or not we have a tomorrow."

Drummond fluffed his pillow. "Maybe if we got some sleep?"

"I don't suppose you've remembered who you work for?" Charlie
asked, on the remote chance that his tactic had had some effect.

Drummond yawned. "Perriman Appliances."

"And what's your job?"

"Deputy district sales manager for the North Atlantic Division. I
demonstrate the appliances in the showroom, then go on-site with
building owners to—"

"So you said." Charlie sighed.

He turned away from Drummond, continuing to pace in hope that
the motion would stir up a new idea. Helen might have one. He yearned
to call her—apart from his predicament. He had long accepted the
horseplayer tenet that all of life is six-to-five against—until the moment
she asked him out for a beer. The problem was that almost certainly he
and Drummond had been followed after meeting her: In all likelihood,
Drummond was right about the Department of Housing worker on the
sidewalk outside the senior center. And if Lenore was under surveillance . . .

In any case, Helen already had told Charlie that there was no sure way
to stimulate lucidity. Back at the senior center, she likened lucidity's random occurrence to a basketball player of middling ability sinking four
consecutive shots from three-point range. If there were an explanation,
no one knew it. Sometimes, however, strong mental associations trig-

gered latent memories. In this respect the Alzheimer's sufferer was like the Vietnam veteran with post-traumatic stress disorder—show him a helicopter, he's back in Saigon. Because the Alzheimer's sufferer's memory could be damaged, inoperative, or gone, however, finding such a precise mental association was a crapshoot, at best.

But a crapshoot was far superior to Charlie's other idea—doing nothing. He resolved to reel off the names of every United States president in office since Drummond's birth, the major events in history during that time, and anything else Drummond might associate with government work.

Charlie took a deep breath, spun back at Drummond, and exclaimed, "Franklin Delano Roosevelt."

Drummond was fast asleep.

Frustration joined the exhaustion and angst already blackening Charlie's mind. He wanted to fly at Drummond and shake his memory back into operation.

Rest at least had a track record, he reminded himself.

Drummond was curled into the fetal position. Charlie would have bet that the old man slept on his back in the classic coffin pose, arms crossed at right angles over his chest. Careful not to jostle him, he slid the comforter out from beneath him. Close proximity to his father had always given Charlie something of a full-body itch. But no longer, for some reason, or at least not now. Gently, Charlie covered him. He twisted the knob on the nightstand lamp in slow motion so the snap wouldn't wake him, then he tiptoed to his own bed. The springs whined as he lowered himself onto it, but not so loud that Drummond could have heard.

Drummond sat bolt upright, eyes bulging with terror.

"What is it?" Charlie asked, catching the panic himself.

"Beauregard!" Drummond cried.

"You mean the dog?" After Charlie left home, Drummond took in two retired dog track greyhounds, John-Paul Jones, who lived two or three years, and Beauregard, who lasted about a year longer.

"We forgot to get someone to look after him while we're away!"

"No, no, it's fine. Beauregard is—" Charlie stopped short of saying, "dead," seeking to soften it. He was clumsy with euphemisms. "Beauregard's with Mom."

Drummond's face twisted in mystification. "Now how would Beauregard have gotten all the way down to Monroeville?"

It sounded awfully Alzheimer's-y, but Charlie had a feeling it was a major clue. The envelope with the first of his mother's Social Security checks had borne a forwarding label; originally the check had been mailed to Monroeville, Virginia.

He got up and paced some more, trying to make sense of it.

He'd been a month shy of four when she died. He remembered a woman with the grace of a princess, the grit of a tomboy, and a whimsy all her own. She liked rain. No matter how cold the water was at Brooklyn's Brighton Beach, she let out a whoop and plunged in. The two of them never went on mere errands, they went out in search of adventure. And found it—at the time, Charlie believed riding in the shopping carts at FoodLand compared to the Paris-Dakar Rally.

He couldn't recall her funeral—just Drummond sitting him at the kitchen table and soberly relaying the details of the accident. Charlie's theory was either time had eroded the recollection or he'd blocked it out.

Tonight he developed a new theory: She never had a funeral.

"She's still alive, isn't she?" he asked Drummond.

"Who?"

"Mom."

"How could that be?"

"If she didn't in fact die."

"She was hit by a bus in San Francisco in eighty-three, killed instantly," Drummond said. His delivery was pat, much the same as when he detailed his duties at Perriman Appliances.

6

In a dark bedroom only slightly larger than its full-sized bed, Mickey and Sylvia Ramirez slept.

The telephone changed that.

Mickey looked first to the clock. 5:56.

Usually he slept until the alarm buzzed at 7:05. Then he needed three cups of coffee to dissipate the haze of semiconsciousness. Adrenaline made coffee superfluous now. Good tips often came early, before word could spread and odds could plummet.

"Fucking horseaholics," Sylvia groaned.

Mickey was well aware that people had trouble believing he had a wife at all, let alone a beauty like Sylvia. Olive skinned, with leonine features and a chute of lustrous black hair, she reminded everyone of the queens and princesses on the canvases of El Greco or Velázquez. A few minutes with her, though, and everyone realized Mickey was no luckier in love than at the track.

The phone was just inches from his pillow, atop the stacked milk crates he used as a nightstand. Sylvia always insisted on answering, her aim being to prevent other horseaholics from putting ideas into his head. By the numbers, he admitted, she was justified. So far. But it was only a matter of time, he believed, until the big score that would bring the apartment of her dreams—"the one with separate bedrooms," she liked to say.

As was their custom, he rolled out of the way and she swung wildly at the phone. Once she got a handle on the cordless handset, she answered with an indignant, "Hello?"

The entirety of her face bunched furiously toward her nose, telling Mickey who was on the line. In Sylvia's mind, Charlie was to gambling what the Devil was to sin.

"Like the rest of the fucking world at this hour, he's asleep now," she said. "But just one thing before you go, Charlie Horse: Fucking thanks a lot for Great Aunt Edith. That money was supposed to be my sofa."

Mickey could hear Charlie's pleas as she plunged the handset toward the cradle. He grabbed it in time to save the connection.

"Man, how many fucking times I gotta tell you not to call here?" he said. This was for Sylvia's benefit, which Charlie would understand. He wouldn't have risked stirring Hurricane Sylvia, especially so early, unless something big was up.

Taking the handset, Mickey shot off the bed and out of the room. Sylvia was content to roll back to sleep, thank goodness.

The linoleum in the narrow hallway froze his bare soles. He entered the compact living room, which also served as his office, and pulled the door shut delicately, so the click wouldn't wake four-month-old Alfonso—the living room also served as the nursery.

"The less you know, the better," Charlie was saying, "but I need you to help me get hold of my mother or Grudzev's going to be the least of my problems." It did not sound like the man was calling with any sort of tip. It did sound like he'd been at the bottle.

"Your *mother*?" Mickey whispered for the sake of the baby, four feet away. "Wouldn't you be wanting a lady with a crystal ball to get hold of her?"

"Listen for five seconds, please?" Charlie said, as sober as Mickey had ever heard him. "The first of her Social Security checks was forwarded to me from general delivery, Monroeville, Virginia. And last night, my father said something that led me to believe she's actually still there."

"So, you're thinking, what? Your mom, who's rich enough that she doesn't give a shit about seventeen hundred bucks a month, can solve your problems?"

"For our purposes, that sums it up."

"I'm guessing you tried calling four one one?"

"Every permutation of Isadora VanDeuersen Clark I could think of.

The closest I got was an Isaiah Clark in Arlington, which isn't in any way close. I know if anyone can find her, it's you."

"Directory assistance operators are amateurs," said Mickey, the once and future PI. He lowered himself into his swivel chair at the computer table that, lately, doubled as a diaper-changing table. He toggled a switch and set his hard drive purring.

"Fasten your seat belt," he said to Charlie. "I know a back way into the online databases the directory assistance operators use. Unpublished numbers they can't access, I can, with just a click of the option key."

His browser opened. A mouse click and three keystrokes and he was in the national master directory. A few more keystrokes and he relayed, "Nothing listed or unlisted for her. But, relax, we haven't even gotten started."

Placing his icy feet onto the radiator, he accidentally knocked a rubber bath duck from its perch atop the diaper pail. It squeaked softly on impact with the rug. Baby Alfonso awoke in full-on wail.

"Hang on," Mickey said to Charlie.

He stuffed a hand through the crib slats and rubbed the crown of Alfonso's head. As usual, the baby was back asleep in seconds. But now Sylvia was marching down the hallway.

"Hey, man, can you call me a little later at the office?" Mickey asked Charlie.

"I might not be able to, actually, because I might be dead."

Mickey didn't take this lightly. Charlie had been calm in comparison when detailing Grudzev's cup-of-sand threat. "Okay, okay," he said, mouse-clicking his way to the board of elections Web site. Its information-rich database was available only to qualified election officials. Mickey could access it thanks to a guerrilla Web site that generated functioning election official pass codes.

"I thought we were through with this shit, Moby Mick," Sylvia yelled from the other side of the hollow plywood door. She maintained it was thoughtless to speak inside the nursery while the baby slept.

"Charlie, hang on one more sec?" Mickey said.

He balanced the handset atop the hard drive and stepped out of the room, head lowered. The appearance of supplication usually helped.

"It's not the horses this time," he said.

Her eyes were hot coals. "I don't care if it's the weather. You said you don't want your son knowing you associate with the likes of that deadbeat."

Mickey winced. Charlie probably had heard her. This was gracious, though, compared to things she'd said before to his face. Mickey's concern was Alfonso.

Indeed, the baby began to cry again.

"Nice work," Sylvia said, as if it were Mickey's fault.

Mickey rushed back into the nursery, simultaneously picking up poor Alfonso and the handset. He saw that, in his absence, the board of elections site had linked to and automatically opened a PDF of the elaborate paperwork required, in light of all the Social Security benefits fraud, for a change of address. It requested that Isadora VanDeuersen Clark's checks be forwarded to Charles Clark at 305 East 10 Street in New York City. The original address was General Delivery, Monroeville, Virginia. No news there. But the form stated, in oversized bold caps, that if the original address were a post office box or general delivery, the applicant needed to supply a physical address below. So to learn Isadora VanDeuersen Clark's actual whereabouts, in theory, all Mickey had to do was scroll down.

"What's going on?" asked Charlie and Sylvia, almost in unison.

"Just a sec," Mickey told them both.

Sylvia stomped into the room. Mickey's back was to her. Still, her look made him wither. "One more second, please," he begged, scrolling furiously toward the address.

"Okay . . ." She eyed the ceiling for about one second, then seized the computer's power cable, shifting her weight toward the outlet, to pull the plug with maximum dramatic effect.

"Stop, please!"

She did. But only to twist the knife. And what could he do? The crib stood between them—not that he could overpower her if he wanted to. He knew of no way to persuade her. Out of spite, she usually denied even his simplest requests, like "Pass the salt?"

"Tell her you're trying to help me find a place in Virginia," Charlie said.

Sylvia heard. "Really?" she said with enthusiasm. She relaxed her grip on the power cord.

Mickey's own look of mystification gave up the game. Sylvia reared back and jerked the power cord as if starting a lawn mower. The plug whipped past him, a prong grazing his cheek. The hard drive fizzled. As the screen faded to gray, however, he was able to make out Isadora V. Clark's street address.

7

With the address firmly in his memory and corresponding bounce in his step, Charlie hurried from the parking lot pay phone and down the still-dark breezeway. Night Manager A. Brody sprung out of the vending machine room, directly into his path.

"Top of the morning to you, Mr. Ramirez!"

Although the vending machine room was just a few steps from the office, Brody was bundled into a coat, scarf, and hat. And he hadn't purchased anything.

He'd been waiting.

Swallowing against an upsurge of dread, Charlie said, "Top of the morning back at you."

"You have rather fair hair for a Ramirez, don't you?"

"My mother's Swedish."

Brody laughed derisively. "Listen, I've had so many weird middle-of-the-night check-ins that a man giving a fake name counts as fairly normal, especially if a second person's waiting in the car. I can't see the parking spaces around the corner from my office, but while you were checking in last night, I could distinguish the rumble of your car from that of the highway. Most people, fearing car thieves, don't leave their vehicles running. Unless there's *someone else* in the vehicle."

"Is there a charge for a second person?" Charlie asked, hoping the objective of this third degree was merely the collection of a few bucks.

"No, up to four can stay at no additional fee. I wanted to share with you the message in a fax I just received from the FBI. They're seeking two fugitives, an older man and one about your age. And height and weight and hair and eye color."

"Thanks for sharing," Charlie said. By it he meant, "What do you want?"

"I'll tell you what, a thousand in cash, and if someone asks me, a man matching your description may or may not have checked in here in the middle of the night—it was dark, you were all bundled up, who could tell?"

A thousand dollars was a small price to avoid capture. Charlie wished he had it. He fished the wallet from his pants and flipped it open to display bills totaling $157. He saw no need to mention the twenty he always kept in a different pocket. "This is what I have, and going to an ATM won't do either of us any good, even if I had that much in my account."

"What about Daddy?"

"Obviously you're a highly observant individual. Notice how, like last night, I'm wearing just a sweatshirt even though it's, like, two out?"

"The point?"

"I had to leave home last night in a rush—you can imagine how that happens, when you're a fugitive. My father was in the same rush. He left home in pajamas, or, to the point, without his wallet. I only have as much cash as I do because yesterday I was thinking about buying a bus ticket to South Dakota."

Brody deliberated, his breath rising from the dimly lit breezeway and into the predawn darkness. Finally, he cast a porcine hand and pinched the bills from the wallet.

Eight minutes later, Arnold Brody was swiveling anxiously in his desk chair when a dark blue Chevy Caprice sailed into the lot. Out darted two men. A strong gust of wind blew their overcoats open, revealing gray suits. The driver, in his twenties, was pale, with a stern countenance, like a wolf's. He was what Brody had expected of a federal agent. The passenger, in his early forties, had a jock's thick torso, gone soft in the middle. His big face was pleasant and suntanned, showcasing a sparkling grin. He looked more like an insurance salesman or a golf club pro.

"Mr. Brody, I presume," the driver said.

"Good to meet you." Brody stepped out of the office and extended a hand.

The driver did too, but only to flash an FBI badge identifying him as Special Agent Mortimer. His partner's ID showed him to be Special Agent Cadaret.

"Sir, where's their car?" Mortimer asked.

"They were clever about that," Brody said. He pointed to the back end of the building. The nose of the gray Buick peeked from behind it, twinkling silver in the nascent sunlight. "They parked all the way down there, even though their room isn't anywhere close, so the car would be hidden from the road."

"We appreciate the detective work, sir," Mortimer said. "Which room are they in?"

"Do you mind a quick question first?" Brody asked.

"Please," said Mortimer.

Brody looked to his shoes to convey his reluctance to broach the topic to such men of altruism. "The fax mentioned a reward?"

"That's right." Mortimer turned to Cadaret. "It's what, ten thousand?"

"For each of them."

"Room one oh five," Brody said, fighting an urge to sing it.

8

Mortimer wandered down the parking lot, stealing glances at room 105. The curtains were closed and the lights were off. He looked for telltale shadows or flickers. He saw none. The gap between the door and the threshold was clear. Likely the rabbits were in bed.

He positioned himself behind a brick column directly across the breezeway from their room. The column would hide him from their view. Another motel guest might think he was examining the structure, that he was an engineer or an aficionado of architectural kitsch, perhaps. Fortunately there were no guests around. But any second, one might appear. And because of the strong wind—the gusts turned the breezeway into a block-long flute—Mortimer wouldn't have the luxury of being alerted by the sound of the unbolting of a door. Accordingly, he drew the Walther from his coat with no more fanfare than if it were a cell phone, and he held it close enough to his chest that his lapels hid it. The gun was loaded with subsonic ammo and sound-suppressed, and its report would be no louder than a quarter falling into one of the vending machines' coin-return slots.

Cadaret pulled up in the breezeway two feet before the room, flattening himself against the wall—though not too flat. A passerby might guess he was waiting for his wife, using the bricks to scratch his back maybe. He reached sideways and banged on the door three times.

There was no response.

Mortimer took a quick look around. Still no one about. He signaled this to Cadaret.

Cadaret knocked twice more and said into the door, "Charles and Drummond Clark, Special Agents Mortimer and Cadaret, FBI."

Again, nothing.

Mortimer listened for a creak of weight shifting on carpet. He heard none.

"We know you're not responsible for the taxi driver," Cadaret said. "We're here to get your assistance in finding out who is."

Mortimer aimed his Walther at the zero in the plastic room number mounted at eye level on the door. His overcoat still concealed the weapon from all points of view except that of whichever rabbit would open the door. By the time Drummond or Charlie Clark glimpsed the gun, a hollow-point round would have entered his head, driving him back into the room. Cadaret would follow and, with his own .22, take out the other Clark.

As Cadaret crept closer to the door, Mortimer scanned the area. He shook his head, informing Cadaret the coast was clear.

Cadaret whirled and kicked the door inward. The wind masked much of the smash. Leading with his gun, Cadaret dove to the carpet and rolled, coming to a halt on one knee, planning to shoot both men.

He fired no shots. Instead he turned and beckoned Mortimer. Warily, Mortimer stepped in. Cadaret appeared to be alone in the room.

Brody must have gotten the number wrong, Mortimer thought, until Cadaret directed his attention to the rumpled comforters and blankets. Not only had someone clearly lain in each bed, particles of cinder—no doubt from the house on Prospect Place—and similarly shaded smudges remained on the sheets and pillowcases.

Cadaret rose slowly, his gun aimed at the closed bathroom door. There was no need to discuss the plan—Mortimer got it from Cadaret's eye movements.

Nodding his acknowledgment, Mortimer tapped the room door shut behind him and stole toward the bathroom. Adrenaline slowed down time, sharpened his senses, and left him swollen with an exhilarating sense that he could shape circumstances to his will.

He knelt by the bathroom door and prepared to fire his Walther twice—and only twice. He was confident no additional rounds would be required.

He counted to three with his fingers. On three, Cadaret lowered a shoulder and flew at the door. It flew inward, ripping the shower curtain from the rod above the bathtub, rings and all. Everything clattered into the tub, which, like the rest of the bathroom, was empty.

"Did you find them?" Brody asked, and just as soon wished he hadn't. The agents' demeanor said enough.

"We suspect they took someone else's car," Mortimer said.

Impossible, thought Brody. "There are just three other rooms rented. All of them are on this side of the inn. And look—" Stepping out of the office, he pointed down the breezeway. Three cars were parked outside their respective rooms.

He considered, though, that while he had been sitting in his office pricing widescreen TVs online, the fugitives might have sneaked around the back of the building to his own car. He felt the blood drain from his face.

"Are you okay?" Mortimer asked.

"I don't know," Brody said, bolting for the other side of the building.

Rounding the corner, he could see that the Reserved: Management spot was empty. He stopped and placed his hands on his knees to prevent himself from collapsing under the weight of his own stupidity. How had he gotten it into his head that shaking down fugitives would provide them with a sense of security?

Mortimer and Cadaret rounded the corner behind him. "Mr. Brody, can you give me the make, model, color, and tag number?" Mortimer asked.

Brody sighed, thinking not of the car, which was late in life, but the value of its occupants. "It's a red, ninety-three Toyota Cressida, Jersey plate T-E-N dash P-I-N."

"We ought to be able to get a statewide be-on-the-lookout alert on the system in a matter of minutes," Mortimer said, hurrying to his car, presumably to effect the BOLO from a computer. "We'll get it back for you." His cool failed to buoy Brody. The fugitives would have to be idiots to keep the car long.

Brody returned to the office with Cadaret. "You may have information, whether you realize it or not, that can help us," Cadaret said as they sat down.

Brody couldn't think of a thing that would be of use to them. Desperate to increase his reward prospects, however, he added insights and innuendo as he recounted his chat with Charlie, including Charlie's admission that he was on the lam and thinking of going by bus to South Dakota. Wherever possible, Brody sprinkled in what little else he knew, like that the old man was wearing pajamas.

Cadaret asked, "Have you told any of this to anyone else?"

"No, of course not."

"Good," Cadaret said. His words were punctuated by a muffled blast.

Brody's eyes fell on the gun Cadaret was aiming at him.

Then came a searing pain unlike anything Brody ever had felt, and all at once the world was cold and black and—

Cadaret posted a BACK IN FIVE MINUTES sign in the office window. Watching from the driver's seat of the Caprice, Mortimer dialed a local number. One ring and a man answered, "Road service and towing."

"Hi, I've got a dead battery," Mortimer said.

"No problem, man. Where are you at?"

"Montclair, at the library."

"I got a guy I can get there in fifteen, twenty minutes."

"Great, thank you." Mortimer hung up and opened the door, admitting Cadaret.

They drove onto the New Jersey Turnpike as soon as the paramedic van pulled up at the motel office. Three men, clad head to toe in white medical garb, exited the van. While the first tidied the office, the second and third removed the corpse. They got a chuckle out of the A. BRODY placard beside it—Cadaret had removed the letter R.

9

No sign welcomed Charlie and Drummond to Monroeville. The northwestern Virginia town appeared to have no signs at all. Or buildings, houses, or power lines. The Toyota Cressida's replacement, the burgundy Ford Taurus Charlie drove, was alone on what, according to the map, was Monroeville's only road, a crudely paved, single-lane straightaway through an eternity of dense, towering pine trees. Monroeville had no streetlamps either. And because of the shadows cast by all the pine trees, the town could have used some, even at ten on a cloudless morning such as this.

"I remember Mom liked the outdoors a lot," Charlie said, "but enough that she could have become a forest hermit?"

"I don't know," said Drummond, taking the question at face value. "Now that I think of it, there is one thing I do remember about her: She was a smoker." He said *smoker* with disdain.

Charlie had lost count of how many times this morning Drummond had recalled that she was a smoker and gone on to condemn the habit. All Charlie had learned otherwise was that the three of them used to take wonderful outings to the Prospect Park Zoo when he was in his pram. Which smacked of cover story. He gave up on questions while still in New Jersey.

Pine trees flew by for several more miles, and he was beginning to wonder if they'd left Monroeville, or Virginia for that matter, when he saw that the road terminated ahead at a pair of tall, rusty doors in a high stone wall.

He stopped the car at the doors. He couldn't see over them or over the wall, just through the gaps between the hinges. All he saw was more forest.

To the left sat, at a slant, a small gatehouse. Many of its wooden roof and wall shingles were missing and the remainder were beset by rot. The lone window was cracked and caked with muck. Above the door, hardened pine sap formed outlines of letters that had since fallen off; Charlie was able to make out 1 Loblolly Blvd.

"That's the address I have," he said, "but she can't live here."

"Why not?" Drummond asked.

"For one thing, no one's been here for a hundred years."

The gatehouse door creaked open, giving them both a start. A string bean of a man unfolded himself through the tiny aperture. Although the pine boughs overhead diffused the sunlight, he squinted, transforming his pale and craggy middle-aged face into a roadmap of wrinkles. He hadn't shaved in a few days and his graying black hair, while not long, was chaotic. A disproportionate belly swelled his soiled khaki windbreaker imprinted with MHFC SECURITY.

Charlie rolled down his window. Air blew in that was cold and redolent of pine. The guard's approach brought the smell of liquor.

"Gentlemen, it is my pleasure to welcome you to the Monroeville Hunt and Fish Club," he said as if he'd learned it by rote. "How may I be of assistance?"

"We're looking for Isadora Clark," Charlie said. Off the guard's blank look, he added, "Supposedly she lives here."

"Nobody lives here, sir. No humans, that is."

"Maybe she's a member of the club or something like that?"

"She married to a member of the Plumbers and Pipe Fitters?"

"I don't know."

"Well, that's who belongs here. Any case, the rule on club grounds is no ladies."

Pine trees flew the other way on Loblolly Boulevard until, finally, Charlie spotted a filling station. The pumps still said ESSO. The faded yellow-clapboard general store at the back of the property predated horseless carriages. There was just one vehicle in the dirt lot that had tires, a rusty pickup. What mattered was the place was still in business and it had a pay phone. Better, the pay phone was outside the store on the rear wall; Charlie was keen on being seen by as few human beings as possible.

While Drummond waited in the car, Charlie fed a handful of change into the pay phone's coin slot, then spun the rotary dial. By the second long ring, a sticky foreboding crawled over him. In the hours before the betting windows opened, when the tip trade was at its peak, Mickey was something of a legend for answering his cell phone before the end of the first ring. Even though it added fifteen minutes to his commute, he rode the bus instead of the subway because some of the subway tunnels blocked his cell reception.

By the fifth ring, Charlie suspected Mickey would never answer a telephone again. Hoping he was wrong—as well as praying to that anonymous entity he called upon when one of his picks was neck and neck with another horse—he dialed Mickey's office line.

The phone was picked up in the middle of the first ring.

Along with profound relief, Charlie exhaled, "That address can't be right."

"This isn't Mickey." The voice was deeper than Mickey's and solemn enough that guilt kicked Charlie in the stomach; if not for the phone cord to cling to, he might have fallen.

Boiling over with rage, Charlie sat at the wheel of the Taurus, gas pedal even with the floor, the filling station rapidly becoming a faded yellow speck in the rearview.

Drummond looked over as if Charlie were the one with lucidity issues. "Did you get the proper address?" Drummond asked.

"Do you know what they mean at the track by a stooper?"

"It rings a bell. I think. Maybe not."

"Stoopers comb the floors and the corridors, picking up tickets in hope of turning up a winner that was mistakenly crumpled or tossed before the race officials took an infraction into account and revised the order of finish. A little while ago, while stooping in the Big A parking lot, my friend Mickey found a ticket from yesterday's eighth race for a hundred bucks on a filly named Tigertown. Tigertown won, paying nine to one. The paramedic's opinion was that, in his excitement, Mickey died of a heart attack on the spot."

"I'm sorry, Charles."

"Same," Charlie said. For now his remorse took a backseat to retribution. "And we're not the only ones who are gonna be."

"Who else?"

"There has to be some way to make it look like a person had a heart attack that'll be missed in a conventional autopsy, right?"

Drummond pondered it. "Had someone given your friend chocolate?"

"Why?"

"I—I don't know."

For Charlie's purposes, that was as good as a toxicologist's report. Getting a free Hershey bar would have made Mickey's day.

"I assumed someone did *something* to him," Charlie said. "So I asked myself, What the hell was I thinking about dragging Mickey into this?"

"You needed the address."

"I know that. I meant, why hadn't I taken into account what happened to the taxi driver, Ibrahim Wallid, who was an innocent bystander in comparison? One difference that occurred to me is Ibrahim Wallid posed a threat as a witness. But Mickey Ramirez? What did Mickey know? Just a wrong address for Mom—an address that's supposedly a decrepit hangout for chauvinistic plumbers and pipe fitters."

10

Charlie pulled off Loblolly Boulevard about a mile short of the club gate, then let the car roll into the woods.

"We're not going to be able to go far with all these trees," Drummond said.

"I was thinking we'd park here."

"It would have been legal to park on the roadside."

"I don't want anyone to be able to see the car from the road. We're trying to *sneak* onto the club grounds."

"I see. Good thinking."

They'd had the identical conversation a minute ago.

Having found a place to leave the car, they headed into the woods, batting aside boughs and crunching through mounds of crisp leaves and pine needles. A woodland novice, Charlie slipped and fell several times.

Drummond was as nimble as a stag, despite the comically oversized lime green down coat lent to him in Brooklyn. He also wore turquoise slacks and turquoise and glittery gold shoes, the outfit they'd found in the bowling bag in the backseat of Brody's Toyota. Charlie now considered that the pajamas Drummond changed out of might have been less conspicuous.

A quarter of a mile brought only more trees. Charlie had expected a No Trespassing sign at least. "I don't suppose you have any idea where we are?" he asked Drummond.

"In the woods in Monroeville, Virginia," Drummond said in earnest.

"I know that. I guess I was hoping you'd blurt out something like, 'the forest surrounding the Monroeville Secret Agent Encampment,' or 'uninteresting frontage to convince interlopers there's no point in continuing.' But I'm afraid you're right."

The surroundings seemed to concur. There was the swish of trees in the light breeze and the trill of a few birds who'd either stayed here for winter or thought it far enough south. But there were no sounds of civilization, even at its most secretive.

Deciding to try a different approach to the club, maybe closer to the main gate, Charlie said, "I hope we can find the way back to where we parked the—"

He caught sight of a stone, at eye level, glistening in one of the few bits of sunlight able to breach the ceiling of branches. He flew toward it, until, thinking better, he slowed and approached with caution.

The stone was one in a wall of unmortared fieldstones, the type of wall the colonists built and identical to the one at the club's main gate. Logistics suggested that the two were connected. This section extended through the woods for another half mile or so, then took a ninety-degree turn and went on at least that far.

"Building an enclosure this size in Colonial times would have required the participation of everyone within a hundred miles for years," he said, abuzz at having been right. "But I'll bet this was put up much more recently, like when someone decided that an old-looking stone wall would draw less attention than electrified high-tensile wire."

"Should we see what's on the other side?" Drummond asked.

"As long as we're here, why not?"

Charlie struggled to find handholds and footholds. Gasping, he reached the top of the wall. Drummond was already there, breathing no harder than usual.

"You're getting your money's worth out of your Y membership," Charlie said.

Drummond stared past him and said nothing. His reserve was not due to his condition but, Charlie realized with a start, the huntsman standing on the other side of the wall. The man's camouflage field coat was classic deer hunting attire, but he looked like he made a living blocking linebackers rather than fitting pipes. Also the shiny black semiautomatic rifle he pointed at Drummond would tear apart a deer. Or a rhinoceros.

Really he was a guard, Charlie suspected. And hoped.

"Both of you, slide down real slow, then stand with your backs against the wall," the man said.

11

They rode in a six-wheel all-terrain vehicle, their captor at the controls in a motorcycle-style seat, Charlie and Drummond dead-bolted inside a cold, dark, and windowless trailer, hands pressed against the icy metal walls and floor to brace against the bumps and jolts. Through a small ventilation grate, Charlie watched the browns and yellows of the woods give way to the uniform pale green of a golf course.

The three-minute ride ended with a skidding halt on damp grass. A rasp of the bolt and the guard opened the trailer, revealing a wall of red and brown bricks set in a herringbone pattern. With a flick of the rifle, he gestured for Charlie and Drummond to exit the trailer.

As Charlie slid out, and his eyes readjusted to daylight, he saw that the bricks comprised the first story of a three-story, oak-framed Tudor mansion nearly a city block long, topped with a steeply pitched red tile roof that was a mountainscape of gables and dormers and cut-stone chimneys. Charlie had anticipated an impressive clubhouse but nothing of this scale or majesty.

"That way," the guard ordered. It was as much as he'd said since ordering them against the wall to submit to a weapons search. He pointed his rifle at a stone staircase that wrapped around one side of clubhouse.

The stairs brought the three of them to a polished limestone portico that ran the length of the building, with tall, perfectly cylindrical columns every five or six feet. Inside it, their footfalls sounded like applause.

Halfway down, they crossed paths with two men in their late sixties, wearing expensive tennis shoes and the sort of warm-up suits in fashion at Wimbledon. Flushed from a match, they both smiled, one giving a crisp military salute and the other offering a bright "Good morning." In reply the guard uttered a deferential, "Sirs." With far too much cordiality, Drummond said, "Hello, how are you?" Charlie simply nodded, while studying the players' reactions to the assault rifle at his and Drummond's backs. They appeared to find Drummond's bowling pants and shoes of greater interest. As they passed, they resumed a discussion of whether it was late enough in the day for cocktails. Charlie wondered what *would* have fazed them.

At the portico's end, the guard directed him and Drummond up a short brick pathway. It led to a flagstone terrace that had the dimensions of a Broadway stage and overlooked an expansive garden, beyond which were a trio of grass tennis courts and, after that, a good percentage of Virginia.

A silver-haired woman in a wheelchair rolled over to meet them.

12

Charlie hadn't anticipated that she would be paraplegic, but it rated as a background detail. That his mother was really alive was almost as great a shock as her "death" had been. She looked to be in her early fifties, but unless Social Security were in on the deception, she was sixty-five. As ever, she was trim, her features were sharp, and her sea-glass-green eyes radiated intelligence. She wore a buttery blouse, a cashmere cardigan, and tartan riding breeches. Even with the wheelchair and the woolen blanket atop her legs, she had such windblown vitality that he might have believed she'd just come from breaking a horse—which she used to do on the ranch in Montana, where she grew up.

Or so he'd been told.

"It's them, definitely," she told the guard.

The guard looked from her to Charlie and back again. Probably the resemblance alone convinced him. He lowered his rifle, allowing Charlie and Drummond onto the terrace.

Crossing the flagstones to meet her, Charlie felt an otherworldly weightlessness. He considered that the guard had in fact shot him against the stone wall, and this was some sort of afterlife.

"Never in the thousands of times I dreamed of this were you so handsome, Charlie," she said. "And this can't be a dream, because Drummond's here."

Drummond didn't react.

She turned to him with the mischievous grin Charlie remembered. "Of course I'm just joking, Drummond. It's wonderful to see you."

"Same," Drummond said vaguely.

She reached up to Charlie. He leaned into a courteous if tentative embrace. Then she wheeled to Drummond, presumably for the same.

Stepping sharply out of the way, Drummond asked, "Where's the dog?"

She looked to Charlie.

"Bit of a story there," he said.

"Well, I'm in the mood for a story." She turned to the guard. "Lieutenant, you can leave them with me."

He dropped an eyebrow. "Ma'am?"

"My son and I need to chat." *Son* left a glow on her.

"Yes, ma'am." The lieutenant withdrew to the portico.

"Alone," she added.

He *yes, ma'am*ed again and departed. Or gave the appearance of having departed; Charlie had a prickly feeling that the guard was hiding somewhere, finger on a trigger.

Drummond wandered across the terrace. He fidgeted with a loose rock in the balustrade, seemingly disturbed by the way it spoiled the symmetry. The far tennis court caught his attention and riveted him.

Nobody was playing.

Watching him, Isadora shook her head. To Charlie, she said, "After you showed up at the main gate, the good folks in the office did a little digging. I was shocked to hear about his condition. It's awful—I don't know what else to say. We also learned about the trumped-up FBI charges. If you can bring me up to speed on a few things, we ought to be able at least to solve that." She waved him toward the nearest of several sets of cast iron chairs.

"I wouldn't complain," Charlie said, mustering delight. His reserve lingered. Sure, she was like the long-lost mother of fairy tales, and it seemed safe here, but . . .

"But first you probably want to know why I'm not in a box underneath six feet of dirt?"

He took a chair. "It did cross my mind."

She rolled up opposite him. "I hadn't expected it would be today, but I always knew that someday we would meet again, and that you would want to know why—" She looked away, fighting tears.

He found it heartening. "It's okay. This is already a way better explanation than *It was just business, nothing personal.*" Which was how the conversation had played out in his imagination.

She smiled. "Most of what you already know is true. My parents—your grandparents—spent their entire lives in Billings. I was their only child. I used to be a swimmer and would have been an Olympic swimmer if I'd been three hundredths of a second faster. Other than my occupation, I kept nothing from you, until—" The tears got the better of her.

She didn't move to stem them, not even when they cut into her blush. She rummaged through her purse, producing a cigarette case and a gold lighter. Charlie knew the lighter's signature flask shape; vintage Zippos occasionally made it into Broadway Phil's, the pawnshop he visited more often than he cared to. She snapped open the lid, spun a flame from the spark wheel, sucked it into her cigarette, then took a long drag. Her eyes dried and her composure matched the cloudless sky.

Either she had extraordinary resilience, Charlie thought, or he needed to find out her brand of smokes.

"I always imagined that when this day came, I would be much older, or at least more mature, and prepared," she said. "Also, I would have had my hair done."

He smiled. "Your hair looks nice now."

"You're sweet. So tell me then: How much do you know about the spy game?"

"Bond movies," he said sheepishly.

"Actually, that's a fine place to start. You see, in reality, James Bond wouldn't last a week on the job. An egomaniac with weaknesses for cars, girls, and booze? An enemy could exploit any of those to get him to give up the crown jewels. That said, I enjoy Bond movies. If only covert operations took place at the Casino de Monte Carlo. In reality, the job is mostly paperwork. The action, what there is of it, rarely gets more glamorous than bad coffee with a frightened local in a place with lousy ventilation—and that's if you're lucky enough that your man remembers the appointment. But the brief moments when we do learn something—'product' that actually advances our position—make it worth it." She nodded at Drummond, who remained fixated on the tennis court. "You might be interested to know that he likened the job to playing long shots at the track."

Self-consciousness shrank Charlie. "I'd imagine the men and women in the clandestine service have slightly loftier motives than us guys at the track."

"It's about patriotism less often than people think," she said, putting him at ease. "I do care about our country, but my reason for getting into the game was the thrill, or perceived thrill. As a girl, I'd read too many of the Bond *books*. Once on the job, I had my share of bad coffee and some successful operations. You need to know about two of them. The first commenced August 27, 1977: I met your father at a lunch in conference room Seven C at Langley. One week later, we were in Peshawar, Pakistan, as honeymooners."

"Pakistan in August? Was Death Valley booked up?"

She grinned. "By 'honeymooners,' I mean husband-and-wife cover. He posed as a mortuary supplies salesman—if ever you're trying to keep a low profile and a chatty neighbor asks your line of work, that one's a great conversation ender. I was Suzy Homemaker, utterly obsessed with American soap operas—again, to ward off neighbors. Really we went to Peshawar for bridge."

"And by 'bridge' you mean . . . ?"

"The card game." She laughed. "Our prime asset was a Pakistani tea magnate. His home in Peshawar was the top floor of the charmingly old-world Dean's Hotel. He and one of his mistresses hosted couples' bridge nights there. Pakistan's nuclear program was then in full swing, and among the bridge players were many of the swingers."

"So you and Dad were never married? It was only your cover?"

"The agency is known as 'the world's most expensive matrimonial service' because of all the men and women who work so closely together in deep cover and then wind up that way in real life. Your father and I always had maintained a professional relationship, but near the end of our tour, something happened—"

"*I* happened?"

"Please know, dear, that once the shock wore off, we were delighted. And by the third trimester, we could hardly contain ourselves."

Charlie was almost touched. He decided it best to keep his sentiments in check until the part where she faked her own flattening by bus.

"We came around to the idea of getting married for real," she said.

"We wed in Las Vegas, at a chapel called Uncle Sam's, fittingly. Then we went back east and gave settling down a go—bought the house on Prospect Place, a six-piece living room set, even chose a china pattern."

"But?"

"Yes, the 'but' . . ." She took another long pull at her cigarette and glanced at Drummond. He continued to watch the tennis, or lack thereof. "Your father and I had the difficulties in adjustment most new couples do. Also, a legitimate domestic situation is a quantum leap from the life to which we were accustomed. Embassy soirées notwithstanding, spying is a state of war. What made your father a good spy—and he's a natural—is what made him a poor husband. He had what the Buddhists call 'right mindfulness,' an eternal and unflagging attentiveness to what's going on. The problem with that was, to him, outside work, *nothing* goes on. So what I got at home was the dullest guy on the block, who viewed being the dullest guy on the block as fantastic cover. I'd complain, and he'd quote from scientific studies that showed that people are conditioned to ignore their environment, that if something is mundane, they tune it out. So, he maintained, it would be in our interest to be even more mundane."

"Well, he mastered it," Charlie said.

His mother laughed, and he couldn't help joining her.

"And, though I can't think of any," she said, "I may have had a failing or two of my own. Surely he wasn't entirely to blame for our discord. In any case, I'd decided that you and I would leave, but I hadn't worked out the precise escape route. Then Moscow Station called with what sounded like a good initial phase . . ."

She was forced to halt as a distant whine turned into raucous thumps. Over the treetops appeared a helicopter, its fuselage emblazoned with NEWS RADIO.

"Gracious, this is the fourth medevac this week," she said against the ruckus. "We'd best get inside while we still have our hearing."

She started toward the portico. Charlie went to fetch Drummond. The helicopter aimed for the far tennis court, the one Drummond had been watching. Charlie noticed for the first time that it had no net. Unease coated him.

"You think it's *them?*" he had to shout.

"No," Drummond said. He stared with childlike fascination at the swirl of grass and leaves caused by the helicopter's descent.

Charlie wasn't at all assured.

The helicopter's skids touched the court, and two paramedics jumped from the cabin. Shimmering with each rotation of the main rotor, they slid out a gurney bearing an unresponsive patient. The first paramedic was a diminutive brunette, no more than twenty-five. The other was a weary-eyed Hispanic man in his early fifties. They unfolded the legs and wheels from beneath the gurney with a synchronization and fluidity of thousands of repetitions, which comforted Charlie.

But how about the patient? Probably around fifty, he had gray hair and an athletic build. His face was largely veiled by an oxygen mask, dark glasses, and the brim of his fishing hat.

The tumult now made it impossible even to shout to Drummond. Charlie tugged at his elbow and gestured with urgency toward the portico.

13

With Drummond in tow, Charlie followed Isadora through a mono-lithic bronze door into the clubhouse's cathedral-sized entry hall. Cloaked in elegant gray velvet curtains, three-story windows admitted only stray particles of daylight. The floor was a pool of black marble. As Charlie's eyes acclimated, trophies sprang from the dark mahogany walls—a lion, a boar, a herd of antlered animals, and an elephant with tusks big enough to bracket a car. Breathing in the bouquet of cigars and old leather, Charlie reflected that at least the Bond movies got the locations right.

As large as the entry hall was, it was hushed. The hiss of Isadora's rubber wheels reverberated into a shriek. "Let's go to the tea parlor, it's a bit cozier," she whispered—any louder, it seemed, and the echo might loosen bits of ceiling.

The tea parlor was indeed cozy compared to the entry hall; still it was as large a room as Charlie ever had been in that wasn't public. Fluted columns sustained a high ceiling and framed ten bays, each adorned with hand-painted battle scenes. Friezes repeated in half-moons over the doors and over a stone fireplace almost as big as his bedroom. A waiter wheeled an antique silver trolley, laden with tea and pastries, to "club members," as Isadora referred to the casually dressed men and women, all in their gray years. The members occupied about ten of the fifty or so tapestry-upholstered sofas and chairs. The quantity of muf-fled reports from the other end of the clubhouse suggested that pistols and trap shooting were much more popular at the "club" than tea.

"Charles, I may have rushed to judge assisted-living facilities," Drum-mond said. "Is *this* Holiday Ranch?"

"This is the Monroeville club, Drummond," Isadora said. "You've visited several times before." He looked at her as if she were a mile away. "It's a residence for injured and retired intelligence officers, and it serves as a medical facility in a pinch, when an injury treated at Bethesda Naval or Hopkins might make unwanted headlines or, worse, enemy intelligence."

"Yes, yes, of course," he said.

But he appeared confused. He even walked with uncertainty, as if a misstep might trip a mine.

"Why don't you sit, dear?" She pointed him to a sofa.

He let himself fall into it. At once, his head toppled to his shoulder and he began to snore lightly. She seemed relieved.

Charlie noticed that Drummond's fly was halfway down. "Any chance there's a room for him here?" he asked Isadora.

"I'm sure he'd say that this place isn't big enough for the two of us. But hopefully he can be assigned to another club once we get to the bottom of our inquiry." She waved Charlie into the adjacent chair and pulled up beside him. "Now, where was I?"

"About to die."

"Right." She laughed. "Officially, I was the second assistant secretary at the embassy. Really, I went to Moscow to run Nikolay Trepashkin, a Federal Assembly member notorious for chasing American skirts. The idea was he'd point me to a mole we suspected the KGB had in Washington, then I'd come home to you. But trouble arose with what should have been the simplest part. Usually when Trepashkin had a message for me, he wedged it behind the sink in the men's room of a drab little bar off Pushkin Square."

"You went into the men's room to get it?"

"Actually, he signaled it was there by moving a flowerpot to one side of his windowsill. At that point a male cutout—that's a messenger who knows as little as possible about the works—retrieved the document and loaded it into another dead drop, a slot behind a loose brick in a playground wall. Then another cutout took it to the desk of a busy hotel on the Donskaya and sent it to the embassy in the guise of junk mail."

"It wouldn't have been easier to send it straight to you?"

"The short answer is no; the other team was too resourceful. On my last day in Moscow, Trepashkin had a document important enough that he signaled for a face-to-face. I procured a bland Zhiguli and parked on a busy block—cars are good for meetings on short notice because the space is small, controllable, and two people in a car don't arouse suspicion. But he didn't conduct adequate countersurveillance, and the other team ordered a 'discontinuation of his existence,' as they liked to call it. Their gunmen drove by and obliterated my car while he was getting in. He died while saying, 'Hi.' When they doubled back to get his attaché case, they took me for dead too. As you've probably surmised, they were wrong. The director decided to make it appear I *had* died, though. I was exfiltrated in a casket; the agency even dug a grave and put up a tombstone beside my parents' in Billings. The reason is, in the time between the shooting and the gunmen's return, I'd peeked into Trepashkin's attaché case and learned who the mole was. But the director wanted the Ivans to think we'd learned nothing, so that they would leave their man in place and we could play him. For years, we succeeded, with one enormous exception: I couldn't see you. I did keep tabs on you, and I longed to see you. Probably that's why, when the Social Security Administration exposed a facet of my cover that the agency had failed to take into account, I went against my better judgment and had the checks forwarded to you. My rationale was the money might come in handy, and perhaps, in some infinitesimal way, allow you to feel your mother's love."

Charlie wanted to feel it. But her story wasn't quite adding up. "The mole must be collecting Social Security himself by now," he said.

"He died four years ago. Natural causes, of all things."

So why, Charlie wondered, had she remained out of touch?

As if having read his thoughts, she said, "Unfortunately my resurfacing still opens the national security equivalent of Pandora's box. All that I'm allowed to say in that regard is, I'm working on it. When I was notified that you were here, I pleaded for the opportunity to tell you the little I've told you. I'm glad we had this time. Unfortunately it came at a cost."

She peeled the woolen blanket from her lap, revealing a pistol. She took it up by its bulky grip, aiming in the general area of Charlie and Drummond.

Two or three of the other members looked over. They regarded the weapon no differently than if it were a teacup.

Charlie felt as if a veneer had just been stripped away, revealing the world as dark and cold and cruel beyond his most cynical appraisals. "With parents like the two of you, it's amazing I didn't end up really fucked up," he said. "Oh, wait, I did."

Isadora's eyes showed nothing of her feelings now. Drummond remained contorted on the sofa. A bit of light bounced off her stainless steel barrel and hit his eyes. It had the effect of a splash of cold water. He sat up.

"I just remembered something," he said.

"What?" asked both Charlie and Isadora, curiosity trumping all.

"Izzy, I was glad when you left."

14

It was a storybook sunny morning in the Caribbean, or so Alice surmised when her bedroom door opened, allowing her a glimpse of the daylight-flooded hallway. Not only had Hector and Alberto locked her in last night, they'd bolted the window shutters closed to prevent her from jumping three stories to the sea.

Hector admitted a small man wearing a neatly pressed white lab coat. "This is Dr. Cranch," the servant said, then returned to the hall, locking the door behind him.

Cranch lowered himself onto one of the two plastic benches fused to a molded plastic picnic table, the bedroom's only furnishing other than the air mattress on which Alice had slept—or was meant to have slept. Hector and Alberto had taken everything she conceivably could use as a weapon, including her sandals and underwear, leaving her only the cocktail dress she still wore.

"I'm afraid we won't be having much fun with you, Alice, given that you've already confessed," Cranch said. He was an American, with a cherubic face and big, soft blue eyes that had surely drawn no end of coos when he was a baby but played as creepy on a wan fifty-year-old. Like his lab coat, his grooming and attire were meticulous—too meticulous. The laces on his shiny black wingtips were tied into loops so perfectly symmetrical, he might have used a ruler. "For this morning, I'd like to get through the formalities, like your real identity, your rank within MI6, the code name and details of your operation, and so forth—you know the drill."

"No, as it happens, I don't know any drill," she said. She sat down across from him and looked him in the eyes. "You need to understand: I only 'confessed' so Nick wouldn't have Jane butchered further by—"

"Mr. Fielding bet me a very expensive bottle of rum that you'd say as much," Cranch cut in. "I've lost. I expected more from you than one-oh-one-level denial."

He was a professional inquisitor if she'd ever known one; she'd known many in eight years in the business.

"So obviously you're stalling," he said. "Why? If your backup team doesn't receive your happy signal by such and such an hour, they chopper in an extraction team? You'd be wise to let me know. All of it."

Indeed, docked three miles away at Martinique's Pointe du Bout was a yacht purported to belong to a pair of retirees from Sussex, and if Alice failed to signal them by seven tonight, via either phone or—the usual—Facebook post, her backup team would storm Fielding's island in the guise of drug enforcement authority agents with a warrant for Alberto's arrest. They would "happen on" her in the process.

She hoped it wouldn't come to that. She'd known from day one of rehearsal that Fielding subjected everyone in his close circle to these trials, often taking pages from Torquemada's book. She was prepared. Unless Fielding or Cranch had a source within her group (highly unlikely, given the paucity of evidence against her), she could maintain her innocence, then resume her investigation of Fielding with relative impunity.

"This is a nightmare," she said, dabbing tears. "What can I do to convince you?"

"There is one way," Cranch said. "Did you happen to notice the coffinlike device Hector and Alberto wheeled into your bathroom?"

"It would have been hard not to."

"Do you know what it is?"

She allowed her jaw to tighten, as if to counter a chatter. "No."

"It's like a polygraph machine, just simpler and more effective."

Really she knew all about the "water bed," including a bullet-points bio of the KGB Mengele-wannabe who'd devised it. The tank's twenty-five-centimeter-deep basin was filled with enough tepid water that an interrogation subject, stripped naked and forced to lie inside, had a mere two centimeters of clammy air to breathe once the casket-style lid was closed. After just an hour, it was common for subjects to fall into a semipsychotic state. Their subsequent interest in responding truthfully to interrogators' questions was like a drowning man's desire for a life ring. Alice had been subjected to the water bed for two hours during her training. As it happened, it stirred fond memories of the sensory deprivation tank she'd enjoyed at a California spa a few years earlier. The KGB's black-out goggles and earmuffs enhanced the experience, she'd thought.

Regardless, if it came to torture, Cranch might extract the truth from her. No one could withstand every instrument of torture, and surely this character had more where the water bed came from.

"So the thug on the Malecón spoke like a cliché thug," she ventured. "Isn't it common knowledge that they all get their lingo from the same television programs?"

"I seem to recall reading something along those lines," Cranch said. "And I imagine that Mr. Fielding would grant you that. Actually, it occurred to him that the Malecón episode was staged only after he'd already learned—by a fluke—that you were a spy. What happened was, while you were supposedly spending Christmas with your friends in Connecticut, he came into possession of an audio file with a voice that sounded like yours, except with an American accent. He had it checked. The voiceprint matched. Lo and behold, you spent your holiday in Brooklyn posing as a social worker named Helen Mayfield."

Shock made Alice feel like she was about to implode. She hid it, but it didn't matter. She'd been caught climbing into the cookie jar.

15

The pool was a conundrum. Fielding called it a *pool* for lack of a better term. There were probably smaller lakes. Through a physics-defying feat of engineering, two of its five sides extended over a high cliff, giving swimmers the sensation of being at the edge of a flat Earth. Its installation had run him more than four million dollars, not including the bribes and headache remedies attendant to half the population of Martinique protesting the bulldozing of a thousand-year-old Carib burial ground. He wondered whether it was worth it. He was, after all, a beach man.

His doubt was dispelled this morning, when the sight of the pool knocked his prospective customer's breath away.

The thing could pay for itself today, Fielding thought, several times over.

His prospect, Prabhakar Gaznavi, an Indian real estate billionaire, sat across the antique crystal table in the middle of the pool, atop a level, ninety-five-square-foot coral reef, accessible by the gangway from Captain Kidd's *Adventure Galley*. Word was the portly Gaznavi's stomach was the way to his wallet, so the breakfast buffet included twin eggs Benedict (a specialty of the sous chef, with eggs from a native hen and those of a beluga sturgeon), Swiss chocolate waffles with raspberries picked and put on a plane in the Willamette Valley hours ago, and four enormous platters of fresh local fish and a fifth with a nearly-as-fresh salmon from Nova Scotia. Also there were a raw bar; a pile of langoustine tails; an entire roasted rib eye; nine giant silver shell bowls, each with a different tropical fruit, and a tenth with the fruits in a medley;

and the usual pastries, along with Gaznavi's reputed favorite, cinnamon rolls, their trails of steam still pointing the way to the oven.

Gaznavi helped himself to just a single cinnamon roll. "I'm sorry," he said, "I'm on a diet." Fielding had known that ahead of time too, otherwise he would have had the head chef recalled from vacation so the kitchen could ready the A menu.

"How's your appetite for treasure?" Fielding asked.

"Much stronger," Gaznavi said.

In the world of treasure hunting, as little as an anchor from a lesser-known shipwreck could net six figures and land the diver on magazine covers. Fielding's in-box brimmed with fat checks written by complete strangers more interested in a share of the glory than investment. They never asked where the money went. There were no regulations beyond taxes, and Fielding paid his taxes in full and without fail. Nowhere in his filings, though, did he mention the gifts certain investors received: illegal munitions.

"The gift that I hope will persuade you to invest in the Treasure of San Isidro Expedition, LLC," he told Gaznavi, "is a Soviet-made atomic demolition munition."

"I'm interested," said the Indian, who was the chief benefactor of the United Liberation Front of the Punjab, a violent Islamic separatist group. But he seemed no more interested than he was in his cinnamon roll—he'd taken only a token nibble. His droopy eyes and sagging cheeks were set so that, even when jolly, he appeared sullen.

This guy must clean up at poker, Fielding thought.

Fielding snapped into salesman mode. Smiling to warm the table a degree or two, he said, "It has a ten-kiloton yield *and* it's portable. During the Cold War, the Soviets' invasion plan for Europe called for deployment of these babies at bridges and dams, to keep defending armies at bay—that sort of thing. And if the West came East, the Russkies had ADMs waiting in underground chambers—think nuclear land mines."

Squinting through shimmering bands of light projected by the pool, Gaznavi asked, "Is it one of the Karimovs?" He was referring to the two bombs Uzbekistan's President Islam Karimov admitted had gone missing during the Soviet Union's dissolution.

Fielding saw an opportunity to impress with his expertise and, at the same time, discredit his competitors. "Actually, there are no Karimovs," he said.

Gaznavi flicked a speck of frosting off his lapel. "I saw the speech myself."

"President Karimov's speech?"

"It was on CNN."

"I saw it too. He said a couple of nukes had been misplaced."

"I'm confused, Mr. Fielding."

"Call me Nick. If I had friends, they would."

"Nick, if *you* heard him say nukes had been misplaced . . . ?"

"If a politician in that part of the world says something on the record, that proves it's untrue," Fielding said.

Gaznavi emitted a phlegmy chuckle.

Pleased, Fielding added, "There's no way that a nuclear weapon could be *misplaced*, if you think about it."

"I don't know. Hundreds upon hundreds were transported from the outlying republics on ancient coal-powered trains and Russian trucks that stall every other kilometer. For all to have made it home safe and sound would be an unprecedented logistical feat—and the Russians are famous for tripping over their own red tape."

"Except when it comes to a nuclear warhead. Losing one would be tantamount to NASA forgetting where it parked one of the space shuttles."

"What about the three suitcases?" Gaznavi said. He meant the three suitcase-sized nuclear bombs reportedly pilfered from an undermanned Eastern European storage facility in the late 1990s by members of a Russian organized crime family, then sold in the Middle East.

"A fairy tale, Mr. Gaznavi. What chance is there that over ten years, as little as a firecracker would go undetonated in the Middle East?"

"Please call me Prabhakar," Gaznavi said, tearing into his cinnamon roll. "Now tell me this, Nick: You make it sound impossible to obtain a Russian nuclear weapon. So how'd you obtain one?"

"A little while back, a Moscow military insider sold me AK-seventy-four bullets from the Ukrainian stockpiles for ten cents each. He put them on the books as 'vended to a private party at eight cents apiece' and pocketed the difference, which added up to a hundred million rubles. Then he tried to buy himself a summer place in Yevpatoriya and found that, real estate exploding like everything else there, a hundred-million rubles could no longer buy much more than a peasant's izba."

"So he started thinking bigger than bullets," Gaznavi said through a mouthful.

"Exactly. The trouble with nukes is there are extensive records for each one, including serial numbers for even the most insignificant screw, plus the Russians keep Bible-length logbooks. We made every last bookkeeper wealthy enough to afford a seaside home in Yevpatoriya. As a result, a two-hundred-kilo crate of artillery shells at the storage facility in—Dombarovskiy, let's say—now has the curriculum vitae of a uranium implosion *Aftscharka* Model ADM. And I have a two-hundred kilo crate that really contains the *Aftscharka*."

"An awful lot of work."

"If only being a bum-kneed, middle-aged surfer paid as well."

"So what is the number that you have in mind?" Gaznavi asked. He appeared more interested in the handle of his teaspoon.

Fielding wasn't fooled. Not only was Gaznavi's sentence clumsy, it was also the first in which he'd passed up the opportunity to contract verbs, indicating that he'd scripted and rehearsed the line in his head, maybe even in front of his mirror this morning.

"Nothing," Fielding said. "It's free—if you invest just ninety million dollars in the treasure hunt."

"I am interested," Gaznavi said.

Despite the dispassion—again Gaznavi's delivery was as flat as the pool—Fielding heard the words as a song, in large part because Gaznavi ate the remainder of his cinnamon roll in one gulp, then helped himself to another.

All that remained was the inspection. Gaznavi had brought along a crack nuclear physicist, who was currently in the arcade, wowing the staff with his PlayStation prowess. Fielding was about to suggest they fly right now to the bomb's hiding spot, when Alberto set a latte before him, a signal—Fielding never drank any sort of coffee.

Fielding decoded the message on the accompanying napkin, two sentences penciled in tiny letters on the border. He told Gaznavi, "I can take you to the *Aftscharka* but not until tomorrow morning."

Gaznavi's brow fell in such a way that there was no mistaking his disappointment. "The more *minutes* I spend here, the greater the chance of actionable intelligence that can be used against the ULFP."

"Not to mention against good old Trader Nick," Fielding added. His much greater concern was that Gaznavi's feet would get cold.

"You must have one hot date," Gaznavi said.

The devout Muslim would regret his words a short while later, when one of Fielding's assistants revealed to him that the delay was due to the death of Norman Korey, who'd been a father figure to Fielding.

Korey was a beloved husband, father of four, grandfather of eleven, championship Little League coach, and a district vice president of the Benevolent and Protective Order of the Elks. He had succumbed to pneumonia at eighty-eight. His funeral service would fill the First Baptist Church in Waynesboro, Virginia.

Fielding had never heard of him. The news of the funeral resulted from the assistant's search of today's Virginia area services that were crowded enough that Fielding could lose Gaznavi's people and anyone else keeping tabs on him.

His actual engagement was forty miles away, in Monroeville.

16

Although he had a Pilates physique and the latest scruffy-chic haircut, the waiter's frilly blouse and loose-fitting knickers gave him the appearance of having just stepped out of the eighteenth century. He led two men in contemporary business attire into the tea parlor and over to Isadora's table. With a start, Charlie recognized the pair as the too-jolly gunman and the pale driver last seen at the intersection of Fillmore and Utica in Brooklyn.

"Officers Cadaret and Mortimer of the Defense Intelligence Agency," the waiter said by way of introduction.

"Glad to meet you," Drummond said cheerfully.

So much, Charlie thought, for his hope that the recollection of the day Isadora left had triggered Drummond into battle readiness.

"We've met, actually," Charlie told the waiter. He locked plaintive eyes with Isadora on the remote chance of stirring her maternal instincts—if she had any. "If you hand us off to these guys, *Mom*, you'll be discontinuing our existence."

"It's not like that at all," she said.

"They've already shot at us, like, fifty times."

"In an effort to halt a ten-thousand-pound stolen truck. I'm aware of all of it. They just need to find out what you know."

"If I knew anything, why the hell would I have come here?"

"I've been assured that if you answer their questions, you'll be let go."

"Where? To the target end of the shooting range?"

The waiter interrupted with a pointed clearing of his throat. From his breeches he produced a distinctly modern pistol. With it he directed

Charlie and Drummond out of the tea parlor and into a wide, white marble hallway. And what choice was there but to proceed? Mortimer and Cadaret fell in behind, and Isadora brought up the rear.

Just down the hall, the party came upon a taproom, which, if not for electric bulbs in the sconces and modern contraptions behind the bar, could be a London public house circa the Crimean War. A smattering of patrons ate and drank in secluded mahogany booths and at a pewter-topped bar. Of course no one blinked at the pistol pointed at Charlie and Drummond, not even the helicopter pilot or the paramedics.

Hungrily eyeing the servings of bangers and mash set before that trio, Drummond asked, "Are we having lunch here?"

"We'll be continuing down the hall," the waiter said.

Charlie proceeded with the feeling that his legs were sinking into the floor—the same heaviness felt in nightmares when there's no choice but to face the horror ahead.

The hallway terminated at a fifty-foot-long ramp covered in Persian carpet. The group descended, coming into a narrow corridor with the antiseptic scent and fluorescent colorlessness of a hospital.

"First room on the left," the waiter said.

The brass plaque beside the doorway was engraved CONFERENCE ROOM. Through the open door, Charlie took in a spartan table and chairs, bare brick walls, and a rubber flooring possibly chosen for the ease with which blood could be wiped off.

The entrance to the conference room was blocked, briefly, by a man in surgical garb, wheeling an instrument cart. He pushed through the swinging, steel-plated door directly across the corridor, revealing a full-sized operating room with a multitude of beeping monitors and machines. Seven members of a surgical team hovered around the operating table. On it lay the man who'd been carried off the helicopter, now apparently under general anesthesia.

The scene momentarily captured the attention of everyone in the corridor.

Except Drummond. He shot a hand into his half-opened fly, withdrew the rock he'd been fidgeting with on the terrace, and threw a fastball. It struck Cadaret in the jaw with a crack that caused everyone but the patient to jump.

While the others reeled, Charlie realized, with a rush of euphoria, that Drummond was *on*.

Cadaret collapsed, banging the operating room door inward. Drummond pounced on him, pried the gun from his shoulder holster, then rolled onto the operating room floor. He bounced up into a kneel, sighted the weapon, and squeezed out a shot. The report was thunder in the windowless chamber. A red starburst appeared on the front of the waiter's frilly blouse. Gun still in hand, he fell dead, revealing matching splatter on the corridor wall behind him.

In the operating room, the surgical masks were puckered by expressions of alarm. Everyone looked to the surgeon. "Evacuate to recovery," he said as if it were self-evident.

In the corridor, Isadora wheeled herself into a position so that the left side of the thick steel doorframe shielded her from Drummond's fire. Pressing himself against the right side of the doorframe, Mortimer reached his gun into the operating room and fired three times in rapid succession. The unsilenced shots seemed to shake the building.

The first bullet kicked up a strip of linoleum from the tile on which Drummond had been kneeling. Drummond leaped away, to the patient's left, vanishing behind a fireproof cabinet with the proportions and bulk of an industrial refrigerator.

Mortimer's second round hammered the metal-plated face of the cabinet, at Drummond's chest level. The bullet ricocheted, toppling an instrument stand and causing surgical instruments to ring against the floor tiles. The dense cabinet or its contents absorbed the third shot.

Charlie thought he could retrieve the fallen waiter's gun. While Mortimer and Isadora were preoccupied with Drummond, he would dive for the weapon, snatch it, and roll to the safety of the conference room. Taking a deep breath in preparation, he was struck bodily from behind.

The next thing he knew, he was being propelled into the operating room by Mortimer. Although his shoes remained in contact with the floor, he had the feeling of being thrown off a building.

"What are you thinking?" Isadora screamed from the corridor.

Ignoring her, Mortimer shoved Charlie ahead.

They rounded the big cabinet, bringing Drummond, who knelt behind it, into view. With uncanny calm, Drummond tracked Mortimer through his gun sight. Charlie realized that he was being used by Mortimer as a shield.

"Put the gun on the floor," Mortimer ordered Drummond. He gathered Charlie closer for emphasis.

Drummond fine-tuned the barrel and tightened his squint.

He wouldn't dare shoot, Charlie thought. William Tell wouldn't.

Drummond pressed the trigger. Mortimer too. The booms and the flashes were indistinguishable.

Mortimer's bullet struck a side of the bulky cabinet, denting the heavy-gauge metal, then it bounced off and disappeared unceremoniously through the door to the dressing room. Drummond's bullet tore the air inches to the side of Charlie's jaw and knocked Mortimer off his feet. He keeled backward, hot blood from his jugular spraying Charlie, then slammed to the floor and lay on his back, unmoving. The angle of his neck declared he wasn't playing possum.

Charlie was left awhirl in shock and stupor and, mostly, umbrage: How could Drummond have taken such a risk? Through it all he saw a faint gleam pass over Mortimer.

Drummond appeared to see it too. He spun toward the doctors and nurses, now transporting the patient by gurney through swinging side doors into the recovery room. Drummond fired at them, eliciting screams of horror.

From within their midst toppled a uniformed club guard, a boxy man with a fresh bullet hole in his forehead. The floor knocked a gleaming revolver from his hand.

Recalling Isadora's description of Drummond as a natural, Charlie's umbrage evaporated. Had William Tell been as good a shot, he would have had no famous dilemma.

Spotting Isadora's wheels inching through the doorway, Charlie dropped behind the vacated operating table. Drummond, her likelier target, jumped behind the stalwart fireproof cabinet. Neither had a shot at the other.

The pandemonium dissolved to just the mechanized humming and intermittent beeps of the machines. The acrid gun smoke faded. The room brightened. Charlie was reminded of the moment at the end of a party when everyone realizes it's time to go.

"Try not to kill me for a minute, Drummond, dear," Isadora said. "I need to speak to the two of you."

"You want a minute?" he said. "Does that mean you expect your backup here in forty-five seconds?"

She wheeled the chair tentatively with her left hand. She held her gun with her right, letting it dangle from her index finger by the trigger guard. "My backup is here already." She pointed to the boxy guard, face-down in a pool of his own blood.

Still Charlie didn't chance budging from behind the operating table. Drummond, too, held fast behind his cabinet.

"I was ordered by my superiors to hand you over to these men," Isadora said. "I didn't have the vaguest idea it would turn out like this."

"Do you expect us to believe that you were just obeying an order?" Drummond asked.

She gasped theatrically. "Don't tell me you've given up on your belief that obedience is next to godliness?"

"I just have a hard time imagining you listening to anyone."

"Well, I did, *sir*. I heeded our club manager, who believed these men were DIA on a legitimate operation, and he's a sphinx when it comes to bona fides—or, I should say, he *was* a sphinx." With a grimace, she nodded at the slain waiter. "I expected you weren't in for a rollicking time of it in debrief, but that's the game. As for you, Charlie, if I hadn't agreed to turn you over, I would have been charged with aiding and abetting federal fugitives and obstruction of justice, for starters. Still, I agreed to it only after I was given complete assurance that you would, truly, walk away."

Charlie took it for granted that she was lying. "Don't sweat it," he said. "These mix-ups happen all the time."

Drummond seemed to soften. "So who are they?" he asked her.

"In hindsight it would appear DIA was just cover, and at the least they co-opted the club personnel," she said. "The manager and security guard positions at a glorified nursing home don't generally merit the highest pay grades."

With a grunt of agreement, Drummond stepped out from behind the fireproof cabinet. He checked the double doors to the recovery room. She inspected the corridor. "The guards here mostly patrol the grounds," she said. Both she and Drummond seemed satisfied that there was no imminent danger.

"So what do you think this is about?" he asked.

"I would imagine a secret that you either know, knew, or unwittingly have stumbled onto," she said.

"That narrows it down to a stack's worth."

"I might have an idea. First, there's something our son needs to know."

Charlie felt safe in rising from behind the operating table.

She turned to him. "In our trade, Charlie, good and evil often blur to the point that it's impossible to distinguish the two. At home, the oil and the water made a better couple than your father and I. On the job, I would stake my life that he's on the good side, anytime, in sickness and in health. So we can rest assured that the culprit in this case is—"

A gun boomed from the corridor and her head snapped sideways.

17

She was dead.

Charlie broke free of horror's grip and threw himself to the safety of the back of the operating table. On the way down he glimpsed the lieutenant who had initially brought Drummond and him to the clubhouse. The man was ducking into the conference room across the hall. He must have been hiding there. And evidently he'd been co-opted sometime before that.

In retreat to the back side of the fireproof cabinet, Drummond fired twice more. His bullets came within inches of the lieutenant but damaged only the conference room door.

Isadora slumped in her wheelchair like a rag doll. Her purse tumbled from her lap, cigarette case, lighter, keys, and change spilling out and bouncing away.

Charlie's seconds-old fondness crumbled into heartache. "Coming here might not have been such a good idea after all," he said, nausea reducing his words to mutterings.

"Let's take a moment for a silent prayer," Drummond said.

Charlie, who'd never known his father to utter so much as grace before a meal, peeked out from behind the operating table. With an index finger held to his lips, Drummond nodded at the corridor. Charlie saw no one, but he heard a dull groan of floor tile—one man, maybe two, creeping toward the operating room.

Drummond snapped the selector on Cadaret's pistol to an automatic setting, aimed at the wall between the operating room and corridor, and flattened the trigger. He delivered a burst of bullets into the wall, brass casings arching over his right shoulder. From the other side of the wall came a man's agonized shout, followed by a heavy flop of body against floor. A second man—a guard who was younger and even brawnier than the lieutenant—dove past the operating room doorway. The lieutenant hauled him into the conference room in advance of Drummond's fire.

The duo initiated a hail of their own gunfire. Charlie pressed himself so low to the floor that he could taste the lemon in the cleanser. Even with his hands over his ears, it felt as though the reports would blow his eardrums.

The guards' target was Drummond. Their bullets turned his cabinet's facing to pegboard, but failed to hit him, thanks to computer hard drives within it, as well as a gurney, a steel rack full of monitors, and an anesthesia machine with the dimensions of a floor safe—he'd gathered the lot around him. Still, he wasn't fully shielded: One shot ricocheted off the ceiling, causing a steel tray atop the anesthesia machine to spin away like a Frisbee, giving flight to several loaded hypodermic needles. A few stuck in the ceiling. Drummond dodged the rest. Meanwhile more bullets pierced the cabinet and reached the monitors, resulting in an eruption of glass and sparks from which he could only turn away and shield his eyes. Additional rounds shredded the linoleum tiles and filled the air with particles of the glue that had adhered them to the subfloor.

Squinting into the resulting gritty green haze, Drummond returned fire. Two shots drove the guards back into the conference room. His next pulls of the trigger resulted only in flinty clicks.

Charlie hoped Drummond was merely pretending to be out of bullets, that a ruse was in the works. But Drummond dumped the gun onto the anesthesia machine beside him and dropped to the floor, obviously searching for another weapon.

The lieutenant and the junior guard scrambled into the operating room, ducking in and around the machinery with the clear intent of flanking Drummond. Like Charlie, they probably expected Drummond would obtain another gun.

As they closed in on the anesthesia machine, Charlie made out the barrel of the boxy guard's shiny revolver against a baseboard, well out of Drummond's reach. Mortimer's gun lay by his body at the entrance—the guards blocked Drummond from it. Drummond's last option was

Isadora's gun, still dangling from her hand, also beyond his range. Charlie thought about going for her gun himself. To move from behind the operating table all but guaranteed the guards would obliterate him.

Drummond stepped out from behind his cabinet, head lowered, hands empty. Charlie glimpsed a thin plastic tube connected to the anesthesia machine, caught on Drummond's right sleeve. The guards shared a look of self-satisfaction.

Drummond placed his hands before him, as if to raise them in surrender. Isadora's Zippo dropped from his left sleeve and into his left hand. He spun the spark wheel at once, transforming the invisible gas flowing from the thin plastic tube into a spray like a dragon's breath. The operating room turned orange.

Charlie averted his eyes; the guards' primal howls painted the picture more than adequately. A burst of gunshots followed.

Charlie looked to find the corrupt lieutenant dead on the floor. Also, Drummond had obtained the lieutenant's gun and used it to put an end to the other conspirator.

Simultaneously, a cardiac event monitor, the size of a kitchen television, hurtled through the air, thrown from behind Drummond by Cadaret.

"Dad!" Charlie shouted in warning.

Drummond looked to him, too late. The monitor crashed into his upper back, staggering him. Then Cadaret pounced. Other than a welt where the rock from the balustrade had struck his jaw, the killer appeared in the peak of health.

He grabbed Drummond around his rib cage and rode him down. Drummond's head banged into the floor, costing him his hold on the gun taken from the guard. He ended up flat on his back. Cadaret sat astride him, preventing him from regaining the gun.

Drummond somehow sat up, like a jack-in-the-box, surprising Charlie. Cadaret appeared to have expected as much, but his eyes bulged with shock at what flashed in Drummond's hand: the biggest of the hypodermic needles from the anesthesiologist's tray. Drummond thrust it deep into Cadaret's shoulder and hammered the plunger, flooding the killer with anesthesia.

Presumably.

Nothing happened.

Cadaret laughed. "Must be a placebo." He pried the needle from his shoulder, tossed it aside, and snatched up the guard's gun.

Fighting off queasiness, Charlie lunged for Isadora's gun, prying it from her still-warm hand just as Cadaret pressed a thick muzzle into Drummond's temple.

"Drop it!" Charlie called out, glad to have kept the tremble out of his voice. From a crouch behind the instrument cart, he fixed the side of Cadaret's head squarely in his sights.

Cadaret didn't flinch. Nor did he bother to look. "Whatchya got there, Charlie? Mom's Colt?"

Charlie noted the rearing horse etched onto the grip. "That's right."

"Poor choice of names, in my opinion. It should've been Bronco or Mule, the way it kicks. My guess is, by the time you get off a decent shot, the three of us will be dead of old age."

"Go ahead and shoot him, Charles," Drummond said, as if growing bored. Probably he sought to calm Charlie.

Charlie suspected that the full contents of the anesthesia machine wouldn't calm him now. The Colt's grip was uncomfortably coarse, the heaviness of the pistol startling. He had blasted away with the gamut of weapons in virtual reality, but the only actual gun he'd ever held fired water. It was difficult just to keep the Colt steady. Although Cadaret was a mere twenty feet away, Charlie had no confidence he could hit him.

"Yeah, go ahead, Charles," Cadaret said. "But if you do, know that even if, somehow, you get a bullet into me, I'll put two or three easy into Papa Bear's head, and at least one through that flimsy cart you're squatting behind and into your red zone."

He was articulating, practically verbatim, Charlie's concerns.

"He's afraid of you, Charles, or he wouldn't be gabbing," Drummond said. "At this distance your bullet will probably kill him before he's able to process that you've pulled the trigger. At worst it will knock him well beyond the point of being able to do anything to me, except by happenstance."

Charlie resolved to fire.

Cadaret spun at him and pressed his trigger first. At the same instant

Cadaret's eyes rolled up into his head, leaving them white. The anesthesia had kicked in.

Still the pressure of his finger against the trigger resulted in a blast from his gun.

A bullet bored into the ceiling directly above Charlie, dusting his hair with bits of soundproof tile. Cadaret crumpled to the floor.

Drummond said to Charlie, "Fine stall tactic."

Charlie couldn't tell whether he was kidding. Through a general daze, he replied, "Thanks, I was worried the fear I was going for wasn't quite playing."

Drummond hurried to his feet. "Now comes the hard part," he said, plucking the gun from Mortimer's corpse.

18

In the dressing room, Drummond burrowed through scrubs cabinets. "I worked up an escape route," he said, as if that were something he usually did, like turning on the lights when entering a dark room. He tossed Charlie a surgical gown, cap, pants, a mask, and a pair of disposable booties.

"You want to leave disguised as doctors?"

"As it happens, it worked for me at a similar facility in Ulaanbaatar, a couple of years ago, just after the Tiananmen Square protest."

Charlie began to put on the scrubs in the faint hope that his father's plan was more substantive than the Marx Brothers' plot it smacked of. Clearly a high percentage of Drummond's mental channels were open. At issue were those that weren't. He never said "a dozen" if he meant eleven or thirteen; only twelve. Similarly he used "a couple" exclusively for 2.000. The Tiananmen Square protest was not a *couple* of years ago, not by anyone's measure; Charlie had been in grade school at the time.

As if sensing Charlie's misgivings, Drummond added, "In Ulaanbaatar, my life came down to getting through a single door. It had granulated tungsten carbide locking bolts and eight inches of steel and Manganal hard plate—or enough to repel a tank. Opening it from outside required an eye scan, a thumbprint match, and a numeric code. But opening it from inside required only knowing how to use a push bar, which I did, and no one saw me do it. As you may have noticed, there are hardly any surveillance cameras here, and obviously the guards are elsewhere. The security in these places is geared toward keeping people out, not in. Our job is to get away without being noticed, and that's all about camouflage." He launched himself toward the exit. "You'll see as we go."

Charlie's concerns were allayed. Until Drummond inexplicably bypassed the exit door and headed back into the operating room. Charlie stumbled after him toward the recovery room. The doctors and nurses were startled as Drummond smashed through the double doors.

"All of you come with me except your patient and you and you," Drummond said. With Mortimer's gun, he pointed to the anesthesiologist and a nurse—the two men closest in size to himself and Charlie.

Charlie realized that Drummond's idea was to pose as part of an evacuating surgical team, while retaining its original number and composition. Once more he felt better about the idea's cogency, but he wondered whether incorporating the doctors and nurses added too many variables, not least of which was their cooperation.

No sooner did the thought strike him than the surgeon instructed his team, "We're not going anywhere." With a bold step forward, he told Drummond, "Our first responsibility is the well-being of the patient."

"I'm aware of that, sir," Drummond said. "It's my hope that the club's security force is aware of it too. Now, please?" He indicated the door.

The surgeon stood fast.

"Sir, what's your name?" Drummond asked.

"Rivington."

"Dr. Rivington, I don't want to shoot you, but I will if you don't do exactly as I say." Drummond waved his gun at the rest of the men and women. "That goes for every one of you."

They all shuffled into the operating room. Following alongside Drummond, Charlie could practically see the fear rising off them.

"Now I want you to place that man on a gurney," Drummond told them. He pointed to the unconscious Cadaret. "Put an oxygen mask on him, plus the fishing hat and the sunglasses your patient had on, and a blanket."

Charlie didn't entirely understand the thinking, but it wasn't the time for Q & A. The doctor act would play better, he guessed, with a patient, and Cadaret was a more manageable prop than the real patient.

While the members of the medical team readied Cadaret, Drummond threaded an IV stand through the handles of the recovery room doors. If the nurse and anesthesiologist sought to thwart the escape, they would have to break down the doors.

Next Drummond snatched the handset from the wall-mounted intercom and dialed 9. When it was answered, he exclaimed, "This is Rivington in the OR. We have a code green!" Then he tore the intercom from the wall.

19

The "surgical team" hurried up the ramp to the lobby. Drummond brought up the rear, his gun trained on the real doctors and nurses from beneath his surgical gown. Charlie was glad Drummond had assigned him, along with the scrub nurse, to push the gurney. The solid side handles enabled him to appear steady.

At the top of the ramp, the clubhouse resounded with taproom chatter and the occasional ring of silver against china—none of the hurried tread of guards' jackboots or the rattle of rifles he'd been bracing for. He considered that the club members, accustomed to the sounds of gunfire from the various ranges, had been given no reason to think anything was out of the ordinary—and *ordinary* encompassed a lot at this place.

As they turned onto the marble hallway, the scrub nurse narrowly avoided ramming her side of the gurney into a member—one of the tennis players Charlie and Drummond had been marched past in the portico on arrival. He wore a madras sport coat now and was drinking scotch from a tall glass. Given their surgical caps and masks and gowns, Charlie put the odds of the man recognizing them now at astronomical. The problem was that the fright in the scrub nurse's eyes was like an alarm beacon.

The tennis player hopped out of her way. "Code Green?" he asked.

"Yes, sir," she said tremulously. It came off as urgency.

"Godspeed," he said, raising his glass to exhort the team.

Only at the Monroeville Hunt and Fish Club, Charlie thought.

"This way," said Drummond, pointing to the door across the hall—the library, according to the letters chiseled into its marble archway.

Because going to a library made no sense, Charlie expected the big oak door to veil something else, hopefully the armory.

The door indeed opened to a library, a lofty room with leather-bound books crammed into creamy pine shelves so high that three tiers of balconies were necessary to access them. Inside, two octogenarians sat hunched over a backgammon board the size of a suitcase. They nodded to the team in polite greeting and returned to their game. In their time here, Charlie thought, they probably had seen so many surgical teams rushing past that the sight rated as less compelling than double twos.

Within the bookshelves on the far wall was a round-topped door leading to the terrace. The frosted glass transom and side lights offered no clue whether club guards—or the National Guard—waited outside.

Drummond gingerly drew the bronze handle, the door opened inward with a lengthy creak, and he peered out.

"Okay," he said, beckoning the team.

Charlie was last onto the empty terrace.

"Now to the tennis courts," Drummond said, starting toward the path. The "news radio" helicopter sat quietly on the far court.

"Can you hot-wire a *helicopter*?" Charlie asked, curious as much as anything. He took it for granted Drummond could pilot one.

"Most helicopters don't require keys," Drummond said. "There's nothing to—" He was interrupted by a loud and spine-chilling rifle bolt lock-and-load.

Charlie turned around slowly, as did Drummond and the doctors and nurses. The older of the two backgammon players stood in the library doorway, eyeing them down the barrel of an enormous rifle— quite possibly the one used to bag the elephant in the entry hall. He said, "Those of you who would rather not be on the receiving end of an eleven-millimeter round, place your hands in the air."

Isadora's Colt was tucked into Charlie's waistband, beneath his gown. He raised his gloved hands because, like the doctors and nurses, Drummond was raising his.

Swinging the rifle toward Drummond, the backgammon player asked, "Are you pretending not to remember me, Drummond?"

"I think you've mistaken me for someone else, sir," Drummond said, his voice raspier and a half-octave lower than usual.

Not a bad play, Charlie thought. In all the surgical garb, Drummond could be almost anyone.

"It's Carlton Otto, old man," the backgammon player said. "I was on the plane that got you out of Ulaanbaatar!" He called into the library, "Archie, where in the blazes is security?"

This was the kind of luck that caused veteran gamblers to leave the profession, Charlie thought, when the palm of Drummond's right glove exploded into rubber scraps. A bullet—somehow he'd maneuvered the barrel of his gun into the glove—flew high, smashing apart the transom. Glittery shards rained onto Otto, sending him sprawling back into the library.

Charlie looked on in wonder. At the same time, like the doctors and nurses, he dropped to the flagstones in fear of return fire from Otto's veritable cannon. Another shot by Drummond kept Otto inside.

But the escape plan was in critical condition: From the clubhouse roof came a siren—a fusion of whine and honk so shrill that Charlie wasn't sure whether it was an alarm or a weapon. Inquisitive members appeared at windows overlooking the terrace.

Drummond scooped Charlie up from a flagstone by the nape of his gown. "Push the gurney to the helicopter," he shouted over the siren. "I'll cover you."

The heavy gurney would turn what might be a ten-second dash down the winding path into a gravel-ridden ordeal. "But the doctor game's up," Charlie reminded him, hoping he didn't require the reminder.

"We need him," Drummond said of Cadaret.

Charlie couldn't imagine why. But on account of all the other things he'd experienced today that he would have thought unimaginable, he demurred.

20

While sliding Cadaret's bulk from the gurney and onto the cabin's bench seat, Charlie watched Drummond free the rotor blades from their restraints, leap through the right cockpit door, and strap himself into the pilot's seat without glancing at the complex seat belt. Instead he swatted switches on the overhead console, illuminating the instrument panel.

Charlie took a moment to marvel: Just yesterday, he'd thought parallel parking was his father's greatest skill.

Turning his attention to the instrument panel, Drummond became a flurry of switch throwing. With one instrument came a loud, harsh drilling noise. He pulled one of the headsets from the overhead center post and popped the cups over his ears.

Worming his way from the cabin into the cockpit, Charlie didn't need to be instructed to do the same. The headset reduced the remaining second or two of drilling to a mild drone. He heard clearly as Drummond explained, into his pipe-cleaner microphone, "That was the fuel valve, a dead giveaway someone's about to take off in your helicopter." With a wispy grin he indicated the clubhouse. "Unless you can't hear it over your rooftop alarm sirens."

Charlie smiled—the revelation that his father had a lighter side was almost as startling as the revelation that he was a spy. Fastening himself into the copilot's seat, Charlie had the sensation of sitting beside someone he'd just met for the first time.

Although this was Charlie's first time aboard a real helicopter, PlayStation's version had familiarized him with some of the controls, including the cyclic, the stick that tilts the rotor blades in order to direct the ship, as well as the collective, the big lever between the pilot and copilot seats that governs ascent. Drummond rolled the motorcycle-handle-style throttle atop the collective, then placed a finger on the starter button. Charlie assumed Drummond would now press the button, the engine would bellow, the ship would throb, and they'd bound into the sky.

But Drummond had more switches to flick and buttons to press. Other than the toggles overhead labeled FAN and XPNDR—which Drummond avoided—Charlie couldn't guess their functions. ENDCR? RMI? INV? Most of the dials and gauges and other glass bubbles on the instrument panel had no labels at all.

When Drummond finally pressed the starter button, the engine whine drowned out the siren. Now everyone on the club grounds knew both precisely where Drummond and Charlie were and what they were up to. Still, the ship sat on the tennis court, with Drummond continuing to tweak the instruments.

Helicopter takeoff wasn't as simple as PlayStation portrayed it, Charlie thought, or even as simple as an Apollo launch. Unless one of Drummond's blocked mental channels was to blame.

"Would there be a way to speed things up," Charlie asked, "if, say, hypothetically, more bad guys were about to show up any second and shoot at us?"

Drummond tapped the temperature gauge. "Overheating during the start can cause catastrophic engine failure, which would be worse."

"Sorry, don't mind me," said Charlie. Feeling his face redden, he turned away, focusing intently on the altimeter.

It read 0 feet, of course.

Drummond cracked the throttle. Fuel howled into the engine. The rotors awoke. The blades tingled. The helicopter went nowhere. Drummond was fixated on the temperature gauge.

Charlie noticed a flash of light from the terrace. Without ado, Drummond jerked open his window, drew his gun, and fired. More than a hundred feet away, a guard grabbed at his shoulder and toppled over the balustrade. A rifle fell from his hands, its scope catching the sunlight and replicating the flash Charlie had seen a moment ago.

"Forgetting how you even spotted him, I wouldn't have thought that shot was possible," Charlie said.

His attention back on the instrument panel, Drummond said, "The hard part is acting like I do it all the time."

No, Charlie decided, definitely not the same guy he'd known from 1979 until today.

Four more guards had streamed out of the library, rifles in hand. Drummond glanced from them to the temperature gauge. Of the two, the temperature gauge appeared to trouble him more.

"No choice now," he grumbled.

He snapped two more switches and wrenched the throttle. The engine responded with a roar. The blades reached full chop, raising dirt and grass all around. He jerked up the collective. With it went the nose, followed by the skids. Every part of the ship down to the lug nuts trembled.

"Let's get some air," he said, punching the cyclic.

At once it seemed like the ship was falling upward. Past the club-house. Past the treetops. Into a white explosion of sunlight.

On the terrace, uniforms billowed in the helicopter's wash as the men traced the path of the helicopter with their rifle barrels. Their muzzles lit up like flashbulbs. With white knuckles, Charlie grabbed onto the center support strut and braced for the bullets.

They struck immediately, but without the rammed-by-an-asteroid effect he'd expected—it was more like birds pecking at the fuselage.

After five or six such pecks, a rope of blood whipped past his eyes, splattering against his window and peppering his face with warm droplets. He looked anxiously to the pilot's seat.

Drummond was unscathed. "Our passenger," Drummond explained, with a tilt of the head. "Upper thigh, apparently not serious, thankfully."

Charlie turned around to see Cadaret stirring, as if in the midst of a bad dream. The seat cushion beneath him had turned crimson. Beyond basic humanity, Charlie wasn't sure why Drummond cared. He decided not to distract him with questions.

The pecking continued. Charlie held his breath, if only because it allowed him to do something besides thinking about a midair explosion.

The pecks dwindled as the helicopter continued skyward. When the altimeter read 1,700 feet, the guards quit altogether.

Charlie took a deep breath of the cabin air. It was rich with the waxy aroma of aircraft hydraulic fluid people often associate with going on vacation. He admired the plush carpet of treetops below. The old yellow general store appeared quaint. The rhythmic thumping of the rotors became a song of respite.

It was interrupted by a sickly gasp from the engine.

Abruptly the ship yawed to Charlie's side. The first aid box on the wall behind him popped open, raining supplies. Everything else that wasn't tied down, including Cadaret, drummed the right wall. Charlie grabbed a strut to keep from hanging by his straps.

Drummond maneuvered the cyclic control stick and worked the foot pedals, but he couldn't right the ship. His eyes mirrored Charlie's bewilderment.

"What was the thing I was worrying about?" he asked.

The timing was so preposterous that Charlie wondered whether Drummond's newly debuted lighter side included practical jokes.

That notion died as the engine fell quiet, and in its place came a loud, high-pitched horn. The row of warning lights over the instrument panel blazed red, as did the temperature gauge. The flapping of the blades began to slow, to sickening effect. And that was nothing compared to the ground racing nightmarishly upward. The air rushed past like fighter jets.

Any panic Charlie had ever felt before was an itch compared to this.

Fighting it, he took hold of the collective from Drummond, who slumped in his seat, stupefied. The lever felt like it had been fixed in concrete.

So much, Charlie thought, for his familiarity with helicopter controls. He had a better chance of landing a car from a thousand feet.

He expected scenes from his life to flash before his eyes.

Cadaret surged from the cabin. Although woozy, the killer squeezed through the gap between the pilot and copilot seats, then dove, slamming the collective to the floor.

"Right pedal!" he screamed to Drummond.

"Yes, yes, thank you," Drummond said, stomping his right foot pedal.

With a groan, Cadaret grabbed Drummond's knee. He manipulated Drummond's foot as if it were a marionette, reducing pressure on the pedal.

Although the gauges still indicated the engine was dead, the rotor blades sped up. Their rich buzz returned. The ship entered a steady glide.

Charlie's jubilation was tinged by disbelief. "How is this possible?"

"Autorotation," Drummond said, as if recalling an old friend.

"Yeah," Cadaret said, pulling back on the cyclic. "Still we're going to dig a giant hole in the ground unless we can slow the hell down."

The helicopter's nose bumped up and the flight path flattened out. The vertical speed indicator dropped to 1,100 feet per minute, which sounded like a lot but didn't feel it. Charlie suspected he'd been in faster elevators.

"Not bad," said Cadaret. "Now if she'll just level off a wee bit more, cocktails are on me once we—"

Out of nowhere a tall pine tree bit into the helicopter's Plexiglas windshield. Green needles that felt like nails filled and darkened the cabin. Charlie shielded his eyes. There wasn't time to think past that. The ship bouldered through branches. The main rotor was snagged by the tree trunk and snapped off. A stout bough peeled away the roof. The ground hit like a giant mallet.

21

A surreptitious peek into the Waynesboro Airport air traffic control database suggested the helicopter had dropped precipitiously within a thirty-mile radius of the Monroeville club. Front Royal, Virginia, the nearest town, was a likely place for Drummond to surface if he survived, and Fielding had a feeling that he had; the old man had a knack for it.

Fielding drove down Royal Avenue, the two-lane main drag, passing non-brand-name fast food restaurants and two-story federal buildings that had been nice, once. The glory days of this little burg had come to an end fifty years ago, he estimated, based upon the chipped and fading Coca-Cola advertisement on the side of a vacant bank.

He pulled his rented Chrysler into a parking space in front of the Rose & Crown. The century-old tavern exuded cheery light, warmth, and tinny Sinatra but little of the usual barroom chatter. Parked in the vicinity were just three cars, all of which looked like they belonged to old men.

Fielding would have enjoyed going in for a rum or two and a cigar nevertheless, but he'd stopped only to see if anyone else would do the same. The pickup truck that had been behind him zoomed past.

He backed out of the spot and circled back to the top of the block. He parked among the relative crowd of vehicles outside his actual destination, Eddie's, a tin-sided boxcar diner. He sprung out of his car and, although he had a pocketful of change, bypassed the meter, where two hours cost a dime.

Inside the diner, many of the old checkerboard floor tiles were missing. From behind a chrome cash register dulled by years of grease, a fossil in a chili-speckled white apron nodded a welcome. Fielding tipped an invisible hat in response. A mailman and two mechanics or plumbers sat at the lunch counter, which was equal parts Formica and cracks; the men were pontificating about the coming Bowl games. The tables were a third filled by the range of the local social spectrum. Fielding, who was only recognized in towns with glossy society magazines, drew looks from most of the patrons, but none conveying familiarity, fortunately.

He approached a window booth, where a prematurely gray itinerant business type with a dour expression was eating alone. Eyeing his bowl, Fielding asked, "How's the chili?" He waited for the correct response.

"Best I've had in years," the man said. "The guys at the counter told me Eddie's arm hair is the secret ingredient."

"How could anyone resist after hearing that?" Fielding sank into the cushioned bench across from the onetime Green Beret who went by Bull.

"Honored to meet you, sir," Bull said, reaching across the table.

Fielding shook his hand, cold and clammy from nervousness. Fielding engendered this reaction often—and after all these years, he still got a kick out of it. "So let me guess," he said. "The rent-a-drones are still only giving us nature footage?"

The drones were five-inch-long robot reconnaissance planes the Army had in development at Virginia Tech, where the director of the Center for Objective Microelectronics and Biomimetic Advanced Technology was hamstrung by three alimonies and two child support payments. He had been happy to "lend" the drones to a "visiting researcher" in exchange for a "donation."

"Just the dense canopy of treetops so far," Bull said. "No helicopter or any sign of it, if that's what you mean."

"I was hoping for a picture of a five-foot-eleven man with white hair."

The former soldier looked away. "I'm afraid all we've come up with is a signal from the beacon in Cadaret's wristwatch."

"What's wrong with that?" Fielding asked.

"If the rabbit had been thinking clearly, the first thing he would have done is toss that watch out of the helicopter. Or toss Cadaret."

"But the rabbit isn't thinking clearly."

Bull lowered his voice. "Sir, he took out five professionals, escaped from the Monroeville club, and stole a helicopter."

"That stuff is second nature to him," Fielding said. "If he'd been thinking clearly, he would have taken out the five professionals then simply picked up the phone and dialed Burt Hattemer."

Bull input a hasty message on his BlackBerry. If any of the diners saw, they would take the display for an online simulcast of a hockey game with digital stick figures representing the players. A few keystrokes and clicks later, he told Fielding, "Okay, two of the hounds are on their way to the wristwatch."

When Charlie awoke, he felt like he was floating in the air with thousands of diaphanous bits of light in orbit around him. He'd previously thought seeing stars was just the stuff of cartoons. It was the most magnificent and glorious experience imaginable, he decided, when—WHAM—he found himself prone on the cold forest floor.

The stars were gone, replaced by trees as far as he could see, and it felt like his head had absorbed the majority of the helicopter's impact with the ground.

He tolerated the pain to take inventory of himself. His mouth tasted of dirt. His nostrils were caked with it. His skin was burned and scraped in multiple patches. The rest of him stung. Although slick with blood, his appendages remained attached. Incredibly, everything seemed in working order.

Fifty or sixty feet away, Drummond was pacing by what remained of the helicopter. The crumpled fuselage lay on its side, looking like it originally had been constructed of papier-mâché. Drummond appeared to have suffered only scrapes. Of course, if half his ribs were broken, would he show it?

His gun was trained on Cadaret, who sat in the dirt, arms behind him, wrapped around the trunk of a tree and bound at the wrists by wire—probably from the helicopter. Blood trickled from his mouth, welling at his collar.

"Who hired you?" Drummond asked. His eyes were still sleepy, and he spoke clumsily, hunting for words as if English were foreign to him.

"It's need to know and a day player like me doesn't need to," Cadaret said. He was oddly chipper.

Drummond took a running step and kicked him in the jaw. The killer's head snapped back. His mouth went slack and reddish vomit spilled out.

"Again, who hired you?" Drummond said.

"How about I tell you what I *do* know?" Cadaret said, his congeniality intact.

Either he'd learned to disregard pain, Charlie thought, or he liked it.

"Fine, fine," said Drummond.

"They call my office voice mail. The caller poses as a buddy wondering what I'm up to over the weekend. If he mentions the Jersey Shore, I check my Hotmail for instructions—the details of the op will be imbedded in a piece of spam hawking diet pills. If he says Hamptons, I service a dead drop."

"And?"

"And I do the job, my bank balance goes up, I fly down to my vacation house on St. Bart's, and spend all my time hunting for carpenters and roofers and painters to undo whatever the hell the latest hurricane's done."

"That's it?"

"That's all I know."

"That's nothing." Drummond toed the dirt, preparing for another field goal attempt with Cadaret's head.

Cadaret appeared no more alarmed than if Drummond were preparing dessert. Probably he would act the same way before a firing squad, Charlie thought. But whether or not another blow to the head bothered him, it could leave him unconscious. Or worse.

"Dad, don't!" Charlie called out. He tried to stand. Pain grabbed every part of him that flexed. The ground seesawed.

Keeping the gun fixed on Cadaret, Drummond stomped over. His look of annoyance was that of someone interrupted during study. He declared, "This is war, and only one thoroughly acquainted with the evils of war can understand the profitable way of carrying it on."

Charlie recognized this as a ragged version of the wisdom of Sun Tzu, the centuries-dead general whose wisdom Drummond used to recite impeccably, apropos of everything from current events to why a boy needed to make his bed every morning.

"I'm not thoroughly acquainted with the evils of war," Charlie allowed, "but he's useful only if he can speak, so how profitable can it be to knock him senseless?"

"Good point," Drummond said. "Thank you."

He trotted back to Cadaret with a benevolent air. Then swung the gun by the barrel. The heavy grip cracked the bridge of Cadaret's nose, creating a spring of scarlet and leaving his head bobbing.

"Great," Charlie said, putting it at fifty to one that Cadaret clung to consciousness.

But there he was, sitting upright and vigorous as ever. Wipe the blood and the pine sap off, comb his hair, tighten his tie, and he could be delivering a sales presentation.

Drummond pointed the gun's muzzle at the inside of Cadaret's knee. "Who hired you?" he asked again.

There was every reason to believe that Drummond would pull the trigger. Still, no trace of panic in Cadaret. Maybe he thought of losing the kneecap as a cost of doing business; he could get a replacement, maybe a bonus along with it. He said, "Sir, basic as that information is, I do not have it, the reason probably being that I might fall into a situation exactly like this one."

Drummond nodded. "Fine, fine. Who hired you?" He seemed entirely unaware that he'd just posed the question.

Cadaret's eyes widened with—of all things—trepidation.

Charlie followed Cadaret's stare to Drummond's trembling gun hand. Drummond added his left hand to steady the gun. He could have used another hand still. No wonder Cadaret was afraid: Normally Drummond could shoot the head off a pin at this distance. Now, it was three to one that he would miss the kneecap and hit something irreparable. And even money that he would create a wound that didn't conform to Spook Interrogation Standards—and one from which the flow of blood couldn't be staunched in time to preserve Cadaret's life.

"Dad, please, put the gun down, just for a second?"

"Why would I do that?"

"I think your subject just remembered some more."

"Yes, that's right," Cadaret exclaimed.

Drummond lowered the gun.

Cadaret looked to Charlie with unmistakable gratitude. "I was in Atlantic City last night, I got a text message with an encrypted number, and I called it from a secure line," he said. "A middle-aged woman with a Midwestern accent told me to fly immediately to the Red Hook Heliport in Brooklyn, where I'd be met by a young guy called Mortimer. He would ask me if I was with Morgan Stanley and I was supposed to reply, 'Regrettably, yes,' and then we'd grumble about the stock market. So I flew, we met, we grumbled, then we headed for a precinct house near Prospect Park. On the way, we got word to intercept a *Daily News* truck. You know the rest."

"Do you know who the woman with the Midwestern accent works for?" Charlie asked.

"Nope. Probably she doesn't either; probably she's just a cutout. But an educated guess would be a government—or someone able to buy into a government. Pitman and Dewart—the kids who tried to take you out on your block—used Echelon to track you here." Cadaret stressed "Echelon" as if it proved his case.

"Does Echelon mean anything to you?" Charlie asked Drummond.

"Just tell me what I want to know," Drummond told Cadaret, punctuating the demand with a wave of his gun.

"You got it, sir," Cadaret said. "It's a bunch of drab office complexes around the world that everyone takes for call centers or whatnot. Really it's a network of listening posts code-named Project Echelon, sponsored by the United States and some allies."

"Oh, that, right, right," Drummond said, though clearly he had little idea, if any, what Cadaret was talking about.

Charlie gestured for Cadaret to continue.

"It records billions of domestic and international phone calls from homes, offices, pay phones, cells, sometimes even walkie-talkies," Cadaret said. "Once sound is captured, a word like *uranium* or *Osama* raises a red flag. Voiceprints can raise flags too. Somehow Pitman got your voiceprints added to Echelon's hit list early this morning. A few hours later, when you called Aqueduct Racetrack from a pay phone, he tapped into your conversation real-time, so of course he knew where you were. He texted Mortimer saying you were probably on your way to do some 'hunting and fishing.' "

"And since the average joe can't just surf on over to the Echelon Web site, you think these guys are government?" Charlie asked.

"Exactly."

"Foreign?"

Cadaret spat a piece of hardened blood as if it were a sunflower seed. "Or American and, for the usual reasons, keeping it black."

"Black for the usual reasons." Charlie looked off, pretending to chew this over. He was reluctant to expose his ignorance. Fuck it, he thought, that toothpaste was out of the tube. "Let me just clarify two things: What are 'the usual reasons,' and what do you mean by 'keeping it black'?"

"Whether you're the Mafia or the CIA, killing people is illegal," Cadaret said. "And if you're the CIA, your problem is it's easier than ever to get caught. So you go 'black'—you leave nothing to link what's being done to the organization doing it. And if Mr. Clark here's outfit stands to get wind of it and take you to task, you go blacker still. You make it look like an accident, if you can."

"His outfit?" Charlie said.

"The Cavalry," said Drummond. Remembering, it seemed.

"Actually, I think they disbanded," Charlie said.

"It's just a nickname."

"Okay?" Charlie waited for more.

"Clandestine operations . . ." Drummond couldn't summon anything else.

"They're a legendary special operations group," Cadaret said. "Probably CIA, maybe SOCOM, but who knows? Whichever, you'd find them on the books, if you could find them on the books at all, as 'Geological Analysis Subgroup Alpha' or 'Research and Development Project Twenty backslash Eighteen' or something like that."

"Isn't CIA already secret enough?" Charlie asked.

"If only." Cadaret laughed. "Bureaucracy and oversight have a way of effectively revealing the best-laid clandestine plans to their targets, let alone gumming up the works. At the end of the day, it's best for everybody if the bureaucrats and overseers are lulled into complacency by an hour-long PowerPoint presentation on the subject of geography, allow-ing the spooks to get down to their real business."

"So other than geographical analysis, what's the Cavalry's business?"

"It's hard to say how much is apocryphal, but word is that they recruit the ballsiest of the best and the brightest, and they run covert ops that no one else can—or would dare. The one you hear the most is that, in the mid-nineties, they replaced the king of one of the less-stable Arab countries."

"*Replaced?*"

"One day the king jumped off his yacht for a quick dip. When he climbed back aboard, he was literally a new man."

Things were beginning to make sense to Charlie. Turning to Drum-mond, he asked, "So Clara Barton High graduation day, when you had that appliance expo in Tucson you couldn't get out of, were you really in the Red Sea in a frogman suit?"

"What appliance expo in Tucson?" Drummond said.

"So how do we call out the Cavalry?" Charlie asked Cadaret.

"To me, the most astounding thing in all this is they haven't tried to get hold of you."

"We've been trying to be hard to get hold of lately," Charlie said.

"We use the horses," Drummond said.

"I think that's the other cavalry," Charlie said. A fraction of a second later, it dawned on him that he'd missed the patently obvious for years. Playing the horses was about a thrill, and thrills were practically anath-ema to Drummond—at least the Drummond he knew. Taking him aside, Charlie asked, "Or is *that* why you always bought the *Racing Form?*"

"Right, right, the *Daily Racing Form.* There was something in the ads."

"That could be more than just an interesting piece of information, couldn't it?"

Drummond brightened. "Do you have today's *Racing Form?*"

"As my luck would have it, today is probably the first day in ten years I didn't buy it. But if I had, what would I find in the ads?"

"A number for us to call maybe."

"Placed by this Cavalry?"

"Possibly."

It wasn't a lot to go on. Still, at the end of the long, dark tunnel Charlie's life had become, a bulb flickered on.

He looked around, trying to determine which way east was. The general store was to the east—after all the driving, he had no doubt about that. They might find the *Daily Racing Form* there—it was sold everywhere there were gamblers, which is to say it was sold everywhere. Alternatively, they might access it online or find transportation to someplace else that sold it.

The trees partitioned the woods into narrow alleys, and those alleys formed a maze. Charlie had dreamed of camping and outdoor adventure as a boy. The closest he got was reading about it. He'd spent maybe eight weeks of his adult life outside urban environments, and most of that time was at racetracks. Still, he remembered that the sun travels west. He looked up. The treetops obscured the sun. But the shadows were shifting slightly, clockwise, enabling him to determine west.

"Dad, what do you say we take a walk?"

"Do us all a favor and let me go along with you," Cadaret said.

"Your gang will be here soon," Charlie said. "Probably too soon."

"They'll be looking for *you*. And they'll find you. If I'm with you, I can vouch for the fact that you don't know anything."

"So? Didn't they kill my friend for knowing only the address of the Monroeville club?"

"Ramirez?"

"Yeah."

"That was just a math thing. He added up to better off not alive."

Guilt and horror pummeled Charlie anew. He felt a hand on his shoulder and jumped. Drummond wanted a private word.

"Let's not leave him like this," Drummond whispered.

"You really think he can help us?"

"No." Drummond retrained the gun on Cadaret.

"What the hell are you doing?"

"Neutralizing him."

"*Neutralizing him?* You and I would look like lasagnas now if it hadn't been for him."

"Making no mistakes is what establishes the certainty of victory, for it means conquering an enemy that is already defeated."

"Listen, I don't mean to diss the *Big Book of Bloodshed,* but what's he going to do if he's stuck here? I've got a twenty-dollar bill that says you know some good tying-guys-up knots."

Drummond relented with a grunt.

With more wire from the helicopter, he bound Cadaret at the ankles, knees, and thighs; and in the time most people take to tie a pair of shoes, he near-mummified the assassin from waist to shoulders.

Standing by and watching, Charlie wondered why Cadaret had put forth such a specious argument on behalf of being freed. Did he really expect them to trust someone who murders people for a living?

His eyes fell to Cadaret's five-buck wristwatch: not the sort of watch he would expect on someone who has a vacation house on St. Bart's.

23

"**. . . and the** code name of the operation?" Cranch asked.

He'd been firing questions all morning. He hadn't touched his water. He'd seldom shifted from his perch on the plastic picnic table bench. He would put most robots to shame, Alice thought.

"Lothario," she said, her reserve diminishing.

"Is that a reference of some sort to Mr. Fielding?"

"To the best of my knowledge, it was generated at random, but, you know, sometimes the kids on the desk get frisky."

"And the skipper?"

"Harold Archibald." She shook off exhaustion. "Surely you have Hal on your spook scorecard?"

"Why don't you fill me in? The complete details, please."

"Senior officer, made a name for himself in the MI6 drug trafficking ops in the early eighties, subsequently fast-tracked with tours in Abu Dhabi, Prague, Paris, and Geneva before being given the keys to Counterproliferation back at the Firm."

"Personal?"

"Public schoolboy—Epsom College and Magdalen College, Oxford. From a line of intelligencers. Granddad was Naval, Dad an MI5 officer in Logistics—"

Cranch snorted. "You can do better than that, Alice."

"Do you think I could just make up 'MI5 officer in Logistics'?"

"No, but I think you can give me something I can use. Does he drink? Does he do drugs? Does he do teenage boys?"

"All right, all right. He's a good man. He devotes much of the little free time he has to charitable work. He's been married for twenty-odd years to a well-liked estate agent named Mimi. They have three children who aren't in any way brats—"

Cranch craned his neck across the table. "However?"

Alice fought an inclination to recoil. "However, an officer who worked for Hal in London was shifted to Nairobi last February. She was in her fourth month of pregnancy. It's been said the baby boy bears quite a resemblance to him."

If Cranch were to dial Harold Archibald, Alice knew, he would ring a telephone located at 85 Vauxhall Cross in London, the headquarters of the Secret Intelligence Service. If Archibald were at his desk, the forty-nine-year-old would probably answer, and, with his crisp, impeccably modulated Oxbridge accent, flatly deny everything she'd said. He would almost certainly add that he'd never heard of her. If pushed, he would purport to be a mid-level analyst whose greatest transgression in life was staying for a third pint at the tiny local down the block from the St. Alban's commuter rail station before his two-minute drive home to the cottage he shared with his mother. And that would be the truth.

Alice wasn't really MI6. She wasn't even from Britain—but, as it happened, New Britain, in central Connecticut. Her actual employer was the National Security Agency of Fort Meade, Maryland. She'd absorbed enough of London during a six-month tour, however, that she could fool even actual MI6 agents. Feeding Cranch her contingency MI6 story bought a few hours, maybe the night—because of the time difference, much of England already had left the office for the night. By the time Cranch debunked her yarn, her backup team might be here. Had better be here. Cranch's willingness to torture her suggested Fielding meant to extract whatever he could, then snuff her.

She weighed revising her fundamental guiding principle that hellish situations in the lives of her aliases beat any quiet minute in her own.

That philosophy had originated when she was eleven, a star student, actress, and athlete regarded by her parents, teachers, and hordes of friends as an indomitable firecracker. Then she tackled a murder case that was baffling local law enforcement. The victim was her father.

On a cold night, in an unlit parking lot across the street from a bustling New Britain pub, Stanley Rutherford had been shot in the head through the open driver's side window of his car. An insurance salesman named Bud Gorman emerged as the prime suspect. Gorman's wife was rumored to be Stanley Rutherford's mistress, and he was at the pub for hours before and after the shooting. No one witnessed him leaving the pub, however, and an extensive search of the area yielded no gun.

Although Alice's encounters with Gorman over the years were limited to greetings in the church parking lot and on the soccer field sideline, she had a strong sense that he was no murderer. She told her mother so. Jocelyn Rutherford had a potent mind and rectitude to match. She would have cried foul on Gorman's behalf from the beginning, Alice thought, if not for the shock and grief.

"It's plain as day he did it," Jocelyn said. "It's just a question of time until they get something on him."

"But how could he have hidden the gun?" Alice asked. "The police even searched the sewers."

"There are any number of good explanations. For one, he could have hidden it in his own car, then dumped it on his way home—into the lake, maybe, or buried it in the woods behind his house where it would be impossible to find."

Alice thought it odd that her mother, shrewd as she was, would imagine that a man with the eyes of suspicious neighbors and law enforcement agents hot upon him would go into his woods and bury anything.

After school the next day, Alice begged out of soccer practice and rode her three-speed to Gorman's street, snuck into the woods behind his house, and searched until it was too dark to continue. She found nothing. She searched there each weekday afternoon over the next week to the same result. She quit the soccer team and, later, the school production of *Jesus Christ Superstar* so she could continue searching. On her twenty-second afternoon, she spotted a pile of leaves and sticks arranged just so. The gun was buried beneath it.

She rode home and confronted her mother, who tried to strangle her. Alice fended her off with the steak knife she had at the ready. Her bicycle stood at the ready too, outside the kitchen door. She jumped on and pedaled to the police station. Both Jocelyn Rutherford and her lover, Gorman's wife, Martha, were sent to prison for twenty years.

Alice was left desolate—on good days. She spent her free time alone at the library, where she became captivated by Jingde legends, particularly the story of the Buddhist monk Bodhidharma, who fell out of favor and had to flee the court of the Liang emperor Wu in 527. Bodhidharma sought refuge at the Shaolin Monastery, where he faced a wall for nine years without uttering a single word. Afterward he wrote the book of Shaolin kung fu.

Letting schoolwork and friendships fall by the wayside, Alice immersed herself in the relatively solitary martial art, working on card-throwing more than anything. After hundreds of attempts, she acquired the ability to sling an ordinary playing card across her foster family's garage with enough force that a corner would lodge in the cork dartboard. With thousands of repetitions, she could deliver the card to the target at approximately thirty miles an hour, so fast it cracked like a whip. About one-third of the time it landed in the bull's-eye. Throwing at slightly higher speeds and with greater accuracy, Shaolin masters actually could stab an adversary with a card or even—by striking certain minute pressure points—put him into a coma.

Alice failed to find refuge with the Shaolin. A decade later, she finally found a measure of sanctuary: the job of covert operations officer. Deep cover roles allowed her a departure from her life of weeks at a time, sometimes as long as a year.

Now, thanks to Fielding, she stood to depart her life permanently.

Too much of a good thing, she thought.

24

Charlie was famished, dehydrated, and otherwise spent. Worse, his sweat had seeped into his wounds, along with sap, turning each step into its own ordeal. They had negotiated underbrush and low-hanging branches for miles. Even Drummond was breathing hard.

Finally the woods thinned, providing a glimpse of the general store's yellow clapboarding. It felt like coming upon an oasis.

Charlie stopped behind a bush to study the area. The only vehicle in sight was the rusty Chevy pickup, in the same spot as this morning. The dirt lot and vast, colorless fields surrounding it offered hiding places. Although Drummond had been mostly cloudy throughout their trek, often humming discordantly, Charlie looked to him now to devise a tactic for approaching the store.

He found Drummond ambling out of the woods.

Praying this meant his countersurveillance software was firing, Charlie caught up to him.

"What are they called again?" Drummond asked.

"Who?"

"Those birds."

"What birds?"

"Woodland birds with brown camouflaged plumage. Known for their degree of challenge as game . . ."

"I hope you don't mean *snipes*?"

"That's it, snipes, thank you."

Charlie's heart turned into a jackhammer.

"They search for invertebrates by stabbing at the mud with their bills with a sewing-machine motion," Drummond went on.

"What made you think of *snipes*?"

"The woods, I guess. An interesting piece of information is the first sewing machine was invented by a French tailor in 1830. He nearly died when a group of his fellow tailors, fearing unemployment as a result of the invention, burned down his factory."

Crossing the field, Charlie couldn't shake the mental image of himself and Drummond seen through crosshairs.

As Drummond ushered him into the store, there was a gunshotlike crack.

Just the door—Drummond had let it fall too fast into the frame in his rush to inspect the snack aisle.

Charlie's relief lasted maybe a second. The store itself, with five tall aisles and a crowd of large, free-standing racks, had a dark-alley feel. The reedy teenager behind the counter seemed to be the only person present. *TUCKER* was stitched onto his gas station attendant uniform shirt. Tobacco ballooned one of his cheeks. His sleeves were rolled up past his biceps, revealing a tattooed likeness of racecar driver Dale Earnhardt and a second tattoo of a dagger dripping blood.

After the bodega on Ludlow Street, Charlie couldn't help wondering whether Tucker was a plant. He quickly dismissed the notion. Vaudeville would do a Tucker with greater subtlety.

When his index finger reached the end of a paragraph in the sports section, Tucker looked up, spat a string of tobacco juice into an oilcan, then took in Charlie and Drummond. Most of their scrapes and bruises, along with the tears in their clothing, had been impossible to cover up.

"How y'all doin'?" he asked warily.

"Better, now that the hunting trip from hell is over," Charlie said.

"Been there," Tucker said with understanding. "So whatchy'all be needing?"

"For starters, do you sell any clothes?"

"Yes sir, there's tons down there." Tucker waved at the central aisle.

Like the other aisles, it was crammed floor to ceiling with all manner of provisions. This was the sort of store where it's a challenge to find something they don't carry, and where there almost always was a *Racing Form.*

"And magazines?" Charlie asked.

With his newsprint-blackened finger, the kid pointed to the far wall, where a magazine rack ran the length of the store.

Following Charlie to it, Drummond asked, "We were on a hunting trip?"

Thankfully Tucker was engrossed again in his newspaper.

"If being the prey counts," Charlie replied.

The magazine rack was packed with hundreds of publications. Few weren't pornography. The *Daily Racing Form*'s iconic bright red masthead shone like a beacon. While pleased to get it in hand, Charlie felt a trickle of depression that the publication central to his existence was used by clever and righteous men to transmit messages without fear that anyone of consequence would see them.

The masthead appeared to perk up Drummond. He pulled a copy from the rack and flipped as if by habit to the classifieds, which ranged from offerings of services to personals and want ads.

"So I'm guessing it won't be as simple as '*Wanted: spy to come in from cold*'?" Charlie said.

"It would be encrypted."

"Any idea how?"

"Bank code, maybe?"

"What's bank code?"

Drummond shook his head as if to align his thoughts. "I mean book code."

"Okay, what's book code?"

"Take this here." Drummond pointed to the ad placed by Theodore J. Tepper, a lawyer specializing in quickie divorces. "The numbers in his address or phone number might really be page numbers."

"Of a book?"

"The first letters of the fourth lines of those pages, say, would spell out the message to us."

"What's the book?"

"We would need to know."

"If your friends know we're on the lam, would they expect us to go find a Barnes & Noble? We were lucky just to get the *Racing . . .*"

Charlie let his voice trail off as Drummond thrust a finger at the ad below the divorce lawyer's.

Stop Duck Hunting! (212) 054–0871

"*Duck* means Drummond Clark," Drummond exclaimed.

"How's that?"

"If you drop out all but the letters beside D, U, C and—?"

"Got it," Charlie said with mounting excitement.

Drummond's brow bunched in skepticism. "On second thought, it doesn't feel right."

"Why not? You're being hunted, the Cavalry's trying to stop it, and this can't be a real ad. If you're an animal rights advocacy group, the *Daily Racing Form* is the last magazine you'd expect to rally support, save maybe the *Daily Cockfighting Form.*"

Drummond tried to find the handle on what was troubling him.

Charlie stabbed at the 212 area code. "Also the area code's Manhattan. Where we were when the *Racing Form* went to press."

"There are a lot of organizations in Manhattan."

"But the only thing anybody hunts for there are apartments that rent for less than two thousand bucks a month."

"Radio silence is maintained during all battlefront operations," Drummond said. Another recitation.

Regardless, Charlie got the point. "What's to lose by calling them?"

Drummond's eyes widened in alarm. "On the telephone?"

"The Ministry of Voiceprints, right. How about if we have the kid over there speak for us?"

Drummond shrugged. Which was better than a no.

They approached the counter. While pointedly unfolding a twenty-dollar bill, Charlie said to Tucker, "I was hoping you would call a number for me and ask when and where the meeting is. It's, how can I put it . . . ?" He writhed in discomfort, as he imagined someone calling about an AA meeting would.

"No problem, sir," said Tucker, happily accepting the twenty.

Charlie wrote the number between the greasy fingerprints on a scrap sales receipt. Tucker uncradled the wall phone, mouthed the numbers to himself as he read them, then dialed. Charlie made out a faint ringing followed by a greeting from a deep male voice.

"Afternoon, sir," Tucker said into the mouthpiece, "I'm calling for a customer who wants the info for the meeting." He listened for a moment, studying Charlie and Drummond meanwhile, as if per something the man on the other end was saying. Placing a hand over the mouthpiece, he said to Charlie, "He needs the name of your calculus teacher at Clara Barton." If Tucker thought the request was strange, he kept it to himself.

Huddling with Drummond, Charlie asked, "What do you make of that?"

"A false subtraction cipher, maybe," Drummond said.

"What is a false subtraction cipher?"

"I— It's on the tip of my tongue."

"Hang on for just a bit, sir?" Tucker said into the phone.

Charlie asked Drummond, "Could it just be a straight question?"

"Why would they do that?"

"If they suspect we're too addled to remember what false subtraction is. Also it's the sort of information that wouldn't have made it onto any database. But you might have told it to a friend." Drummond had followed Charlie's progress in math like other fathers did their sons' accomplishments on the ball field.

"I'm sorry, Charles, I just . . ." With a hangdog look, Drummond sought refuge in the *Racing Form.*

"Mrs. Feldman," Charlie told Tucker.

Tucker repeated the name into the phone, listened, and relayed to Charlie, "The meeting's at seven thirty at the Montezuma Restaurant on a hundred sixty-fourth."

"Dad, Montezuma Restaurant?"

"A Mexican restaurant?"

If the clock above the refrigerated shelves was accurate, it was now 2:10 P.M. Charlie estimated they could make it to New York by 7:30—if he drove like Dale Earnhardt. Which would entail having a car. The Cavalry man had had no reason to think they were on foot, but surely he knew, as soon as his phone rang, where they were.

Charlie turned to Tucker, "Can you ask if he means tonight, or—?"

Tucker was glaring at the receiver, as though that would chasten the man on the other end of the line for the abrupt hang-up.

Charlie huddled with Drummond. "Could 'Montezuma Restaurant on one sixty-fourth' be code?"

"What isn't code, really?" Drummond said.

Charlie might have considered the question profound, but Drummond's eyes were bobbing along with the hot dogs on the roller grill.

Charlie reflected that he and Drummond had demonstrated proficiency with the Drummond Clark-to-Duck cipher. So maybe the Cavalry was rolling with it.

From a spinning rack stuffed with road maps, he plucked one that included Monroeville and its environs, then tried to apply the cipher to 164th Street.

There was no 1st Street in the area, no 6th either. No Route 4, no 4th Street, no 4th anything. There was a narrow Country Route 1 ten miles north of Monroeville. Also, a few miles up Country Route 1 was a tiny blue soldier icon, labeled MONUMENT. And by dropping certain letters from Montezuma Restaurant . . .

Charlie's thoughts went to an old track axiom: "If you hear hoofbeats behind you, it's a horse." He felt the horse's breath on the back of his neck.

But what about the time of the rendezvous? 7:30 would mean five and a half hours to kill. Or to be killed—7:00 helped, but not enough; 0 would mean midnight, by which time their bones might be licked clean by buzzards; 3:00 was doable.

If they had wheels. Drummond could surely hot-wire the old pickup parked outside. But absconding with it would entail either bringing Tucker along or incapacitating him so he couldn't call the cops.

"Charles, what do you say I treat you to lunch?" Drummond said, digging a sheaf of bills from his bowling pants.

"Is that the motel manager's money?" Charlie asked, delighted as much as anything by the measure of justice in recouping his $157.

"No, the fellow who also lent us his wristwatch."

They'd strapped Cadaret's watch to a stick and floated it down the first stream they came upon. When tying him up, Drummond must have "borrowed" his wallet too.

Five hundred dollars bought four hot dogs, two big bottles of Gatorade, the road map, two pairs of dungarees, two coats, a pair of sneakers for Drummond, and the decrepit 1962 Chevrolet short bed Tucker probably would have happily parted with for just the price of a fifth hot dog.

The truck's engine coughed rheumatically on ignition and the tailpipe sprayed the yellow clapboards with black oil. But soon enough, Charlie and Drummond were on their way to the monument, at fifty miles an hour, and in excellent spirits.

"All things considered," Charlie said, "we really owe that Cadaret a nice note."

25

According to the map, the '62 Chevrolet short bed needed to rattle and gasp just one more mile to reach the monument. At the wheel, Charlie imagined the government vehicle that would meet them and bring them in from the cold. He had no idea whether the Cavalry would send a sleek government car or a helicopter or something clandestine— a VW Love Bus, for instance. Whatever they sent, even another rusted-out '62 Chevrolet short bed, he was sure he would luxuriate in the ride.

Drummond was smothering his second hot dog with a fourth packet of ketchup.

"Trying to get more condiments into your diet, Dad?"

"An interesting piece of information is that four tablespoons of ketchup have the nutritional value of an entire tomato."

That actually is sort of interesting, Charlie would have said. But just as the pickup was about to chug past the weed-colored Battle of Staunton Historic Monument sign, which was mostly hidden behind tall weeds on the roadside, he spotted it. He pumped the brake and jerked the steering wheel, heaving the truck onto a long, bumpy dirt road that wound through thick woods. The tires kicked up so much dust, the truck appeared to be chased by a sandstorm.

"So much for stealth," he said.

"Oh," said Drummond, squeezing the last molecule of ketchup from the packet.

The driveway terminated at a ramshackle blacktop. Some two hundred parking spots ran along one side of a much longer field of overgrown grass that was golden in the afternoon light.

Drummond's nostrils flared. "There's no one here," he said.

Indeed, the only sign of life was a few ravens perched on a statue of a soldier on horseback, about fifty feet into the field. Charlie pulled into a space close to the statue, at the center of the parking strip. "We're still five minutes early," he said.

"Five minutes? That's all?"

"What were you expecting?"

"An hour at the least."

Charlie wasn't sure what to make of this. Drummond's internal clock had been off by decades lately. But his intuition couldn't be discounted. "Would you ideally have allowed yourself time to conduct one of those countersurveillance things, or to work up an escape route, something like that?"

"Of course. When is the meeting?"

"Uh, five minutes from now."

Drummond pushed open the passenger door. The hinges croaked, scaring off some of the ravens. He lowered himself to the asphalt and edged toward the field. His eyes jumped around, as if he were watching the battle that had taken place here.

Trailing him, Charlie saw little and heard only the chatter of the remaining ravens and the rustling of tall blades of grass.

"What am I missing?" Charlie asked.

"There's no one here."

"Maybe I screwed up the deciphering. If you were trying to bring us in, what sort of meeting place would you choose?"

"Someplace crowded, like a train station."

"That's what I was thinking too."

With a shrug, Drummond waded into the high grass, running his palms along the tips as if stroking a cat. His interest went to the man on horseback, a soldier from the Civil War era—the tip-off was the visored cap with the distinctive forward-sloping top—who was sculpted at about twice the size of life and cast in bronze. A real, wooden-wheeled cannon from the same period sat on the ground a few feet to his side.

"Any chance this is one of those dead drops?" Charlie asked. "Maybe they hid directions here to the real meeting place?"

"Maybe." Drummond peered into the mouth of the cannon. It was plugged.

He wandered around the granite pedestal, gazing up at the statue. The soldier would have been unrecognizable even to Civil War buffs because of the raven droppings.

"You know what's interesting?" Drummond said.

"What?"

"On equestrian statues, if the front hooves are off the ground, it signifies the soldier died in battle. If just one hoof is raised, he died later of wounds related to the battle."

If they were going to learn anything here, Charlie thought, the soldier would have to tell them himself.

"If all the hooves are on the ground, like this one," Drummond continued, "it means the man died in his sleep."

"You think it's possible they just missed that turnoff?" Charlie asked.

"It's possible." With a yawn, Drummond lay down on the granite pedestal, using the horse's stout left front leg as a headboard.

Hoping Drummond's nonchalance indicated they were safe, Charlie took a seat beside him.

Ten minutes passed, another raven was the only arrival, and anxiety began clawing at Charlie's stomach lining. Nudging Drummond from a light slumber, he said, "It's not like they could have been caught in traffic."

Drummond shrugged. He still seemed entirely unconcerned.

It no longer offered reassurance. "Maybe we should drive to the next town and call the number in the ad again," Charlie said.

As the words left his lips, a black Dodge Durango roared down the driveway toward the field. The dust and glare made it impossible to see into the sport utility vehicle. Charlie looked to Drummond.

He was fast asleep.

"Looks like we're in business," Charlie said, rousing him.

Opening his eyes, Drummond regarded the Durango with only passing interest, if any—it was hard to tell.

Charlie expected the Durango would park near the pickup truck. But it veered away and drove to the far end of the field, pulling into the farthest possible spot.

"Could it just be someone else?" he asked.

He bet himself Drummond would shrug. He won the bet.

The Durango's driver's door eased open. A compact man of perhaps forty edged out. He had a dark brown flattop and wore a mossy-oak camouflage suit. His slow, deliberate movements made his circumspection obvious, even from the monument a hundred yards away. He might just be a hunter. As for his hesitation? He didn't have a hunting permit? Or maybe he was indeed the Cavalry's emissary, the camouflage was part of his cover, and his unease was attributable to the fact that he saw no one—the giant statue blocked Charlie and Drummond from his sight, and the lone vehicle in the lot, the rusty pickup, could well have been abandoned here years ago.

Charlie considered leaping up and waving. Intuition held him in place.

The Durango's passenger and rear driver's side doors sprung open. Out darted two more men in camouflage. Following Flattop, they dropped onto hands and knees and shot into the high grass.

Through gaps between stalks, Charlie glimpsed the man who'd been in the backseat. He was young, no more than twenty-five, with the slight build and serious look not of a hunter but a scholar. His pistol glinted. Charlie entertained the idea that this was some sort of intelligence analyst, pressed by exigency into field duty.

Then a gust of wind parted the grass, revealing the man who'd been in the passenger seat.

Cadaret.

Shock ran through Charlie like a sword.

"Dad, we've been set up," he exclaimed. "And that's the best-case scenario." The worst one he could think of was that Cadaret and his men had intercepted the Cavalry.

Drummond looked up. "That's a shame," he said, then tried to get comfortable again against the bronze horse's shin.

From the Durango's end of the field came the whipcrack of a gunshot. Its low echo skittered along the top of the grass. The ravens leaped into flight. The bullet stung the bronze soldier's left elbow, turning the hardened excrement in its crook to a puff of white. The horse's barrel-thick left front leg shielded Drummond from all but a dusting.

Charlie pressed himself against the inside of the horse's right front leg, some primitive survival apparatus enabling him to coil himself so he wasn't exposed to the shooters. A second round splashed dirt onto the pedestal, pelting him like buckshot. Loath to move, he angled his eyes to Drummond.

On three occasions, peril had transformed Drummond into a superhero. He was incited now, but only in the manner of someone whose rest is being disrupted.

26

Their gambit was plain to Charlie. From behind a mound at the far end of the field, Cadaret took a shot every few seconds. His objective wasn't to hit Charlie or Drummond—although that would have been perfectly acceptable—but rather to hold them in place behind the statue until Flattop or Scholar flanked them. Capitalizing on the rises and dips in the field, that duo had crept to within sixty or seventy yards, still too far to fire with any accuracy. At twenty-five yards, they probably would be able to split an aspirin.

Charlie hoped someone driving along County Route 1 would call the cops. The road was barely traveled, though, and the monument was far enough away that the gunfire might not be heard over an engine. If a good Samaritan heard and came to investigate still, he would find only hunters, as common in these parts as teenagers in a suburban mall. And if he investigated further, he'd die.

Charlie tried to conceive a more proactive solution. Every avenue his mind took ended with the sober realization that outmaneuvering professional killers on a battlefield was even further from his expertise than landing a helicopter.

Then there was Drummond.

"Hear those bullets, Dad? These guys are playing your song."

"How about we shoot back?" Drummond put forth, as if it were a novel idea.

"We have Mom's gun." Charlie patted the Colt in his waistband. "But I think we're going to need more than that."

A bullet bored into the horse's right shoulder and exited its left breast, buzzing directly over Drummond's head. Drummond hunkered closer to the pedestal but otherwise appeared untroubled.

Charlie was troubled enough for them both: He'd figured the bronze statue was impenetrable. "We need to get down," he shouted over the echoing report.

Drummond didn't seem to follow. Rather than take time to explain, Charlie wrapped his arms around him and heaved them both off the front of the pedestal. They flopped onto the ground, putting the pedestal between them and the shooters.

The ground appeared to have received a fresh dusting of snow. In fact it was particles of raven excrement. Lovely, Charlie thought.

Some of the particles had filled the letters chiseled into the face of the pedestal.

GENERAL PIERRE GUSTAVE TOUSSAINT BEAUREGARD, 1818–1893

A bullet chimed the horse's right cheek, ricocheted, and struck the pickup truck, shattering a headlight.

Drummond appraised the damage with a thin smile and said, "As Churchill put it, 'There is nothing so enjoyable as to be shot at by one's enemy without result.' "

Charlie asked himself, How did it come down to this? "Didn't Churchill have a drinking problem?"

"Give me the Colt, please."

Charlie saw a glow in Drummond's eyes. Had a mental association with Beauregard the dog triggered him?

It could have been an association with raven crap, for all Charlie cared. Electrified, he handed over the gun.

Drummond pivoted to his left and squeezed off two quick shots.

The first missed by a wide margin, judging by the puff of dirt. Still, it sent Flattop diving for the cover of high grass. The second met him there. Red spouted from his leg, and he dropped from sight.

If not for fear of breaking Drummond's concentration, Charlie would have cheered.

Whirling to his right, Drummond trained the Colt on Scholar, now scurrying across a patch of barren ground about forty yards away, and fired. The bullet merely trimmed the high grass to Scholar's left.

Not an ideal time for Drummond to prove human, Charlie thought.

Drummond tweaked the barrel and snapped the trigger again. The result was a feeble click. "It wasn't fully loaded," he told Charlie. "Give me the Walther."

"I don't have it."

"Where is it?"

"The glove compartment."

"This isn't the time for your jokes."

"In the car, you were rocking back and forth, obsessing with ketchup, and the gun was just kind of balancing there on the seat, so I thought it'd be for the best . . ."

Drummond's eyes slitted, which Charlie read as fury.

"It might have been for the best, actually," Drummond said.

He outlined their escape plan.

27

"The problem with that is the huge likelihood I'll get shot," Charlie said.

"I'd say only fifty-fifty," Drummond said coolly.

"Oh, okay, great."

"What are our chances otherwise?"

"Way worse," Charlie admitted.

A bullet gonged the horse's throat.

"All right, I'm getting ready," Charlie said.

He forced himself into a sprinter's stance, which wasn't as simple as placing a hand here and a foot there. Anxiety had the effect of doubling the force of gravity. He worried that when the time came to run from behind the pedestal, he wouldn't be able to move, and their window of opportunity would slam shut. He clung to the hope, dim though it was, that some savior would arrive and render this brutal plan unnecessary.

Drummond crouched behind him. A bullet spat chips of granite. The bitter scent of cordite filled the air.

"What was the name of that catcher on the Mets when they won the World Series back in eighty-six?" Drummond asked.

"Gary Carter," said Charlie, unsettled by the introduction of the topic.

"Just think about him."

"He was pretty much the slowest runner in the majors."

"I know."

"So, what? You're saying this could be worse? I could be as slow as Gary Carter?"

"No, I just hoped it might take your mind off the other business."

It had.

Charlie looked over his shoulder to convey his gratitude. Drummond was pivoting in the opposite direction, his eyes locked on the pickup truck, his knees tensed to spring toward it. His would be by far the harder role, yet he was aglow, like he'd just stepped out of an adrenaline shower.

Awe burned away the remainder of Charlie's anxiety.

Drummond gave the go order—"Execute!"

Charlie surged out from the pedestal, faster than he'd imagined himself capable.

A bullet cleaved the air inches in front of his eyes.

To keep going, he thought, would be insane.

Out of the blue, however, a spirit took possession of him—that's how it felt—a spirit who saw things in greater depth and definition, and in slow motion. Both Flattop and Scholar appeared clearly in his peripheral vision, jumping from their hiding spots to capitalize on the open shot at him. In his new perception, they rose as if weighted, and the twinkle of the waning sun on their gun barrels was as slow as a turn signal. They pulled—tugged, it seemed—their triggers. He had the sensation of seeing, hearing, and feeling everything that followed: the crashes of firing pins, the jolts of explosive in the primers, the white heat gobbling the powder, the flames screaming through the flash holes, the propellant blasting, the cartridges groaning under pressure and expanding and swelling and bulging and, finally, the bullets bursting out of the barrels. He watched the plumes of flame balloon from the muzzles and the guns themselves sashay backward. He heard the booms of the projectiles as they exceeded the speed of sound, and he saw them revolving on their way toward him.

He didn't just dive, he took off; gravity no longer seemed to have sway over him. He landed after just ten feet, behind the barrel of the cannon, because that's what Drummond's plan called for. Rocks cut into his palms, his forearms, and his chin. No big deal.

Whatever had lodged in his left calf, though, returned the world to its normal pace. A hatchet, it felt like. Spotting the hole in his dungarees, he realized it was a bullet. And, holy fucking bloody damned Jesus, he hadn't imagined a bullet could hurt even a hundredth as much. The thing seemed to be setting him on fire from the inside. He wanted to tamp it somehow and to scream in pain. He lay still, facedown, as if dead. That was part of the plan too.

Vomit, tasting of a stale convenience store hot dog, erupted from his esophagus, burning its way up his throat and into his mouth. He couldn't very well spit it out if he were dead. So he let it seep out. It welled on the ground by his face. Each time he inhaled, bits went up his nostrils.

Bullets whacked the opposite side of the cannon, kicking the ground into a brown-gray haze. But the big gun shielded him, as Drummond had said it would. A solid hit to one of the brittle wooden wheels might bring the ton of bronze crashing down on him, though. He managed to lie still, his eyes slits. Out of a corner of one of them, he spotted a blur: Drummond, running through the grass, toward the pickup truck.

Cadaret leaped up from a cluster of stalks at the far end of the field and fired three times. Drummond dove for the blacktop. Cadaret's bullets kicked up the grass.

Drummond lunged to the safety of the passenger side of the truck. The engine block would now protect him. Theoretically.

Scholar and Flattop rammed fresh clips into their guns and joined Cadaret in firing at the truck. They made a punch card of the wobbly hood, dislodging it.

The steel slab banged down onto Drummond, sandwiching him against the asphalt. Luckily. The hood protected him when more bullets brought bits of glass raining from the windshield, and more rounds burst apart the headlight caddies, causing the lamps within them to explode.

Without letup in their fire, the three gunmen closed in. The pickup's grille, side panels, engine, mirrors, and roof rang like a steel band, and the whole chassis staggered. With a report as loud as the sum of those preceding it, the gasoline tank exploded into a mound of fire. In a blink, the fire swelled to the size of a house, encasing Drummond along with the entire truck. Just as fast, it receded into puddles of flame and burning pieces of upholstery scattered about the parking lot.

The wind thinned the smoke, revealing the truck's charred remains. And Drummond. The hood that shielded him had been cast aside. He lay flat on his back on the asphalt. His chest, swamped in shimmering crimson, had ceased to rise and fall.

28

Cadaret strode onto the blacktop, followed by Flattop and Scholar. With a twisted grin, Cadaret aligned his pistol for a game of "shoot the can" with Drummond's head.

"Enough, enough," Charlie cried from the ground behind the cannon. "How many times do you need to kill him?"

Cadaret whirled at him, gun leveled.

Charlie tried to stand up. Each movement made it feel like he was being shot in the leg again. "Look, our plan was shit. You win," he said, hobbling to the blacktop, where the wide-eyed stares said he'd succeeded in playing dead. "If you'll let me live, I'll tell what you want to know."

Flattop and Scholar looked curiously at Cadaret. He flexed his shoulders.

"What do we want to know?" he asked Charlie.

"About the shootings."

"What shootings?"

"Yours," Drummond said, reaching up from behind Cadaret and surprising him by grabbing hold of his belt. Using Cadaret as a counterweight, Drummond rose to his feet, then threw his forehead into the killer's temple with a resounding crack. Cadaret crumpled, unconscious, into Drummond's arms.

Both Flattop and Scholar swiveled toward Drummond and fired. Flattop's shot flew wide. Scholar's was absorbed by Cadaret—now Drummond's shield—fatally.

Drummond lifted Cadaret's limp hand, the gun still in it, and pressed the trigger. With a blast, a bullet plunged into Flattop's chest. Convulsing as if he'd instead absorbed a jolt of electricity, he fell to the parking lot. Another twitch and he lay still, for good.

Drummond pivoted Cadaret's body a few degrees and fired again. A round slammed into Scholar's right collarbone, sending him reeling with a wake of blood.

He remained upright by grasping Charlie's neck and holding tight. He settled directly behind Charlie, breathing heavily, his chest pressed against Charlie's right shoulder blade—probably to staunch the flow of his blood. He used the crook of Charlie's neck to prop his gun, to get a shot at Drummond. Charlie couldn't so much as flinch without risk of a bullet in his own head.

Scholar's problem was that Cadaret's body shielded Drummond. Also Drummond was trying to shoot him. But Drummond's only shot was directly through Charlie. Charlie had an ugly suspicion that that didn't rule it out. A recent "interesting piece of information": A bullet passes easily through the human diaphragm.

Stuffing the hot muzzle into Charlie's ear, Scholar said, "Please put the gun down, Mr. Clark."

Without hesitation, Drummond let Cadaret's pistol fall. And without having to be asked, he tapped it with his sneaker, sending it rasping over the asphalt. It stopped inches from Scholar.

"Thank you, sir," Scholar said.

His excessive deference was either one of those military things, Charlie thought, or just odd.

Drummond studied Scholar and said, "I know you, don't I?"

"Possibly." The young man seemed indisposed to chat.

Drummond persisted. "You're the kid who speaks ten languages?"

"Only if you include English."

"Belknapp, right?"

"Yes, sir."

"Aren't you supposed to be infiltrating Muslim graduate students at Cal Tech?"

"It's holiday break. I'm in Idaho, snowboarding. As it were."

"So, really you're spending the holiday putting me to pasture. Why?"

"Orders from 'Hen' himself, sir."

Charlie couldn't help exclaiming, "You two work together?"

"Apparently one of us has been made redundant," Drummond said.

"Why? Are they afraid you might talk about what went down at the office Christmas party?"

Drummond looked at Belknapp. "I wouldn't imagine the rationale filtered down to your level?"

Belknapp glanced around, as if trying to determine the location of a microphone. In a low voice, though not without conviction, he said, "The greater good."

"Hard to fathom," Drummond said. "Are you sure your orders came from *Hen*?"

"You're suggesting I was false flagged?"

"That 'Stop Duck Hunting!' ad could have been placed by anyone with a passing knowledge of our simple letter-drop cipher."

"Yes, sir, it was supposed to be easy for you and your son to find. The minimal code was just to make it seem like an actual covert correspondence. Had you been at the top of your game, you would have gravitated to the ad for Theodore Tepper, our fictitious divorce lawyer. And simple false subtraction of the saddle numbers in the day's first race from the alphabet value of the letters and the digits themselves in his address would have netted you the same Manhattan telephone number."

Drummond nodded, convinced. "Well, let's not belabor this, then."

Belknapp kicked Charlie's shins out from under him. Charlie wound up on smarting knees, on the jagged asphalt. Belknapp's muzzle bit into the base of his head.

Charlie looked up at Drummond, plaintively. "That's it?"

"Yes," said Drummond.

With a muffled report and a trail of gore, a bullet emerged from the lower left part of Cadaret's belly, the area over the diaphragm. Belknapp's head snapped backward, taking his body along. As he came to rest on the blacktop, blood arched from the socket where his right eye had been.

"I wish I hadn't had to do that," Drummond said, withdrawing his Walther from the small of Cadaret's back. "For what it's worth, Charles, your surrender was very convincing." Retrieving the Walther from the pickup truck—along with smearing ketchup on his chest—had been the essence of Drummond's plan; Charlie's role had been diversion.

Marshaling his faculties just to process the fact that the risky plan had actually worked, Charlie said, "I have lots of experience with cowardice. For what it's worth, you play a mean dead."

"I would have been more than just playing if not for that," Drummond said, eyeing the dislodged hood that had protected him from the explosion. "How's your leg?"

"Okay, except it feels like it might snap if I take another step."

Drummond knelt on the blacktop and gently rolled up Charlie's left pants cuff, purple and soggy with blood. On its way in and out of the denim, the bullet had carved a groove on the outside of Charlie's calf.

Drummond said, "I wouldn't say it's nothing, but . . ."

"A paper cut by the standards of your industry?"

"Best not to worry about it." Drummond pulled a set of keys from Flattop's pocket. "Now, if our brief helicopter ride taught us anything, it's that you ought to be the designated driver."

Limping after him to the Durango, Charlie tried to ignore the repeated detonations in his leg. "When in Spook City . . ." he exhorted himself.

If there's such a thing as a lucky gunshot wound, Charlie thought, he'd been lucky because the wound was in his left leg rather than the one used to press the pedals. He drove the Durango from County Route 1 onto a side road where it was less likely to be spotted.

Drummond sat on the floor of the spacious passenger footwell. Like Charlie, he'd replaced his bloody and torn clothing with one of the business suits that had been among the gunmen's belongings. Charlie watched him power on the fresh-from-the-factory-case prepaid cell phone also found in the gunmen's things.

"So who does a person typically call when his own CIA special ops group is trying to neutralize him and his son?" Charlie asked.

"There's a reports officer at headquarters whose job is to monitor everything, down to the number of bullets expended," Drummond said, his voice fluctuating according to the bumps and ruts in the road. "I don't think it would be wise to call her, though. In light of the way the fellows have been posing as FBI and DIA, we can conclude that she either signed off on the operation, she was bullied into it, or she's had a bad fall down a flight of stairs from which she won't recover."

Charlie started to grin, until realizing Drummond wasn't kidding. "Wouldn't the FBI or the DIA want to know what the *fellows* have been up to?"

"There are a number of agencies who would, and to whom we could turn. All have twenty-four-hour panic lines manned by veteran agents. The problem is those lines will be canvassed."

The cell phone beeped its readiness.

"So what does that leave us?" Charlie asked. "Greenpeace?"

"Burt Hattemer." Drummond clearly expected Charlie to know the name.

Charlie felt the discomfort of dinnertimes past, when his ignorance of current events, other than sports, was bared by Drummond's choices of conversation.

"He's the national security advisor," Drummond said matter-of-factly, probably masking his disappointment Charlie hadn't known. "He's been a friend since college, and I would trust him with my life."

"So wouldn't it occur to the fellows that you'd call him?"

"I imagine he's at the top of their list. We can reach him without their knowledge, though." Peeking over the window line, Drummond pointed to a part of the shoulder shaded by particularly thick treetops. "Pull over there."

He punched an 800 number onto the phone's keypad. Charlie brought the Durango to a halt in time to hear ringing. A fuzzy recording of a Scandinavian-accented woman blared through the earpiece. "*God dag,* you have reached Specialties of Sweden, bakers of the world's finest *flotevafler—*"

Drummond hit 7-6-7.

"Please hold," said the recording. On came whiney strands of an instrument that sounded to be a cross between a sitar and a fiddle.

"*Nyckelharpa,*" Drummond said fondly.

Charlie felt a familiar chill. "Wrong number, by any chance?"

Intent on the nyckelharpa, Drummond shook his head.

Charlie looked at the sky. No sign of search craft. Nothing but the setting sun, which seemed grimly metaphorical. "So you called a bakery?"

Drummond pressed a palm over the mouthpiece. "In ninety-nine, Burt and I went to Stockholm under nonofficial cover, posing as venture capitalists. Specialties of Sweden was in the red without prospect of a turnaround. We bought it because it abutted the Iranian embassy. When the workers went home, we drilled through one of our exterior walls and into what the Iranians thought was a secure conference room. We planted microphones, and the Iranians never caught on, so Burt's 'venture capital firm' kept the business. The number I input, seven six seven, is S-O-S, alphanumerically. In a few seconds, I'll input a code, known only to me. Then both numbers will be routed only to him. First, the system determines our location."

Charlie's doubt gave way to wonder. "How?"

"A cell phone can be tracked to within a few feet by triangulating its signal strength with the three nearest cell towers."

The recorded woman returned. "To continue in English, dial or say 'two,' *pour français*—" Drummond dialed 10.

"What language is ten?" Charlie asked.

"There is no ten," Drummond said. "It's the first part of my code."

"To place an order, dial or say 'zero,' " said the voice. Drummond hit 16. "To track a shipment—" Drummond hit 79. "If you know the name of the person you are trying—" Drummond entered 11. "I will now transfer you to—" Drummond added a 3 and a 5, then snapped the phone shut.

"We ought to hear from him in a few minutes," he said confidently.

Charlie was convinced of the validity of the system, but not of the code. It started with 10, 16, and 79—his own date of birth. Hardly a spy-like choice. "Any significance to one oh, one six, seventy-nine?" he asked.

"Only if you add the other four digits, one one three five, or eleven thirty-five in the morning—thirty-one minutes after you were born, or the precise time you and I first met, in the waiting room at Kings County Hospital. For a distress code, you choose a number you can't forget."

Charlie laughed to himself. He judged it prudent not to explain why, but out of his mouth anyway came, "Don't get me wrong. If Mom did anything, she showed that you deserve Espionage Parent of the Century. But you *forgetting* my birthday was about the closest thing we had to an annual tradition."

Drummond retained his composure, probably with considerable effort. "Regrettably, there were times where the goings-on at the office meant you were short shrifted."

"It might have helped if I'd known why."

"For security reasons I'm sure I don't need to explain, children of intelligence officers are told, at most, that Mother or Dad is a functionary at the State Department. I hope it makes some difference now that you do know."

"Some." Charlie felt the hurt of the eight-year-old who believed that his father cared more about a line of cheap washing machines. For the truth to make enough of a difference, he thought, somebody would need to travel back in time and have a talk with that kid.

"Looking for a crutch?" Drummond asked. He sucked at his lower lip, which Charlie recognized as an effort at self-restraint.

"Ever have one of those days where you find out your dad's a spy, your dead mother's really alive, a spy too, and then she gets her head blown off? I'm just trying to put things in perspective."

"You can write off your situation to circumstance or plain old bad luck. Throw up your hands, go seek solace in a bar—most people would understand. Just remember, that's the easy way."

Yes, of course, the Easy Way. Drummond used to speak of the easy way, the same way fire-and-brimstone preachers do the Road to Perdition. Charlie would have recognized the words just from the cadence. As always, they sent vitriol coursing through him.

"It's not like I came up with the idea that a person's upbringing has a bearing on his life," he said.

Drummond tightened his tie. "There's a point of accountability for everyone. Others have been dealt far worse hands and still found a way to prevail."

Charlie loosened his tie. "Like you, you mean?"

"One might make the argument."

"But you had Grandpa Tony."

"If you really want to know the truth, Tony DiStephano—"

"Tony Clark, you mean."

"I do mean DiStephano. 'Clark' was just part of his cover. He was really an old Chicago mobster in witness protection who we used for messy jobs."

Charlie sagged in accordance with the feeling that air had just been let out of him. He'd always thought of his grandfather as an oversized teddy bear. "Beautiful," he said.

"It could have been far worse. Your actual grandparents were charming, cultured, life-of-the-party Park Avenue sophisticates—"

"Well, thanks for shielding me from that shit."

"It was an act." Drummond reddened a shade more than Charlie had ever seen. "Really they were traitors. They spied for Stalin with the Alger

Hiss silver spoon flock. An American war hero spent the last four days of his life hanging from a hook in a Leningrad meat locker as a direct consequence of an encrypted postcard they sent to their handler at the Ministry of State Security. When Whittaker Chambers named names, they were blown. They fled to Moscow, leaving me alone. I was five."

For the first time, Charlie saw Drummond's inner workings as an assembly of human rather than mechanized parts. He felt himself beginning to understand him now, and sympathizing. To an extent. "Then I'd think that you, of all people, wouldn't have left your son alone all the time."

Drummond wiped his mouth with a sleeve, as if clearing the way for a forceful rebuttal, when the cell phone chimed.

30

Six minutes earlier, E. Burton Hattemer had been sitting in a conference room in the Senate Hart Office Building while a staffer enthusiastically detailed a solar-powered, robotic surveillance device that looked, flew, and perched just like the barn swallows prevalent in the Middle East. "The prototype can be done for as little as thirty million," she told the roomful of Senate Intelligence Committee members and advisors.

Hattemer wanted to say: Christ, that kind of cash could get us ten decent human spies and a hundred times the actionable intel.

Six years on the Hill had taught him that it would be more effective to partition the sentiment into gentle memos in the coming months when the Appropriations Subcommittee appointed a Robot-Barn-Swallow Task Force, the task force delegated a special panel, and the special panel prepared, drafted, and redrafted its recommendation to the committee.

Feeling his cell phone vibrate, he fished it from his suit pants. The LED flashed a reminder to pick up tulips for his wife at the florist in Potomac.

Hurrying out of the conference room, he said, "I beg everybody's pardon. I've got to attend to a geriatric digestive issue." Who here would want to know about that?

The florist—or SOS—message appeared when the switchboard in Stockholm activated a virtually undetectable shortwave band. "Tulips" was Drummond Clark. Three years had passed since Hattemer had communicated with his old friend other than by greeting card. That he would get in touch in this fashion, now, suggested Drummond's life was in peril and that it was an inside job.

Executive Order 11905, signed by President Ford and bolstered by Reagan with EO 12333, banned assassinations by government organizations. Yet spies continued to die of the flu, falls from terraces, or boating accidents with far greater frequency than people in other professions, in large part because men and women at the very highest levels of government believed themselves to be above the law or turned blind eyes or deaf ears in the name of the Greater Good—a sorry euphemism, Hattemer thought, for sacrificing ideals in order to mop up inconvenient messes. And that was when there was oversight at all.

For the sake of discretion, he took the stairs down to room SH-219. The two flights hurt like hell, or about as much as he'd anticipated. He'd been forced to abandon fieldwork when his deteriorated hips were replaced with six pounds of metal alloys, making the constant air and Jeep travel impractical. Still, it took him another two years to hang up his trench coat.

Protected by armed guards around the clock, few places on Earth afforded more secure communication than SH-219. Essentially a windowless steel vault, it blocked electromagnetic eavesdropping and prohibited signals from escaping. Every morning it was swept for listening devices with an attention to minutiae unseen outside archaeological digs. Even the electrical current was filtered.

Hattemer sat at the armchair at the inner prong of the giant, horseshoe-shaped table. On the olive-green wall behind him were the seals of the various intelligence agencies. Before him was a wall of high-definition monitors, the face of a system the Senate Intelligence Committee members liked to refer to as "state-of-the-art." In fact, state-of-the-art systems lacked many of its classified bells and whistles. A few keypunches could bring him into locked video conference with American intelligence officers operating anywhere from the United States to the United Arab Emirates. He could access all the classified computer networks. He could view satellite imagery of just about any place on the planet, either from vast archives or in real time. And if the pictures were inadequate, a program easier to use than text messaging, in his estimation, enabled him to dispatch reconnaissance drones.

He elected to use a device whose listing in the Intelligence Committee budget—"sound reproduction instrument"—always rankled him. It was, in laymen's terms, a telephone.

Drummond opened the cell phone and raised it to his lips, but said nothing.

A brash young woman's voice burst through the earpiece. "Jimmy, that you?"

"No," Drummond said, "Willie."

"This ain't two-five-two, oh-two-seven, oh-four-four-six?"

"Sorry, ma'am, no. Good day."

Drummond didn't merely hang up; he disconnected the call by tearing the battery from the back of the phone.

Charlie was mystified. "What? Was the phone about to self-destruct?"

"We can't use it again," Drummond said. "Even when it's off, it emits a signal."

"Then how will we get the call from your man in Washington?"

"That *was* him, with more than a little voice alteration interposed between his handset and my earpiece."

"I may have missed something."

" 'Willies' is a proprietary shorthand for hostiles. When I said, 'No Willie,' it was a recognition code that signified I wasn't under duress. His 'ain't' in turn let me know that no one was holding a gun to his head. 'Good day' was my sign-off that his message had been received."

"I'm guessing you've left out the part about what the message was."

"It was the number he said he'd meant to dial." On the cover of the killers' road atlas, Drummond wrote "*2520270446.*"

"So will we need to get another phone to call it?" Charlie asked.

"No, we won't need to make any more calls. We just subtract my 'distress code' number from it."

"A billion, five hundred thirteen million, four hundred seventy-nine thousand, three hundred and eleven?"

Drummond did the math on paper. "Not bad," he said.

"You spend seven days a week handicapping . . ."

With a look of either mock dismay or actual dismay—Charlie wasn't sure which—Drummond again wrote out:

$$2520270446$$
$$- \underline{1016791135}$$

This time, he tabulated it as:

$$1514589311$$

"Actually, we use what's known as false subtraction," he said. "In this case it means you have a series of ten separate subtractions. For instance, when you subtract six from zero four numbers in, you don't borrow from the column to the left, you just invent the ten. Or when you subtract nine from seven—you pretend the seven is a seventeen. False subtraction adds an extra layer of security and makes the math simpler, once you get used to it. The total here is a sort of alphabetical equivalent of 'one hick.' The number fifteen equals the letter O, fourteen equals N, etcetera. Now, 'one hick' doesn't sound very encouraging, but it's probably the closest safe house Burt had at his disposal." He flipped through the atlas. "Ah, there's a Hickory Road about twenty miles north."

The light at the end of Charlie's tunnel burst back on at high wattage. With energy to match, he threw the Durango into a U-turn.

"So what's the deal with this 'Hen' guy?" he asked.

"From the Cavalry?"

"Yeah."

"First, I need to tell you one more thing."

"What?"

"What I said about Grandpa Tony?"

"Yeah?"

"You won't tell him that you know, okay?"

A shiver ran the length of Charlie. "There's no chance whatsoever of that happening," he said haltingly. Grandpa Tony had passed away eight years ago, and not only was there a funeral, Charlie and Drummond both were pallbearers.

"Thank you," said Drummond.

"So who's Hen?" Charlie asked.

To no avail.

31

Cranch continued firing questions, and Alice volleyed with enough information to create the illusion of cooperation. Eighty percent of the information was useless, but it would be impossible for him to determine which was which.

"What about Drummond Clark?" he asked. "How did you get him?"

"We used a Meals on Wheels van."

"So that wasn't a real Meals on Wheels van?"

"It was, once upon a time, in Albany. One of our people got it from a junkyard. It still ran. Just needed a little work on the brakes was all."

"Were the Meals on Wheels volunteers your people too?"

"Glorified cutouts, really. They believed Clark was an embezzler and that we were a special investigative unit of the IRS."

"What did you want with him?"

The objective of Alice's actual operation, code-named "Marquis" (as in *de Sade*, an explicit reference to Fielding), was to investigate Fielding in general and, specifically, to determine whether he'd hired Lincoln Cadaret to assassinate Roberto Mariáteguia, an NSA officer who'd penetrated the Shining Path in Peru. Mariáteguia was found bound to a desk chair in a Lima hotel room, having been bled to death by leeches. The gruesome scene yielded no link to Fielding, but certainly it was his directorial style. A more tangible link was that the contractor who'd built Fielding's three-hundred-thousand-gallon swimming pool recently had installed a smaller version for Cadaret on nearby St. Bart's, gratis. Alice had found her way onto a murky trail that led to veteran Company man Drummond Clark. NSA had intercepted numerous communications from both Mariáteguia and Fielding to Perriman Appliances, where Clark nominally worked. Her hope was that Clark would shed some light on Mariáteguia. Her "holiday" in Brooklyn provided only more questions, though, and the unexpected news of Prabhakar Gaznavi's visit required she hurry back to Martinique before she could get any answers.

"Drummond Clark works for Perriman Appliances," she told Cranch, hoping that with only slightly expurgated truth she might elicit the true nature of Fielding's interest in Clark. "We know Fielding worked there from ninety-one to ninety-four."

"Thousands of people worked for Perriman Appliances during that time period."

"We also know about the CIA entry Clark leaves off his résumé. We wanted to learn his connection to Fielding. But as you know if you heard the audio, the closest thing to a secret I uncovered was that Clark's son goes by Charlie, rather than Charles."

"One just has to know the right questions." Cranch balled his hands as if they contained a magic key. "I expect to be getting on a private jet to go debrief Mr. Clark shortly. Maybe you'll get to listen to some of that audio."

Until now, Cranch had given Alice no indication that he cared whether she lived or died. Yet here he was trying to impress her. And in so doing, she realized, he'd let slip a bit of information that might prove critical.

32

At Hickory Road, thick woods dissolved into a secluded pastoral valley. Charlie turned the Durango in at 1 HICKORY, the mile-long lane's only sign, onto a gravel driveway that wound through hundreds of acres of serene pasture neatly fenced by weather-grayed rails. After several more miles, the driveway ended in a cobblestoned circle and a large stucco-over-stone colonial farmhouse with a commanding view of old-growth orchards and a barn that almost had to have been the basis for the Wyeth painting. Everything was copper as the sun sank into the hazy foothills of the Blue Ridge Mountains.

As he turned off the engine, he heard only a mild breeze, the whinnying of horses, and the soft-shoe of a stream. Nudging Drummond from a nap, he said, "If we need to hole up somewhere while Hattemer straightens things out, this wouldn't suck."

"*Burt* Hattemer?" Drummond asked, as if there had been discussion of several Hattemers. Clearly the nap had not recharged him.

"Christ. Please don't tell me he's really one of them?"

"*Them?*"

"The people you used to work with who keep trying to kill us?"

"Right, right, of course. No, we're okay. Burt's a good friend."

Despite the assurance, Charlie thought only of how Hattemer might prove their undoing. There was an H in Hattemer, and an E. But at least there was no N. If his name were Hatten, Charlie would have insisted they drive the hell away this instant.

"Come on inside before y'all catch your death," came a squawky voice.

It belonged to the man who stood atop the marble front steps, hold-ing open the door. Seventy if a day, he wore a parka over long underwear surely purchased in his beefier years; the bottoms hung like pantaloons until sucked into high rubber boots. In and around his assortment of puckers and pits and creases was a cheery face topped by a thicket of white hair.

Ushering Charlie and Drummond into the vaulted foyer, he said, "I'm Mort, the caretaker, and I'm it for the staff here during winter months, so don't be cross if your suppers are nothing fancy."

Entering, Charlie was struck by an anxiety he couldn't explain. He hoped it was just a reflex born of being attacked everywhere he'd set foot the last two days.

He took in the foyer, furnished with an antique drop-leaf table, a tall pewter vase, and a series of framed ornithological watercolors. The lus-trous pine floorboards were as wide as diving boards. If this room were representative of the home's decor, interior design enthusiasts would pay admission to see the rest.

"Whose place is this?" he asked Mort.

"Sir, all I can tell you is he's an oilman named MacCallum from up in Alaska."

"You mean that's all you're allowed to say?"

"No, sir. Except for he's a friend of Mr. Hattemer's, it's all I know. Mr. MacCallum's never once set foot here."

Charlie suspected that he now knew at least as much about MacCal-lum as Mort did.

"Why don't y'all come on here into the den and take a load off?" Mort said, leading the way.

The floor of the massive "den" was covered by a pair of rich Oriental carpets—probably no single Oriental carpet on Earth would have been big enough. The walls, with refined checkerboard wainscoting, boasted more art than many galleries; the glass and pewter frames mirrored the flickering within the stone fireplace, making the brass banquet lamps unnecessary. Charlie ogled a Breugel snowscape.

Drummond remained behind in the doorway, seemingly lost.

Mort was so hunched that he barely needed to bend in order to draw a log from the brass rack on the floor. With a sibilant grunt, he tossed the dry wood onto the andirons. The fire flared, turning the room a soft ochre and revealing what Charlie deemed the home's most attractive feature: the pair of scallop-rimmed dinner plates, set on the bar, each with a hearty turkey and cheddar sandwich and a pile of potato chips—the upscale, kettle-cooked kind.

"There's your suppers," Mort said. "Help yourselves to whatever you want to drink—the fridge behind the bar's loaded with cold beer and pop. If you're still hungry, y'all're welcome to try your luck in the kitchen. Also there's clothes and anything else a person could ever need in the mudroom. And if y'all're okay with that, I'm gonna go on up to bed—the beasts here like to get up and eat their breakfast way too darn early. Mr. H. oughtta be here in a half hour or thereabouts."

Charlie understood his misgivings now.

Suppers.

During his ten-second phone conversation with Hattemer, Drummond hadn't indicated Charlie was with him. Yet Mort had been instructed to prepare two suppers.

"Hey, Mort, just one more thing?" Charlie asked.

"Sir?"

"Was it Mr. H. himself who called you?"

"That's right."

"Did he tell you how many people to expect?"

"Four, I think."

"*Four?*"

"Y'all plus him and Mr. Fielding."

"Who's Fielding?"

Mort turned to Drummond. "Fella you and Mr. H. work with, ain't that right, sir?"

"Could be," Drummond said. "I don't know a lot of the men in Refrigeration."

In a mirror, Charlie caught Mort shooting a bewildered look at Drummond. Mort didn't know anything, Charlie concluded.

Mort dug a sticky-pad message from a pocket and read, "*Nicholas Fielding?*"

Drummond shrugged.

"Also Mr. H. said Willie wasn't gonna be able to make it," Mort added.

"Can I see that, please?" Charlie asked.

"Yours to keep," said Mort, handing over the piece of paper.

"Thanks," Charlie said. "Thanks for everything, Mort."

As Mort climbed the stairs, Charlie studied the handwritten message:

5:30: MR. H + NICHOLAS FIELDING + NO WILLIE.

No Willie was Hattemer's safety code, meaning Nicholas Fielding, whoever he was, was no threat. As far as Hattemer knew. From the name Nicholas Fielding, however, three letters jumped up at Charlie:

H, E, and N.

Charlie fought to keep from gasping while Mort was in earshot. As soon as Mort was upstairs, Charlie showed Drummond the note, jabbed a finger at the pertinent characters, and said, "According to Belknapp, it was 'HEN' who ordered the hit at the battlefield."

"Which one was Belknapp again?"

"The last one."

"Yes, yes, I see." Drummond appeared more interested in—and to have greater appreciation for the significance of—his sandwich.

Hoping to squeeze even a drop of information from him nevertheless, Charlie blocked his path to the plate. "What are the odds that this Hen isn't *that* Hen?"

"Odds?"

"Higher than the sky, in my professional opinion. Plenty of names have H, E, and N in that order. Howard Beckman, the detective, for one. But how many Hens do you work with?"

Drummond put a hand on his chin to think.

Charlie decided not to bother waiting for the results. "In either case, we can't just drive off now," he said. He was surprised not to be panicking. Maybe his nerves were shot. "We'd just cross paths with them between here and Hickory Road."

"All right then. Can we eat?"

"As soon as one of us works up an escape route."

33

As they crossed the dusky meadow behind the house, Charlie went over his idea. "So we stay and hear what Hattemer and this Nicholas Fielding have to say. Worse comes to worse, we make it look like we tried to get away in the Durango. Really, if we manage to saddle a horse, we go on horseback. What do you think?"

"Okay," was the extent of Drummond's feedback, sadly.

The barn was built of pine planks and painted the classic, rustic red. Inside, the musky scent of horses commingled wonderfully with the sweet smell of hay. It was too dark for Charlie to make out much beyond the expanse and many large shapes. Flipping on the lights might alert Mort to their presence here, so Charlie waited until his eyes adapted, then slipped in. Drummond lingered by the entryway, hungrily contemplating the green apples piled into a thick-slatted barrel.

In the stalls, five horses slept, all standing. The first three were tall and slim, with chiseled faces on long necks: Thoroughbreds. Charlie passed them by. Thoroughbreds have two gears, Park and Locomotive. If he were to attempt to ride one, the odds said he'd be left on the ground with horseshoes permanently stamped on his face.

In stall four was a draft horse; Charlie recognized the characteristic giant hooves and weightlifter's shoulders. CANDICANE was engraved on the beveled-edged copper plaque on the stall door. If the Thoroughbred is a racecar, the draft horse is the family station wagon, the horse used to give grandkids and greenhorns the steadiest ride. Candicane's swayed back and droopy lips indicated she'd held that job for years.

In the last stall was Giovanni, a Thoroughbred who conjured a Ferrari.

So Candicane was the man. Charlie hoped her name reflected her temperament. Despite all his time at the track, he'd never ridden a horse. He'd learned a few things though. Chiefly, those scenes in Westerns where a novice jumps onto a horse and rides off: complete malarkey. Just getting a saddle on would be an ordeal.

Candicane's eyes opened at his approach. He dangled an apple across her stall door. She bared her teeth, which brought ax blades to his mind. He willed himself to keep steady. If she detected his fear, she would whinny her displeasure, which could domino into bedlam in the barn. She sucked the apple from his palm with what felt like a kiss. He was charmed.

"I hope we can still be friends when I saddle you," he whispered.

Equipment bloomed from the walls and ceiling in the adjacent tack room. Charlie unhooked a saddle and groped for bridle, brushes, and the rest of what he anticipated he would need. Returning to Candicane, he opened the stall door and entered inches at a time so as not to spook the thousand-pound beast. She stepped sideways to accommodate him.

He'd seen grooms ready racehorses hundreds of times. Unfortunately, his attention was usually on the conversation—as sources, grooms ranked second only to attendants in the owners' and trainers' parking lot. One thing he had picked up was that a small bit of dirt caught between the hide and the saddle blanket or saddle pad could do to a horse what the pea did to the princess. So he brushed Candicane, delicately. She responded like a thousand-pound kitten, snorts in place of purring.

"Okay, Candi, now for your saddle blanket," he said with rising confidence.

Having witnessed this relatively simple step so many times, he thought failure was impossible. As he opened the surprisingly large blanket, he reconsidered: It would be easier to get a tarp over a building. He set the top of the pile forward of her withers, then worked out the wrinkles as he spread the rest toward her tail, the grooms' method. The reason they did so, he realized, was that it allowed her hair to run in its natural direction. Again, Candicane snorted her contentment. Still Charlie was wary of losing his teeth as a result of poking her in a wrong spot, and he had no idea which spots those were.

He lowered the saddle onto her as carefully as if it were a soufflé. She cozied into it. He let the straps and stirrups cascade down her flanks, then knelt to put them in place. Even in broad daylight, it would take hours just to figure out how to lace the straps in and around the rings. And still she might be girthy, a discomfort horses remedied by kicking. His eyes wandered to her hooves. This close, they were anvils.

He looked over the stall to Drummond, who leaned against a strut, on the verge of dozing again. "I don't suppose you've ever hot-wired a horse?" Charlie whispered.

"Not that I recall."

"That could still mean that your appliance dealers convention in Rochester was a cover for equestrian training so that you could pose as an Arab prince, right?"

"I can tell you that the amount of blood in a horse's body is generally one eighteenth of its total weight."

"Here's hoping we don't put that to a test," Charlie said. He settled for tying things together wherever he could.

Twenty-one minutes later, a sleek, black Lincoln seemingly materialized from the night and parked in the cobblestoned circle in front of the house. Watching from the foyer, Charlie was reminded of a vampire.

There were three prospective outcomes now. One, the Lincoln had indeed come to the rescue. Two, it hadn't, but he would get the answers he needed, and he and Drummond would get away. Three, they wouldn't get away.

The driver's door popped open, revealing a man who, by virtue of being in his early forties, probably was Fielding. Whoever he was, he was too handsome to be Hattemer's driver, or anybody's driver this side of Sunset Boulevard. This was Lancelot with golden hair and a lower body-fat percentage. He didn't just step onto the driveway, he landed, the way a superhero came onto the scene, sculpted jaw set in determination, fists clenched, and eyes burning with a zeal to set things right.

Not your prototypical killer, Charlie thought. But who was? The late Cadaret's neighbors on St. Bart's probably thought he was a helluva guy.

Lancelot blazed around the hood, plucked open the passenger door, and lent an arm to a thickset, older man. Hattemer. Charlie recognized him from somewhere, maybe the news—in which case it probably was a piece he'd seen while waiting for the sports report to come on.

Hattemer's full head of silver hair was combed neatly into place, his flannel suit was crisp, and his tie was dimpled with precision. None of that set him apart from all the hustlers and shysters on Capitol Hill, but there was an undeniable geniality etched between his jowls, and his sharp eyes were full of a certain reassuring gravitas. He was one of the good guys—Charlie felt it.

Still Charlie's circumspection remained high as he opened the front door. As he'd been reminded too many times at the track: Even when you know, you don't know.

Hattemer squinted through the blob of exterior lights. "Charlie, it's good to see you," he said with a warmth that couldn't be artifice.

Charlie allowed that Hattemer had just done some simple checking, then reasoned, thoughtfully, that Drummond and his son could stand some supper.

With a wave at Lancelot, Hattemer added, "I took the liberty of bringing along Nick Fielding, who was your father's protégé and has been the acting chief of the agency's Geographical Analysis Ecosystem Subcommittee since your father went on the disabled list."

While leading them into the foyer, it dawned on Charlie that he knew Nick Fielding, or rather knew the name. "Aren't you a treasure hunter?" he asked him.

"That's just schtick," Fielding said.

Charlie was unnerved. It didn't seem like the sort of secret Fielding would allow someone to just walk away with.

"Gentlemen, I need to tell you something straight off," Charlie said. "My father's watching us through a rifle scope, and the way he's been lately, he's liable to plug all of us if you don't hand over your weapons now." Really, Drummond was stashed safely out of earshot, probably taking a post-supper nap.

Hattemer and Fielding exchanged glances so precise that Charlie wondered whether they were explicit communications, an appraisal of his claim perhaps. These men almost certainly had been trained to spot lies via shifts of eyes or fluctuations in rate of speech, nervous movements, and more ways he couldn't begin to guess. Thinking of the card players' saying—"After the first few minutes, if you don't know who the sucker at the table is, it's you"—he cursed his gall in imagining he could fool these men.

"We understand," Hattemer said.

"We regret it's come to this," added Fielding.

Charlie's self-assurance rebounded. "I'll need you to step against the wall and shrug off your coats, one sleeve at a time," he said. This was the technique the lieutenant at the Monroeville club had used.

Fielding and Hattemer wriggled out of their suit coats, tossing them forward onto the floor before Charlie remembered to ask. The closest thing to a weapon the coats contained was Fielding's cigar case. But removing the coats brought into plain sight the rugged gray pistol tucked into Fielding's waistband. If Hattemer carried a firearm, it was disguised as a fountain pen in his breast pocket.

Charlie had heard of pens capable of discharging a single .22 caliber bullet. Better to appear the fool than be shot to death by a pen, he thought. "Please put the pen and the gun on the floor," he said.

They did, and he knelt and gathered up what appeared to be an ordinary fountain pen and a SIG Sauer. Rising, he executed a rendition of the Monroeville pat down, turning up a thin billfold on Hattemer and, in Fielding's pockets, some change and the Lincoln's keyless remote. He weighed taking the lot, but decided against it; his disinclination to appear foolish was compounded by a sense of futility. If it came down to a fight, he thought, himself armed with the SIG Sauer and everything else, versus Fielding armed with nothing, the smart money was on Fielding.

"Charlie, know that we're here to help," Hattemer said.

"So let's put our cards on the table," Fielding said. "As you've probably anticipated, in one minute, we can have a backup team here with enough pop to take over certain small countries. In addition, we're painfully aware that Duck is not watching us through a rifle scope. He'd never play it like that. My guess is he's resting somewhere."

Charlie's stomach fell so violently that Hattemer and Fielding must have heard it. The team a minute away probably heard it.

"We also know he sketched you a schematic," Fielding said.

"A schematic, what schematic?"

"Of the Device, of course." Fielding spoke as if Charlie were a child.

"Actually, I have no idea what device you mean."

"Please, I had people watching when he showed it to you."

"Is this something that happened when I was, like, ten?"

"No, twenty-seven past two yesterday afternoon."

"The washing machine he drew on his hot dog wrapper?"

"You know that that wasn't just a washing machine."

"Then what was it? Or am I better off not knowing?"

"You're absolutely better off not knowing," Hattemer interjected. "Nick, he doesn't know."

Seeming to have reached the same conclusion, Fielding softened. "Then, ironically, he needs to learn now, if he's going to help us."

34

Fielding paced in front of the mantel, the sputtering fire transforming him into a kinetoscope leading man. "In the late sixties our Special Forces left crates of ammunition on the Ho Chi Minh trail for the Vietcong," he said.

Hattemer perched on the sill of one of the bay windows, his attention wavering—clearly he'd heard this before. Charlie sat on the sofa, rapt. "Wait, I thought the Vietcong were the bad guys," he said.

"The ammo was doctored so it would misfire," Fielding said. "That's where your father first got the idea for the operation that was later codenamed 'Placebo.' He began it in the seventies as an off-the-books joint project of the agency's counterproliferation division and counterintelligence. A few years later, when he and his team had perfected the technology, they used some Saudi spare change funneled through a Swiss venture capital shell and bought a failing Argentine appliance manufacturer."

"Perriman?"

"Of course you know all about Perriman, including that it has offices worldwide. What you probably don't know is that those offices serve as bases for our people, under cover as Perriman employees, to sell specially modified appliances."

"Are we talking washers with a 'detonation' setting?" Charlie asked. He noticed Hattemer smile. Fielding did too, but it appeared forced.

"Sort of," Fielding said. "The atomic demolition munition we work with looks like the innards of a washing machine, and the weights of the two are about the same. So washing machine housings make excellent concealments, and Perriman's network allows for ease of trafficking. What we do is simple: We sell the bombs to terrorists, rogue nations, third world potentates, and any other lunatic with the means and inclination to detonate a nuclear weapon."

"The bombs are duds, then?"

"Well, it's a bit more complicated than that." Fielding stopped pacing. "Nuclear weapons technology is readily attainable from open sources, but it's the production of the fissionable material necessary to give a bomb its bang that's beyond the capability of our customers, not to mention most major industrial countries. Duck's team found a way to make worthless, run-of-the-mill depleted uranium pass muster at the point of sale as the good stuff—highly enriched U two thirty-five."

"What happens when the customers take their new washer home?"

"That was the basis for the decision to replicate the *Aftscharka* ADM. The Russians had built it with the uranium pit deep in place. To fiddle with the uranium requires a complex dismantlement procedure well beyond our customers' capabilities."

"And if the customers try to detonate their new bomb?"

"If one of our *Aftscharkas* is triggered, it still yields some bang. More than *some* bang, actually. Each packs about a hundred pounds of plastic explosive, which is standard issue to generate critical mass in uranium implosion weapons and enough to take out a small building. So, assuming our customers survive the blast, they won't immediately know anything was wrong with their weapon. Later, when they find out that they blew up just the small building as opposed to, say, a third of Calcutta, they have no way of determining why. But hopefully it doesn't get that far. From the moment we make a sale—if not sooner—we have eyes or ears on our customers. We try to plausibly round them up or neutralize them before they blow up *anything*. In the worst-case scenario, characters who might otherwise have gotten their hands on a real nuke detonate the equivalent of a few sticks of dynamite. And the thanks are due to your father."

From his windowsill, Hattemer added, "No one outside of our circle will ever know it, but Drummond Clark is one of America's greatest heroes."

Charlie felt a stirring of filial pride, along with a spring of optimism:

These men weren't just Drummond's allies, they were staunch admirers. A peaceful resolution seemed a possibility after all.

"We should add it is our *hope* that no one outside of our circle will ever know about his heroics," Fielding said. He resumed pacing at a rate that pointed toward agitation. "The problem is that a crude sketch of a washing machine to you, Charlie, could be damning evidence to a Pakistani ISI agent who, in the guise of a tourist in Prospect Park, strikes up a conversation with Duck about the hundred-fifty species of trees there. There are other guys like me who peddle *Aftscharkas*—one of them plays the role of a rival arms dealer, another purports to be a disgruntled Russian general, another still poses as a Senegalese pirate. I've never met any of them. From his perch at Perriman Appliances, where each and every bomb was manufactured and prepped, your father was the only operative who knew everybody on the roster, not to mention every name on our entire client list. In hindsight, that information should have been compartmentalized. That's hindsight though. Now, from the standpoint of national security, he is the very last person the United States can afford to have Alzheimer's."

"What did he tell the Pakistani agent?" Charlie asked.

"That was just a hypothetical. To our knowledge, he hasn't told anybody anything yet. But it's only a matter of time until he does, or until he picks up the phone to order dinner from that little Vietnamese place on Bedford and inadvertently dials an old customer in Pyongyang and rattles off the names of our players in East Asia, or breaks the news to the man in Pyongyang that his vaunted ten-kiloton Equalizer could barely blow up a straw hut."

Charlie felt his blood rise. "Help me put this in perspective. If one of your guys gets shitfaced and becomes a risk to blab, what do you do?"

"If one of our operatives were to get that drunk, we'd dry him out before he could fall into the wrong hands." Fielding's measured cordiality seemed to belie impatience. "If one of our people is subjected to as little as the gas necessary to pull a wisdom tooth, we send a babysitter along to the dentist's office. Over the last seven weeks we've had a team—a top-notch team—monitoring Duck from a house up the block on Prospect Place. But it proved inadequate. On Christmas Eve, he went wandering, which had happened before. But this time, the Meals on Wheels people and the kindly social worker who took him were really MI6."

"Helen Mayfield?" Charlie said in utter astonishment.

"Fortunately Helen—or Alice or whatever her real name is—is relatively benign," Fielding said. "She'd been investigating my alter ego, Trader Nick, who's essentially a red herring, and she learned nothing of consequence from Duck. The issue is, whoever gets hold of him next time won't be benign, and he'll be broken like a piñata."

Charlie tried to set aside the Helen bombshell. "So, in cases like this, you're just taking the candy out of the piñata before the bad guys can?"

"I wouldn't know. There aren't cases like this. Usually, with older operatives, keeping secrets is practically ingrained. You also have to take into account the relative sensitivity of their secrets: Generally, when these men and women leave the field, they spend years consulting for us or for outside firms. During that time, classified technology advances at a head-spinning rate, and decades have passed by the time they begin to fail, at which point they could dictate their memoirs to an ISI agent and it would cause little damage, if any. This simply hasn't been an issue. Until now."

Charlie wondered whether, in his zeal to remedy the matter with bullets, Fielding had missed the obvious alternative. "Has anyone just taken my father to a doctor?"

"He saw specialist after specialist at CIA Medical Services." Fielding leaned against the wainscoting's chair rail, as if wearied by the recollection. "He was prescribed rivastigmine, galantamine, memantine, and everything else with even a snowman's chance in hell of slowing cognitive decline. All, sadly, to no avail."

"What about the new experimental treatments in the news? Wouldn't the CIA have the resources to get him in on any of that action?"

"We could pull strings, sure. In Japan they've had nice results using histone deacetylase inhibitors, but only at the early laboratory animal testing stage. The Swiss have had some success boosting HSF1 levels. In worms. It will be three to five years before they can say the same for humans, if things proceed without a hitch."

Charlie suspected Drummond had information pertaining to medical advances in Geneva, Switzerland, that Fielding did not. But by saying so, Charlie sensed, he would terminate Drummond's prospects of getting there. Instead he asked, "So why not just put him in one of your secret agent nursing homes for three to five years, or however long?"

"As you and he have demonstrated, they're not all that secure," Fielding said.

"The Monroeville Hunt and Fish Club's the gold standard?"

"Even Langley has trouble with leaks, and that's with a thousand times the security. Duck would be a lightning rod in the best of those places. And we can't take risks with Placebo. It's not just any secret. It's the kind you die to keep." Fielding looked to Hattemer. "Were Duck in his right mind, he would take the L without hesitation."

Hattemer's eyes fell precipitously, as if the subject repelled him.

Charlie said, "I'm guessing you don't mean the train."

"L, as in lethal pill," Fielding said.

"My father has one of those?"

"As do I, in a ceramic bridge over the farthest two upper molars, with a spring-loaded release activated by the tongue. The capsule itself dissolves in saliva, releasing saxitoxin, which acts in fifteen to twenty seconds."

"Oh." Charlie had learned all that he'd hoped to. He burned to stay and put forth an argument on behalf of Drummond's preservation, but he suspected he stood a better chance arguing on behalf of Marxism here. It was time to get galloping.

The discomfort with which Hattemer shifted kept Charlie rooted, however. The case was about to move to a higher court, Charlie felt. One with a soul.

35

Hattemer descended heavily from the bay window and strode between Charlie and Fielding. Pivoting to face Fielding, Hattemer asked, "How hard is it to imagine that when Drummond was standing at the brink, lucid or otherwise, he wasn't keen on the abyss?"

Fielding's golden brows nearly crisscrossed. "It's possible in the way anything is possible," he said.

Hattemer looked at Charlie. "Nick here has never been keen on trusting sensitive matters to oversight, and I don't fault him for that to a certain extent. You find yourself with a sinking ship, you want to do something besides twiddle your thumbs while a bunch of bureaucrats in a conference room a thousand miles away have their general counsel draft memos to all the appropriate committees so that a vote can be taken on whether to get a 'finding.' And meanwhile someone, or someone's aide, may leak the story to the *Washington Post*. So when whoever Nick had keeping tabs on me found out that I was going home sick this afternoon, he deduced that those of us whose job it is to provide oversight were now aware of his 'situation' and, accordingly, the dreaded wheels of bureaucracy were about to start grinding. With no choice but to play by the official rule book, he asked for the chance to aid me in my determination of whether there were sufficient grounds for the National Security Council to consider a waiver to the Executive Orders prohibiting assassination. There are some folks on the council who'll say that the secret takes precedence, and that this, sadly, is one of those cases where ideal ends come at the cost of morally dubious or dangerous means." He turned back to Fielding. "I, however, believe it's our obligation to take care of Drummond. I don't care if it means putting a hospital bed in Fort Knox."

Charlie wanted to leap up and applaud. The prevailing seriousness limited him to a negligible smile, and perhaps even that was too garish: Fielding seemed to take a measure of him and dismiss him as nothing, all in a glance.

"We've had enough trouble in the past two days," Fielding told Hattemer. "Any more and we risk word spreading to what extent our ordinary appliance salesman is no ordinary appliance salesman. The entire operation could be blown. He made a decision in his choice of career to place the service of his country before his own life."

"The 'L' is taken when in enemy hands," Hattemer said. "I was under the impression we're on the same side he is. On our side, when our people are in trouble, the fundamental guiding principal is We Take Care of Our Own, even if that means moving a mountain."

"We *are* taking care of our own, the hundreds of our operatives and the millions of innocent citizens whose lives are in the balance as long as he keeps getting up in the morning."

Hattemer nodded. "Some of them might die. Or they might not. Either way, we don't set aside our ideals whenever it's convenient."

"Sometimes in this business, taking care of our own means *taking care* of them." Fielding pantomimed shooting a gun. "We may not like it, but we do it—you know that."

"Well, we can't do it, under any circumstance." Hattemer's face reddened. It seemed Fielding had stepped on an especially sore spot. "Think about what Ryszard Kuklinski said when he fled the Soviets: 'America is the *only* country in the world which does not abandon its people.' If our people *ever* worry about being burned by their own, they'll be less willing to take risks. Then we'll be trounced, because the bad guys like risk too much, and because we'll have ceded the high ground. The high ground isn't just the most secure place to be, it's what makes us the good guys."

Again Charlie felt like clapping. Fielding did clap. It looked and sounded so. But afterward a wisp of bluish smoke rose from his hands, from an aperture in what Charlie initially had taken to be the Lincoln's keyless remote.

Hattemer hit the floor like a felled oak, blood springing from his chest. While struggling to staunch the flow, he died.

Shock pinned Charlie to the couch.

"He left me with no choice," Fielding said, as if seeking absolution. "The ship is indeed sinking, and he was the proverbial fifth man in the lifeboat. You're familiar with that proverbial lifeboat, yes?"

"Don't know that one," Charlie could only mumble.

"If there are five men in a lifeboat that holds only four, you have to toss one man overboard. If you keep all five, you see, the boat sinks and everyone drowns."

Charlie felt like saying, "I give that a three, on a scale of one to ten for Justifications for Playing God." But the ideological mania—or possibly just plain mania—burning within Fielding would not be doused by any sort of reasoning. "Got it," Charlie said instead, as if he meant it.

Fielding seemed mollified. He pushed a thin, metal-jacketed projectile into the "keyless remote," then aimed the weapon at Charlie.

"Now, where is he?" Fielding asked.

Charlie looked away and considered his options. He watched the last log in the fireplace roll over, smothering the flame.

With resignation, he said, "Upstairs resting."

36

With the keyless remote aimed at him, Charlie was forced to return the SIG Sauer, surrender the Walther he'd wedged into the back of his waistband, then silently precede Fielding up the stairs.

They came to a wide, dimly lit hallway lined with pastorals in oil and seven tall doors. Fielding turned with shoulders raised. Charlie pointed to the farthest door.

Fielding trod the creaky planks as gingerly as a cat. Charlie followed, just as careful to be quiet. Cooperating now was his only chance of survival.

At the door, Fielding waved Charlie ahead. Charlie gripped the crystal doorknob, twisted it without a sound, then tapped open the door. With the curtains shut, the room was nearly black, but the spill from the hallway sconces was enough to reveal, in silhouette, the man beneath the comforter on the four-poster bed, a halo of white hair against a pillow. Fielding inched past Charlie and into the room.

Charlie believed his greatest advantage was that Fielding wasn't expecting him to try anything. Elbowing his fear aside, Charlie backed into the hall and took a silent step toward the stairs.

He heard the snap of the light switch in the wall plate back in the bedroom. No light came on. Of course. He'd yanked the fuse twenty minutes ago. Still, in a second or two, Fielding would know he had captured not Drummond but Mort.

Charlie ran for all he was worth. To the landing. Fourteen stairs in four bounds. Then into the bathroom beside the den. He jumped onto the toilet seat—he'd closed it ahead of time. He dove through the already-raised window, landing in a prickly hedge behind the house.

Bouncing to his feet, he raced to the toolshed. The open Durango sat on the structure's far side, driver's door open, engine idling softly, dashboard dimmed to nothing, and headlights off. Charlie flew in.

Now, conspicuous was desirable. He popped on the high beams, slammed the accelerator for maximum tire squeal, then tore into the gravel driveway.

Once the hilly driveway dipped to a point that the Durango was out of sight of the house, he swatted off the headlights and slowed to as close to a crawl as first gear would allow. He turned onto a pasture, then bobbed for about a hundred yards to a onetime hay barn, parking on the side that faced away from the house.

He opened the driver's door, in slow motion, for fear that the sound would carry over the open fields, slipped out, then closed the door just as gingerly. With an armful of winter clothing and other provisions found in the mudroom, he stole to the barn's side door and ducked inside.

Candicane was waiting. Drummond was dozing between a pair of horse blankets in the hayloft.

37

Charlie led Drummond and Candicane out of the hay barn. "Where were you?" Drummond asked at normal conversational volume. The fallow fields between them and the house had the acoustics of an amphitheater. In addition, the night was extraordinarily quiet; snow had begun to fall, and the flakes could be heard tapping down individually.

"I was doing what I said I was going to do," Charlie whispered.

"Oh."

Charlie helped him onto the saddle, then pressed his own shoe onto one of the stirrups and winched himself aboard. Squeezing in ahead of Drummond, he draped the horse blankets over their legs for warmth, then gave a rendition of that fusion of cluck and kiss with which jockeys started racehorses.

And they were off!

The ride was bumpy at first. It smoothed out as Candicane picked up the pace. At top speed, perhaps fifteen miles per hour, though she began to breathe hard—nostrils venting shafts of steam—Charlie felt like he was aboard a hovercraft. The house on Hickory Road shot aft. Quickly it was a flicker on the horizon, then it was swallowed by the night.

Charlie directed the horse to the trailhead at the base of the ridge. A hand-painted trail marker pointed to Bentonville, a dot of civilization two miles due east over the Massanutten Mountain, according to the atlas he'd used in formulating his plan, though possibly much longer along a windy, wooded trail. The hope was to obtain a vehicle in Bentonville.

Innumerable bends and inclines slowed Candicane to little more than a trot, but the trail seemed as familiar to her as her bit. Woods enveloped them. Charlie hadn't known that darkness could be so black. Or silent. Peace and quiet, he reflected, is an oxymoron to city dwellers accustomed to the soothing drone that's the sum of the subway, thousands of motor vehicles, and millions of people. He took in a deep breath of pine and felt flush with satisfaction at his escape. At all times, he kept a hand within reach of the saddlebag. When readying Candicane, he'd packed his mother's Colt, reloaded by Drummond with some of the armory's worth of bullets found in the Durango.

Candicane's mane now glistened with snow. Flakes turned to steam on impact with exposed parts of her hide. She slowed when a small stream came into view. Her breath was ragged.

"Maybe we should let her have a quick pit stop," Charlie said.

"Maybe," Drummond said, with misplaced decisiveness.

At the bank, Candicane halted and plunged her nose into the water. Charlie watched her shadow bobble on the far side as she drank. He noticed sharp impressions of hooves in the quarter-inch of snow there.

Anvils for hooves.

A rush of nausea nearly knocked him out of the saddle. "Oh, Jesus," he said. "We've somehow doubled back over our own steps."

If this troubled Drummond, he didn't show it, or say anything.

"Fielding and his backup team have to have figured out our game plan by now," Charlie tried to explain. "To track us, all they need to do is follow gigantic hoofprints through fresh snow."

"I see."

"I don't suppose you have any idea of what to do?"

"Get going?"

"I'm with you on that. The thing is, without knowing which way to go, it's fifty-fifty we gallop smack into them."

Drummond looked at the stream. The spots of light bobbing atop the water appeared to transfix him.

"Dad, at least help me get our bearings."

"Do you have a compass?"

"No, but don't you have some 'interesting piece of information' about moss—you can tell north by the side of the trees it grows thickest, something like that?"

"We need to find north?"

"East, actually, but north'll do the trick."

"All the times we went camping, you never learned how to use the North Star?"

"We never went camping."

"Oh."

"What about the North Star?"

"If you draw an imaginary line from it to the ground, you have true north."

"What if it's cloudy, like it is now, and you can't see the North Star?"

"If a crescent moon has risen before the sun sets, its illuminated side faces west. If it has risen after midnight, the bright side faces east."

"Okay, what if you can't see anything. Like now, for instance?"

"You'd need a compass."

Charlie was light-headed in reflection of his own shortsightedness. He could have had a compass—five of them, probably. As Mort had promised, the mudroom had anything a person could ever need. Charlie had had a pick not only of sizes in coats and hats, but styles. He packed the saddlebag only with bottles of water and a bag of trail mix. He added Hattemer's fountain pen, for no reason other than general utility. *A fountain pen!* But he left behind enough tools to start a hardware store. He never even thought of a trail map; surely that mudroom had a drawerful.

He clucked Candicane back into drive, sending them splashing down the center of the stream. "Hopefully this puts their idea of our course at a coin toss," he said. "And maybe we can spot another trail marker or a rooftop or a road."

"Or a compass," Drummond said.

Snow accumulated, thickening both Charlie's coat and hat by an inch in places. It provided unexpected insulation, but it burned the skin between his sleeves and gloves and at his collar and his extremities were numb. Drummond never complained, but he alternated between shivers and coughs. Poor Candicane wheezed with each step. All this was better, certainly, than getting caught by Fielding's team. Charlie sensed, though, that they were delving into woods so vast that, for all practical purposes, there was no other side; survival would be an issue even if Fielding and his men called it a night.

Probably Drummond had the answer. Stuck inside his head. In exasperation as much as desperation, Charlie turned around, locked eyes with him, and said, "Beauregard." He would have shouted it if not for the risk of divulging their position.

"Who's looking after him while we're away?" Drummond asked.

The best they could do now, Charlie thought, was stop and rest.

Ahead, the bank sloped up to a plateau shrouded by trees. "Why don't we hang out up there until the sky clears one way or the other and we can figure out which way's which?" he said. "Maybe rig up some kind of shelter?"

"Good idea."

Charlie suspected Drummond's response would have been the same to a suggestion that they go for a swim.

At the top of the slope, Charlie tethered Candicane to a tree and covered her with one of the horse blankets without any difficulty. Drummond sat at the plateau's edge. From forty feet up, the water looked like a shimmering band. An otherworldly vapor rose to be absorbed by the blackness. Drummond watched as if it were a thriller.

Charlie found a fallen branch that was about four feet long—just right. He drove its sharp end through the snow and into the ground so that it stood parallel to Drummond's left side. Drummond didn't appear to notice. Charlie planted a second, similarly sized branch a few feet to Drummond's right. Next he balanced the other horse blanket across the tops of the branches, so that it hung over Drummond like a tent.

Only now, with his view blocked, did Drummond take note of Charlie's efforts. "What are you doing?"

"Making a shelter."

"Good idea."

Charlie weighted the corners of the blanket with rocks. He tossed in small sticks and pine straw to serve as a floor—without it, he figured, the snow would melt beneath them and they would get as wet as if they had gone swimming.

After much tweaking, he finally lowered himself into his construction. He was gratified that it didn't collapse. It felt wonderful to take the weight off his legs, weary and chapped from the riding, and the horse blanket's fleece lining served as a balm to his frozen and cracked skin. There was barely enough room for both him and Drummond, though; the closeness was uncomfortable. And that didn't even rate as a problem in the dismal greater scheme of things.

"Well, here we are camping, Dad," he said. "One for the category of Be Careful What You Wish For, huh?"

"I wish we had gone camping," Drummond said.

It sounded heartfelt, but Charlie dismissed it as another automatic response.

38

Fielding sat at the wheel of his rental car, driving to Bentonville on a calculated hunch. His BlackBerry showed live feed of three Apache helicopters preparing for takeoff from York River Gardens, a half-completed vacation condominium development in mid-Virginia that was purportedly in Chapter Eleven. As Fielding knew, its gray brick exterior, intentionally left unpainted, really housed a sort of Special Forces à la carte. York River Gardens was one of several such outposts around the country maintained by the Office of Security.

To Fielding, the Apaches' bloated engines, floppy rotors, Bigfoot skids, fins, guns, and launchers all looked to have been attached during a game of pin the tail on the donkey; it was hard to imagine the ships getting off the ground. But as he could attest, having flown in several, they could reach twenty thousand feet and two hundred miles per hour. Also they were ideal for searching the Blue Ridge. The dense canopy of trees there could hide a house painted Day-Glo yellow from the drones—and most helicopters—but the Apaches had extraordinary turret-mounted sights with three fields of forward-looking infrared. Unless the night warmed to 98.6 degrees Fahrenheit, the old man and the punk would be seen. The helicopters' sensors relayed to Fielding's BlackBerry that the current ground temperature was 28.41 degrees.

The Clarks could dig in or seek the cover of a cave, but either would leave them vulnerable to trackers. More likely, Fielding thought, they would attempt to flee the ridge. Once they showed as little as a nose, the thirty-millimeter chain gun located under each Apache's fuselage could pick them off at 625 rounds per minute. And if they were out of range of the guns, an Apache Hellfire missile could obliterate their entire ridge.

"Actually, one Apache's plenty," Fielding said over the phone to Bull, who was at Hickory Road, liaising with York River Gardens in order to augment the five-man team he already had combing the ridge.

"But, sir, we'll need to cover as much as forty square miles," Bull said.

"More, by my math. The problem is a resident woken up in the middle of the night by one of those behemoths can imagine a reason for it being there. Three of those behemoths and we're all but writing the lead for the Associated Press manhunt story that Abdullah bin Zayed al Saqr will read at breakfast."

"Got it. What about trackers?"

"It depends."

"York River has a unit that can pick up a trail on a dry cement floor. No one will ever see them—"

"Trackers are a good idea." Fielding didn't want to waste time discussing how, time and again, manhunts had proven the futility of deploying trackers unfamiliar with a specific area. "Let me just see if I can scare up anyone around here first."

When instructors at the Farm say a student has "a good nose," they mean an analytical ability seemingly independent of the five ordinary senses, the intangible "it" quality vital to being a good operations officer. In 1994, lacking such a nose, one of Fielding's fellow first-year "Perriman Appliances sales associates" walked up to the wrong Jordanian roadblock and was halved by a fifty-caliber round. On the same desert road, Fielding held back, for reasons he couldn't articulate, even with the luxury of hindsight. The best he could summon for his incident report was, "It didn't smell right."

Tonight, on pitch-black Virginia country roads about which his GPS offered only the most cursory information, he followed his nose through Bentonville—a hamlet comprised of a metal-roofed church, a couple of tiny stores, and a post office that shared space with a construction company. At the live bait shack at the end of town, he turned up an unlit dirt road leading into the mountains. It brought him to a solitary, shabby, corrugated steel Quonset hut with neon Bud signs in the windows and ten-point antlers above the door. This was Miss Tabby's, according to the metallic letter decals running down one side of the doorframe. A jukebox had the place throbbing to a rockabilly beat.

Fielding parked among the forty or fifty vehicles, mostly pickups. He popped open his collar button and loosened the knot of his tie an inch or two, to where it would be hanging after a shitty day at the office and a couple of grueling hours in traffic. As someone who'd just endured such a drive would, he hauled himself out of his car with a groan and rolled the kinks out of his neck. Despite the fresh snowfall and towering, aromatic pines all around, the muddy lot reeked of stale beer and urine.

The door beneath the antlers opened onto a bar faced with split logs and gaps where other logs had fallen off. Every barstool was occupied, as were all the chairs at fifteen or twenty tables. In the orange-plum glow of illuminated brewery promotions, another three dozen men and women stood elbow to elbow. More still played pinball, darts, or pool. Through a mass of cigarette smoke at the far end of the room, Fielding saw mere forms around a pool table. Among them, he sensed, were the men he wanted: meth men. The Blue Ridge was littered with methamphetamine labs. Many of the cooks were descendants of the notorious Blue Ridge moonshiners. Like their ancestors, they were expert hunters and trackers who were vicious in defense of their turf. They thought nothing of unloading rifles on sheriffs. And most were expert shots.

Wandering their way, Fielding practically felt a breeze from all of the heads turning. It wasn't that anyone recognized him. It was because he was wearing a suit.

Once upon a time, when entering rough-and-tumble places, he was tempted to dress down or affect a tough guy's swagger. Experience had taught him to shun artifice whenever he could. The closer to his base of experience he could play it, the less he needed to fabricate; the less he needed to fabricate, the more convincing he could be. Here he would try to pass himself off as a Capitol Hill lawyer, a breed he knew well—too well, he lamented. Should anyone ask, he would say he dealt "Tina"—a fashionable name for meth in crystalline solid form—to subsidize his own fun. Probably they wouldn't ask; they would just assume he was ATF or DEA.

Seventy-five cents got him into a game of eight ball, but only because that was the house rule—he may as well have set a shiny badge down on the pool table along with his three quarters, given the players' standoff-ishness. He was pleased to see several of them were missing teeth, a hallmark of meth usage.

While playing, he didn't participate in their conversation about the bowl games. He kept looking to the door. Twice he asked his partner, "Sorry, man, are we stripes or solids?" A few times he stepped away and grumbled to himself. Picking up a bottle of Heineken and a double shot of rum from the bar, he forgot to collect his fourteen dollars in change. This was obviously a man preoccupied.

When he felt the others' curiosity peak, he tossed back the rum and stormed out of the bar.

Halfway to his car, he sensed a man approaching from behind. He whirled around, the way someone who was scared would. As he'd hoped, it was one of the pool players, the gaunt kid who'd been his partner. Twenty-five or so, he wore a Lynchburg Hillcats baseball cap with the bill low, shading his bland features and drawing attention to sideburns so chunky Fielding suspected they'd never come in contact with scissors.

"Oh, hey," Fielding said, with fake relief.

"Hey, I was just wondering if everything's okay with you, man?"

So he was the meth men's scout.

Fielding kicked at the ground. "Sure, fine, whatever. Thanks."

"You staying around here?"

"I've gotta get all the way back up to Georgetown tonight. Fucking breakfast meeting first thing mañana."

"Mind me asking what brung you all this way?"

Fielding looked him in the eyes. "I'm guessing you're not a cop, right?" Sideburns would have to be in world-record deep cover: He was missing most of his upper teeth.

The kid chuckled softly. "I work construction, mostly."

"There's a guy, I don't know his name," Fielding said, his relaxed stance and tone befitting the release of catharsis. "Thin, like twenty-five or thirty, buzz cut, lot of tattoos. He works out of a trailer on the ridge north of here, sometimes he does a little business here. Know who I mean?"

"Dude, that's, like, half the guys here," Sideburns said with a grin.

Fielding regarded his new friend with gratitude for the bit of levity. "I started out tonight driving to his place, but, like a mile before the turnoff, around Hickory Road, I saw a government-looking car pull over and park. Two suits got out and headed into the woods. So I figured it probably wasn't the best idea to stick around. I hoped I'd see my guy here. And, mostly, a friend of his." He lowered his voice. "*Tina.*"

This elicited a knowing look. "Her, I think I've heard of," Sideburns said.

"Yeah?"

"I might be able to find her for you."

"Dude, that would be huge!"

"I just wanna know one thing. Those suits. You get a look at them?"

Fielding wasn't fooled by Sideburn's casual manner. The meth man's underlying alarm was as obvious as sirens and strobe lights.

"Just a couple assholes in gray suits is all I can tell you," Fielding said.

With a little prodding, he provided physical descriptions of Drummond and Charlie that would have been good enough for a blind man.

Sideburns hurried back in to the other pool players. Fielding followed as far as the bar, then made a call using his BlackBerry.

"Ginger, you there?" he demanded into the mouthpiece.

"You got the wrong number, amigo," came a young man's voice.

Fielding hung up and happily ordered another beer. His use of "Ginger" signified all had gone according to plan here. "Amigo" meant that Dewart and Pitman, who'd answered, would now start monitoring all analog and digital traffic to and from Miss Tabby's.

In the next three minutes, Dewart and Pitman captured nine telephone calls and relayed the gist of them to Fielding's BlackBerry. The callers included the bartender, checking that her grandson had done his Bible study, and a plumber leaving with a prostitute—he told his wife he was having car trouble. Sideburns and another pool player also made calls. Both left messages urging local familiars to call back ASAP. A third player texted someone located on the ridge a hundredth of a latitudinal degree north of Hickory Road:

DEA fux on prowl 2nite!!! get ready to play D bro!!!

39

Charlie was woken by a rapid crunching of hooves through snow. His sleep had been so deep, he'd lost the ability to gauge how long it had been. Still, he was exhausted, and dehydration had left him woozy. The rest of him was sore or stiff. Seeing he was alone in the tent, panic jolted him to alertness.

He looked outside to find Drummond scurrying back from the tree Candicane had been tied to.

"Where's the horse?" Charlie asked.

"On her way home, I'd imagine," Drummond whispered. Her bulky blanket was draped over his shoulder.

"What, were you cold?"

Drummond pointed at a looming, black hill. "Listen . . ."

Charlie distinguished the far-off beat of helicopter rotors from the rhythmic patter of the stream.

"They'll have infrared," Drummond said. "The horse was too big a target."

"What about us?"

"Not with the horse blankets over us, if we pack snow onto them. We can appear no more anomalous than ripples on a pond."

Charlie didn't see the entirety of the plan. But Drummond was clearly back online, meaning the plan was almost certainly good.

Drummond spread his horse blanket flat on the ground and began packing powder on top of it. Charlie tugged the other blanket free of its makeshift tent poles and anchors.

"How long do you think we can hide here like this?" Charlie asked.

"We'll have to move, otherwise they'll find us. Once you've put about two inches of snow on top of the blanket, get underneath it. Use the Velcro straps on the underside to fasten it at your wrists and ankles and to your belt, if you can."

"But we still don't know which way to go."

"East is that way." Drummond pointed.

"How do you know? Is it that moss grows on the north side of trees?"

"It does. It also grows on the south, east, and west sides. What I did was, I took the steel clip off the fountain pen in the saddlebag, flattened it, magnetized it by rubbing it through my hair, then dangled it from a shoelace. It pointed to the nearest magnetic pole, which is, of course, north."

"Oh, that old trick. Good, I was worried you wouldn't find the fountain pen."

With the snow-packed horse blanket covering him, Charlie crawled after Drummond. They moved slowly enough that the snow, for the most part, stayed in place on top of the blankets, providing extra insulation from the cold. The problem was the frozen and jagged terrain. Charlie's suit pants offered little more protection than another sixteenth of an inch of snow would have. His bones became circuitry for shivers. Factoring in an increasingly potent wind, he considered that his body temperature might drop to thirty-two degrees on its own.

He turned his thoughts to Gary Carter of the New York Mets.

It helped.

When the wind reached enough of a howl that no one farther away than Drummond could hear him, Charlie said, "So, Dad, I have some office scuttlebutt to catch you up on." He filled him in on the happenings at the house.

Drummond's pace through the snow never varied nor did he act shaken or surprised in any other way. "Around the time I went on disability, there was an NSA operator named Mariáteguia in Lima who, we thought, had figured out what we were doing," he said. "Word was that the Shining Path discovered him as a traitor and executed him, though I suspected Nick somehow was behind it—I never got the chance to look into the matter. In any event, what you've described tonight is ample evidence that Nick is resorting to tactics that put him at a level with the most contemptible of our enemies. I have to say, though, that in my case, he's not entirely wrong."

"What are you talking about?"

"I *am* a liability."

"Please don't tell me that you've gotten me into the frozen middle of nowhere and made a compass out of a pen clip and a shoelace just to pop your L-pill?"

"When I first made plans to go to Switzerland, the lapses had barely begun. Now, I could fall into enemy hands and be utterly defenseless."

"There are how many Americans, three hundred something million? Out of that many, we ought to be able to find enough people to look after even you."

"But the cost and the risk—"

"What about '*We take care of our own*'? To have heard Burt Hattemer tell it, it's a cornerstone of democracy."

"That's not wrong either."

"Well, the problem is good old Nick and the rest of your Cavalry kids got the lesson *somewhere*," Charlie said, in bitter realization of exactly where, "that business comes first."

Drummond said nothing. For several long seconds, Charlie heard only lashes of wind against them and the squeaking of snow as they crawled through it. He suspected that, in spite of the conditions, his father was simmering.

"I see your point," Drummond said. "It's valid. Also, I've been remiss, and I'm going to rectify it."

The contrition threw Charlie. "Rectify what?"

"Alzheimer's disease shouldn't be fatal to a thirty-year-old. I'm going to take care of *my* own."

Charlie appreciated the sentiment. Unfortunately, Alzheimer's disease, on top of the circumstances, probably dictated the sentiment would be fleeting.

"No doubt Fielding will pin Burt's death on me," Drummond said. "What we need now is to buy some time."

"You know somewhere that sells that?"

"Brooklyn. If we can just get a vehicle—"

"And drive to Brooklyn? Why not just save gas and drive right to Langley?"

"Brooklyn's so obvious that, ironically, it will provide an element of surprise. Also I have a safe house there that no one else knows about. For years, under an alias, I've rented one of the little offices in the back of the Desherer's building."

For more than a century, Desherer's Sweet Shop on Bedford Avenue, with its iconic art deco front, was a favorite destination of every kid in Brooklyn. Every kid except Charlie, that is, and not by his choice. "So all of the times I wanted to go to Desherer's, your litany of horrifying facts and figures about sugar . . . ?"

"I didn't make those up. But I did have an ulterior motive. Desherer's is as crowded as any place in the neighborhood. If I were wary of surveillance, I could enter the candy store, then exit from the offices having changed my hat or coat or face. It wouldn't have done to run into you there or have the people who worked there see you with me."

As they crept down a dark slope, Charlie reflected that as he learned more of the truth, the corresponding scenes from his youth were no longer as bleak.

"I've always kept a flight kit there in case I ever needed to disappear," Drummond said. "It has travel documents and enough cash to tide us over until we can draw on the Bank of Antigua account."

Charlie sensed that another bleak scene was about to be re-rendered in Technicolor. "What Bank of Antigua account?"

"The numbered account with eight million dollars. Remember, I told you—"

"Yeah, I know, but at the time I figured you were delusional. With all due respect, you're okay now?"

"Just a bit chilly."

"The thing is, you said you made the money at Perriman."

"Correct."

"But at Perriman, you really were just an appliance salesman, right?"

"When I started there, as a loyal company man would, I elected to take my bonus in stock options, which were close to worthless in the aftermath of the *Chubut* fiasco. But my end of the business ended up being very profitable—bombs that cost relatively little to make sold for hundreds of millions—and it was least conspicuous to keep the profits in Perriman, so the stock price increased."

"So why didn't you ever buy a new car? Or a new château?"

"My role was middling sales executive, not multimillionaire arms dealer. Also, there was nothing I needed. The Olds is reliable; I rarely drive it more than five thousand miles per year—"

"Well, if you want to get me a Christmas present this year . . ." Charlie felt giddy in spite of the enormous odds against surviving to spend a dime of the fortune.

"There is one hitch," Drummond said.

"It's eight million in Antiguan dollars?"

"You'll need to leave the country, likely for an extended period of time. You'll be able to say no good-byes, and while you're away, you can't have contact with anyone you know. You won't be able to maintain connections to any aspect of your current life."

Charlie considered shedding his current life a significant net gain. Only one negative came to mind: He would miss having that beer with Helen. Which was silly, of course. She was a spook. Probably she'd meant to poison the beer.

"I suppose I can handle it," he said.

The tree limbs and needles began to hiss. A helicopter rose over the hillcrest.

Mimicking Drummond, Charlie stopped and became a random mound of snow on the hillside. As the helicopter thundered overhead, the only movement on the hill was that of snowflakes stirred by the rotor blades.

The ship flew on to the ridge behind Charlie and Drummond.

The racket receded into the usual babble of wind and woods.

"Get up now, both of you, nice and slow," came the voice of a man behind them. Charlie saw the shadow of a machine gun. "Hands up high where I can see them."

40

Charlie rose inch by inch, so as not to spur the unseen gunslinger into precipitous use of his trigger. Charlie was confident that Drummond had had the presence of mind to take the Colt from Candicane's saddlebag when he took the fountain pen. When Drummond stood and followed the instruction to put his hands up, however, Charlie saw no hint of the gun.

"I could stand another fifty-fifty proposition," Drummond said. Charlie understood this to mean Drummond required a diversionary tactic, like at the battlefield.

"Zip it," the stranger barked.

His black-lacquered machine gun was distinguishable from the night by a filament of light. Although Charlie saw him only in silhouette, it was obvious the barrel of his machine gun was shaky. Probably not coincidentally, the man was chattering furiously—oddly, without making any sound. He collected himself sufficiently to steady the barrel, point it at Charlie, and get out, "Time to say your prayers."

An idea struck Charlie. "Sir, first, there's one thing that, legally, I need to inform you," he said.

"What?"

Charlie looked past him, in the direction the helicopter had flown. "Our helicopter has you locked in its sights."

The stranger peeked over his shoulder at the dark sky. "I can't even see it anymore."

Drummond's bullet hit the man in the head. He fell dead long before the brash report ceased bouncing around the ridge. Charlie was at once sickened and glad the diversion worked.

"Are you okay?" Drummond said.

"Better than him," Charlie said numbly.

"We need to hurry." Drummond scrambled back to his horse blanket.

"You think he might have a car around here somewhere?" Charlie asked.

Drummond packed snow into the bald spots on his blanket. "Maybe, but that shot was probably heard for miles. If there's a road down from here, they'll block it."

Charlie pulled his blanket back on with all of the joy of getting into a cold bath.

"Fine diversionary tactic, by the way," Drummond said.

"The old there's-someone-behind-you trick? Who'd have thought it would work?"

"It wasn't that simple. There was nothing distinctive about his appearance or dialect. Yet you deduced he wasn't in league with the helicopter. How?"

"Oh, that," Charlie said. "Lucky guess: I didn't hear anything when he was chattering. I got the sense he was missing a lot of teeth."

"Ah, symptomatic of methamphetamine usage?"

"Like a big, old red nose is to whiskey."

"I see." Drummond rolled onto his haunches, pulled his blanket over him, and shoved off.

"Fine diversionary tactic, by the way" was as much commendation as Charlie ever would have expected. "The young and impressionable profit more from constructive criticism than puffery," Drummond had long maintained—an adage Charlie speculated had been originated by a childless Spartan. With a coping sigh, he resumed crawling downhill. The ground seemed particularly coarse and cold.

"You have a good nose," Drummond said. "I was thinking of the first time I saw it. At the office, when you were ten. I let you go down to the basement. Do you remember?"

"No." Charlie braced for a recounting of an early trip down the Easy Way.

"There was another stairwell, down to the subbasement, but we'd walled it off before we moved in; we needed to keep the existence of the subbasement secret from the legitimate employees. And none of them ever guessed a thing. But you said, 'Dad, there's a secret room down here!' I asked, 'What makes you think that?' You just shrugged, so I dismissed it as childish fantasy. On the subway home, though, you blurted out, 'The closet opens inward!' Which was the key. We'd made the stairs to the subbasement accessible by what appeared to be a utility closet, which was kept locked. You'd noticed there were no hinges on the outside of the frame. You intuited that the door opened inward—which closet doors customarily do not—meaning the door led somewhere. Ten months we'd been there and no one had thought of that. I had it fixed that night."

Drummond was fond of citing ability to frame underachievement. Charlie girded for the inevitable drop of the other shoe.

Drummond said no more.

When they'd crept another hundred yards downhill, Charlie considered that Drummond had told the story in appreciation. It kindled in Charlie a good feeling, like winning. He wouldn't have thought such a nice moment could arise from capping a meth head, but there it was.

As they forged onward, the terrain didn't bother him as much.

At a back table at Miss Tabby's, Fielding read the message, forwarded to him by Pitman. Two minutes ago, a man on the ridge texted the pool player:

TEH 2 DEA FUX R HER

"There are some who will tell you that with all of its haste and lack of punctuation, text messaging is the death of communication via the English language," Fielding told Pitman over the phone. "This message, however, is evidence of its singularly descriptive powers."

" 'DEA fux' is singular," agreed Pitman, adding a chuckle.

Obviously the kid was just sucking up.

"What I meant was the readout of the latitude and longitude of the guy's cell phone to three thousandths of a degree," Fielding said. "Shakespeare couldn't have done any better."

"Oh, that, of course. I put the hunting pack into a lasso perimeter around the coordinates."

"Good. Also, it occurred to me that the rabbits must be using tarps or something like that, layered with snow, to mask them from the infrared. So pass along word to the boys in the hunting pack that if they step on a mound of snow and it says 'Ouch,' shoot."

41

Still shrouded by the snow-packed horse blanket, and on hands and knees that felt frozen solid, Charlie followed Drummond to the edge of a cliff. As the branches overhead thinned, he braced for a sky full of search craft.

Other than a few unhurried snowflakes, he saw only blackness. Below was farmland, miles of it, dormant aside from an old truck meandering along a narrow road, headlights every so often revealing a dark house or outbuilding.

"I like that one," said Drummond, pointing to an enormous dwelling, with three parallel gambrel roofs intersected at right angles by a pair of A-frames. It appeared as if five different houses had been roped together.

Someone had gotten carried away with their Design Your Own Country Mansion software, Charlie thought. He understood that Drummond's appraisal wasn't based on aesthetics, though. No lights burned in or around the house. The long driveway wasn't plowed. There might be a vehicle they could use, a weekend station wagon perhaps.

Reaching the house would require a simple two-hundred-foot downhill crawl—simple, providing no sniper lay in wait.

That threat made the relatively slow descent feel like a prolonged freefall. Charlie began perspiring for the first time tonight. Halfway down, his shirt was soaked through. The wind, no longer impeded by woods, threatened to freeze him in place.

They made it to the cornfield at the base of the slope. Here a sniper would have seen the field, in Grimm brothers fashion, sprout two grown men. Drummond let his frosty camouflage fall so that it conformed to the ground, taking on the appearance of just another patch of snowy field.

While shedding his blanket in the same fashion, Charlie picked up, on his periphery, the silhouette of a stout man with a rifle. His heart leaped, and the rest of him followed.

Drummond simultaneously drew the Colt and whirled around.

At what proved to be a scarecrow—a good one, replete with dungaree overalls, plaid shirt, worn cowboy hat, and a hoe that, in the dark, at a certain angle, could be mistaken for a rifle.

"If I were a crow, I would have been scared to death," Charlie said. Embarrassment burned sensation back into his cheeks.

With a brief smile, Drummond stole toward the house, choosing a route through the darkest shadows. Still shaken, Charlie tramped after him. Halfway, without explanation, Drummond veered toward the barn, an archetypal, apple-red two-story with a gable-roofed hayloft.

The sliding door was unlocked. Drummond raised the latch and threw his weight into the handle, grinding the wheels through a season's worth of decaying leaves. The building released a shaft of stale air tinged not with the hay Charlie had anticipated but gasoline. The source was a vintage Jeep Wagoneer. With its wooden side panels, the old sport utility vehicle fit the classic barn the way a round-back sleigh went with an Alpine chalet.

"I should be able to start it, provided it starts at all," said Drummond. He felt his way through the darkness and opened the driver's door.

"Let me get this one?" Charlie said. He jangled the keys suspended from a hook on the inside wall.

The Wagoneer's dome light showed a lopsided grin crease Drummond's face. "Maybe I ought to learn more about the Easy Way," he said.

And so it was that—shivering, windburned, cut, aching, and painfully aware a Hellfire missile might at any moment turn the barn to splinters—Charlie, for the first time he could recall, shared a laugh with his father.

42

If any among the handful of drivers on the Stonewall Jackson Memorial highway—a narrow, winding country road—were to look into the four-door GMC pickup, they would have seen a heavyset, prematurely gray-haired man at the wheel. Wearing an insulated red flannel shirt and a scuffed Hillcats baseball cap, Benjamin Stuart Mallory, known to colleagues as "Bull," hoped to pass for a worker on his way home from the late shift at one of the area mills.

On the seat beside him, hidden beneath his coat, was a glossy black Steyr Tactical Machine Pistol, the weapon of preference in testosterone-fueled crowds. The shooting he was planning would be passed off as crossfire in a meth dealer turf war. He liked that the Steyr was light and small enough to be held in one hand, yet capable of delivering the same firepower as a submachine gun. Its primary disadvantage was accuracy, but even if 90 percent of his rounds went awry, he could still do the job several times over.

He turned off the road at the position Pitman had texted him, a driveway leading to a darkened, tin-roofed farmhouse, a half mile below the ridge where the slain meth cook had been found. Bull parked in such a way that a passerby might think he'd stopped to collect his mail.

He lowered his window enough to allow the nose of the Steyr out, then took up his PVS-29. The difference between this monocular and a typical night scope was its proprietary light intensifier that amplified more electrons and thus delivered an unbelievably bright and sharp image. He'd once asked one of Langley's "Toy Makers" exactly how many more electrons. "Thirty-eight thousand bucks worth," the man replied.

From a hundred yards away, on this overcast and particularly dark night, an ordinary scope would have enabled Bull to distinguish only the gender of the occupants of the vehicle presently approaching, and maybe not even that much. The PVS-29 turned night into a hazy afternoon, meaning he would have little difficulty recognizing rabbits Drummond and Charlie Clark.

The vehicle was a late-model Toyota coupe. At the wheel was a young woman in her mid-twenties, fair-haired with a roundish face. Pretty enough, Bull thought, that it was peculiar she was out so late alone. Of course the rabbits might be hiding below the window line, one of them poking a gun into her hip. Also peculiar: she was speaking; she was too young and too normal-looking to be talking to herself.

When the Toyota was within seventy or eighty yards, he saw a glint of a cell phone bud in her ear. Her brow was knitted. Her lips pursed, then opened into the shape of an O, and finally snapped shut.

" 'Mom!' " he repeated to himself as the Toyota shrieked by.

A minute later came an SUV, an old one. Again he focused on the driver. A young man, also by himself, between twenty and thirty years old. At nine P.M. in areas such as this, where residents woke with the sun, 80 percent of vehicles were driven by lone men, and of them, 90 percent were between twenty and thirty. At a hundred yards, the driver looked like Abbott or Costello, whichever was the fat one. In other words, no resemblance to Charlie Clark, whose photo glowed on Bull's BlackBerry. Also the fat man was singing too boisterously for someone who'd been carjacked. Bull read his lips too: "Stayin aliiiiive." He let Abbott or Costello stay alive.

A few seconds later came an even older SUV, a late-seventies Jeep Wagoneer. In the front seat were two men. The driver was white, between twenty and thirty. Of course. He wore an old hunting cap, side flaps down. Hats of any sort ignited Bull's suspicion, especially when worn in a heated vehicle. But the Wagoneer was old enough that the heat had probably given out years ago. Parts and labor for a new heater core would run more than the old Jeep was worth.

When the Jeep was close enough, Bull saw that the driver, unlike Charlie Clark, had a buzz cut. Maybe old Drummond had come into possession of a pair of scissors, or a hedge trimmer even, and sought to alter the shape of his son's head. Probably he'd learned that trick on day one of Disguise. Then there was the driver's beard, like a billy goat's, the sort seen on the up-there mountain folk. Whenever people see a unique feature on a person, Bull knew—and Drummond Clark certainly knew too—they fixate on the feature rather than on the person. A fingerful of elementary adhesive, chewing gum even, followed by a few hair clippings, and a man had a beard that would surely have strangers asking, "Does he know a woman who finds that attractive?" or "How does he manage to keep it out of his soup?"

Bull had mere seconds to make up his mind whether to fire. He devoted the time to the passenger, slumped in an awkward recline, as if passed out. His face was pressed against the window so that it was effectively hidden. He too wore a hat, a cowboy hat, with a wide brim that hid all except for a few dark strands of his hair. Drummond might have adhered his son's relatively dark hair clippings over his own white hair beneath the hat line. Drummond wasn't nearly as beefy as this redneck though.

Patrons of Miss Tabby's, Bull reckoned.

Once the Wagoneer had passed, he texted the license plate number to Pitman and Dewart, just in case.

An hour later, Dewart received confirmation that a traffic camera at the Virginia-Maryland border photographed the same license plate. He passed the pertinent information to state troopers in the vicinity, who soon found the Wagoneer in a rest stop parking lot, empty except for the well-dressed scarecrow in the passenger seat.

43

At dawn on weekdays, ten piers full of commercial fishing boats brought Brooklyn's Sheepshead Bay to a boil. One by one they joined a bobbing traffic jam to the day's best fishing spots. With them always was the forty-five-foot stern dragger *Sea Dog*. Every so often she bypassed the good fishing spots, and her captain ignited the pair of supplementary ten-cylinder diesel engines hidden in her belly. No one guessed it, what with the *Sea Dog's* dented hull and ungainly array of masts and poles and tangled netting, but she could cruise at twenty knots, meaning Nova Scotia could be in sight in time for breakfast the next day.

"Ideally we can take the *Sea Dog* to Halifax," Drummond said to Charlie, who was still unable to resist running his fingers through the stubble that used to be his hair. They were in a gas station minimart a few miles into Maryland, weaving around hanger racks of Baltimore Orioles souvenir T-shirts, heading to the pay phone to call the *Sea Dog's* captain.

Every few seconds a big rig blew past on I-95, rattling the flimsy building. The only other customer was a middle-aged man focused on keeping a low profile himself; he was selecting condoms. The woman at the register appeared poised to nod off. As benign as the two seemed, Charlie no longer regarded anyone without suspicion.

"From Nova Scotia we can obfuscate our trail with a stop at Saint-Pierre et Miquelon, the French territory ten miles southwest of the Burin Peninsula," Drummond said. "There we should have no difficulty finding cargo ship passage to Europe." Their eventual destination was a clinic in Geneva. "And if at any time before we're at sea, I start blathering

about the Merrimack River or for whatever reason you're unsure of
what to do, where do we go to ground . . . ?"

On the drive from Virginia, Drummond had drilled Charlie on con-
tingencies which, unlike a Fairview Inn, were not on the law enforcement agencies' Fax Blast list. As if reciting a mantra now, Charlie replied,
"Fleabags, flophouses, and whorehouses."

"Correct," Drummond said.

"Sounds like it would make a good TV show, doesn't it?"

Amused, seemingly in spite of himself, Drummond deposited two
quarters into the coin slot and dialed a Los Angeles number. Fifty cents
bought three minutes of talk time to anywhere in the United States.
After one fuzzy ring, a synthesized voice said, "You have reached a number that is either not working or has been disconnected. Please hang up
and try your call again."

Undaunted, Drummond remained on the line and hit 2.

Nothing happened.

He waited two seconds, then hit 2 twice more.

"Three," came the synthesized voice again. Then the line went dead.

"Excellent," Drummond said. Turning to Charlie, he added, "Don't
worry, it's not contingency plan time yet. The captain of the *Sea Dog* is
a former operative of the old school, which is to our benefit, because
Fielding and his team are better equipped to pick up the trail when sili-
con chips are involved. 'Three' is the number for the dead drop where
we'll book our trip."

44

The Chevy Malibu, which Drummond acquired in Delaware, gobbled up the remaining miles to New York State. Finally, Brooklyn rose at the far end of the Williamsburg Bridge, the twinkling lights and two-in-the-morning vapor giving the city the appearance of a distant solar system. At the wheel, Charlie blinked repeatedly to keep exhaustion from locking his eyelids shut.

"A salty Coleridge?" asked Drummond from the passenger footwell.

He was doing the crossword puzzle from the Newark *Star-Ledger*. Before Charlie could even place the name *Coleridge*, Drummond had filled the boxes of 44 Across with "ancient mariner."

"Not that a wrong answer makes a difference," Drummond said. "Forty-four is what matters, the approximate latitude of Halifax." He pointed to the puzzle. "This will be our message to the captain."

Charlie suspected Drummond was in the midst of one of the rarer episodes of lucidity, several hours in length. Another thirty or forty minutes was all they would need in order to take care of business and hit the sea.

They crossed into Brooklyn, quickly nearing the dead drop site. "If we can, let's find a spot on this block," Drummond said, pointing to a bustling nightclub.

Charlie had assumed they would leave the car someplace out of the way, like a dark alley. This block was dicey to begin with, and it looked like Hoodlums Night at the club. "But if the Cavalry finds the car, they'll know we're here," he said.

"They'll find it, there's no doubt about that. Our hope is that when they do, the car will be at the chop shop to which our accommodating car thief will have driven it. Most of those establishments are in New Jersey and Westchester. Make sure to leave the keys in the ignition."

"Got you. Leave the motor running too?"

"Now you're learning."

Charlie clambered down the stairs into the Atlantic Avenue subway station. There was a chance, he thought, that the Baltimore Orioles fleece he had on—purchased at the minimart—could give him away. But at least it wasn't the Yankees.

Drummond, who'd put on a new ski cap as well as a canvas barn jacket he'd found by the Wagoneer, descended at a more leisurely pace, fifteen or twenty steps behind Charlie. They didn't appear to be together—or at least, that was the idea.

Charlie made it to the vending machine first, bought a Metro Card, pushed through the turnstile, and entered a tunnel that amplified the footfalls of the few other passengers and the sporadic shrieks of far-off trains. He emerged onto a drafty D train platform. The small crowd of prospective passengers had the hollow eyes and restlessness of having been waiting too long.

In a security mirror, Charlie saw Drummond scratch his left shoulder, the "all's clear" signal. Charlie fell into step with him to the men's room at the far end of the platform.

"What if it's out of order?" Charlie asked. Out of Order signs dangled from subway restroom door handles as often as not.

"We have a backup," Drummond said, pointing to the trash can beside the men's room door. Stout metal legs raised its base an inch above the floor. "It's easy to leave an envelope beneath it without attracting any notice, while tying a shoelace for instance. The problem is, contrary to popular belief, the platform is cleaned regularly."

The men's room was open, fortunately—unless the stench were taken into account; the ventilation grate looked to have been degrimed last in

the '70s. Assuming his appointed position at the sink, Charlie rinsed his
hands and tried to breathe as seldom as possible. The spotty mirror gave
him a view of an empty room in which the white tile walls and floors
were grayed with filth and the ceiling tiles had greenish stalactites—of
what, he didn't want to guess.

Drummond entered, heading straight into the stall in order to place
the vinyl pouch that had contained the Chevy Malibu owner's manual
and now held the crossword puzzle turned cipher.

"What if, for any of fifty reasons, this place gets shut down after we
leave?" Charlie asked.

"The cutout either will have a key or some other idea," Drummond
said as he placed the pouch in a cavity behind a loose wall tile. "Speaking
of things going wrong, you need to know that once the captain gets the
note, he'll have someone use the ten digits I added to the puzzle—the
phone number of the Mykonos."

"The diner on Bedford?"

"Right. If the trip's a go, Stavros will flip a switch and light the neon
waves of steam above the cup of coffee on the sign. We'll be able to see it
from Desherer's. A help wanted flyer inside the door, on the other hand,
means we need a new ride. But at the least, there will be handwritten
instructions at the base of the flyer."

That all this sounded reasonable to Charlie spoke to the way his
thinking had adapted in a day. "So I guess we always had to get dinner at
the Mykonos for work reasons?"

"No, we only went because Stavros was a friend of Tony's. You didn't
like it?"

"Just not the food."

"Sorry, I never thought about it one way or the other."

"It's not a big deal. It never killed me."

"I probably wasn't as attuned to that sort of thing as I might have
been. That, at least, I can make up to you."

"That's okay—you don't have to cook." Charlie winced in recollection of the few times Drummond had tried.

"I know. I said 'make up to you.'"

"What do you have in mind?"

Drummond exited the stall, thumbs-up—the drop was successfully loaded. "I was wondering if you would like a ski house in the Swiss Alps," he said.

Charlie was delighted, probably as much as he ever had been. "Let's find out."

45

The chrome-banded façade of Desherer's Sweet Shop was, in Charlie's opinion, dazzling. Tonight was the first time he'd seen the rear of the building, which was essentially a pile of soot-blackened bricks. There were nicer tombs, he thought. Roomier ones too. Trailing Drummond into the alley required stooping and turning sideways to fit into a narrow, clammy passageway. Six steep steps, carpeted with moss and pungent with mildew, brought them down to a squat steel door. Drummond extended his fingers into one of the many dark crevices alongside it.

"I'm sort of surprised an actual spy's safe house has a hide-a-key," Charlie whispered. Neighbors slept above, street traffic was barely audible; the loudest sound was the clicking tread of a rat in a nearby alleyway.

"A retinal scanner, like the ones at the office, might have been a bit conspicuous here," Drummond said.

Charlie joined in the search. When his fingers struck something slimy and jiggly, he yanked out his hand. An old rubber glove flopped out after it.

Drummond caught the glove. "Good work," he said.

From the glove, he removed a key, then unlocked the door to the onetime storeroom, releasing a shaft of air redolent of fresh chocolate, bubble gum, and red licorice—a louvered wall was all that separated the back offices from the candy store. The aroma was enough to catapult anyone into the fondest childhood memories. As he followed Drummond in, Charlie's memories were of standing outside Desherer's big front window, drooling a puddle. Drummond meanwhile was across the street at the Mykonos Diner, collecting their take-out containers of dry meat loaf and boiled potatoes, or something even less exciting. Just making it inside Desherer's now felt like a victory.

Hearing a car approach the front of the store, Drummond eased into a shadow and flattened against the side of a tall file cabinet. Charlie ducked beneath a window, his foot inadvertently sending a box of malted milk balls rattling across the floor.

The car drove up at a slow pace, on patrol, or on the prowl. High beams pierced the blinds that hung inside the store's big front windows, making a display worthy of the Fourth of July out of the chrome counter and its myriad jars of colorful candies, and throwing huge shadows onto the walls and ceiling in the back storeroom.

"*Them?*" whispered Charlie, pressed against dusty floorboards.

"More likely just a routine police patrol."

Whoever it was drove away. The store seemed blacker than before.

Drummond unlocked the door to the last in the row of five small offices that had been built out from the storeroom's back wall. On entering, he twisted the coin advance handle on a gumball machine. A soft lightbulb within the globe blinked on, revealing four walls of warped wood paneling stained an orange-brown not found in nature. The file cabinets and bookshelves pressed against the paneling appeared to be all that held it up.

Drummond knelt and examined the small cube refrigerator. Nodding his satisfaction that it hadn't been tampered with, he pulled the door open and removed an armful of Chinese take-out containers—aluminum trays with waxed cardboard tops. He set them on the cracked leather desk blotter and pried off the lid of the topmost. Charlie backed away. The odor was like a punch in the nose.

"This is nothing," Drummond said. "An agent of ours in Berlin used to leave microfilm hidden inside dead rats in his cellar. And times I had something really important to hide, I submerged it in here." He tapped a stout wooden door, which swung inward, revealing a tiny bathroom that made the one at the subway station seem spiffy. The toilet bowl was filled with brown water. Or brown something.

"You've made the eight-year-old Chinese food seem appetizing," Charlie said.

"Actually I have a feeling you'll find it mouthwatering," Drummond said with a smile. He pried away a slab of congealed chicken and peanuts, revealing a plastic-wrapped brick of twenty-dollar bills and another of hundreds. "Not incidentally, the peanuts aren't peanuts. They're uncut diamonds."

Charlie found Drummond's smile infectious.

This was the Christmas morning they'd never had.

"Actually, it's the most beautiful dish I've ever seen," Charlie said.

Laughing, Drummond took the top off another container of now-petrified lo mein. The odor was fresh flowers as far as Charlie was concerned. Drummond removed a block of noodles to expose documents including two blank United States passports and two more United States passports with his photograph inside. The names were Bill Peterson and John Lewis.

"Are these your emergency aliases or pseudonyms or whatever?" Charlie asked.

"Bill Peterson is a fabrication, pure and simple. John Lewis took some doing. He was born in Altoona, Iowa, in 1947, then was committed to an insane asylum in Des Moines in 2002. So he's not going anywhere. I 'borrowed' his social security number in order to get a duplicate of his birth certificate sent to an accommodation address I set up for him in Stamford, Connecticut. Then I used the birth certificate to get the passport as well as a Connecticut driver's license, and, over time, all this—" He popped a hardened layer of rice from the next container and poured onto the desk blotter Fairfield Textiles LLC business cards belonging to "John Lewis" as well as cards of others in the textile industry, receipts, a New Haven library card, about ten department store charge cards, and another ten ordinary debit and credit cards. "Most of these cards work, but using them in the next couple of days will be too risky. We may as well send Fielding a note saying 'Wish You Were Here.' Still, this one could be vital." He tapped a Sears card.

"In the event of an emergency where we need a blender?"

"In the event we want to draw on the account at the Bank of Antigua. It's a numbered account, so there's no link to my name. Do you think you'll be able to memorize the number on the card?"

Charlie glanced at the sixteen digits. "For eight million bucks, I could memorize all of *Moby-Dick*."

Drummond regarded Charlie with what looked like contentment; Charlie wasn't entirely sure, never having seen that expression on him before.

"Charles, please know I never wanted you to be in the position of having to flee the country," Drummond said. "As it stands, though, I'm grateful to you for having gotten us this far. And I'll be very happy to have you along." He thrust out his right hand.

Charlie clasped it with matching energy. Still, the handshake felt lacking.

It was interrupted by three raps at the door between Bedford Avenue and the vestibule the offices shared with the candy store.

"This is the police," came a man's voice from the sidewalk. "Please come out now or we'll be forced to come in."

Charlie flashed back to his clumsy, boxes-of-malted-milk-balls-rattling move when the car drove past. He groaned inwardly.

"I can take care of this," Drummond whispered. He put the lid back on the container of cash and diamonds, then grabbed a card from the pile on the desk. "Stay put for just a minute."

He stepped out of the office, blending into the darkness of the corridor leading to the vestibule. He reappeared for a moment, red, then white, and then blue from the flashing light bar on the patrol car. Then he vanished into the vestibule.

Charlie heard him padding down thick rubber matting. He heard too the raspy slide of the bolt, the groan as the door opened, the tinkle of a little bell on top of it, the influx of the Brooklyn night, then Drummond delivering a very convincing, "It's okay, officers, I'm Bill Peterson. I'm a tenant here. With too much work due tomorrow morning, unfortunately." What sounded like a brief exchange of formalities between him and the policemen came next, followed by another jingle of the bell as the door fell back into its frame, the relocking of the bolt, the patrol car rolling away, and, finally, Drummond ambling back down the dark corridor.

"So did you have to buy tickets to the PBA dinner?" Charlie asked.

There was no response.

"Dad?"

Out of the darkness came a stocky young man. Charlie knew him as MacKenzie, but his name was really Pitman—assuming Cadaret hadn't lied about that too. Pitman held the Colt that had been tucked into Drummond's waistband seconds ago.

"Dad had to go to a meeting," he said.

46

Pitman pried a block of wood from a corner of the bookshelf. It matched the triangular braces on the shelf's other corners. He shook it until a small transistor-like gadget fell out and onto the desk blotter. An eavesdropping device, guessed Charlie, who sat at the desk per Pitman's promise to shoot him if he didn't.

With the butt of the Colt, Pitman smashed apart the gadget, then swept away its remains, along with the Chinese food containers, sending them clattering against the fake-wood paneling and then to the floor. Spreading the charge cards out onto the blotter, he asked, "Okay, which one is it?"

Evidently he'd overheard what Drummond said about the Bank of Antigua and was looking to get in on the money himself—how else to explain his furtive solo entry coupled with the destruction of the eavesdropping device? His problem was Drummond never identified the card by name; he'd merely tapped it.

"Which one is *what*?" Charlie said.

Pitman grabbed him by the collar and thrust his face toward the desktop. The bulb of Charlie's nose flattened against the blotter. The cartilage was a hair's breadth from exploding when Pitman jerked him to a stop.

"Why make this hard on yourself, Charlie?"

"I don't know what you want," Charlie said, trying to buy time to think.

No doubt Pitman could torture him into revealing it was the Sears card. Probably the spook knew dark artistry that would hurt just to hear about. And even more disturbing: Once Pitman got what he wanted, he couldn't risk Charlie breathing a word of what had happened.

"I know it's not one of the gas station cards, because you can't buy a blender at a gas station," Pitman said. "So, which is it? Nordstrom's? Spiegel? Sears? JCPenney?"

Charlie felt the heat of Pitman's scrutiny with the mention of each. "Really, I have no idea what you're talking about," he said.

"Do you have Alzheimer's too? I overheard your entire conversation."

Pitman gripped the Colt by the barrel and appeared only to flick it. When the handle struck Charlie's nose, though, it felt like a wrecking ball. Hot blood burst from his nostrils, he saw at least two of everything in the room, and he wanted to shriek. But while shrieking would release some of the pain, it would get the neighbors' attention, and draw the police. Then Pitman would simply flash his G-man badge and drag Charlie somewhere else to torture him.

Which would foil Charlie's nascent escape plan.

So instead of shrieking, Charlie dug his nails into the wooden frame of his chair, sucked back the blood, and said, "Oh, I get it, you mean the numbered bank account."

"So pain helps jog your memory. Good." Pitman positioned himself so he stood directly above Charlie. He took Charlie's right ring finger in a tight grip, then raised it as high as he could in preparation for plunging it into the sharp edge of the desktop. "I'm going to break your fingers, one at a time, until you tell me which card it is."

Charlie had no doubt the maneuver would break his finger. The question was whether it would break the finger *off*. "Okay, okay, okay! Uncle!"

Pitman let Charlie's hand fall but kept the gun pointed at him. "Which?"

The bright red Sears card sat in the very center of the blotter. Trying to block it from his consciousness, Charlie inched a hand toward the JCPenney card. The nose of the Colt mirrored his motion.

"JCPenney?" Pitman asked.

"Yeah," Charlie said in defeat.

He grabbed at his nose, as if to staunch the blood. In the process he elbowed the JCPenney card. It skidded off the desk and clicked to the floor. "Sorry," he said.

As Pitman knelt to pick up the Penney's card, Charlie snatched the Sears card, wound up, and fired it toward the bathroom. Its flight was clumsy—end over end, as opposed to the laser beam he'd envisioned. The motion caught Pitman's eye. He looked up from his kneel as the card landed, with a splash, in the toilet bowl—or, as Charlie thought of it, the bull's-eye.

"It was the Sears card, wasn't it?" Pitman asked.

Charlie looked away and said nothing.

"I should have known from the way you avoided looking at it." Pitman stood and pointed the Colt at him. "Get it out and lick it clean."

Charlie rose. From the desk, Pitman matched his movements with the nose of the Colt. Fearing another pistol-whipping, Charlie steered clear of it.

When in range of the bathroom, he lunged, grabbed the handle of the flush chain hanging from the overhead cistern, and pulled as hard as he could. Water rushed into the bowl with astounding power. The Sears card would almost surely go down the drain.

Pitman dove headlong from the desk and toward the bowl. Charlie threw all his weight against the inside of the bathroom door. The face of the door met Pitman's jaw squarely with a sound neighbors might have mistaken for a bowling ball that had fallen from the top shelf of a closet.

Pitman toppled backward. Still he managed to keep the muzzle of the Colt on line with Charlie's face. Until he slipped on a greasy take-out container top. The base of his skull smacked into a sharp edge of the desktop. He collapsed to the floor.

47

Charlie knelt over Pitman and jostled him back into consciousness. Pitman's eyes opened and he appeared to regain focus. Charlie flashed the Colt. "What happened to my father?"

"I don't know. How long have I been unconscious?"

"Like, ten seconds."

Pitman inched a hand toward his waistband.

"While you were out, I put that SIG Sauer P two-two-eight of yours in a safe place," Charlie said. "Now, where'd they take him?"

"I don't know."

"You're lying."

"You memorized the number on the Sears card, didn't you?"

"Is the number your price for information?"

"It could be."

"Why would I trust you?"

"What choice do you have?"

Charlie eyed the Colt.

Pitman laughed. "If you fire that in here, either half the neighborhood will hear it and call the cops, or the cops will hear it themselves, and after I identify myself and explain the situation to them, you and I will go somewhere else and take our sweet time on your recollection of the account number."

"All right. I'll use this then." Charlie uncradled the telephone on the desk.

"For what?"

"I'll say you came here to apprehend my father's retirement fund, rather than apprehend me—I'll bet you didn't even tell anyone you'd heard me with your bug."

"Who can you call?"

"Anybody. Your colleagues will hear me whoever I call."

"Then they'll know you're *here*."

"Then they'll know *we're* here, you mean. And they'll put you in jail for a long time. If you're lucky."

Pitman rolled his eyes.

Charlie dialed the number of a second-rate bookmaking service in Vegas, listened to the menu, then hit 0 to speak with a live operator. As usual, Muzak kicked in. The first-rate places were staffed with operators who answered straightaway. Charlie clung to the hope that he could sway Pitman without having to say another word—if the Cavalry were to learn Charlie's location, his plan was dead. Him too, in all likelihood.

Pitman sat against the desk, blasé as ever. Obviously the spook had let it get to this point because he saw the bluff.

Charlie decided: Better to cede the round and hang up before it was too late.

"Fine, fine," grumbled Pitman. "Fine." He rubbed his jaw.

With manufactured nonchalance, Charlie dropped the handset into its cradle.

"They took your father for a debrief," Pitman said.

"Is that a euphemism?"

"No. They do intend to neutralize him, but they need information first. They're worried that in the time since he figured out what was going on, he secretly spread out a security blanket. They're jetting an ace interrogator up from the Caribbean."

"What do you mean by a 'security blanket'?"

"Like, a timed drop."

"And what do you mean by a 'timed drop'?"

"A dead drop that will be cleared after a set time period unless he's around to put a stop to it. Then the contents go to, say, the *Washington Post*."

While such a measure was practical, Charlie suspected that Drummond's patriotism would have precluded it. "Where did they take him?" he asked.

"I heard Cuba," Pitman said, rubbing his jaw again.

"Not the island?"

"No, it's someplace around here. That's all I can tell you."

"How can I get more information?"

"Call four one one," Pitman said. His hand shot from his jaw to Charlie's stomach.

It caught Charlie off guard and felt like a blow from a heavyweight. Pitman sprang up, tackling him hard about the rib cage. Charlie tumbled backward. His right wrist smacked into the thick steel trunk of the gumball machine lamp, costing him his hold on the Colt. It fell onto the desktop and slid to within inches of Pitman.

Snaring it, Pitman said, "On second thought, you may want to call nine one one." He curled a finger around the trigger and aimed the gun at Charlie.

The odds were that a professional like Pitman would reclaim the Colt. Charlie had bet on that beforehand. And been right. Accordingly it was with gusto that he yanked the lamp's power cord, plunging the room into total darkness. Then he whisked Pitman's silenced SIG Sauer P228 from the back of his own waistband, leveled it, and pulled the trigger. The gun nearly kicked out of his hand. The plume of flame lit the office, showing Pitman lifted by the shoulder and thrust into the wall. He slid to the floor and lay still, apparently unconscious again, blood darkening his shirtfront.

Another time, Charlie would be in shock. Now, all he thought about was getting to Drummond. He recognized it was a long shot. Which buoyed him: For once he had relevant experience.

Part Three

The Triggerman

1

Pitman was lying on the office floor, still breathing but unconscious, when he began to intermittently glow green. It was the reflection, Charlie realized, of the neon sign sputtering on across the street at the Mykonos Diner. The *Sea Dog* was a go.

Sitting at the desk, Charlie tried to devise an alternative plan. His approach was no different than if he were playing the horses, which begins with an evaluation of the past—the speed, the endurance, and the style demonstrated by the horses during their previous trips. The next step is to create a mental picture of them competing in the forthcoming race. To Charlie's surprise, his thinking wasn't just clear but electric. Adrenaline strengthened his focus and quickened his acuity, which had the effect of slowing the pace of the rest of the world, allowing him to weigh options he otherwise might have overlooked. Like nuclear fission.

He recalled a story Drummond used to tell in which the scientists arrived for work at the secret headquarters of the Manhattan Project. A lot of the early atomic bomb research was conducted at Columbia University, on Manhattan's Morningside Heights, in a subterranean complex built solidly enough that vibrations from the adjacent IRT subway line wouldn't disturb the hypersensitive instruments.

The entrance was in the campus grocery store in the basement of Furnald Hall, an undergraduate dormitory. All day long students and professors bought coffee and snacks. The students had no idea that the cashiers from whom they finagled six-packs were really employees of the U.S. Army. No one suspected that Gibby, the dim stockroom guy, held the key—literally—to the Allied nuclear effort. When Gibby was sure no one was looking, he admitted certain "professors" to the employee washroom. Within the far toilet stall was the entryway to a tunnel leading to a secret warren of offices and laboratories. When the war ended, the complex was sealed off to prevent radioactive leakage. Or so everyone was told.

When Drummond used to talk about the Manhattan Project, it was with the same patriotic pride he reserved for D-day and the lunar landing. Tonight it seemed significant to Charlie that, unlike the Normandy beaches and the moon, the Manhattan Project facility was two blocks from Drummond's office. Also, dropping letters from *Columbia* netted *Cuba.*

Charlie imagined a subterranean complex of sparkling modern laboratories, teeming with scientists in gleaming lab coats, corridors patrolled in lockstep by guards in crisp unitards. Then he applied what he'd learned the last two days: Odds were, to avoid drawing attention, the Cavalry would keep personnel to the absolute minimum, and their security force would more closely resemble the small Manhattan Project unit in the grocery store. Which meant they would be susceptible to attack.

All at once, Charlie had an idea of how to carry it out.

"I hope you're okay," he said to Pitman. "We have a lot of work to do."

2

Alice heard a baby crying in the next room. She knew that Iraqi interrogators, believing no sound induced greater psychological stress, were fond of piping recordings of wailing infants into the cells of their subjects. It certainly would explain the twinkle in Dr. Cranch's eye when he'd left the room a few minutes ago.

"I'd estimate you've told me ninety percent of what I want to know," the interrogator had said. "Most likely the omissions are the result of fatigue and the shock of your having been discovered. So let's table our discussion until you've had a chance to get some proper rest."

Since the Dark Ages, sleep deprivation had been recognized as an effective means of coercion. In most modern civilized countries, it was an illegal form of torture. Alice knew from experience that after seventy hours, her electrolyte balance would go haywire. She would lose her ability to think rationally. She would say things she shouldn't. Thankfully, she'd learned this during a training exercise. If the same were to happen here, people would die. And she'd be number one.

As Hector peeked through the transom, a far better scenario presented itself. The nominal butler stood on the other side of the door, a Beretta tucked into the waistband of his too-tight white linen uniform trousers. He'd been peeking through the transom more often than the position of watchman warranted. That he was on duty tonight, rather than the more resolute Alberto, was a stroke of luck.

Twenty-five or so, Hector was tall and dark and built like a Greek statue, with chocolate-brown eyes, waves of glossy black hair, and sparkling teeth. But these classically handsome parts went together poorly, like stripes and checks. He was unaware of it, or at least he didn't let it impede his efforts as a lothario. Not only was he a chronic flirt but he often called Alice "baby." Who calls the boss's girlfriend "baby"?

Still, under the current circumstances, seducing him wouldn't be easy.

The door opened and he entered to clear her dinner. His eyes took their usual extended tour of her sleeveless dress.

"Hey, baby, how was the grub?" he asked.

She tried but couldn't think of a single come-on that hadn't been uttered or performed a zillion times in a zillion cheesy singles bars. Also the crying infant from the next room, evidently a looped recording, was hardly Barry White.

"My compliments to the sous chef," she said finally.

God, what a flirt, she thought.

Yet he lingered, tensing his arm muscles more than was necessary to lift an empty plastic bowl. In doing nothing, she realized, she was doing all that was required.

"Hector, I'm bored," she said.

He flashed his Romeo smile. "I'd entertain you myself, but . . ."

"How about bringing in a TV?"

"The doc said no TV. Sorry, baby."

"Just for a little while? I won't say anything."

"I ain't worried what you'd say, I'm worried what the boss would say. The smallest TV in this place is, like, fifty inches. How'm I gonna explain why I'm lugging that shit in here?"

"How about a portable radio, then? I'll make it worth your while, Hector." She visualized Rita Hayworth batting her eyelashes, then tried it herself.

Flattery tinted his beefy cheeks. "They say you're a dangerous lady."

"What am I gonna do with a radio?"

"I don't know—build a bomb?"

She would put a radio to better use than a bomb. She could sling a channel selection dial at him with nearly the same lethality as a Shaolin throwing star, which wouldn't draw the attention from the household that an explosion would.

"At least something to read?" Her real aim was a deck of cards.

"He specifically say no books, no magazines, no nothing to read."

"Bloody hell!"

"Baby, I wish I could."

Alice sighed. "At this point, I'd be happy just for a pack of cards."

He shrugged, probably just averse to saying no again.

"Even in maximum security prisons, they let inmates play solitaire," she said.

"I know, I know, but—"

"What if I play strip solitaire?"

"How do you play that?" he said with indifference. He was a poor actor.

"Each time I lose a hand, I remove an article of clothing. And I only have one article of clothing."

"You're probably super-crazy-good at solitaire."

"How about if I start out with the dress off? Will that do it for you, baby?"

Hector grinned, and still was grinning when he returned with a deck of Bicycle cards in hand. A bonus: Bicycles had "air cushioning," plastic coating intended to prevent cards from sticking to one another. To a card thrower, it was a full-metal jacket.

She rose to accept the deck. "Hector, have I ever told you that you're my favorite person?"

He held back. "The dress," he reminded her.

She unbuttoned the dress and let it spill down her bare breasts and hips to the carpet. Hector's mouth fell open like a mailbox.

He dumped the cards on the picnic table, then turned away, probably to hide the protuberance at the front of his trousers. Still, he would be able to draw and fire the Beretta well before she could throw a card.

Putting on a lackadaisical air, she took up the deck and extracted a joker from the top. She pinched the center of the card with her thumb and ring finger, as firmly as she could without creasing it, and placed her index finger on the far corner. Card-throwing power is generated by the wrist, but the key to the throw is finesse: The wrist needs to be as relaxed as if propped up by a pillow. She inhaled deeply, filling her lungs and stomach, then exhaled slowly. She bent her arm ninety degrees at the elbow, bringing the joker toward her abdomen. With a motion similar to that of a Frisbee toss, but much quicker, she released the card. It sliced the air, likely in excess of fifty miles per hour, toward Hector. The whipcrack alerted him. Just as a corner of the card bit into his jugular. The "crying infant" next door masked his cry.

Alice leaped at him, landing a blow to the side of his head. He sagged beneath her, out cold. She took his Beretta and cell phone, hauled him into the bathroom, used her full strength to lift him into the "water bed," then lowered and bolted the lid. There was no water in the basin, which was fine—the idea was containment. The villa was big enough that ten minutes would pass before any of the other household staff members or security guards would miss him. If she couldn't escape in that time, she never would.

"Don't turn on the water," came his muffled plea.

To her ear it was serendipity. "But, Hector, that would be like a cone without any ice cream."

"Please." His deep breathing was an unmistakable precursor to anxiety-induced hyperventilation. "I'll tell you what you want to know."

"What do I want to know?"

"Señor Fielding's really CIA."

"CIA *what?*"

"The real deal: spy, covert ops man—whatever you call it."

Two days ago Alice more readily would have accepted this—the Drummond Clark connection begged the question. Now she was inclined to dismiss Hector's information as preposterous. And she hoped it was. What CIA officer would sic the likes of the Knife on an innocent little girl? Hector certainly sounded like he believed what he'd said, though. A CIA link also might explain Fielding's willingness to subject her to torture. Most criminals feared backlash from intelligence agencies, who famously took care of their own—often, on learning their captive was such an agent, the thugs released him at once and gave him a first-class ticket to wherever he wanted.

"Hector, the way this will work best is if you tell me something I don't already know," Alice said, twisting the knob on the face of the tank. Water swelled the hose running from the showerhead into the basin, splashing Hector.

"Okay, okay, okay." He began to sob.

She turned the water off. "Off for now," she specified.

"You know about the old CIA guy you talked to up in Brooklyn?" he asked. "Señor Clark?"

"I know a lot about him. Do you know something I don't?"

"You know Fielding's gonna snuff him?"

"Why?"

"Something he knows, I guess."

She scoffed. "CIA men don't usually snuff one another." But of course she was here in the first place because Fielding allegedly had Lincoln Cadaret snuff an NSA man, Mariáteguia—probably because of something Mariáteguia knew.

"He's not doing it himself."

"He contracted Cadaret?"

"The St. Bart's guy, yeah, I think so. And a bunch of other heavy-duty guys."

So Fielding was a spook who played the role of villain with too much verité. Which happened: When the CIA let the kids play without supervision, things had a way of going *Lord of the Flies*. Fortunately there were other organizations providing checks and balances, the NSA in this case. Fielding would be brought to justice. Case closed.

Except for the immediate matter of Señor Clark's continued existence.

"Is Clark still in Brooklyn?" she asked.

"Who knows? His kid's got the hit teams running all over the map."

"*Charlie?*" Alice liked Charlie—she genuinely had been looking forward to drinks with him. She had assumed, however, that he lacked the capacity to care for his father in the best of circumstances.

"He's giving them fits, that dude."

Alice intended to marvel at this later. Now, she had a phone call to make. "Hector, I need to go now," she said, patting the lid. "If you just let yourself relax, it can be quite tranquil in there."

Hurrying into the bedroom, she heard his screamed protests. Wonderfully muted. He could shout his lungs out, and no one outside the bedroom would hear him.

She rushed back into her dress and crept into the hall as far as an empty guest room. Once inside, she grabbed the plastic liner from the trash can and wrapped it around Hector's gun and phone so they would stay dry. She loosed two thick cords from the curtains, knotted them together, and tied one end to the frame of the elephantine mahogany bed; then, gripping the free end, she lowered herself out the window, down three stories of the villa's shadowy exterior, and into the warm, starlit Caribbean.

The throaty gurgle of a motorboat froze her.

So much for her plan of swimming to the dock and borrowing Fielding's vintage Chris-Craft.

Taking a deep breath, she let herself sink underwater. The Chris-Craft passed overhead, propellers on each side of the stern churning ropes of bubbles. In seconds, the launch was far enough past that she felt confident in resurfacing.

She made out Alberto standing at the helm and Cranch perched on a bench in the stern, clutching an overnight bag. This was more good luck. When Cranch had said he expected to be getting on a private jet to debrief Drummond, she'd focused only on the security lull that might result. Now she might be able to tail him.

Treading water, she unwrapped and flipped open Hector's cell phone. She dialed the office of a supposed Potomac, Maryland, insurance agency, ringing a phone on a yacht docked in Martinique's Pointe du Bout. Her chief answered with a chipper, "Good evening," the optimal greeting.

"It's Desdemona with a bow on top," Alice said. "I need you to get the quick maneuvers gang to wrangle the fastest jet possible at Aimé Césaire Airport in Martinique and have it ready in twenty minutes tops for a game of follow that plane."

3

Charlie's plan of attack called for experienced soldiers. To recruit them, he descended from the rickety elevated subway station in Brooklyn's Little Odessa. Had he not been to Little Odessa before, he might have believed he'd arrived at the neighborhood's namesake in Russia. Cabbage, onions, and potatoes boiled in pots at sidewalk kiosks. Caviar vendors were as prevalent as Starbucks were in other parts of town. The street signs, the restaurant names and menus, and even the listings on the theater marquees were in Cyrillic. The impassioned chatter on the sidewalks was in Russian. There were bearded old men in Cossack hats and wrinkled women in babushkas out of the pages of Tolstoy.

To blend in, Charlie bought a fake fur Cossack hat from a street vendor. Then he waited in a dark doorway down the block from Pozharsky, the celebrated blintz joint named after a seventeenth-century Rurikid prince—the place was so old and run-down, though, the joke was the prince had been named after it. Pozharsky's kitchen ran at full steam until four in the morning, catering to two distinct groups, Kingsborough Community College students requiring second dinners and Russian gangsters kicking back after a night's work.

Charlie's vigil was rewarded when a red Cadillac Eldorado bombed into a handicapped parking space in front of Pozharsky and six men poured out. Leading the way was the menacing Karpenko, Grudzev's muscle. The way things had been the past two days, Charlie now thought of Karpenko's as a friendly face.

Behind Karpenko, Grudzev and four other Russians bobbed into the eatery. Sticking to shadows and lagging far enough behind to avoid notice, Charlie followed.

The thugs converged on a big, wooden corner table covered with decades worth of knife and fork carvings. The eight undergrads seated there had just been served steaming blintzes and pierogi. At the sight of the new arrivals, they grabbed their plates and vacated, going to the end of the line to wait for another table.

Paying the students no notice, Grudzev and his cronies heaved themselves onto the chairs. Grudzev corralled a plate left behind by a panicked coed and took up a gooey cheese blintz as if it were a candy bar. To the waitress, something of a Ukrainian Dolly Parton, he said, "Tatiana, I want your melons."

"The restaurant have no fruit, Leo," she replied in earnest.

Karpenko laughed, pounding the tabletop with such force that a water glass flew off and shattered against the faded harlequin floor tiles. He didn't stop laughing until Charlie slid into the vacant seat beside him.

The Russians all glared at Charlie. Activity and conversation at surrounding tables lulled. Charlie saw a young couple drop a twenty on their table and hurry off, their egg creams not even half finished.

"You here to pay up or you fucking suicidal?" Karpenko asked. His English was slightly better and less accented than Grudzev's.

"Yes to the first part, maybe to the second part," Charlie said.

Karpenko's hand dipped under the table, to a gun tucked into his shiny tracksuit pants no doubt. Two days ago, fear would have frozen Charlie. He still felt fear, but it was relegated to the background by his sense of mission.

Looking past Karpenko, he said to Grudzev, "I have your money. I also have a business proposition for you."

4

Holding his breath against the wake of musky cologne and garlic, Charlie followed Grudzev up a narrow flight of stairs to an empty private functions room. Charlie smarted in nine or ten places from the "pat down" Karpenko had administered in search of a wire, resulting in the temporary confiscation of his new cell phone.

They sat at a table and Grudzev opened the shopping bag from Yuri's, the convenience store up the block, where Charlie had bought the prepaid cell phone. The Russian dumped out the stack of hundreds and flicked through it with the practiced dexterity of a bank teller. An hour ago the money had been in a Chinese take-out container. He grunted his approval.

"And now, how about a way to make that seem like chump change?" Charlie asked.

"This better no be a fucking horse."

"I'm totally over that action." Charlie paused to look around the room, as if wary of snoops himself. "Here's the story: My father, who has Alzheimer's, gets out of bed at four yesterday morning. He forgets he's on sick leave and goes to the office. Perriman Appliances."

"Cheap crap."

"I know. That's why they're way the hell up in Morningside Heights. So, anyway, nobody's in yet when Dad shows up. He's sort of in a daze, and he goes down the stairs to the basement and opens a closet that's supposed to be locked. It leads to another flight of stairs, then into a tunnel and, next thing he knows, he's in the old Manhattan Project complex. I don't know if you know, but during World War Two—"

"Yeah, yeah, I saw thing on History Channel." Grudzev slid his chair closer to the table. "I thought that place was sealed off."

"It's supposed to be. But some Columbia scientist types have gotten in. Evidently they're planning to moonlight as arms dealers. My dad's an old physicist. He could tell that they'd put together a ten-kiloton atomic demolition munition. You know what an atomic demolition munition is?"

"Of course, ADM." Grudzev's flat nose twisted as if he smelled a rat. "Why you telling me this?"

"You deal weapons. You could retire on this, right?"

"Or get killed before I can spend *this*." Grudzev patted the sweatpants pocket that contained his new stack of hundreds. "What's in it for you?"

"Dad wandered out and went home a little while later, before anyone saw him. But they snatched him back tonight—to sweat him would be my bet. When he talks, he'll be in real trouble. And so will I."

"So why you come to me instead of cops?"

"I didn't think the cops would give me a twenty percent finder's fee."

Grudzev flicked a dismissive hand. "Craziness," he said, as if announcing a verdict.

Charlie had anticipated the Russian would be drooling by now. What had gone wrong? Poor acting? Was the tale just too preposterous? Despite Karpenko's frisk, did Grudzev suspect a sting? Perspiration sprung from Charlie's scalp.

Grudzev said, "*Ten* points, maybe."

"Twenty is fair," said Charlie, hiding his delight at being back in the game. "You'd never figure out how to get into the place without me. Also, I could take the deal to Bernie Solntsevskaya."

Grudzev was impassive at the mention of his rival. "Thing is, if I am these Columbia guys, I worry you out blabbing now, so I close up shop, like, now."

Charlie placed his chin between thumb and forefinger, striving for the appearance of the pupil contemplating the wisdom of the master.

"If I can get men and guns—*if*," Grudzev said, "I give eleven points."

For reality's sake, Charlie argued for fifteen and caved on twelve.

5

Things were going too smoothly, Alice thought.

Within ten minutes of her call, the backup unit had fished her out of the Caribbean. On the yacht ride to Martinique, she used a Birdbook encrypted communication system to cable HQ the lowdown on Fielding, then she took a hot shower, ate a sandwich, and changed into a fresh linen suit. An NSA agent, meanwhile, having paid off a Martinican air traffic controller, learned Cranch's flight plan—Newark, New Jersey. And one of the Caribbean desk jockeys at HQ tapped into the FAA radar system in case of deviation.

Just ahead of her now stood a Cessna Citation X, its navigation lights giving the medium-sized jet the appearance of a constellation on the dark airport tarmac. The aircraft could cruise at Mach 0.92, reach an altitude of 50,000 feet, and cover 3,500 miles. Equally nice, Alice thought, was the chardonnay in the onboard bar.

She ascended the fold-out stairs and entered the twenty-five-foot cabin, which consisted of six leather seats—each dwarfing most recliners—a kitchen, a bar, and a bathroom complete with a shower. Setting her briefcase on the floor by the foremost of the six seats, she caught sight of Alberto outside, hurrying from the runway where Cranch's plane had just lifted off. Ordinarily Fielding's man stood every inch of his six four. The way he hunched now, eyes locked on the tarmac, suggested he'd seen her and was pretending he hadn't. This wasn't so much bad luck, she thought, as proof of Murphy's Law.

She jumped down the stairs and ran after him. "Alberto, wait!"

Accelerating, he shoved a hand into a pocket. Probably not for a gun:

He'd be afraid to use one in sight of the many airport workers, passengers, and crew members. When she caught up to him, he had drawn something far worse: a cell phone, presumably to speed-dial Fielding and blow the game.

"Don't do it!" she said to his back. "I can give you fifty thousand dollars in cash. I have it on my plane."

He turned around. He shared Hector's dark, chiseled features. But while Hector's assembly had gone awry, Alberto had been put together to perfection and, more pertinently, hardened through hours in the dojo with Fielding. She wouldn't dare engage him without a weapon.

"Fifty K no do me no good," he said. "Señor Fielding would keelhaul me—you know that."

"Fly with me, so I can be certain you won't contact him. When we land, once I get out, the pilot can take you wherever you want."

"I want the cash you got, plus another two hundred K wired into my account before we leave here."

"That I can take care of with the iPhone I have onboard in, like, a minute."

"Fine."

With a satisfied smile, she returned to the jet. He followed at three paces. Two problems remained. First, her briefcase contained just $5,000. Second, even with all the money in the world, she couldn't trust Alberto.

The cabin door of the empty aircraft opened onto the small kitchen and the bar, which was copper plated, like those in most luxurious ship's galleys. Passing the bar, she opened the briefcase on the first seat. No fool, Alberto stayed in the doorway, from which he easily could retreat at any sign of chicanery. He drew his gun and propped it on the bar.

She thought about making a grab for the SIG in her briefcase. The better choice, she decided, was the powerful stun gun concealed by an iPhone casing. She plucked it from her briefcase and powered it on.

"Hector's got one of those," he said.

"An iPhone?" She turned to face him.

He had dropped behind the console, out of sight save his sturdy brown hands and the big barrel aimed at her. "No, a Taser disguised as one. Drop it."

With a groan, she let her fake iPhone fall to the floor. Staring into his barrel, she raised her hands tremulously into the air. She also pressed the big key on the face of the iPhone with the toe of her shoe. The copper-plated bar conducted a current of approximately one million volts. Alberto crumpled to the carpet, his gun falling away from him. Muscles quivering, he lay across the doorway, preventing the pilot and copilot from boarding.

"I have some baggage," she told them.

6

In an out-of-the-way corner of Little Odessa, Charlie found a peeling four-story building whose hand-painted sign read гостиница, and in smaller letters beneath that, as if in afterthought, the translation: HOTEL. According to the same sign, the establishment rated five stars.

He slid three tens and a five through a chute in the bulletproof glass encasing the front desk. In return he received a room for the night. The hotel also let by the hour. If all went according to plan, his stay would be less than that.

A drinking song warbled from one of the rooms as he made his way up the stairs. As a result he nearly missed the chirp of his new cell phone.

He answered, "What?"

"That you, professor?" came Grudzev's voice.

"You can talk to me at my office, mister," Charlie said, snapping shut the phone.

The exchange meant Grudzev and his men and guns were a go—a triumph. Charlie recognized it was only a small part of the battle, though.

He hurried up to his small, third-floor room, which, while surprisingly tidy, smelled like a butcher's shop. What mattered was the casement window, or, for his purposes, the escape route. The roof of the adjacent massage parlor was a short jump. He unlocked the handle and let the window glide inward a half inch. To get out in a hurry, he would need only tap it the rest of the way and jump through.

Taking a seat on the magazine-thin mattress, he dialed the number of the *Washington Post* on his cell phone. He reached a night operator and conveyed enough urgency to be transferred to a junior reporter, the lone person on duty in the newsroom at this hour—3:43, according to the phone. The clock radio bolted to the nightstand was flashing 12:00.

"This might be hard for you to believe—it's hard for me to believe," Charlie told her. "I've been targeted by a black ops group working under the auspices of the Central Intelligence Agency. The thing is, if I can disclose what they've been up to, their secret will no longer be a secret, which means they'll no longer have incentive to 'neutralize' me. So I was hoping you've got a free megabyte or two on your tape recorder."

"Better you start with the broad strokes," she said. "You have to understand, we get a lot of these calls."

Charlie took "these" to mean "crackpot." "Have you ever heard of the CIA covert ops unit known as the Cavalry?" he asked.

"No. What's the story?"

"They began in the early nineties as a collaboration between the agency's counterproliferation division and counterintelligence, then they went deep black, and, it turns out, too deep."

"How so?"

"First, let me give you a small amount of background?"

"How small?"

"One column inch?"

"Okay." The woman emitted a low-energy laugh.

"In the late sixties, our Special Forces scattered boxes of ammunition along the Ho Chi Minh trail for the Vietcong—"

A key snapped open the door bolt, startling Charlie. The ancient floorboards in the hallway were so whiney he'd anticipated he would be able to hear a caterpillar's approach. The door popped open, and in sailed the man who introduced himself the other night as Smith, attorney with an expertise in negligence suits against boiler manufacturers. His real name was Dewart, Charlie had learned since. It took a beat to recognize him with the swollen face, which was Drummond's handiwork. As was the right wrist—stabilized now in a splint that permitted him full use of the hand. In the hand was a sound-suppressed SIG Sauer.

"Why would our Special Forces leave ammunition for the Vietcong?" came the reporter's voice. She sounded intrigued.

Dewart pantomimed for Charlie to hang up.

Charlie glanced out the window. A man now stood just below, on the massage parlor roof, apparently inspecting the elevated water tank.

Charlie sighed in dismay. "Listen, I'm sorry to have bothered you," he told the reporter. Over her protest, he ended the call.

"What do you say we go grab a cold one, sport?" Dewart said.

"Gee, that'd be fun," Charlie said.

He followed him out of the room, head lowered in defeat.

Really he was elated. He'd counted on their coming. He wanted them to think he'd gone to ground at an out-of-the-way fleabag. He wanted them to believe he'd gone so far as to plan an escape route to the neighboring building. Hopefully they'd heard every word of his call to the *Washington Post* and accordingly believed he would have spilled the beans if Dewart hadn't broken into the hotel room when he did. In fact, Charlie would have revealed little, if anything, that the reporter couldn't have found in the archives of her own paper. But if the Cavalry thought of Charlie Clark as a bean spiller, they would worry that the call to the *Washington Post* wasn't the extent of it and that their secret could be making its way into the blogosphere now or onto the morning news. So they would question him. And the response he had at the ready would enable him to get to Drummond.

Dewart didn't ask him anything, though. On the way out of the hotel, all he said was, "The car's just up the block."

As he drove them out of Little Odessa, Dewart listened to music on the car radio, humming along. "Silent Night," of all things.

When the song ended, he unpocketed a pill bottle and tipped two white capsules into his mouth. "Your old man did a number on my wrist, I'll tell you that," he said, swallowing the capsules. He chased them with a mouthful of bottled water, then glanced at Charlie. "You've probably done painkillers before, right?"

Ignoring the implication, Charlie shook his head.

Dewart guzzled more water. "The pharmacist said cotton mouth was one of the side effects, but this is ridiculous."

Charlie looked out at Manhattan's sparkling skyscrapers as they began to appear from behind the big dark shapes on Brooklyn's side of the East River. Maybe Dewart was waiting until they reached "Cuba" to ask questions. Or maybe he just lacked the requisite clearance.

Instead of taking either the Williamsburg or the Brooklyn Bridge, the most direct routes to Manhattan, Dewart followed the Brooklyn shoreline north, into a stretch of darkened warehouses and factories. The East River here was notorious as a gangland corpse depository. Charlie began to think he'd wildly miscalculated. He contemplated opening his door and leaping out. With no traffic to contend with, the car was cruising at fifty. To strike the pavement at that speed would be to do Dewart's job for him.

Dewart swung the car toward the Queensboro Bridge's Manhattan-bound ramp. With an eye at the rearview, he said, "Well, if anyone tailed us, they've perfected the invisible car."

Charlie smiled as if amused, but really because he was pleased to be going across the East River rather than into it.

Dewart continued into Manhattan, traversing Central Park at 86th Street. He parked on West 112th, between Broadway and Riverside. By day the block was a ruckus of chatter and honking and boom boxes. Now, at 4:10 A.M., the only signs of life were a gypsy cab prowling for a fare and a few Columbia students who had stayed in town through Christmas break.

Dewart prodded Charlie toward the Perriman Appliances' building. The six-story Georgian postwar was faced with a creamy granite browned by the Manhattan air to match its neighbors, a mid-sized apartment building and a parking garage.

Inside, Perriman was as shoddy as Charlie remembered. Cramped offices surrounded the support staff's network of plastic workstations. The stagnant air smelled of copier toner. The poor souls who answered the phones and tabulated the legitimate end of the business probably hated this place, by design—diminishing the chance that curiosity would lead them downstairs to the moldy basement and over to the grimy utility closet, then down the flight of stairs the "utility closet" opened to.

Charlie and Dewart took precisely that route, arriving in a subbasement nearly as big as a hockey rink. Unlike the basement—which had been stacked with file boxes, worn-out furniture, and old computers no longer worth the expense of hauling away—the subbasement was free of clutter. No reason to maintain the pretence here, Charlie thought.

At the far wall, Dewart pressed a cinder block, which slid aside, revealing a small scanner. He leaned his right eye into its glass screen. A few seconds later, locks within the wall clicked open. A rusty, seven-foot-high ventilation grate swung outward, exposing a bare concrete tunnel two city blocks long and wide and high enough to accommodate a light truck.

Charlie gazed into the facility in awe of its history. He was also terri-fied—the Cavalry's decision to make him privy to it was effectively a statement that they had no intention of letting him leave. More than anything, though, he was glad he'd been right.

7

The eighteen-year-old who would become known in Columbia lore as Poughkeepsie Pete enrolled at the university's School of Engineering in 1990. From his first day on campus, wherever he went, he marveled at the possibility that the hallowed Manhattan Project tunnels might be beneath his feet. Little was known about the complex beyond its role in the Allied victory. Nothing about the offices and laboratories had been declassified. Entry was forbidden. The facility became Poughkeepsie Pete's holy grail.

He learned that in years past, likeminded students had pried their way past boarded-up parts of Furnald Hall's basement, where the famous grocery store had been. Those who made it farthest entered a dark, cement tunnel, empty but for a few wagon-wheel-sized wooden cable spools stamped U.S. ARMY. After a hundred feet, the tunnel dead-ended. The students turned back, generally thrilled at getting as far as they had.

Trying a brand-new tool, the World Wide Web, Pete found a site with a blueprint of the entire complex. Late one night, he snuck past a campus security guard and into the crew team's indoor rowing tank facility, across the quad from Furnald Hall. He easily hammered through what the same Web site had promised would be a thin plaster wall in the basement.

At the back of a defunct boiler room, using a technique also provided by the site, he picked the lock on what appeared to be a closet door. It opened onto a short tunnel at the end of which he discovered a full-sized laboratory, seemingly frozen in time from 1945. The built-in tables and cabinets had been stripped of all equipment and instruments, save a dusty cathode ray tube. The cathode ray tube later drew dozens of awestruck classmates to his dorm room, where he held court with the tale of his experience. For years thereafter, Columbia students dodged campus security guards to visit "Al's," as the lab became known—Al was Albert Einstein.

A second-year medical student from California thought they were fools. Why didn't they find it odd, he asked, that the same Web site that mysteriously provided the blueprint also provided the method to pick the lock? Or that of the hundreds of kinds of locks, the formidable Manhattan Project complex was protected by perhaps the simplest, a basic pin and tumbler? He suspected the laboratory was real, but utilized as a decoy by someone with extensive knowledge of the complex, the aim being to divert students from the relatively mundane tunnel they'd breeched so often in the past. Although the medical student never had given much thought to the Manhattan Project complex before, he found himself unable to stop wondering what was going on there now.

Determined to find out, on Christmas Eve, 1990, at 11:45 P.M., he accessed Furnald Hall's basement by prying open the shaft of an outmoded service elevator and rappelling down. He sprung the old employee washroom door's intricate lock with a quiet surgical drill. Leaving the door ajar, he crept into the tunnel.

The tunnel ended after about a hundred feet at a grimy cinder block wall. He suspected the rusty ventilation grate there, wadded with a half-century's worth of dust, was really a door—the dead end of a tunnel was an odd place for a ventilation grate. If so, the door probably opened with a retinal scanner concealed somewhere. Even if he knew where, the odds were one in 100,000 at best that his eyeball would open it. If he had brought a torch and five or six tubes of acetylene, or a grenade launcher, the odds would have been a bit better. These were still odds, he thought, that the people inside the complex could live with.

He concealed himself in the core of one of the giant cable spools. He planned to stay the entire weekend, during which time he would not eat. He would drink a minimal amount of a citrus beverage he'd made after reading about it in one of his books on desert survival. The beverage was stored in the small rubber bladder he'd sewn onto his backpack. He'd taken preventive measures so that his bodily waste would be limited to urine, discharged into a tube and stored in the rubber bottle secured to his thigh by spandex bicycling shorts. Just being balled up in the cable spool for so many hours might have been torture, but he'd spent three weekends rehearsing in his small clothes closet. Also he viewed self-deprivation as something of a sport.

His plan hinged on his theory that the tunnel's entry door was outfitted with at least one motion sensor. His backpack contained forty-eight small lab rats. At precisely 12:00 A.M., four minutes after his arrival, he sent the first of his rats scurrying out of the cable spool, through the open tunnel door, and into the Furnald basement, where he'd placed a hunk of cheddar cheese. At exactly every hour on the hour thereafter, he sent another rat on the same course. The first rat was meant to simulate the motion of his own departure. The subsequent rats were intended to make whoever was in the Manhattan Project complex conclude that the motion sensor had gone haywire, then come out to do something about it.

At 9:07 the next morning, the ventilation grate swung outward and two men in business suits emerged. The medical student revealed himself to them and owned up to what he'd done. They invited him into the complex. Although not one for emotional displays, he found himself pumping a fist.

While gloomy, the labyrinthine facility dazzled him. Racing the Nazis to develop "the gadget," the Manhattan Project scientists never got around to decorating or even painting the concrete walls. The medical student would learn that when the current occupants moved in, they had no more time or inclination. But in the early '80s, on one of the chaotic August days that Columbia students all arrived on campus, the custodial alley behind Furnald Hall received a truckload of items confiscated by the DEA from a local drug kingpin—tables and chairs and fixtures befitting the Palais de Versailles in jarring combination with furnishings better suited to Las Vegas. Typical of the resulting scheme was the conference room, with an elegant antique Persian carpet and a contemporary black lacquer table inlaid with a shiny soaring hawk rendered in silver, gold, and bronze.

At the head of the table on the morning of December 25, 1990, sat

Drummond Clark, then in his mid-forties. When brought into his stern glare, the medical student considered for the first time that he might be killed.

"We're undecided what to do with you as yet," Drummond said. "Some of my colleagues have suggested that, as a penalty, you have to work here."

And so, after the usual vetting, Nick Fielding joined the Cavalry.

Now, nearly two decades later, Fielding entered the same boardroom and stood at the head of the same hideous conference table. Snowflakes from the 165th Street helipad still glinted on his suit coat. Drummond sat slumped at the foot of the table, in a chair whose scrolled ironwork formed a pattern of diamonds within diamonds. One of its front legs had been bent so that its occupant couldn't get comfortable. This was a trick as old as interrogation. And it wasn't working: Drummond was fast asleep. If not for the handcuff clamping his right wrist to the arm of the chair, he would have slid to the floor.

"Duck?" Fielding said.

Seeming to snap to, Drummond said, "Sorry, it's been a long night."

"How are you feeling?"

"Fine, fine. Yourself?"

"Not so fine. But I'll be better when I find out if you've spilled Placebo."

Drummond looked him over. "Oh, I thought you were the fellow who was here before."

Probably he meant O'Shea, the guard who stood outside the conference room. O'Shea had fair hair like Fielding. He also had fifty more pounds and twenty less years. Fielding was troubled by his mentor's failure to recognize him, but only insofar as he couldn't tell whether it was attributable to illness or artifice.

8

Ventilators the size of jet engines heaved fresh air into the complex. Still, the tunnel from the Perriman subbasement was clammy, the way Charlie imagined a submarine would be. It ended at an ordinary door, through which Dewart ushered him into a stark, concrete hallway lit with fluorescents that caused the walls to shimmer in a dull blue.

In the sporadic dark offices and meeting rooms on both sides, activity was minimal. Charlie saw only a desk chair roll partly into view and a shadow fluctuate just so. His hope that Drummond was still alive rested in large part on the length of time it took to fly an interrogator from the Caribbean to New York. Twice when he tried to ask questions, Dewart shushed him.

Dewart stepped into the employee lounge, an alcove whose amenities included a spotty coffee urn and a refrigerator on which somebody had taped the note THROW OUT OLD MILK. Still clacking a dry tongue, he opened the refrigerator and plucked out a bottle of Gatorade.

"Have a throne," he said to Charlie, indicating a bridge table surrounded, incongruously, by a quartet of high-backed, gilded chairs that could have come from Liberace's dining room. "Coke or something?"

"I'm good," Charlie said. He sank into a velvet-covered cushion.

This was hardly the interrogation upon which his plan hinged.

Dewart plunked his Gatorade onto the table and sat as well. "So there's a small matter I wanted to run by you, Chuck. We have a recording of a cryptic phone call this evening between you and twice-convicted felon Leonid Grudzev, a.k.a. Leo Kuchna and Leo the Terrible. Do you have any interest in explaining this?"

"Well . . ." Charlie said. It was about time.

"*Well,* what?"

"You're not going to be too happy about this."

"I promise you, I'll be a lot less happy if you don't tell me."

"Okay, have it your way. Once Mr. Hattemer was killed, I figured anyone else in this country with the power to help me probably would be having a bad fall down a flight of stairs or something like that. I called Grudzev because he knows people in low places, and I hoped one of those places might be the new KGB."

"The SVR?"

"That's the one. As everyone's favorite philosopher, Sun Tzu, put it, 'My enemy's enemy is my friend.' I figured if the Ivans knew about Placebo, it wouldn't be much of a secret anymore. I know this isn't the ideal solution, but it's more ideal than getting killed because I know the secret myself."

" '*My enemy's enemy*' is an *Arab* proverb," Dewart spat. He jerked Charlie up from his chair, slung him against the refrigerator, and handcuffed him to the adjoining refrigerator and freezer door handles, slapping on the cuffs with more force than necessary. Then he was off; Charlie heard his hurried footfalls long after he'd disappeared down the corridor.

Charlie had misattributed the "enemy's enemy" quote on purpose: it was misdirection, designed to distract attention from his actual intent. His call to the *Washington Post* and his intentionally clumsy cell phone tradecraft also had been misdirection. As Sun Tzu in fact had counseled, "Even though you are competent, appear to be incompetent. Though effective, appear to be ineffective." If Charlie's incompetence act worked, the Cavalry would worry that spilled beans were now rolling toward the Kremlin. Which meant the spooks would hold off neutralizing him or Drummond. And before they determined that Charlie's story was pure fiction, hopefully Leo the Terrible would arrive and shoot the place up.

9

Leonid Kirilovich Grudzev parked an anonymous cargo van on the uptown side of West 112th Street. Through a windshield steamed by their breath, he and his men studied the Perriman Appliances building, trying to plot a way into the Manhattan Project complex.

Breaking into the appliance company offices ordinarily would take a good three days of casing and planning, Grudzev reflected. Doing the whole deal tonight was additionally complicated by the American popped by Charlie Clark. They'd found the kid in the narrow alley behind the sweet shop, gagged and practically mummified from the waist up in twine. He lay unconscious in the back of the van now, the bullet wound much worse than Charlie had estimated. Despite Karpenko's makeshift compresses and other on-the-fly remedies, the life was spilling out of him. Once he died, his retina would start to decay. According to Charlie, if that happened as little as five seconds before they reached the retina scanner at the entrance to the Manhattan Project tunnel, they might as well turn around and go home.

Grudzev tried to hide his worries from his men. "I'm thinking we go in through the little offices on the fourth floor," he said in Russian. Perriman took up the first three of the building's six stories. One-man travel agencies, tarot card readers, and such had the upper floors. Most building managers, in his experience, were lazy, cheap, or both, and put alarms on only the lower two floors, occasionally the third, and sometimes the roof.

"What if somebody sees us and calls nine one one?" said Pyotr from the passenger seat. The onetime Red Army weapons specialist was so tall and burly it was a wonder the van didn't list to his side.

He and Grudzev both turned to the backseat to Veshnijakov, a veteran second-story man everybody called Bill, short for Chernobyl, a reference to his face, badly pitted by childhood acne. Although too old to scale buildings, he still had the wiles, as they say in the old country, to outfox a wolf.

"A couple roach traps ought to solve that," he said.

Grudzev, who considered himself a religious man, muttered a quick prayer, then pressed a few buttons on the intercom panel at the front door of the apartment building that neighbored the office building. As most New Yorkers knew, getting into a locked apartment building in the middle of the night was as simple as hitting enough buttons on the front door panel until a resident intent on getting back to sleep decided he just wanted to shut the buzzer the hell up. Grudzev was thus in the lobby in twelve seconds.

Many of the wall-mounted mailboxes were swollen with mail. No surprise there: It was Christmastime. Affixed to Apartment 4A's box was a note instructing the residents to contact the post office upon their return to receive overflow items.

Grudzev climbed the stairs and knocked on the door to 4A. When no one answered, he slipped on cotton gloves, flicked a torsion wrench and a feeler prong into the lock, then fished around. Thirty seconds later, he was gratified to hear the faint snap of the bolt skipping free of the doorframe.

The apartment was hot and smelled of dust—good signs in terms of occupancy. He groped for the intercom panel and buzzed in Bill, who would admit the others.

The bedroom had been hit by a hurricane of last-minute packing. Stepping over a skirt and a pair of Bermuda shorts that hadn't made the cut, he raised the window and looked out onto the sliver of an alley between the apartment and the office building.

The one-room Globetrotter Travel office would be a short jump. A mist of streetlight outlined a diagonal grid of metal mesh within the pane there: shatterproof glass, the best kind from the burglar's point of view in such a situation. When knocked in properly, a shatterproof pane falls in one piece, as opposed to a regular pane, which rains bits of glass and gets the attention of everyone within a couple of blocks.

When Grudzev felt certain no one was watching, he climbed out the window and onto the ledge. He stepped across the dark alley, touching down firmly on the far ledge.

Police sirens ripped into the night, freezing him, until he gratefully recalled Bill's "roach traps." To cut down the number of cops available to respond to a call here, Bill had dispatched a man to do a torch job in Riverside Park, a block west, and a second man to heave a garbage pail through one of the storefront windows up by Columbia, to which the university's ass-kissing 26th Precinct gave disproportionate attention.

Grudzev kicked the pane as if it were a soccer ball. Other than a dull thud, nothing happened. Undaunted, he tried hitting the glass with an open palm. The entire pane recoiled and plunged into the travel agency, landing with a muted tap on pile carpet. He slid into the office, then beckoned the silhouettes massed at the bedroom window across the alleyway.

Although loaded down by Kevlar and weapons, the men crossed the gap like birds. First Karpenko, then Bill, and finally Pyotr with the unconscious American cradled in his massive arms. Grudzev helped them into the office. He thought the vapor seeping from the American's mouth a beautiful sight.

Habitually wary of building employees working late, Grudzev used gestures to direct his men into the dark hallway and toward the rear stairwell, clearly demarcated by an illuminated sign. They raced down the stairs to the basement, where, beneath the monstrous growl of the furnace, they were free to speak.

Pointing to the utility closet, Grudzev said, "That's where our guy thinks the entrance is."

It wouldn't open, not even when Pyotr tugged.

"We need to find a service box," Bill said.

"Got it." Pyotr pointed to the box ten feet down the dark wall. "But . . ."

The access panel was padlocked shut.

"No problem." Bill drew a can of Freon from his overcoat and sprayed. The lock glistened but nothing more.

With a condescending snort, Karpenko aimed his AK-74 at the lock.

"No, wait, stop!" Grudzev shouted.

Karpenko held his fire, but he didn't lower the gun. Grudzev sought short, simple words to explain to the trigger-happy brute that they'd yet to spot any heat or motion sensors, and that they wanted to postpone announcing their presence to the Manhattan Project complex security guards until the last possible instant. If the guards could be taken by surprise, they would be limited to the weapons on them—likely sticks and stones compared to what the Russians had. Along with a .357 Magnum and a Walther machine pistol designed for close-quarter combat, Grudzev's XXXL leather overcoat concealed an AK of his own with an underbarrel grenade launcher capable of piercing armor two football fields away. Karpenko packed at least as much punch, Bill carried incendiary devices, and Pyotr was a walking arsenal.

Bill said, "Abracadabra" and struck the padlock with the base of the spray can. The frozen lock shattered as if made of porcelain. Grudzev expected Karpenko's face to be red, but the big fool gaped as if he'd witnessed real magic.

Bill opened the service box and pulled the lever inside. The utility closet door sprung outward, revealing a flight of stairs. Ecstatic, Grudzev led the charge down.

There were no lights in the giant subbasement, but the fluorescent ring in the stairwell was enough to reveal the door-sized ventilation grate on the far wall.

"That's gotta be it, yeah?" Grudzev said.

Advancing for a closer look, Bill said, "The plating's awfully thick for a vent."

"That better be it," said Pyotr with uncharacteristic anxiety.

A glance at the young man in his arms explained it: He'd lost color, and his breathing was barely noticeable.

Bill examined the grate. "Did the horses guy have any idea where the scanner is?"

"No, but I'm sure we'll find it," Grudzev said, keeping private his fear that they wouldn't. Studying the huge, essentially featureless room left him at a loss.

"Maybe hidden inside a cinder block, yeah?" Karpenko said, tapping the wall beside the grate.

"Yeah, could be," said Bill. "A pressure-sensitive or spring-loaded deal. But . . ."

The wall was a good twenty meters of cinder blocks. And who was to say the scanner wasn't in one of the other three walls? With no better option, Grudzev began rubbing his palms along the rough, musty cinder blocks. The others followed his lead.

"Probably at eye level," Bill suggested.

Seconds later, Karpenko pressed a cinder block about six up from the floor and the same distance from the left of the grate. The facing hissed sideways, revealing a scanning module like a telescope eyepiece. Grudzev thanked God.

Pyotr took up the American like a puppet, pulled open his right eyelid, and positioned his eye before the scanner. The machine within it whirred, glowing green, then faded back to black. The ventilation grate didn't stir.

Grudzev said of Charlie, "I'm gonna make that cocksucker eat one of these fucking cinder—"

Locks were heard popping open within the wall.

10

The first shot sounded high caliber, like the rounds in battle footage. As the report resounded along the raw cement corridors of the complex, Charlie envisioned a zealous Karpenko brandishing some sort of shoulder-mounted cannon, and he felt like jumping for joy. With his hands cuffed behind him to the handles of the heavy refrigerator and freezer, he could barely move.

More weapons joined in. Among the blasts and jolts, bullets hissed, whined, and pinged off the walls and floors. Things began to pop and shatter, building to one continuous, deafening peal. To Charlie it was a symphony. Lights flickered and a fog of dust rolled into the employee lounge.

Suddenly, as if someone had thrown a switch, the shooting ceased. The complex settled, the familiar hum of the ventilators and fluorescents returned, and the air regained most of its clarity.

Charlie heard someone approaching the employee lounge. He pictured himself momentarily giving Grudzev a bear hug.

Dewart batted through a dust cloud and entered the lounge. His face was streaked with perspiration and blood. A fragment of ceiling tile clung to the back of his neck.

"Hey," he said flatly.

Charlie was too stunned to muster even that much in response.

Dewart uncuffed him from the refrigerator, nudged him aside, and opened the door. He lunged in for a fresh bottle of Gatorade and drained most of it with his first gulp.

Charlie got out, "What happened?"

Dewart wiped his mouth with his sleeve. "We had three men to their four. They had vastly superior weapons. But one of the guards here was alerted in time for us to put a couple of rifles on tripods and wait inside the tunnel entrance. You see, criminals without qualms about nuclear devastation is a key demographic of ours, so one of their men was really one of our men." Dewart flicked a hand at the hallway.

To Charlie's shock, Karpenko appeared, hauling a giant assault rifle. As most PlayStation veterans would have, Charlie recognized the iconic AK-74 fitted with a big-mouthed underbarrel grenade launcher. Despite the burden, Karpenko stood more erect than usual, his jaw no longer jutting and his eyes shining with intelligence in place of the usual demonic possession.

"Fortunately, Charlie Clark, you have qualms about nuclear devastation," Karpenko said. His accent was now no more Russian than Charlie's. "You went to elaborate lengths to convince us you were the new town gossip, but all you really did was give Grudzev vague details. None of his surviving goons know anything of consequence. And now we'll be able to spin it so I can get in with Bernie Solntsevskaya, who's a much greater threat than Grudzev ever was." The past tense slapped Charlie. "Also, the way things worked out, we were able to save Pitman."

Charlie reflected that his rescue mission had amounted to saving the life of a traitor, almost certainly at the cost of his own life. Through a thick gloom, he said, "Super. Let me know if there's anything else I can do."

11

The interior of the Blue Lion Pub was paneled in mismatched sheets of dark wood, all nail-gunned into place, many of them warped. The effect was more utility shed than pub. Alice had chosen the Blue Lion for its view across Broadway onto West 112th. She'd been sitting by herself in a window booth for half an hour, nursing a pint of Guinness while immersed in a copy of the free weekly she'd taken from the pile in the entryway. Or so the wizened barkeep and three solitary drinkers were meant to think.

Really she was using the neon Rolling Rock bottle in the window as camouflage of sorts while watching the Perriman Appliances building. Earlier she'd followed Cranch there from the heliport. The night vision lenses in her otherwise superfluous eyeglasses allowed her to see him admitted from the dark vestibule to the Perriman reception area by a young man who wore a powder-blue Columbia rugby shirt—but probably was no Columbia student. Although baby faced, he had that boxy build indigenous to ex-military contract agents.

Her job now was to determine the right time to send in her backup unit, augmented shortly after Cranch's arrival by sixteen SOCOM weapons and tactical specialists, all of them in dark gray Nomex jumpsuits with body armor vests, Twaron/Kevlar helmets with protective face covering, night-vision goggles, gas masks, and combat steel-reinforced boots. They were armed with either nine-millimeter Heckler & Koch MP5 submachine guns or Remington 870 shotguns. All carried semiautomatic handguns as well. Their tactical aids included a battering ram, flash bang grenades, Stingers, tear gas grenades, and—probably most useful of all—extension poles with mirrors on the ends for looking around corners without putting the looker in the line of fire. If the Clark exfiltration went according to plan, they would need to fire only a couple of paintball guns. The paintballs were packed with oleoresin capsicum, an upmarket pepper spray.

Alice had no expectation that things would go according to plan. In her experience on such ops, Murphy's Law was a good-case scenario. Her "go" order was to be decided by a number of variables and protocols perhaps best summed up, by her backup unit's chief, as "whenever you feel the time's right."

Shortly after the tactical team arrived, she'd watched Fielding enter the vestibule, then use a key to admit himself to the Perriman offices. She itched to send a couple of troops rappelling through a plate glass window and into the rogue's face, but the time still wasn't right.

A few minutes later, a lanky young man who reeked of the Farm prodded in Charlie. Given what Alice had gleaned of his travails, Charlie appeared in great shape. She again refrained from issuing any orders; Drummond still might be en route or somewhere else altogether. Also, she could afford to hold off because Cranch needed time for his act.

When four men parked a van, studied Perriman as if casing the place, then broke into the neighboring apartment building carrying a fifth man who appeared to be unconscious, she still lacked sufficient cause to order in her team. Upon hearing faint but unmistakable bursts of AK fire, however, a vegetable would have known it was time.

"It's Desdemona with a green light," she said into her cell.

"Desdemona, we've just been ordered to go home," came the voice of her backup unit's chief.

"You're kidding? By who? Nick Fielding?"

"Yes, as a matter of fact, on conference with the interim national security advisor."

"What about our cable to HQ?"

"Pending investigation by the inspector general. Meanwhile, our top brass were briefed by the director of the CIA and now they're basically telling us, 'Yeah, Nick Fielding's *supposed* to be a bad guy—it's his cover.' "

Alice was incredulous. "Great, he'll probably win an award," she said.

Before she could begin to ask any of the questions flooding her mind, the bell on the pub's entry door jingled. Two young men in Columbia sweatshirts strolled in.

"Hang on," she whispered into the phone. "Looks like a couple of boys are about to hit on me."

Sure enough, the young men wandered toward her booth. They wore no coats though the night was arctic. In all probability, she thought, she'd been hit-listed at Echelon or the like. They'd rushed from wherever they'd been lurking when she made her cell phone call.

"We need to talk, Ms. Rutherford," said the stouter of the two.

"Sorry, angel, you got the wrong girl."

"It's okay, Alice, we work for the same uncle you do."

She believed him. The issue was the thinner man's hand, inching past his hip and toward the back of his waist.

"I'm not Alice Rutherford, but I'm looking for her," she said. "I'm Rita Hayworth-Thomas, with National Recon. Here's my ID." She flung a cardboard coaster.

Hardly an air-cushioned Bicycle, it wobbled in flight. It slapped the thinner man in the wrist, barely inhibiting him as he drew a silenced SIG Sauer. But it caused a slight delay, allowing her to loose the Beretta from her shoulder bag and fire first. Her bullet hit his knee as he fired. He fell into the next booth, vanishing behind the high seat back. His round bored past her shoulder and into the top of her seat back, creating a cloud of sawdust.

The other man produced a SIG as well. She shot at him while diving for the cover of the bar. When she came down, her head exploded—or felt like it had. The world began to fade. Just before it went black, she glimpsed the barkeep standing over her, gripping a baseball bat.

12

Fielding sat in one of the comfortable Naugahyde recliners in the observation room, puffing a Señora Dominguez cigar. On the other side of the two-way mirror, at the head of the conference room table, Cranch was getting started. His white lab coat, usually crisp and immaculate, was rumpled. He'd traveled for much of the night, first in the vintage motor launch, which made him seasick; then for three turbulent hours in a small jet; and finally in a helicopter buffeted by a snowstorm. Still, he radiated energy and enthusiasm. He would have flown to the moon on his own dime, Fielding supposed, for the opportunity to crack Drummond Clark.

Drummond was still handcuffed to the theoretically uncomfortable chair at the foot of the conference table. A pneumographic tube had been fitted around his chest to measure his respiration rate, a cuff had been inflated around his left bicep to gauge his blood pressure and pulse, and galvanometers had been clamped onto two of his fingers to detect sweat gland activity. The sensors were wired into Cranch's laptop computer, which was linked to a monitor in the observation room.

"Do you know why you're here, Mr. Clark?" Cranch asked.

"No, but someone said this is the Manhattan Project complex. I'd very much like to see it."

"You've never seen it?"

"No, will I need a ticket?"

Fielding glanced at his monitor. The polygraph registered no deception.

"Actually, I was hoping to ask you about Placebo," Cranch said.

"Placebo?"

"The covert operation. Do you know of it?"

"No."

Again, as far as the polygraph could determine, Drummond's response was truthful.

"If you don't mind, Mr. Clark, I need to ask a few meaningless questions, just to make sure this system is properly calibrated. Could you tell me, please, what year it is?"

"1995."

The yellow, red, and green lines running across Fielding's monitor were identical to those of the previous responses.

"Actually, Mr. Clark, 1995 was a little while ago," Cranch said. "Of course everybody forgets the date now and then, right?"

Drummond sighed. "Tell me about it."

"Actually, it's 2004."

"Oh, right, of course."

"I mean, 2009."

"Oh, right, right, right."

"Excuse me for a moment," Cranch said.

He signaled, and O'Shea opened the door, letting him out. He disappeared into the maze of corridors. A moment later, he trudged into the observation room.

"It's no act," he told Fielding.

"I'm not so sure," Fielding said. "If you hook me up to the poly, I can explain in great detail how purple two-headed men from Pluto and I traveled from another time and shot JFK, and it would read as gospel truth. A number of us can temper our responses that way." He pointed through the mirror. "*He* was our teacher."

"This isn't an issue of true or false," Cranch said. "It's been proven that even subjects with the utmost training and ability respond on some level to meaningful stimuli more vigorously than to nonmeaningful stimuli. If the senility is artifice, and I say something he purports to know nothing about at random, he has no time to ready his defenses. If the information is meaningful to him, like the current year, the polygraph detects it; 2009 read as no more meaningful to him than 1995. If he'd known that it was in fact 2009 . . ." Cranch sank into one of the recliners.

"Okay, so he isn't lucid—where does that leave us?" Fielding asked, even though Cranch's deflated look alone probably provided the answer.

"He won't be able to answer our questions."

"Well, I certainly wouldn't mind sitting here in this comfortable chair and enjoying my cigar until he blinks on. The one little hitch is he may have written down details compromising our *entire operation*—then placed what he wrote in a dead drop somewhere between here and Virginia, to be serviced any minute by God knows who. Isn't there something you can pump into him so we have a chance of finding out at least that much?"

Cranch shrugged. "Even if we were to penetrate his defenses with an absolutely perfect combination of sodium amytal and thiopental or secobarbital, we'd be asking for information he's incapable of retrieving, whether he wants to or not. Also, because methedrine—or a comparable stimulant—is a necessary component in a truth cocktail, we'd risk ratcheting him to acutely confusional on a permanent basis."

Fielding took a long drag of his cigar. He barely tasted it. "I don't suppose there's anything on earth—no contraption, no holistic remedy, no prehistoric fish extract—that can spark lucidity?"

"Not really," Cranch said.

Fielding saw a glimmer of hope. " 'Not really' is different from 'no,' isn't it?"

Cranch's lips tightened. "It was done. Once. In 1916."

"*1916?* By who, Dr. Frankenstein?"

"A Dr. Lovenhart at the University of Wisconsin. He was experimenting with respiratory stimulants, and to his amazement, a catatonic patient, after being injected with sodium cyanide, opened his eyes and answered a few basic questions. It was the first time he'd said a word in months. But immediately thereafter, due to complications inherent with sodium cyanide, he dropped dead."

Fielding stabbed his cigar into the ashtray. "Good, now we have a Plan D."

"There are other, more conventional methods," Cranch said with enthusiasm, but it felt synthetic. "We can try making him comfortable. Playing music has been shown to reduce stress hormones in the blood, which has a tranquilizing effect on the limbic system. Reflexology can—"

"Sorry, I don't see Charlie Clark rubbing his old man's feet."

"Why would Charlie have to do it?"

"That's a very good question," Fielding said. "For two months, Duck was a zombie. But since Charlie's entry onto the scene, he's been Mr. Lucidity."

Cranch looked away, probably to hide his skepticism. "Are you hypothesizing that a professional horseplayer has become the first person in medical history to discover a means of triggering lucidity in an Alzheimer's patient?"

Fielding leaped up. "I knew I had a reason for letting him live."

13

"**So how** do you do it?" Fielding asked.

Charlie had reached the same conclusion science had: There was no precise trigger. But if he could convince them he had the silver bullet, he would likely be taken from the employee lounge to Drummond.

"As I'm sure you know, Alzheimer's sufferers are triggered by family members they haven't seen in a while," Charlie said.

Across the table, Fielding shook his head. "Possibly that explains his mild resurgence at the senior center, when he saw you for the first time in two years. But since then, you've been old hat, otherwise he would have flickered on every time you opened your mouth. Tonight, when I told him that you were here, all it sparked was, 'What's he doing up so late on a school night?' "

"I guess you're right." Charlie hadn't expected getting to Drummond would be that easy. Also, getting to Drummond wasn't enough. Charlie needed to work it so he could get a weapon to Drummond too, or at least get one within Drummond's reach. He cupped his chin in his hands now, trying to appear contemplative. "I guess it has been, mostly, random."

Fielding sat up. "*Mostly?* So then there *is* a kiss that turns the frog back?"

"I'm ashamed to say it."

"Pretend there's a gun to your head."

"Well . . . I'm a disappointment to him, to say the least. You know, he graduated from MIT with a crateful of awards. I barely made it through a year of college. He's a patriot and a hero. I play the horses, and not that well. He's the fastest gun in the East. I'd never even used a gun until yesterday, and the times I needed to, it was a disaster. At best, I was too shaky to shoot straight. Up on the ridge tonight—or last night, I guess it was—he flickered on and snatched the gun away from me just in time to shoot that meth guy—then he led us down the mountain like a Sherpa. When we were attacked at that battlefield, he was napping. I couldn't defend us. Suddenly he grabbed the gun from me and figured out a way for us to escape. While I sat there cowering, he said, 'There's nothing so exhilarating as being shot at without result.' "

"It's Winston Churchill," Fielding said. "I've heard him recite that one before." He sat back, interlacing his fingers behind his head—not the posture of a man who had just seen the light or otherwise had been convinced. "I want to share something with you, Charlie. In all of the years I worked for Duck, he mentioned you just three or four times, and all he ever said was that you were good at math. But I knew a few things about you anyway. One was you always avoided the disagreeable or difficult in life, finding refuge at the racetrack, for instance. Another was you considered seeing him one day a year, on Christmas, to be one day too often. Yet now, lo and behold, you're false flagging Red *Mafiya* thugs, pretending to go to ground at a nowhere fleabag, and blabbing to the *Washington Post* to induce us to capture you, then launching a veritable paramilitary assault on the Manhattan Project complex, all in an effort to rescue your not-so-beloved father. Meanwhile you could have gotten away with a small fortune in cash and diamonds, and millions on top of that if you know where he's squirreled his stock options hoard, as I suspect you do. So I have to conclude something's changed."

Charlie wasn't sure where Fielding was headed. "Maybe he and I got off on the wrong foot for the first thirty years," he allowed.

Fielding stood. "He had us fooled all these years. Everyone always thought that all that mattered to Drummond Clark was getting revenge against his crazy pinko parents. But in the past two days, he's shown something else mattered to him. He showed it with his episodes of lucidity. Each was triggered when his son was in harm's way."

Fielding had hit the nail on the head. Charlie felt it. He felt terrible, too, that he'd failed to see it himself. And he suspected he was about to feel a lot worse.

14

Charlie lay on his back lengthwise atop the conference room table, his wrists and ankles bungeed to its legs. He'd been stripped to his boxer shorts. Most of his skin was covered in goose bumps, and not because he was cold. It was a reaction to the telephone on the chair to his left, a rotary device that could well have been in the complex since the '40s. The cord was plugged into the wall, not at a phone jack but at an electrical outlet. In place of the usual coil and handset was a rubber wire that hissed subtly, like an asp. The ghoul in the lab coat they called Dr. Cranch loomed over Charlie and dipped the copper mouth of the wire toward his face.

"This will deliver a near-lethal amount of electrical current," Cranch said to Drummond, who was handcuffed to the chair at the foot of the table.

"A placebo is used as a control in drug experiments," Drummond said, the fifth time he'd done so since Charlie was brought in, each time with greater distress.

"Sir, we need to hear about Placebo, the operation," Cranch said, "or, more specifically, whom you've told about it." Repetition had progressively deadened his delivery.

"I just don't know what else I can tell you." Drummond sighed.

Charlie wondered whether his rescue effort possibly could have made things any worse than they were now.

"Just a light spray," Cranch said to Dewart, who sat to Charlie's right.

Dewart gave a gentle pull at the trigger of a plastic plant mister. The water was warm, yet the droplets caused Charlie's bare legs to shiver.

Cranch touched the copper tip of the wire to Charlie's right thigh briefly, as if he were testing the ink in a pen. The tip emitted a buzz no louder than a gnat.

Charlie shot straight into the air. If not for the restraints, it seemed, he would have hit the ceiling. Hot, maddening pain filled his blood vessels, and his body began to convulse. It felt like muscles and tendons were being ripped from bones. An involuntary wail rose from deep within him, unlike any sound he would have imagined he could make, or that any animal could.

A velvety blackness materialized around him. A cool and comfy refuge. Unconsciousness. He welcomed it.

Before he could settle in, his spine cracked back onto the tabletop, and he was again in the fierce glare of fluorescent lights. All his joints felt like they'd been dislocated. He tried to breathe. He retched, then inhaled air hot and heavy with the smell of his own burned flesh. His body settled, but a thrum continued inside his temples. Bells rang in his ears. The worst was the stinging in his eyes. Some sort of lingering electrical current?

Cranch and Dewart looked at Drummond, presumably for his reaction. He stared at his shoes as if he sought to avoid seeing his son suffer.

"Please, just talk to Mr. Cleamons," Drummond begged Cranch. "I have his home number in my office."

Cranch looked to Dewart. "Cleamons?"

Dewart shrugged. "We'll find out." He gestured at the two-way mirror: Make a phone call.

Charlie knew who Cleamons was but didn't see how mentioning it would do any good—even if he could move his mouth. Also, they would know soon enough. Lionel Cleamons had been Perriman's district sales manager. He dropped dead one afternoon in his office more than a decade ago.

15

Charles would die, Drummond speculated, if the man in the white laboratory coat used the crude stun device a second time. The younger fellow, to Drummond's left, seemed inclined to do nothing about it. He just sat back sipping Gatorade.

Drummond wondered: Who are these men? Gamblers Charles has fallen in with?

No, something told him. This had to do with his own work.

He recalled passing his office at Perriman Appliances earlier, then being led down the back stairs to this subterranean facility.

The Manhattan Project complex was rumored to extend beneath the Columbia campus as far as West 112th Street, where Perriman was situated.

Or was it on *East* 112th Street?

Yes, East, he decided.

He'd worked there a long time.

How long, five years?

No, more than that. Eighteen. No, no, no, twelve.

He demonstrated the appliances in the showroom, then went on-site with building owners and property managers. He ensured that their specifications were met.

The man in the laboratory coat kept asking about "Placebo." Maybe it was a code for something new in R & D. The new nanotechnology in the wash and rinse cycles? Probably not. Nanotechnology was already trumpeted throughout Perriman's advertising and promotional campaigns.

Could the Manhattan Project have something to do with it?

Manhattan Project . . .

At Columbia University.

Columbia University was originally called King's College. The name was changed for reasons of patriotism after the American Revolution . . .

Which commenced on April 19, 1775 . . .

The shot heard 'round the world . . .

At the Old North Bridge in Concord, Massachusetts . . .

An interesting piece of information about Concord—

Drummond felt his thought process derailing.

It was hard to concentrate to begin with. And Charles's scream still resonated within him.

It reminded him of another scream.

The memory began with dawn, as if beamed from a old film projector, sputtering through the blinds and into the drafty waiting room in the maternity ward at Brooklyn's Kings County Hospital. Drummond was sitting there alone, savoring the silence. For most of the night, the waiting room had been a hive of expectant fathers. Nurses had brought bundles one by one. Each man, seeing his son or daughter for the first time, declared the moment the happiest of his life. Drummond anticipated no such sentiment. He wasn't bent toward giddiness. But that was only a small factor: 2 percent, he estimated. The other 98 percent was fear.

That he felt fear at all was confounding. Displacing fear was second nature to him.

He'd been timid initially, as a boy, a voracious early reader living a largely internal life. But when his parents fled the country without him and a spinster aunt capitulated and took him in, he commenced a campaign to prove his worth. He drove himself to be first in his class, first in his weight group, first at anything—if he found himself walking parallel to a stranger on the sidewalk, he would be first to the corner. He would even finish his ice cream cone before other children. Winning intoxicated him; the greater the challenge, the greater the high. By his first day at Langley, perilous situations practically whetted his appetite.

On learning Isadora was pregnant, however, he felt standard-issue fear, like anyone else's. He was at a loss to explain it. He hungered to succeed as a parent, especially in light of his own parents' record.

In the ensuing months he sought a remedy. The problem, he theorized, was his lack of enthusiasm for the baby—he couldn't summon so much as a spark. Attributing this to insufficient data, he read everything on the subject. The only applicable wisdom he found, repeatedly, was *"If he can afford it, the new father is wise to hire a baby nurse."*

Now, with just hours to go, he was scared as a cat.

The squeal of crepe soles in the hallway outside the waiting room momentarily diverted him from his predicament. Probably it was the nurse coming to update him on Isadora's status. "Another few hours still," she would say—he hoped.

She entered with a swaddled bundle in her arms. "Mr. Clark, it is my great honor to introduce you to your son," she said. She had delivered the line to new fathers thousands of times, but the joy was fresh, and augmented by a particularly musical Indian accent—Gujarati, he was certain of it.

He had thought learning that the baby was a boy might stir him. It made no difference. And the squirming, tomato-headed creature itself kindled none of the love at first sight on which he'd pinned his last atom of hope. If anything, the sight validated his fears.

"Would you like to hold him?"

He put on exuberance. "Of course!"

His arms became stiff as shelves, and on contact with them, the baby began a cry that might have been mistaken for an air-raid siren.

"This is just wonderful," Drummond exclaimed; he could spew lies at a poly and leave examiners swearing he was the second coming of Abraham Lincoln.

Registered Nurse Aashiyana Asirvatham, however, did not appear to be fooled. "It's time for baby's bath," she said, offering Drummond an out.

As soon as the baby was safely away, strangely, Drummond felt a desire to hold him again. Within a few weeks that desire exploded into a dizzying love. Ironically, his challenge became keeping a lid on the sentiment, lest his enemies exploit it.

The memory had the effect of turning night into day in his mind as he sat in Conference Room A at the foot of the table originally crafted for the Jersey City narcotics dealer known as Catman because of his fondness for leopard skin.

Drummond sat up slightly to better get the lay of the land. He maintained the appearance of staring dully. Even if he could get his hand free of the cuff, he would need to grapple immediately with young Dewart, who almost certainly had a sidearm. The guard standing outside the door, onetime IRA heavy Jack O'Shea, would be in the room within five seconds, his own firearm drawn. And of course Cranch had the "hellephone," as everyone here liked to call the torture device. Drummond's own prospective weapons included the chairs and table, though the latter would be too heavy to budge even without Charles atop it. Also within reach were three dry-erase markers, a half-full bottle of Gatorade, and a plastic plant mister, the last item probably purchased at the twenty-four-hour DrugMart at West 110th and Broadway specifically for use with Cranch's device—to Drummond's knowledge, the plants in the Manhattan Project complex were all plastic.

The Gatorade had promise.

16

"**You've left** me with no choice but to increase the voltage to a level he may not survive," Cranch told Drummond.

Charlie craned his neck—the simple act felt like being choked—and glimpsed the interrogator tweaking the rotary dial on the telephone.

Drummond's eyes were glassy and rimmed red. He sucked a finger, as if to pacify himself. He'd never done that before, and, Charlie reckoned, never would, given the unsanitary nature. So maybe he had something in the works. Also, albeit slightly, he had sat up. But where the flicker of hope should have been, Charlie felt nothing. What could Drummond Clark, even at the height of his powers, do to get out of this fix?

"How about this?" Drummond asked Cranch. "By 'placebo operation,' is it possible that your people mean a medical operation performed more for the psychological benefit of the patient than for any physiological effect?"

Cranch sighed.

"Can you at least give me some sort of hint?" Drummond pleaded.

Cranch gestured and Dewart pumped the plant mister five or six times. Charlie's chest glistened. Cranch moved the tip of the wire toward Charlie's heart.

Charlie tried to will himself into unconsciousness.

Drummond sat upright in his chair, abruptly, as if *he* had been shocked. Cranch jumped in surprise. Dewart nearly lost hold of his Gatorade. Like Charlie's, their eyes flew to Drummond.

Drummond took in the room with unmistakable sharpness. "Ernie, why are we interrogating my son?" he asked Cranch. His voice was ragged, like he'd just risen from a long slumber.

Each time he'd flickered on before, Charlie recalled, it was with an awareness of the immediate past. So the Rip van Winkle act was almost certainly an act. But to what end?

Drummond tried to rub his eyes. The cuff snapped his hand back into place. "Or should I be asking, 'Why are you interrogating me?' "

"First, allow me to say that I'm flattered you remember me, sir," Cranch said.

"Dr. Ernest Cranch, you come happily to mind every single time I look in a mirror to shave and see no scar whatsoever from that Croatian hooligan's blade. Now, what is going on here?"

"There's an urgent need that we know whether and to what extent Placebo has been compromised."

Drummond seemed shaken. "Placebo has been compromised?"

"If you could tell us what you last recall of it?" Cranch said.

"Yes. Of course. Tell me, what's today's date?"

"The twenty-eighth."

"Forgive me. Of which month?"

"Forgive *me,* I should have begun there. It's December 28, 2009."

"Good Lord," Drummond exclaimed. "The last I remember, the leaves had just begun to fall."

Cranch's eyes drifted to the rotary telephone, leaving Charlie with a fresh coating of goose bumps. "Mr. Clark, please," Cranch said. "You've had several clear-cut and extensive episodes of lucidity since autumn. Per my clinical experience with Alzheimer's patients, I would expect—"

He stopped abruptly as Dewart slid from his chair, fell hard to the floor, and didn't move.

Charlie supposed either the pain or the painkillers had gotten the better of Dewart. Then the Gatorade bottle rolled from Dewart's hand, and Charlie had a better idea of what had happened: Drummond had just pretended to suck his finger as a means of pacifying himself. Really he tripped the spring-loaded release on his molar and, with incredible sleight of hand, while feigning focus on his shoes, he deployed his L pill. Once Dewart sipped the Gatorade, Drummond stalled until the saxitoxin took effect!

Cranch too eyed the rolling Gatorade bottle, possibly thinking the same thing. The thickest part of Drummond's iron seat back flew into the interrogator's head, crushing his skull from the sound of it.

With the cumbersome chair still cuffed to his wrist, Drummond dove at Dewart's body and snatched the Glock from the dead man's waistband. Bouncing up, he swung the chair as hard as he could into the mirror. The glass exploded like a bomb, spraying thousands of bits into the adjoining observation room.

From his seat in one of the recliners there, Karpenko rushed to take up his big AK-74. Two thunderclaps from Drummond's Glock and Karpenko keeled over, spouting a rooster tail of blood. He fell into the recliner, flipped it over, then came to rest onto its upturned swivel base, almost certainly dead.

A third report from the Glock and the fair-haired guard, surging into the conference room from the hallway, fell as if clotheslined. Blood streamed from his forehead, turning the front of his powder-blue rugby shirt maroon. He was definitely done for. Still Drummond pounced on him. He retrieved a set of keys from the guard's pants pocket, freed himself from the handcuff, then hurried to unbind Charlie.

Incredulity acted as a pain remedy for Charlie. "Good thing I came to the rescue," he said.

The observation room preoccupied Drummond. Charlie followed Drummond's gaze to the smoldering cigar in an ashtray on the arm of one of the empty recliners. The door was open.

"Fielding?" Charlie said.

"Yes."

"Why didn't he shoot back?"

"In his mind, what happened here is a positive step. Now the real inquisition can begin."

17

Drummond took the slain guard's pistol and, leading with it, inched out of the conference room. With leaden limbs, Charlie followed, still clad only in boxer shorts—there hadn't been time to locate the rest of his clothes. The chill of the cement floor bit into his bare soles and shot up his shinbones.

"We'll sneak out through the old east tunnel, to the university campus," Drummond said. "Less chance of running into guards."

The corridor was still and quiet, save the drone of the ventilators. The bare concrete walls meant no recesses or shadows in which an adversary could hide; a mouse would have stood out.

"I need you to cover me," Drummond said, passing back the Glock.

"I'll try," said Charlie. He took the gun with both hands, judging just one frail hand inadequate.

If Fielding or his remaining men were to shoot, they would likely position themselves at one of four corners—there were two corners at each end of the corridor. Charlie pivoted on his numb heels, swinging the gun barrel from one end of the corridor to the other, a motion like a metronome's. He wasn't sure whether it was a good system.

Drummond ran west, or so Charlie thought; his bearings had been scrambled along with the rest of him. He was certain, though, that the tunnel to campus was to the east.

Drummond beckoned from the corner, and Charlie sprinted. Concern that they were headed in the wrong direction took his mind off the pain.

Nearing Drummond, he asked, "Isn't the campus the other—?"

Drummond shot a finger to his lips. "I said that in case anyone was listening," he whispered. "Really we'll go out through the tunnel to the Perriman subbasement."

Again he was on the move, with Charlie left to supply cover fire. The next corridor was identical to the last, with the exception of a six-foot-high metal canister imbedded in the wall. Drummond stopped at it and signaled Charlie.

As Charlie reached him, Drummond pressed his right eye into the scanning module mounted on the wall beside the canister. A laser hummed within it.

Charlie wondered whether the Cavalry had taken Drummond off the guest list. Perhaps while shooting at him throughout the woods and mountains of Virginia all day and night, they hadn't considered the chase would wind up back at the office. The answer came with a hydraulic hiss, as the canister rotated, presenting a compartment like that of a revolving door.

Drummond ushered Charlie in, then crammed in alongside him. The cylinder began to rotate again, groaning beneath their weight. The compartment was sealed by the circular wall, plunging them into total darkness. Halfway around, it reopened onto a galaxy of luminous dials, gauges, and displays. When the compartment was completely open, the conveyance stopped with a mechanical grunt.

Drummond reached out and swatted at a wall panel. Rows of lamps high overhead tingled on, revealing a white rubber-walled laboratory the size of a gymnasium. "For reasons that will become apparent straightaway, this is known as the laundry room," he said, at normal volume.

Charlie followed him into a cityscape of gleaming machines and ducts. He recognized centrifuges, condensers, incubators, and robotic arms; there were exponentially more gadgets whose functions he couldn't guess. On the back wall was a garage door big enough to allow through the motorized pallet truck parked beside it. By Charlie's reckoning this door opened onto the tunnel to Perriman's subbasement. He assumed the door was their destination.

Drummond stopped well short of it, at a row of washing machines. "I don't think we'll be able to sneak out or even gun our way out of here," he said. "But if we arm one of these devices, then threaten to detonate it by remote control, Fielding will let us waltz out; he may even call us a car."

"I thought these don't really do anything."

"The uranium doesn't do anything, but the systems still operate like nuclear weapons insofar as they initiate with ninety-seven-point-eight pounds of penthrite and trinitrotoluene. That would be enough to blast apart a good percentage of this complex."

"Sounds good to me, unless it's at all hard to arm a nuclear weapon."

"Yes and no." Drummond popped open the top-loading lid of a Perriman Pristina model.

Inside, where clothing would go, was a cluster of electrical components. Unlike the nuclear weapons Charlie had seen in movies, this one had no display panel with illuminated digits that ticked down to 00:00. There was just a cheap, battery-powered alarm clock, held in place by what appeared to be wadded bubble gum.

Leaning into the machine, Drummond rummaged through a jungle of wires and tubes and cleared a path to three numeric dials, like those on safes. "These are permissive action links," he explained. "In the Soviet Union, this sort of weapon would have been armed by three men, each knowing just one third of the code."

"What if, hypothetically, you've forgotten the code?"

"If I input the wrong code more than twice, a capacitor will fry, leaving the system unable to detonate," Drummond said. "But we don't need to worry about my memory for once." He pointed to a card adhered to the washer's instrument panel, listing make, model, and energy usage information. From its base he peeled a strip of yellow tape imprinted with a sequence of one- and two-digit numbers. "This serial number's not the actual serial number." Carefully he maneuvered the first dial into place, then began on the second.

Charlie's eyes bounced between the cylindrical entryway and the garage door, anticipating Fielding and company would at any second send one or the other blasting inward.

"Okay, done, except for the clicker." Drummond jogged toward a tool cabinet across the room. "While I find it, why don't you put on a uniform?" He indicated a hanger rack of royal blue Perriman Appliances repairmen's coveralls. On the floor were pairs of rubber boots. "You'll be conspicuous in it once we're out of the complex but not as much as in what you have on now." He meant Charlie's boxers.

As Charlie dressed, a staccato movement sucked his eyes back to the bomb. The second hand on the alarm clock was ticking counterclockwise. Every hair on his body shot up.

"Dad!"

"Sorry, should have mentioned that. I'm intentionally running the timer down to about ninety seconds—too little time for them to retrieve the PAL sequence from the computers and dial in the numbers in reverse, to disarm the device." Drummond crumpled the strip of yellow tape with the "serial number" into a ball no bigger than a pea, then dropped it through a drain grate. "But it will be plenty of time for us to trigger the device, if it comes to that, then get out of harm's way." From the tool cabinet, he dug out what appeared to be a TV remote control. Aiming it at the washing machine, he pressed a button. The conic bulb on the gadget's head glowed red.

The second hand on the alarm clock ticked to a stop at the 6. The hour hand was slightly left of the 12 and the minute hand pointed halfway between the 10 and the 11.

"Ninety seconds on the nose," he said with satisfaction.

Charlie mopped perspiration from his brow. "After all we've been through, it would be a shame to die of a heart attack."

Drummond smiled. "Well, what do you say we go for a boat ride?"

18

The laundry room's garage door rumbled up, revealing the midpoint of the two-block-long tunnel between the heart of the Manhattan Project complex and the Perriman subbasement. Charlie braced for men waiting in ambush. He saw only an empty tunnel. The floor twinkled with flecks of the fluorescent bulbs shattered earlier by bullets.

Drummond pointed to the end leading into the subbasement. "I'll cover you from here until you're safely through the door."

"Won't I need your retina to open the door?"

"On this side, all you'll need to do is use the handle. You'll trip a sensor though, so they'll be onto us, if they aren't already."

"But if I'm inside the subbasement, how can I cover you?"

"You can't, not over the length of the tunnel. That's where the clicker comes in. The big red detonator button is pressure sensitive. If I'm shot, or, for whatever reason, I fall and lose my grip on the clicker, the sequence initiates and can only be reversed manually on the bomb. They won't risk that."

"See you in the subbasement then," Charlie said, the bravado intended to mask his foreboding: This was the most treacherous block he would ever travel.

He reached the end of the tunnel without incident. A simple turn of the handle unlocked the door, and it opened with a gentle push. Holding his gun ahead of him, the way Drummond did, he edged into the silent subbasement.

If not for the fluorescent ring in the stairwell, he would have been unable to see. The scant light silhouetted three splayed bodies, pools of blood glinting around each. He recognized Grudzev's sloped face. The Russian's AK-74 rig was propped against the back of his head like a grave marker. If Charlie had had time, he would have been sick.

He turned back to the door, still partway open, as Drummond emerged with caution from the laundry room. Sudden motion at the other end of the tunnel froze them both.

The door there opened and Fielding entered the tunnel along with two equally solemn guards, both pointing large rifles at Drummond.

Drummond raised his hands. "I'm holding a pressure key to one of the Pristinas," he called to them. He stood a full city block away from Charlie—as well as from Fielding and the guards—but the tunnel's acoustics were such that it sounded as if he were just halfway down a typical hallway.

Fielding leaned an eye into a rifle scope. Two blocks away, Charlie could hear the rattle of the rifle's shoulder strap. Fielding muttered something, both men lowered their guns, then he said to Drummond, "There's no need for this to get unpleasant."

"Then have a pleasant evening, Nicholas." Drummond turned and began walking toward Charlie at a swift pace, though not too swift to jeopardize his hold on the clicker.

"I have some news for you first," Fielding said. Drummond didn't slow. "At the top of the hour, a Department of Transportation camera snapped an image of Patrick Bragg, captain of the stern dragger *Sea Dog*. He was removing a vinyl pouch with a Chevrolet logo on it from beneath a sidewalk plate in Grand Army Plaza; five minutes earlier, another man had placed it there. According to the accident report, Captain Bragg subsequently stepped into the path of a van that jumped a red light. He was killed instantly."

Drummond's eyes darkened, but he said nothing and continued toward Charlie.

"For argument's sake, let's say his death was necessary," Fielding went on. "The argument is there are too many frightening characters out there who need to believe that Drummond Clark is a relatively humdrum appliance salesman as opposed to a spymaster. If you're aboard the SS *International Fugitive,* word could get around, and those characters would start asking questions the United States of America would prefer they do not—and that's assuming you haven't already sketched out the whole operation for them. So I'll ask you now to bear in mind the oath you took to obey the orders of those above you in the chain of command—in this instance our interim national security advisor in Washington—and stand down."

Charlie expected Drummond to whirl back and point out that such an order would never have been issued had the interim national security advisor known that Fielding had murdered the prior national security advisor in cold blood.

All Drummond said was, "Nicholas, I'll ask you to either respect my most basic right or suffer the consequences." He was now a short dash from Charlie—fifty feet at most, a difficult shot now for the men at the other end of the tunnel.

"What about you, Charlie?" Fielding called over Drummond. "There must be something you want? How about I erase Mickey Ramirez's wife from the loose ends list?"

Charlie's heart strings were wrenched. "She just had a baby."

Fielding shrugged. "That happens."

Charlie suspected Fielding would erase Sylvia one way or the other. "There is one thing I want," he said.

"Yes?"

"To be a witness at your trial."

"Okay, then we've run into a wall." Fielding struck a match and lit a cigar. "As it were." He exhaled smoke toward a gunmetal gray plate on the ceiling.

The peal of an alarm bell filled the complex.

"Shit!" Drummond said.

Charlie had never heard him curse.

Drummond held the clicker tight against his belly, took three running strides, then dove for the subbasement. Charlie crouched like a shortstop in order to best haul him in.

Steel slats cascaded from the ceiling, hammering the tunnel floor between Charlie and Drummond with a ringing echo, then forming a solid firewall. There were no discernible gaps between the slats themselves, or between the slats and the tunnel walls and floor. Charlie threw a shoulder. The firewall gave a millimeter, if that, with a condescending clink. "There's got to be a hand crank or some hinge we can shoot?" he said through the wall, even though he was fairly certain the solution was nowhere near that simple; Drummond had cursed after all.

"The motor is inside the blast-proof frame, almost certainly remotely operated. This must be new." Drummond's face appeared at the small view hole, a six-by-six-inch tempered glass and metal-mesh square at head level. His eyes showed defeat. Another first. "Listen, Charles. Fielding knows I won't detonate the device while we're both down here. He's sent his men out the east way, to campus."

Through the view hole, Charlie saw that Fielding now stood alone at the far end of the tunnel, a departed guard's rifle in his hands. Once the guards crossed Broadway to the Perriman offices, they would flank Charlie, robbing Drummond of his leverage.

"So now what?" Charlie asked.

"You need to run."

Although he knew he'd heard correctly, Charlie felt he'd missed something. "What about you?"

"I'll stay here and detonate the device," Drummond said. "Fielding won't expect that."

Charlie's body temperature plummeted. "Of course he won't. It's crazy!"

Drummond's calm dissolved into discomfiting urgency. "There's no way we can both make it out now."

"Come on. After all we've been through, there's no way the dead end is a bunch of slats. You'll figure something out. You always do."

"This may be for the best. Even if we made it out, with the NSC under Fielding's sway, we would have to contend with an army's worth of the kind of men who've been after us. If I stay here, they'll conclude that you and I both died here."

Charlie could only stare, dumbstruck, at the grim visage in the porthole. Although nothing about Drummond's features changed, suddenly, somehow, Charlie saw love in his eyes. And just as suddenly, Charlie's own jumble of feelings disentangled. He felt love for his father too, and he knew that he always would. "Forget it," he said.

"I've had my fair share of time," Drummond said. "At best, with an unprecedented leap by medicine, I'd get two extra years before I start needing to be diapered. And I'd still be a national security risk."

"What about parlaying their fear of a timed drop into some sort of a deal?"

"The only deal I'm going to take is that you can get out of here, go anywhere you want, and have everything you want. There's only one way I'm going to get that deal."

The only thing Charlie wanted was to get Drummond out.

"You're resourceful," Drummond went on, speaking more quickly. "You'll make it out of the country—you'll figure things from there." A tinny clank shimmied the length of the tunnel. "And that's your cue. That's them raising the firewall at the tunnel to campus." More clanks resounded through the complex.

Charlie saw clearly that staying was no longer an option.

He stayed.

"Know always that I love you, Charles," Drummond said with finality.

Charlie was preoccupied with plotting to save him.

Drummond must have seen it. "This is the best way," he said. He turned and strode toward Fielding. The tunnel floor ahead of him flashed pink in the beam cast by the clicker.

Charlie had ninety seconds to get out.

19

Charlie fielded Grudzev's AK-74 on the run. The bullets in its big banana clip could barely dent the firewall. The armor-piercing grenade in its underbarrel, however, might blow the thing down.

He slid to a stop in the stairwell across the subbasement, slamming his hip against the stout handrail. He couldn't afford to think about it. The stairwell was far enough from the firewall that the grenade, while in flight, could have the time it needed to arm. The stairwell also looked solid enough to serve as a shield against the lethal shrapnel that would fly at him if the grenade did its job.

He raised the rifle to his shoulder, found the firewall in the rungs of his front sight post, said a silent prayer to all comers, then absolutely pulverized the trigger.

Nothing happened. The grenade didn't budge.

Was it a dud?

Had Karpenko supplied Grudzev with a neutered AK-74?

Ninety-seven point eight pounds of penthrite and trinitrotoluene would turn Drummond to mist in less than a minute.

Take an extra second, Charlie urged himself.

Check out that little lever just in front of the trigger.

The safety, maybe?

He flicked it downward, raised the rifle, and tried the trigger again. The underbarrel responded with a disheartening *sproing*, like that of a spud gun.

The grenade flew out. It hurtled through the hundred feet or so of subbasement and punched the firewall, creating a colossal, magnificent explosion.

Charlie closed his eyes and still could see the fiery flash. His ears shut down. Pressed flat against the inside wall of the stairwell, he felt a hard gust from the hail of passing shrapnel. He had no idea whether the shrapnel included bits of firewall.

Once the gust subsided, he crept into the subbasement. He couldn't see what damage, if any, the grenade had done. The firewall area was blocked by a mass of dust and smoke.

He took a deep breath, shut his eyes, and plunged into it. The air smelled and tasted like a spent match. He felt his way toward the firewall. Then he felt the firewall itself—where he'd hoped to feel nothing.

He opened his eyes. Through a burning haze, he saw that the firewall remained anchored to the surrounding concrete walls and ceiling—unfortunately, the blast-proof frame had lived up to its billing. The metal slats themselves had puckered outward, however, leading to a cavity at its base big enough for a midsized dog to squeeze through.

Charlie tried, an act of contortion. A steel shard cut into his neck. Another ripped into his sleeve and dug into his arm. At the cost of two strips of skin, he made it through.

In the tunnel, the dust kicked up by the grenade had grayed the air. Using a hand as a visor against it, Charlie made out the forms of two men standing together halfway down: almost certainly Drummond and Fielding—had Drummond revealed he'd triggered the bomb, Fielding would have fled, at the least. Charlie couldn't see enough of their shapes or features to tell who was who. Except for a small circle glowing faintly.

The lit end of a cigar.

Charlie fired the AK. The cigar hit the floor along with Fielding, the splash of sparks momentarily illuminating his rifle and the rage on his blood-splattered face.

One of his bullets sparked the wall inches from Charlie's head. Charlie didn't hear it; he still couldn't hear anything. He countered by spraying more of his own bullets, sending Fielding staggering in retreat. He disappeared into the smog, perhaps into the complex itself, allowing Drummond to run to Charlie.

Drummond shouted something. Charlie couldn't hear what, but

Drummond's urgency made it clear he wasn't suggesting they stick around. Charlie estimated forty seconds remained for them to get out of the tunnel, feel their way across the subbasement, climb two flights of stairs, and exit the building through the Perriman offices. He wasn't sure whether it was possible. But trying beat the hell out of the alternative.

He ran with Drummond for the firewall. Along the way, he emptied his banana clip at the shards around the hole, effectively enlarging it, then cast the spent rifle away. At the end of the tunnel, Drummond stepped aside, allowing Charlie through first. Charlie pulled Drummond out on the other side. Together they raced across the subbasement and into the stairwell.

They were halfway up the stairs from the basement to the ground floor when the detonation came. The stairwell filled with white light so intense that Charlie couldn't distinguish any single object—not Drummond at his side, not even his own hand in front of his face. Although he couldn't hear, he heard the blast, and he felt it in his stomach and his knees and his teeth. The blast current hit like a bludgeon. It snatched him, and in its hold there was no telling up from down, until he came down chin first onto the edge of a stair.

The white light dissolved into swells of hot gray dust and blue-black smoke that stank of burned rubber, inflaming his lungs, and revealed that the walls of the stairwell were buckling, the ceiling was raining chunks of concrete, and Drummond was gone. Utterly vanished. Possibly he'd fallen into the sooty abyss where the bottom five or six stairs had been a second ago.

As Charlie peered into it, the remaining stairs, including those beneath his feet, cracked apart into nothing.

He flung a hand at the stout handrail. Because the lower mooring had fragmented, his weight caused the rail to pop free of the wall. The upper mooring held, enabling him to climb the rail while it swung.

He belly flopped onto the landing, then scurried on scorched—and possibly broken—hands and knees into the Perriman offices.

Other than the billows of white dust, tinted red by the illuminated exit signs, all was as before. Except, of course, the building might come down at any second.

If Drummond had made it out of the stairwell, Charlie figured, he would have headed down the hallway to the front vestibule, which opened onto West 112th Street.

There were no footprints in the fresh coating of dust there.

Charlie felt like slumping into one of the plastic workstations and crying. He hauled himself toward the vestibule. Halfway, he sensed motion behind him. He spun around, his hope reignited, all of his parts feeling like new again.

It was water, spraying from fire sprinklers.

His hearing had begun to return. He could make out the howl of a smoke alarm, though barely. To his ears, it was a drone.

Still he could hear Drummond. At least he thought he could. From the office next to the stairwell, the one whose door said D. CLARK, DEPUTY DISTRICT SALES MGR, N. ATLANTIC DIV. "Is there a fire?" Charlie thought he heard him say.

Charlie bounded down the hallway and threw open the door. Drummond swiveled sharply in his desk chair. A coating of white dust made him look like a baker. He seemed irked that there had been no knock. Taking in Charlie, his demeanor shifted to puzzled.

"Charles, what are you doing here?" His eyes settled on Charlie's Perriman uniform. "Are you working here now?"

20

Charlie led Drummond out of the office, at the same time using Drummond's shoulder to keep weight off a new knee injury relative to which his old gunshot wound felt like a paper cut. The glass-walled vestibule at the far end of the hallway showed West 112th to be as crowded now, in the middle of the night, as it ordinarily would be at midday during a street fair. Dogs yelped at the strange rumbling below-ground. Residents with coats thrown over pajamas gawked, through the haze of streetlamps, at towers of smoke rising from sidewalk grates. Charlie heard them speculating: "student prank," "science experiment," and, the overwhelming favorite, "terrorists."

"My guess would be a cigarette," Drummond said in earnest. "Eighteen percent of all nighttime fires begin when a person falls asleep while smoking."

"My guess would be penthrite and trinitrotoluene," said Fielding, climbing from the dark remains of the stairwell, assault rifle in hand. Dust gave him a ragged edge.

The shock of seeing him hit Charlie nearly as hard as the blast current. He probably would have fallen if he weren't clutching Drummond.

Drummond studied Fielding as if trying to remember who he was. "Interesting theory," he told him meanwhile.

Although the lights were off in the hallway, Fielding's extensive wounds were apparent from blood that slicked much of his face and body. Yet he approached without evident impediment, his rifle blinking orange along with a changing traffic signal outside, his finger on the trigger.

Charlie looked to Drummond for guidance only to find Drummond looking to him the same way.

"Should we tell him about the security blanket?" Charlie asked, intending it for Fielding's ears.

"That is a decent bargaining chip," Fielding said. "An hour ago. In case it comes up in your next life, a man with an honest-to-goodness security blanket doesn't resort to blowing himself up." He flicked his rifle at a bare stretch of hallway. "Now, both of you, back up against the wall."

Charlie raced to conceive a way he and Drummond could defend themselves. There was nothing in reach, save a light switch and the carpet sodden from the fire sprinklers. The people milling outside the front vestibule couldn't see them through the doors and all the way down the dark hallway, and probably wouldn't be able to hear a cry for help, or intervene in any case. The huge bank of fluorescent tubes directly above Fielding's head held more promise: They might come on with enough flash or pop to distract him long enough that his rifle could be knocked away. Also the people on the street might be able to see in. And, at some point, Drummond might blink on too.

As he and Drummond backed toward the wall, Charlie tried to telegraph his intent to him. "Fifty-fifty proposition," he said.

Drummond gave no sign of acknowledgment. But would he under the best of circumstances?

Trying to be discreet, Charlie flipped the light switch with his elbow.

The lights didn't come on.

Glancing up at the dark bulbs, Fielding said, "Talk about your metaphors."

"Actually, it's a better metaphor than you know," Charlie said.

"I'll humor you: Why?"

"My father might be out, but now the whole world can see what you've been up to." With an air of expectation, Charlie peered over Fielding's shoulder, toward the street. He was primed to fly at Fielding if he bought the bluff or for whatever reason turned as little as an eyelash that way.

Fielding only smirked. "This can't be the there's-someone-behind-you trick."

A series of gunshots, in such rapid succession that the sounds blended together, jolted the corridor. Glass shattered with near-matching clangor.

Fielding slumped against the wall opposite Charlie and Drummond.

Charlie snatched Fielding's rifle out of the air. "That worked out a lot better than I hoped," Charlie said, battling disbelief.

Looking toward the street, Fielding's face dropped into an expression of shock. "You—!"

He fell the rest of the way to the floor. Blood spilled from his chest and darkened the water pooled on the carpet. He didn't move, and wouldn't again.

Any relief Charlie might have felt was superseded by surprise of his own, along with apprehension, as the shooter stepped through the newly created gap in the vestibule's inner door.

"Why, if it isn't Helen," Drummond said warmly.

Her hair was red now and matted by what appeared to be dried blood.

"Actually, it isn't Helen," Charlie said, aiming Fielding's rifle at her. He wished taking out Fielding signified that she was on their side. Given her track record, it was a good bet that she had a different agenda.

"I'm really Alice Rutherford, NSA," she said. "I was watching from a bar across Broadway when you were brought in here, Charlie. It got to be a while. Then came that gigantic explosion. I was a little worried."

"I don't mean to be unappreciative," Charlie said. "It's just that, sooner or later, everybody in your line of work tries to kill us. And you . . ."

"I'm sorry I deceived you the other day." She dropped her gun to her hip. "If I'd known then what I do now, I wouldn't have let you set foot outside the senior center—at the least I would have called you a tank."

"And now that you know what you know?"

"I don't know what I can tell you to win your trust in the time we have—or the time we don't have, I should say. The people outside probably have figured out by now where the gunshots they heard came from. And any moment this building, if it's still standing, will be swarming with officers from every intelligence agency you've ever heard of, including my own, who all have you two as numbers one and one-A on their most wanted list. Having just killed the superspy whose orders they have been marching to, there's not much I'll be able to say on behalf of any of us—I'll be on the list too. But if you'll come with me now, and if we can just make it across the Hudson and to Newark Airport, we can get away on the private jet I have standing by with dummy flight plans."

Based on intuition as much as any factor he could identify, Charlie was inclined to join her; he suspected he would have felt similarly had she merely suggested they try to get a cab. "At least a private jet is an upgrade from the places people usually try to kill us," he said, lowering the rifle.

She smiled. "That's a start."

They both looked to Drummond.

"I'd really like to go to Geneva," he said, "for some reason."

"It's possible," she said. "We could try for Polish airspace, where we won't need any documentation. From there, we'd still have the little matter of eluding every law enforcement agency in the world."

"What, no air forces?" Charlie said.

"Not if we're lucky." She stepped into the reception area and raised a window overlooking the alley. The din of the crowd seemed to triple in volume. Sirens of arriving emergency vehicles shook the frosty air.

Drummond turned to Charlie. "Is it too risky?"

"Definitely," Charlie said. "But that works for us."

The Cessna sliced through the clouds above New Jersey and into a golden dawn. The right questions would net the information that the passengers aboard the Innsbruck-bound private jet were a young hedge fund manager and his wife on their honeymoon. Really, Charlie and Alice occupied the overstuffed leather recliners in the cabin, along with Drummond—the copilot, according to the manifest.

"An interesting piece of information," Drummond said, "is Blackbird fighter jets fly so fast—twenty-five-hundred miles per hour—the pilots have to wear space suits."

Charlie and Alice were enthralled, primarily because there was no evidence of such aircraft in the vicinity.

The remainder of the trip brought only clear skies.

As far as they knew.

Acknowledgments

Thanks—the details of which would make this book about eight pounds heavier—to: Richard Abate, John Ager, Elizabeth Bancroft, TJ Beitelman, Tim Borella, Rachel Clevenger, Brian Coshatt, Stacy Creamer, Nik DiDomeniko, Ken Driscoll, Peter Earnest, Sean Fay, John Fellerman, John Fontana, Verna Gates, Phyllis Grann, Randall Griffith, Adam Grossman, Chuck Hogan, Farah Ispahani, Edward Kastenmeier, Joan Kretschmer, Kate Lee, Sonny Mehta, Jackeline Montalvo, Alexis Morton, Stan Norris, Ray Paulick, Nick Reed, Nora Reichard, Jake Reiss, Alison Rich, Fred Rustmann, Sandy Salter, Martha Schwartz, Roy Sekoff, Karen Shepard, Keck Shepard, Richard Shepard, Adrienne Sparks, Bill Thomas, Elliot Thomson, Malcolm Thomson, Adam Venit, John Weisman, Lawrence Wharton, Elizabeth Yale, and anyone else who has read this book to this point.

Please send questions or comments to kqthomson@gmail.com.